THE POISON BALANCE

LUCY GHOSE

CRANTHORPE
MILLNER
PUBLISHERS

First published by Cranthorpe Millner Publishers (2024)

ISBN 978-1-80378-159-4 (Paperback)

www.cranthorpemillner.com

Cranthorpe Millner Publishers

For all my readers and supporters – it means a lot that you are here and have picked up this book. And for anyone who thinks they can't do it or has forgotten who they are – you can, and you are good enough.

*

CONTENT WARNING

This is not a cosy read. Expect sex scenes, bad language, substance abuse, violence, gore and zombies – a lot of them! This book also makes reference to historical sexual abuse.

They were coming. The scalpel fell from Chen's trembling hands as howls echoed across the misty paddy fields.

From the window of his veterinary practice, he saw something black dart across the alleyway between the houses. His eyes strained from the glare of the fluorescent lights overhead. Jittery – that was all he was. He was just tired and overworked. The car across the road was still there. It had been all night. In the dawn gloom, he could just make out the shadowy figures sitting inside.

To find out the truth, he had to do the autopsy. He levered the canine skull open and sat back in disbelief. He prodded the cold, spongy brain tissue. It was covered in a thick membrane of snowflake scarring. There were no abrasions to the outside of the skull to explain the damage, or the seizure that killed it.

As he typed up the report, every now and again he glanced at the vials of green slime next to his laptop. The contaminated river water had to be the reason why the wild forest dogs were dying. When he had gone to collect the samples, he had found dead fish floating among the river reeds, and clouds of algae pooled around pebbles at the shoreline.

The morning sun had turned the sky a milky blue above the terracotta tiles of the house opposite. A black dog scaled over the rooftop, teeth bared as it leapt onto a balcony and into an upstairs room. Screams pierced the air.

Another dog padded down the main street, sniffing the air for prey. Patches of red, raw skin exposed its muscular shoulders and haunches. Its gait was shaky, and its eyes were wild.

A man and woman bolted from a door, making for the riverbank. The dog pounded between the pair to join the snarling pack now circling the man. He raised his knife. One grabbed him by the ankle and yanked him down. It yelped as he sunk the knife into its ribs. The others dived onto him. Chen saw no more of him than ripping limbs and spurts of blood. The woman turned and ran back up the street, wailing as she went.

Chen opened the door and held out his hand. 'Come on.'

She made it to the driveway just as another dog padded out from behind a truck. Its cloudy eyes stared back at Chen and it bundled the woman sideways into the dust. Her screams were silenced by the snapping of teeth. Blood dripping from its jowls, the dog watched Chen and sprang onto the porch.

Chen slammed the door and bit his knuckles, guilt rotting his insides. Claws scrabbled on wood. Gunshots were fired. The thud of a body hitting the deck reverberated through the floorboards. He inched the door open. A red stain spread across the floor around the dead dog.

He looked up to see who had fired but only saw running villagers. He crept out and tugged the animal through the doorway. The earthy smell of hot flesh and blood made his stomach lurch as he hauled the body onto the operating table.

He got to work, searing through the skull. The brain was damaged, just like the other one. He hurried to type up his conclusion.

The printer chugged away, spitting out pages as fists

hammered on his door. He picked up the sticky, wet scalpel from the table. The door splintered on its hinges. The first guy burst in and Chen launched himself at his middle before he had a chance to take a shot. As they tussled, Chen slashed at his face with the dirty blade. He fell back into the other men, spraying the room with bullets.

Muffled shouts came from the men as they scuffled with one another. The man Chen had cut with the autopsy scalpel writhed on the floor, clutching his stomach as he retched up blood. Then he reared up and opened his mouth, saliva dribbling down his chin. He swooped on his nearest colleague to gnash at his face.

Chen grabbed the pages from the printer, and the memory stick from the laptop. He rushed out the back door to the sound of gunfire. As he ran towards the road out of the village, his mind was full of fear. The pack was acting as one to attack. If the dogs were infected, nowhere was safe. If the men who tried to kill him were still alive, he had an even bigger problem. There was only one place left to go: Beijing.

It was a day much like any other when Amy Weston realised the world was poisoned.

'Come on, I thought you were in a hurry to get to work,' she told her sister, pulling her by the elbow into the empty graveyard.

Leaves fell in a last hurrah, spinning to freedom before hitting the path. Gnarled tree skeletons were shedding their blossom on the breeze.

'This was a stupid idea,' Ash said. 'This place gives me the creeps.'

Amy grabbed her hand. 'It's a shortcut. Do you want to be on time, or not?'

Away from the tarmac roads and grey pavements the lie became clear. Everyone was being spun the media tripe of an early autumn, but it was impossible; it was barely June. How could nobody see it?

Everyone else was rushing around, busy being too busy. Life had slowed with lockdown, but the rat-run began again in earnest after the vaccines, and people had gone back to the offices. *Maybe it was not a lie*, she pondered. It was all they had, because there was no explanation.

'We shouldn't have drunk so much last night. I feel like death,' Ash said.

'You'll be right at home here, then,' Amy replied, feeling her sister's grip tighten as they turned the corner. Faceless statues stood like sentries along the path, and leaves cartwheeled past. Amy bent down to pick up a small branch. The brown leaves were spattered with holes.

'Why are you stopping?' Ash whispered.

'See? Summer leaves should not look like this.'

'Not this again,' Ash groaned.

'The poison balance is real. It's not just a theory now. The trees are dying, and we'll be next.'

Ash sighed. 'The people in power would know. They'd be doing something about it.'

On her knees, Amy looked round at a headstone. Most of the engravings had worn away. She stared up at the stone angel looming over her as it balanced on a plinth. Its slender arm was raised to Heaven. The concave profile of its face was missing a nose. Pitted skin and black staining could not hide the beauty of its serene smile. Some weathering was to be expected, but it was one of the newest memorials in the churchyard. In less than a decade, it had aged beyond its years. The hairline fracture around its foot looked like an ankle bracelet.

'Can we go?' Ash rubbed her face. 'The hospital really will fire me at this rate.'

'This is the link,' Amy said, pointing at the angel. 'The statues eroding, the trees with no leaves, the high cancer rates in the hospitals. People can't breathe. You know that – you work there.'

'You're only an intern. Who will believe you?'

'My boss, if he'll let me do some proper research at the lab rather than just make coffee.'

'We need to go,' Ash whined.

Amy sat back on her heels and looked up at her. 'Fuck's sake. If you don't believe me, what chance do I stand? You know what happened to Aanya. Do more people have to die for everyone to listen?' It was too late. Ash was stepping backwards, blinking away tears. 'Fuck. I'm sorry. Let's go out tonight. I'll meet you from work.'

'Whatever. Just don't stay here long,' Ash muttered.

'Love you,' Amy shouted, but she had vanished down the path beyond the tall hedges.

Mention of their dead sister had been a step too far for Ash. Sometimes, the ripples of their past caught up with them both, but every time she just blanked it out. Amy wondered when the day would come that they would have to face it together.

Amy carefully put the twig in her jacket pocket. She had to make her boss listen. What if he refused to take the word of an intern? She got out her phone and turned on the camera to selfie mode. Lining up the statue, herself and the barren trees, she took the picture. She attached it to all her social media accounts and shoved her phone in her back pocket.

Taking a step back, she missed her footing and knocked into the statue. She heard a crack. A diagonal slash appeared across the angel's torso, from shoulder to hip. With a rumble, the statue pitched, tilting towards her. Her wrists jarred as she dived to the ground. She scrabbled away and shut her eyes. The statue crashed onto the path.

Her teeth crunched on grit and she opened her eyes. The smashed figure had landed inches from her legs. She rubbed her scuffed palms, smarting and dotted with blood. The dank smell of mulched undergrowth filled her nostrils.

Hearing shouts, she looked up to see a policeman striding along the path, pointing at her. 'I want a word with you,' he shouted, running now.

Among the rust-coloured leaves laid the angel's thumb. Amy grabbed it. 'You'll have to catch me first, fuckface.' She grinned at the policeman and gave him the Vs. She always loved a chase. Getting up, she ran hard in the other direction, with the calloused stone thumb safe in her fist.

*

Amy checked the time on her phone and groaned. She was nearly an hour late for work. The police car beeped as it pulled away from the kerb and slotted in behind a black taxi. She waved and hurried through the glass doors of the lab foyer. She knew she was lucky to avoid a stay in the cells. Over the years, she had learned how to sweet-talk her way out of trouble. It was a bit early for drama, even by her standards, and far too late in the morning to be any kind of punctual. Could she feign illness? Heavy traffic? Maybe no one would notice.

The lab was silent except for the tapping of keyboards from her colleagues.

'You're late,' a girl with freckles and brown bob said, as she passed. She was barely older than Amy, though having completed her PhD while Amy had not was apparently reason enough to boss her around.

'Sorry, Gabrielle. Is Ron in yet? I need to see him,' Amy said.

'In a meeting. Although, you could help me.'

Amy felt a rush. In the few months she had been there nobody ever spoke to her, let alone wanted her to do some proper work. 'Sure. What?'

Gabrielle held out her coffee cup. 'Can you put two sugars in this? I forgot.' With a smirk, she headed back to her bench. 'Can you believe it?' she said to the guy sitting next to her. 'Ron's dragged that old dinosaur Professor Harket out of retirement to represent us at the UN Air Health summit in Beijing. And there's one spare pass.'

Gabrielle rambled on about how she should go to the summit, how she had reached a research breakthrough, and how Ron could not say no.

After delivering the coffee, Amy found someone had spilled liquid on the bench nearest her and left the Bunsen burner on – again. 'Messy shitheads,' she muttered. Her stomach knotted with jealousy as she tidied up the abandoned experiment, emptying the test tubes down the sink.

With a sigh, she got out her phone and checked her social media. She had a few "likes" from her post at the churchyard. A quick scan of the news websites made her think of her argument with Ash, telling of rising cancer cases and hospital admissions for breathing problems. Then a headline from one of the broadsheets caught her eye: *Poison water blamed for killer dog attacks in China*. Amy scanned the article to read that wild forest dogs, usually scared of humans, had gone on a rampage in a village and broken into houses and attacked residents. "It hadn't rained in weeks", said one survivor. "Then it rained for a fortnight and that's when all my chickens were savaged in the night. My neighbour's horses too. The next day the dogs came for us".

An autopsy on one of the dogs was due to be performed by a

vet from the village, believing the water source, a nearby river, had become contaminated. The whereabouts of the vet had not been established, but he was not on the official list of the dead.

A quick check on the Internet and Amy found there was only one vet's practice in the village. She typed his name into social media – nothing. She had no way of knowing if he was still alive, but with the news article, the leaf and statue fragment, she had more than enough evidence.

'Where do you think you're going?' Gabrielle asked, as Amy marched towards the hallway.

Everyone was staring at her. 'I have to talk to Ron,' she said.

'I told you he's in a meeting. It'll have to wait.' Gabrielle rolled her eyes at her bench partner as she turned back to her computer screen. 'Ron needs his head testing, letting her loose here. It's not the place for the likes of *her*.'

The landline phone began to ring, and Amy knew she ought to answer it, but she stopped mid-step. Did she really hear that right? She strode up to Gabrielle and jogged the back of her chair. 'What the fuck do you mean by that?'

Gabrielle looked round. 'Well, it's not like you take your job seriously, is it? Turning up late. Who even wears gold hoops and trainers to work?'

'I really need to see Ron. It's important,' Amy said through gritted teeth, trying to keep her rage in check.

'Look, some of us are busy here earning our keep.'

The phone kept ringing, but no one answered it. Amy dug her fingernails into her palms and took a deep breath. She always had to work twice as hard as the white girls at school. She had known girls like this, who looked down on her because she did not look like them and did not have a nice cosy home to go back to. Here she was again. Only this time, Amy was making her coffee. 'Actually, I'm on a paid internship,' Amy said.

'Bet I know how you got that.' Gabrielle gave an obscene gesture, jerking her hand towards her mouth. 'Giving Ron a little bit extra, other than his sweetener? He must like a bit of ghetto.'

An overwhelming sensation burned inside Amy. Growing up in care, she had quickly learned survival skills and they stayed like muscle memory. You never forget how to fight when there is no one else to stick up for you. The old Amy would have pinned that bitch down and got her in a chokehold until she said sorry. She was not a teenager anymore, and there was more at stake than just an internship.

Anger tingled through to her fingertips until she could not stand it anymore. Her eyes fell to a test tube rack on the bench. With a sweep of her arm, she sent the glass tubes shattering across the floor. 'Fuck you,' Amy shouted. She picked up the water jug from the table and tipped it over Gabrielle, who leapt to her feet and shrieked. Watching the lab's queen bee gasping in a puddle felt a million times better than smashing her out. Amy looked round the lab to see a few people stifling laughter behind their sleeves. It seemed Gabrielle had upset a few other worker bees besides just Amy. She could make her own bastard coffee from now on.

'Amy,' a voice boomed from the doorway. Her boss, Ron Dean, a short, flush-cheeked man, looked incandescent. Her grin vanished. He surveyed the water and broken glass, then pointed to the hallway. 'My office, now. And will someone answer the phone?'

Amy marched into Ron's office and her breath caught as she found someone already there. A man with haunted, pale blue eyes was leaning back in an office chair with his boots up on the desk. Twiddling a pen through his fingers, he showed no interest in the piles of papers spread out across the desk. He had more of a care to the window, as though devising a plan to launch himself out of it, rather than endure the sudden interruption of company.

'If you want the world to listen, you should stop shouting at it,' he said, his cold stare locked onto her.

Just what she needed: another person telling her what to do. And a total stranger too. 'Thanks for that,' she panted, putting her hands on her hips, 'but I don't need your help.'

His appearance suggested he had about as much reason to be there as she did. He had not bothered to shave his stubble, peppered with early greys; the frayed sleeve of his navy blue t-shirt revealed a glimpse of a tattoo on his upper arm and his black chinos had a hole wearing at the knee.

'So, you're the intern?' He spoke with hints of a clipped accent she could not pinpoint. Biting on the end of his pen, revealed a small gap between his two top teeth. 'Must've been a hell of a bender last night to get a police escort to work.'

With an easy view of the street from his chair, he must have seen her arrive in the police car. She hoped he had not told Ron as she was in enough trouble already. She looked back to the doorway, but there was no sign of her boss. *Where is he?* No doubt he was getting the lowdown of Gabrielle's version of events.

'Have a nice night in the cells?' the man asked with a smirk.

'I wasn't arrested. Not that it's any of your fucking business,' she said.

He shrugged. 'I don't care what you do. But you might want to dial down the weeknight partying if you want to keep your internship.'

'And when I want advice from someone who looks like they just crawled out of a bin, I know who to call.'

He laughed. 'Speak for yourself. I can smell your hangover from here.'

Amy frowned, annoyed with herself that she liked the way he laughed. It had a shy edge to it, which was bafflingly at odds with his brusque manner. 'Who are you? The fun police?' she asked.

The sunlight coming in from the window behind him cast a silver lining around his dirty-blond hair. He gave no reply and watched her as though he had never seen anything like her before.

What is in that stare? she wondered. *Disgust, fascination, or just plain hate?* If she was about to be fired, she had nothing to lose. She reckoned he might be worth a tease. She slinked over and held her wrists out. 'You should cuff me now – get it over with. You might even enjoy it.'

His gaze fell to her exposed skin. He looked away with a grimace and resumed pen-chewing. 'You wish.'

'You have no people skills,' she said. No answer – again. How could silence be so infuriating? 'Who are you, anyway?' she asked, folding her arms.

'It hardly matters.'

Amy's words stuck in her throat. *How could someone think they did not matter?* Hearing a door shut, she realised someone else had come into the office.

Ron walked over to his desk and sighed as he sat down. 'Gabby isn't pressing charges,' he said, looking up at Amy. 'What on Earth possessed you to smash the place up like that?'

She shot a glance at the scruffy man drumming his pen on his thigh. He raised an eyebrow at her. *People skills?* he mouthed.

She turned her back on him. 'Ron, you didn't hear what she—' She stopped herself, knowing there was a fine line between being honest and being a grass.

'Just calm down. Have a seat,' Ron said.

There were no spare chairs. The stranger with the high cheekbones dragged his scuffed boots off the desk, grabbed his jacket and stood up. 'Take my seat. I'm leaving, anyway.'

'Joel, don't go,' Ron said.

'*Joel?* Professor Joel Harket.' As she said his name, recognition clenched Amy's stomach. Now the accent made sense: he was the Norwegian scientist who was going to represent the Foundation at the UN Air Summit. He was the man all the others in the lab were trying to impress. They talked about Professor Harket like he was an old man. His skin had a lacklustre pallor and his eyes were bloodshot, as though he had been on a decade-long piss-up, but he could not be any older than mid-forties. 'But, you—'

'That's me, the man who just crawled out from a bin,' he said, his gaze upon her by necessity rather than choice.

It was obvious Ron had called her into the office to take her

ID pass without causing another scene in the lab. She was used to people giving up on her when she screwed up. From the care homes, to university, it just kept happening. It was pointless apologising, and it was futile to stay. She had turned up late, started a fight in the lab, and massively insulted one of the senior scientists. It was back to pulling pints at that god-awful Irish theme pub. 'Don't worry, *I'm* leaving,' she said, taking off her lanyard. She slammed it on the desk and made for the door.

'Amy, wait—' Ron began to say, but Harket blocked her way.

He was head and shoulders taller than her, and as he cupped her elbow, she froze at his touch. Forgetting how to breathe in and out for a moment, she looked up into his eyes.

'There's just one thing I want to know before you go,' he whispered into her ear. 'What are you doing with that skanky old twig in your pocket?'

Amy broke away from him. She had almost forgotten the reason she needed to speak to Ron in the first place. She thought of the killer dogs and the poisoned water, but she did not have the autopsy findings yet. She needed to start with what proof she did have. Feeling Harket's stare on her, she tried to re-focus and addressed Ron instead, putting the twig on his desk. 'The trees in this city are dying,' she said.

Ron picked off a leaf and held it up to the light. 'Why do you say that?'

'You think this is an early autumn? Seasons don't just alter like that,' she said, buoyed on by his interest. 'Look at the leaves – the burn holes. You know what causes this? Acid rain. The air is toxic and it's killing people. We need to do something.'

'That's crazy talk,' Harket said. 'People don't die from acid rain.'

'If the pH level becomes too acidic and it's already in the water cycle, then the poison balance tips. There might be no going back,' Amy said. 'How will the world survive if we can't drink water, or go out in the rain? It'll burn our skin and our lungs—'

'The poison balance? I think you've been watching too much Netflix, kid,' Harket said.

She gawped at him. '*Kid*? Really?'

'You need proof, Amy,' Ron said.

'There's this.' She put the angel's thumb next to the branch. 'The statues are eroding too fast. One kind of broke as I went past.'

'*Kind of* broke?' Harket repeated, perching on the desk.

She shook her head. 'The statues are eroding from the acidic particles in the air. It's dry deposition at a crazy rate. That statue is only about ten years old.'

'I don't know...' Ron began.

'I've got the evidence. Let me have a bench and prove it. We can present it to the summit.'

Harket stood up, jabbing his finger on the desk. 'Ron, if you send this car crash to Beijing, I'm not going on principle.'

'I'm a *what* now?' she asked.

'Well, look at you.'

'People keep saying that,' she said. 'These hoops are *Cartier*, you know.'

'If you say so.' Professor Harket snorted and looked away.

Ron splayed his hands on the desk. 'Amy, the problem is that research costs money. We're operating on a shoestring here and the cuts from government are making it impossible.'

'If we can explain my theory to the ministers, they'll have to listen, and we'll get the funding.'

'If you're wrong, we'll be a laughing stock. I'm sorry, I can't take that risk,' Ron replied. 'You haven't even got a PhD.'

'I was working on my thesis before I...' She felt too ashamed to finish her sentence.

Harket kicked his heel against the desk. 'It needs more work to be a viable theory.'

She refused to look at Harket. 'Please, Professor Dean? Let me work on it.'

'I wish we could,' Ron said. 'But there's no more room in the lab. All the tables are full.'

Gabrielle's words echoed in her head. Maybe Ron only got funding for Amy because she ticked the diversity box. She needed to prove herself and work twice as hard yet again. 'What about the old stockroom?' she asked. 'I could clear some space, and there's loads of old equipment in there I could use. I'll do it all myself. I won't be any bother, I promise.' Her phone pinged and she started with surprise.

Harket locked eyes with her, daring her to succumb. 'Oh, don't mind us,' he said.

'I need to get this,' Amy said to Ron.

'Social media security blanket,' Harket muttered.

She ignored him and unlocked her phone. Someone had replied to her Instagram post. 'See? I took a photo of the trees in the graveyard this morning and someone has posted back.'

'How cute. You've got yourself a penfriend,' Harket said.

She addressed Ron instead. 'This professor says I can use their computer modelling system if I do some more research. I won't cost you an extra penny.'

'This is on... what is it?' he asked.

'Instagram and TikTok.'

'What in the blazes is TikTok?' Professor Harket asked with a grimace, as if it was something disgusting.

Ron glanced at her and Harket. Drumming his fingers on the desk, he sighed. Then he pointed his pen at Amy. 'Only if you promise to behave from now on. No fighting. Oh, and you're still on the intern salary. You've got one week to come up with something.'

'You won't regret it, I promise,' she said.

'You've got to present your case for the summit, the same as everyone else in the lab. Right?'

'Sure thing, professor,' she said, grinning.

He made an ushering gesture. 'Go on, off you go. You've got a stockroom to clear.'

As she made for the door, Harket reached round her, and their hands bumped against each other's. 'Don't forget your pass,' he said, pressing her lanyard into her palm.

'Thanks,' she muttered, realising they were in each other's breathing space again.

He smirked as he turned the door handle. 'Don't overthink it. Even if Ron's lost us our integrity, I've got manners, kid.'

It was her turn to raise an eyebrow. 'Selective manners at best. And seeing as you never asked, my name is Amy.' Giving a sickly-sweet smile, she breezed out the office.

He slammed the door so hard it bounced back off the doorframe and swung open. She was about to walk away when he started yelling at Ron. 'After all those awards I won for us, this is how you repay me? I'm not going. Ask someone else.'

'You're the best we've got. You owe me.'

'It's too soon, since my wife—' Harket's voice trailed off.

'It's been years, mate,' Ron said. 'How long is it?'

'Since the first lockdown.'

Amy rolled the lanyard cord around her fingers as she eavesdropped in the hall. She ought to go, but something about the professor intrigued her. All her life, people had been rude to her, talked down to her, treated her like the care home scum she had always been. Except for her sister. But the way he looked at her... She could not figure him out.

If he cleaned up a bit, he could easily have some posh career woman, who went on spa days, had her clothes dry-cleaned and owned a riverside apartment. His minimal people skills and dishevelled appearance suggested an aura of chaos that made Amy suspect a happy homelife had eluded him. What was in the eye of that storm?

'Lauren wouldn't want you wasting away like this,' Ron told him, his voice softer now. 'Don't you think it's time to start life again? You're our best bet.'

'I'm not. Look at the state of me. Christ, why are you bothering?'

'You've got the most experience in the field. When you team that with—'

'Little Miss Car Crash? What the hell are you thinking?'

'I'm thinking that's the most spark I've seen from you in ages,' Ron said. 'She's not afraid to get out there and get people noticing her either.'

'Get arrested, more likely.'

'And *you* haven't ever been in a cell?' Ron asked. 'We both know what you were like. You came up with some of your best stuff when you were doing those protests. Maybe we need some of the old you back again. That girl might be the shot in the arm that this place needs – that *you* need.'

'Me? I don't need anything. She's clearly a pain in the arse.'

'She knows her way round social media better than either of us. We can get the investors on board with a bright young thing like her,' Ron said. 'If she's right, we can get funding for global research on pH levels in the sea and air. If you can both stop bickering long enough.'

'I was only going to the summit as a favour to you.'

'A favour? You need to pay the mortgage, I need to pay wages. You need someone with you.'

'I work better on my own. You know that.'

'You are going to the summit with that girl,' Ron told him. 'It's happening, whether you like it or not.'

'As much as I'd like being force-fed a bloody TikTok sandwich,' Harket grumbled.

Amy pushed away from the wall and gave a little hop of triumph, realising she had proper work to do now. The one downside would be enduring Professor Cheekbones and his perpetual bad mood at the summit, but anything would be better than making coffee for messy shitheads.

Mei checked for loiterers beyond the glass door before swiping her key fob. The streets of Beijing, once choked with evening commuters and snap-happy tourists, were dark and empty. Smog blurred the view of the shops opposite.

The tangy, damp air clawed at her throat as she stepped out onto the pavement. She knew she ought to stop and put her mask on, but this part of the city was too risky. Out of habit, she looked up. One day, she hoped to see the tops of the skyscrapers again. She could only count a few floors before the lights were swallowed by mist. Hazy traffic lights sat on green as cars clogged the road.

Everyone used to wear masks because of Covid, and before that, it was SARS. Now the vaccines had been rolled out, the masks were more against protection from the pollution.

By the time she got to the crossing, her eyes stung and her lungs ached. She opened her bag and pulled out her mask. Zipping up her bag, she noticed a light flashing inside: someone had left her a message. They could wait. All she wanted to do was go to the bar, and then bed. Someone in the queue sneezed. The lights changed and she walked fast to get some distance.

She hurried past the white-pillared National Museum. The red flags on the roof were barely visible in the murk. She crossed over to Tiananmen Square by the giant TV screens showing a peach sky and a white sun setting into the clouds. She had not seen a real sunset in a long time, not since she visited her parents in the countryside.

She rubbed her eyes and scratched her arm. Her skin felt tight from the acrid air. Once she got underground, she would be fine. She was almost there – just a bit further. Reaching the avenue where the tanks ran on parades, she rushed past the Forbidden City's towering red walls.

It was by the pillars in the shadows that she stopped. The shutters were down on all the shops, except for one black door. She slotted her ID through the card reader and the door swung open. In the hallway, her heels sunk into the plush carpet. Tempting smells wafted up the stairs. Every possibility was down there. She had been longing for it all day.

She caught sight of her tired reflection in the mirror. She took off the mask and rubbed the marks it had left on her face. Smoothing her hair back, she went down the stairs. In the dark interior of the bar, she headed to the counter, trying to avoid eye contact with the other seated clients. They laid back in scoop chairs, plastic tubes draped across their faces under their noses. The oxygen tubes led to illuminated pods on tables beside them. Bottles of greens, pinks, purples and yellows bubbled away in them. Orchestral music mixed with the fizzling sound of clean air. No one talked. The suits, the business types, were all plugged in, sucking up their respite time. It was a paid privilege to breathe freedom.

'Will it be your usual booth today, miss? Twenty minutes.' He was tall, and his Australian accent was delightful in its difference. One day Mei would ask his name, but not tonight. It could wait until she felt better.

'Thanks,' was all she could muster in reply.

'Which aroma will it be tonight?'

'Mandarin.'

'That'll be forty credits. Please go and make yourself comfortable,' he said as she swiped her card on the reader on the counter.

She went to the far end of the room and placed her bag on the floor. She settled herself into the chair and watched the waiter. He selected one of the coloured bottles on the shelves and began sorting out the tubes.

The oxygen bar used to be a cocktail place, a tourist trap in easy reach of the square, but trippers did not come to the city anymore. She took the opportunity of the waiter's absence to blow her nose. She folded the black contents into the tissue and stuffed it back into her pocket.

The orange jar was in the waiter's hand as he approached. He fixed it in the silver pod on the table and began attaching the tubes. 'Can I assist you with the link-up?'

He always asked that, and she wished he would not. It made her feel grubby, as though she were paying for something illicit. 'No, thank you.'

When he had gone, she grasped the tube laid out ready on top of the armrest. She secured the cannula to her nose and turned the knob on the canister. The bottle in the pod began to bubble. Sweet-scented air flowed up her nostrils, taking her back to childhood summer picnics and trips in the mountains with her family.

She settled back and stared at the mute TV on the wall in front of her. The news was on, the presenter stood outside the barricades at the Square. Her boss, China's environment minister, was hosting the summit and she would be assisting. Her department had spent weeks preparing inventories for the clean air strategy. If the experts all agreed with the action plan they had devised, it might just stop the country's decline.

When she could no longer focus on the picture, her eyelids fell. She came to at the sound of someone fiddling with the clips on her bag. She watched the back of the man's head as he scrabbled around. How could a mugger have walked straight in off the streets unnoticed? She unhooked the tube from her nose, just as she realised she knew her assailant. 'Chen?'

He lunged forwards and hugged her tight. She indulged all her old feelings. Relief and anger flooded her as one, and she jolted back in confusion. 'What are you doing here?'

He glanced at the door and scratched his face with a shaking hand. He was always so composed and immaculate. This was not like him. 'I had to come back,' he said.

Dried blood had left a large smear down the front of Chen's top. He had grey circles round his eyes, and kept looking back to the door as though he expected his worst nightmare to rush in. People were staring. The waiter gave her a nod to make sure she was all right. She held up her hand. *Five minutes*, she mouthed. He nodded and went back to attending customers at the bar.

'What have you done?' she whispered.

'Did you get my email?' He dived into her bag and picked out the phone. 'I need to know – did you get it?'

She wrestled it off him, alarmed at the terror on his face. 'Just sit down, yes?' She put him in her chair and crouched next to him.

He perched on the edge of it, seeming ready to flee any second. 'Is it drugs?' she asked.

He shook his head.

'Why are you stealing from my bag?'

He smiled, but his eyes had lost their sparkle. 'I'm not.'

'What then? Why travel all the way here?'

'I'm a dead man.'

'What?'

He glanced towards the door again. 'Not here.' He grabbed her hand as she stood up to head to the exit. 'Not that way. They'll kill me.'

'Stay here for a minute,' Mei said. She smoothed down her pencil skirt and went over to the waiter. 'I need to get a friend out of here. Do you have a back door?'

He gestured behind the bar. 'Go through the kitchens. The end door leads to the old service tunnels. You should be able to get to the surface from there into the Toki district.'

The red-light zone. *Great*, she thought. Feeling a warm touch on her hand, she looked down. He had taken off a glove. His fingers brushed hers.

'Are you sure you're OK?' His eyes were full of promise and protection.

It had been so long since anyone touched her. The last person who had was sitting in her oxygen booth. 'I'll be fine, thank you.' She signalled to Chen and he scurried over to the bar.

'Hopefully, we'll see you again soon.'

She ushered Chen past the door, cursing the bad timing of her old flame.

Leaning back against the hallway of her apartment, she tried to get her breath back from the race home. As she adjusted her skirt, her fingers felt ripped fabric along the seam. Her shins smarted where she had scraped them climbing out the manhole. It was quite ironic that she had been on her hands and knees in the red-light district. All that for an ex-boyfriend who had wheedled his way back into her life. She had let him. She was not sure who she was more cross with.

As she reached out to turn on the lights, Chen pulled her hand back. 'No, don't. We can't take the risk,' he said.

She gave a nervous laugh, worried at his spiralling paranoia. 'It's fine. We can't stumble about in the dark.' She flicked the lights on.

He held her by the shoulders, his brown eyes full of concern. 'Mei, please. I need you to look at the dossier.'

She frowned. 'What dossier?'

'The one I slid into your bag.' He thrust the bag into her hands. 'The village – it's gone.'

Her stomach lurched. 'What do you mean?'

'The forest dogs – they've gone crazy. Everyone's dead. There are people with guns. They're coming for me because of what I know. There's no time!' He was screaming now.

Mei held his shoulders and smoothed his hair. If she did not settle him, the neighbours would call security. 'It's going to be all right. We'll figure it out.' He started to slump and she only just managed to catch him. 'You're exhausted. Come on, let's get you in the bath. You smell worse than the smog.'

'I've been doing some research. It's the water in the village. The dogs, they—'

'We'll get to that later. Bath, now. You can sleep in the spare room,' she said as she helped him to the bathroom.

'Promise me you'll give it to the environment minister.'

'My boss?'

'There are people who don't want those papers to be seen. Promise me you'll read it and give it to him.'

She was too tired to argue. 'Yes, I will. Go and wash.'

She closed the door behind him. Walking to the lounge, she wondered how he had got all the way to Beijing in just a jacket, t-shirt, jeans and trainers. As she put her bag down on the dining table, she was surprised to find herself shaking. It was not his ranting that frightened her – he would never hurt her – it was his fear, and the blood on his top that was not his. It could be that he was into drugs and had got himself into trouble. As a vet, he had access to all kinds of medicines. They were easy enough to come by in the medical profession.

The dossier would prove if he really was mad. Leafing through the large document, she realised it would take her days to read it all. Time was not on her side. All he had to do was upload it to the Net and the world would see it. Why the secrecy? Officially, the Net was state-controlled but the hackers had found a way round that. They devised a phone app which bypassed the Chinese Internet. Everyone in Asia used Silverweasel. It was illegal, but the Government could not lock up millions of people at once.

She could not give the papers to her boss without checking it herself. No, she would read it and then decide what to do. She had to keep him at her apartment for a few days, just to figure out what was wrong with him.

First, she wanted to make sure the minister's summit notes were all in order. She put Chen's papers back in her bag and spread out her boss's files on the table. By the time she was finished, it was two a.m. There was no time to read his research if she wanted to look at least half-human for the summit.

Listening out for him, all she could hear was silence. She tiptoed down the hallway. The light was off in the bathroom and the spare room door was ajar. She peeped her head round to find him crashed out on the bed, the blue towel around his waist, a damp patch on the pillow from his hair. Was it his love for her that brought him back? It was too late at night, or early in the morning, to find out. She needed to sleep too.

*

Mei woke to muffled coughs beyond her apartment walls. Every morning was the same. All the children in the block had asthma or recurrent bronchitis. Picking up her mobile, she opened the app. The Chinese Air Pollution Index sat at five hundred. She could not remember it ever being at twenty, a "healthy" level as deemed by the World Health Organisation. Rumours on the Net were that the pollution levels were so hazardous, they were beyond a measurable scale.

At the window, she flicked the blinds. Daylight strained on half-power behind a reddish-brown haze. The car-jammed streets below were barely definable. Limos and sports cars bore pockmarks of rust. A white bus drove past, an orange stain covering almost the entire roof.

Tying up her light pink neck scarf, she stared at the dog-eared pages of Chen's dossier laid out on the table. If she wanted to know why he was so riled, the pages held the answer. Scanning through the document, she realised it was unreadable. It was all science jargon, chemistry code and numbers. She would need an expert to decipher it. Maybe he had flipped, and it was all gibberish.

She jolted when the service phone rang. Her boss's limo was outside. She placed the report back on the table and picked up the postcard of Tiananmen Gate with its red walls and curled roof tiles. She wrote Chen a note on the back, telling him to stay there and that she would be back later. Tiptoeing into his room, she found he was just as she had left him. She placed the card on the bedside table. Stroking his hair, she remembered how she used to wake up with that beautiful face. Even in sleep, his forehead was furrowed in worry. She never thought he would, but he had come back to her. Tucking the sheet round him, she told herself everything would be all right. It had to be.

CHAPTER FOUR
Joel

Joel stood in the cavernous lobby, dread filling his stomach. He clipped the visitor badge to his blazer, knocking the hip flask in his pocket. He ached to take a swig from it, but the receptionist was already eying him with distain. It was not the first summit he had been to and was used to advising government, but he had hardly been anywhere since he lost Lauren.

The receptionist pasted on a smile. 'Welcome to the Great Hall of the People, Professor Harket. Please sign in. Everyone else has already taken their seats.' She held out a pen for him.

He tried to keep his composure as he filled in his details. The thought of being with all those people in one room was too much. Ron was expecting him to make a speech – relying on him. He just did not have the heart for it. Why had he let him talk him into it?

He realised he was biting the end of the biro. 'Sorry.' He put it down on the desk. She did not take it.

A bang made him flinch. He turned to the glass doors. Outside, a young guy slammed his hands against the panels, his face taut with rage. The yellow placard he held read: *Clean Air Now*. Other shouting youngsters had massed with him, jostling banners. They were surrounded by riot police in helmets and stab-proof vests, stopping them from entering the summit. Flashes from the press cameras lit up the murky scene.

He smiled. It reminded him of his Greenpeace days when being in a cell meant victory. Until two days ago, his prison had been his flat where he spent blurred days and nights confined in the security of misery. He thought of the hip flask. It was no good. He picked up his bag to leave.

The main doors were blocked by the riot and he struggled to think. His heart raced and he reached for his flask. As his fingers felt the cool metal, a persistent banging made him look towards the front doors. The protestor had reverted to smashing his placard against the glass. Overcome by coughing, he fell to the ground to be leapt upon by police.

That guy had Joel's respect. He was making a difference to the world, or at least, trying to. Joel reasoned that if he could just do his speech, he could go from there – baby steps. Breathe in for four seconds, hold it for four, breathe out for four, hold it for four, breathe in for four...

'I think they're still on the introductions,' the receptionist said. 'If you go with security, they'll take you to your seat.'

He knew this was his crossroads. It was either give up and go back to the flat, or move on. Taking a deep breath, he walked through the scanner. Once he had the all-clear, he looked back to see the protestor grappling with the police. Their eyes met. That guy had the bollocks to take on the communist police. The least Joel could do was walk into a room full of people. He gave him a thumbs-up, before following the security guard down the labyrinth of corridors.

They came to a stop outside some double doors. Applause came from beyond. The guard spoke into his walkie-talkie as he ushered Joel inside. The bright lights in the auditorium disorientated him.

It was filled with thousands of red seats. Of all the places he had spoken at, the sheer display of the place was overwhelming. He needed to be clear-headed. When he was shown to the end of the aisle, he sat down and started to get his papers out of his bag.

The scent of women's perfume and an awareness of being watched came all at once. He looked up to find the olive-skinned intern sitting next to him. She wore big headphones and had stopped halfway through taking notes. At least she had dressed up this time, in a business suit.

'Now who's the late one?' she asked, flashing him a smile. 'I thought I might've seen you on the plane.'

'Part of my agreeing to come was that Ron get us separate flights,' he snapped. With the pretence of flicking through his papers, he hoped she would shut up soon. When he chanced a look at her, she had gone back to studiously writing notes.

A short Asian woman with a dark bob and a pink neck scarf spoke at the podium in Chinese. Headphones were on the hook in front of him. He was just about to put them on when the intern moved in close.

'I'm taking notes so we can report back to Ron,' she whispered. 'Maybe later we can go through what you've missed?'

His hip flask dug in his ribs and he clenched his hands. 'You aren't in high school now, kid. Don't get too cosy. You're just an intern.'

'Whatever you say, *professor*,' she replied, with a knowing look in her eye.

Joel felt an alien sensation of heat rising from his chest, something stirring deep within. Was it anger or something more primal? He was not cut out for this. He was better working alone, not second-guessing what some young upstart with gold hoops and dimples was thinking. 'Take your notes and shut the hell up. I'm going straight back to the hotel after this. Without you.'

She leaned close to him, her knee touching his. 'I expect you'll want to get back to your pipe and slippers. Did you bring them in your hand luggage?'

He almost laughed. He had not been spoken to like that in years. The cheeky little shit. 'We won't be working together, despite whatever Ron told you. I'm here to do this speech and go home. That's it.'

Someone behind shushed them. A man was talking at the podium and the translator relayed his speech at a rapid rate through the headphones. 'Thank you for all coming at short notice. My name is Heng Chung. I'm the environment minister to the People's Republic of China. We have convened this UN Air Health summit because, despite our best efforts, we have reached unprecedented levels of air pollution in our beloved country.'

'Best efforts, my arse,' Joel muttered. He stole a sideways glance at the intern who had resumed taking notes.

'The situation has intensified by encroaching smoke from neighbouring countries, caused by illegal fires from palm plantation clearing,' Mr Chung explained. 'The Japanese volcanic ash cloud has blown straight into our country, meaning the smog will not clear for some time.'

'Any excuse,' Joel whispered, but the girl ignored him.

'The timing is far from ideal. The current cold snap has created temperature inversion, which my assistant, Mei, will explain.' He gestured to the girl with the neck scarf.

She got up and pressed a remote control. The screens at the side of the stage showed an image of the planet. She stood next to the minister and adjusted the microphone. 'Think of the air above the earth in layers. When the temperature drops, a layer of cold, dense air gets trapped beneath a more buoyant layer of warm air. The air near the ground has nowhere to go and pollution builds within it. This results in a thick haze that is hard to shift. If we cannot clear this dirty air soon, the hospital admissions with breathing problems will continue to soar. We want to reduce cancer rates and get the children into school again. We want to get workers back to their jobs.'

'Thank you, Mei.' The minister gestured her to sit.

Joel glanced at the intern's notes. It was the worst handwriting he had ever seen. It was more like hieroglyphics or Arabic. 'What the hell is that?' he whispered.

'Shorthand.'

'Are you kidding? How do you—'

She put a finger to her lips. 'Shh.'

The translator began his quick-fire sentences again. 'China leads the global economy. What happens here affects the whole world. We need support, now more than ever. International tourism has struggled to bounce back after the Covid lockdown and we want to avoid an economic crash on a global scale.'

The audience was silent. Joel looked round the room and the similarly stunned faces. Was China asking for help?

'Our crops are failing due to high sulphur levels in the atmosphere,' the minster said. 'For an economy to survive it needs energy, food security and clean water. Without any one of these, civilisation is thrown into jeopardy. However, we have a solution at hand, which will be discussed later. First, let us hear from some of our invited speakers.'

He took his seat and the Asian girl took over the podium. 'Now please welcome marine scientist Professor Joel Harket, of the Marine and Atmospheric Science Foundation in London.'

The audience clapped as he walked to the stage. At the podium, he made a point of shuffling his papers to buy him some composure time. 'Thank you for allowing me to speak at this summit. You're right in saying that what happens here will affect the whole world. But I'm talking from an environmental point of view. It was the UN itself that recognised that the effects of climate change will be catastrophic if we do nothing. We are rapidly approaching the point of no return. Everyone knows about the winter floods, droughts, melting ice-caps. My concern is what is happening in the sea. The effects of burning fossil fuels above water are reflected beneath the surface, in the ocean. A quarter of all carbon dioxide emissions are absorbed by the oceans. The excess CO2 is changing the acidic chemistry of the sea.'

Spotting his empty red chair, he noticed the intern winding her highlighted curls round her fingers, staring at the people around her rather than taking notes. With a sniff of annoyance, he carried on:

'In two hundred and fifty years, seawater acidity has risen by a third. If we do nothing, the ocean pH levels will more than double by 2100. We must switch to alternative energies before it's too late.'

A cough came from the row of seats near the front. A bald-headed man on the UN climate panel spoke into his table microphone. Marcus Caines was the senior energy adviser to the British Government. 'Professor, nuclear power is a clean energy source. Why do you think we started the co-share energy agreement with China several years ago?'

'Nuclear plants are no great saviour,' Joel said. 'We all know what happens when something goes wrong. Look at the Fukushima disaster. Radioactive water from the Daiichi plant was flowing into the ocean at a rate of three hundred tonnes a day. They couldn't stop it for two whole years. Where do you think all that water went?' He gripped the edge of the podium and looked back at the faces in the audience. 'For years we've been monitoring sea snails, or "sea butterflies" as they're often called. Their shells are being eaten away, corroded by the acid in the ocean.'

Marcus stood up, light dancing off his scalp. 'You're worried about snails while people are struggling to breathe?'

'They're part of the floating plankton system, which all marine ocean-living creatures depend on. In 1990, Greenpeace found cesium-134 in plankton collected outside the twelve-mile exclusion zone around a French nuclear test site. We're screwing up the food chain.'

Marcus gave a sarcastic smile. 'Everybody knows sanctions are in place regarding nuclear testing. Fukushima tests its radiation levels on the beach every day now. It's all safe levels. The beaches there have reopened. There's even a surfing beach there now. Did you know climate policies cost the UK twenty-one billion pounds each year? Just to try and reduce the Earth's temperature by a hundredth of a Celsius. I mean, it's miniscule. Hardly worth it, in my opinion.' He sat down and the audience clapped.

To the left of the Climate panel table, a plump lady with a bob stood up. 'I'm Janice Barber, the UK secretary to the Department for Business Energy and Industrial Strategy. If I might add to the debate: shale gas, if used as the primary source of energy, would generate sixty-six billion pounds a year in tax revenues and reduce carbon emissions by ten times more than the current plan.'

'What of the water contamination threat?' Joel replied in a level voice. 'The sinkholes? With the constant flooding, fracking would create more voids for water to erode under the surface.'

Her chin doubled as she pursed her lips. 'There is no proof that fracking is a threat to the water supply.'

'Not yet,' he replied. 'But once the water supplies are contaminated beyond repair, that's it. As the global warming continues and polar ice melts increase, this will increase the acidity.'

'What does ice have to do with it?' Janice asked, with a dismissive laugh.

'Our lab took some ice core samples recently from remote glacial areas, which are thousands of years old. We found acidic deposit levels in them.' He shuffled his papers. 'We need to be the generation to make a stand and start caring for the world, instead of using it for our own ends.'

Heng Chung had joined him at the podium. 'That was certainly enlightening. Thank you, Professor Harket.'

There was a smattering of applause as he left the stage. There was no way they would be able to make a case to government for the funding now.

'Don't say it,' he said to the intern when he got to his seat, dumping his papers back in his bag. Coming thousands of miles to be humiliated was not worth it.

'I thought you did really well,' the girl said, her eyes bright. 'We need to swap notes on this, because—'

'Don't be getting any ideas. We aren't lab partners, remember?' he whispered.

'Wow, you have some serious women issues.' She adjusted her headphones. 'What does your wife make of you and your people skills?'

'She's dead.'

'Oh, fuck. I'm sorry.'

'Look, Alice—'

'It's Amy.'

'Whatever. Let's just mind our own damned business, shall we?'

She shrugged. 'If that's what you want. But I think everyone's got an agenda and I bet you *he* has,' she said, pointing at the Chinese minister. 'We just need to figure out what it is.'

They were shushed again. He put the headphones back on to listen to a few other speakers, who argued about which country was at fault regarding the forest-clearing fires. Then it was back to politics and arguing and point-scoring. What was the point in all that research if nobody could do anything constructive? He promised himself that at the next break, he would be off. Preferably, to the nearest bar.

The Chinese minister began speaking again, with an air of finality. 'So, we look forward to establishing an agreement next year with all UN nations to sign a global agreement on climate change. Now, to the core business of this meeting. What we propose is this,' the minister said and gripped the top of the lectern. 'We will be firing silver iodide rockets into the sky to induce the rain chemically and clear the air.'

Joel glanced at the intern, who had stopped taking notes. She had a look of horror on her face. 'What?' he asked, nudging her. She shook her head, not taking her stare from the minister.

The minister gestured to the room. 'We want you to go back to your governments and spread the message that China is very much in business.'

So that was what the whole summit had been about: they wanted to use it as a propaganda exercise. Everyone was applauding, except for Joel and the girl. She looked horrified. *What the hell is wrong with her now*? Before he could stop her, she stood up.

'No, you can't,' she shouted.

The auditorium fell silent and a sea of heads turned to stare their way.

CHAPTER FIVE
Amy

Amy felt cold sweat beading on her lip and her fingertips tingled. This was going against all the summit protocols, but she had made it this far. She kept her gaze on the minister. If she backed down now, she knew she would always regret it.

But Ron would kill her. If she messed up now, more people would die, regardless of whether the wild dog attack was a one-off.

'You can't,' Harket whispered.

She chewed her lip in annoyance. 'Don't you tell me I can't,' she hissed. 'I have to.'

The minister searched for the person who interrupted. 'Who spoke?'

'I did,' she said, raising her hand. 'You can't let it rain.'

The minister squinted through the stage lights, as he spoke into the microphone. 'Cloud-seeding is something we are proud of in the People's Republic of China. We have stopped many droughts by this method. We did it in Beijing before the Olympics to clear the air pollution. I assure you, it is perfectly safe.'

She wound the headphone wire through her fingers. 'Doing it so frequently creates a toxic effect in the weather cycle. You're using silver iodide to cloud-seed?'

'Of course.'

'It can cause temporary incapacitation with continued exposure. You're making people ill.'

The girl with the pink scarf leant close to the minister. He put his hand over the microphone as they conferred.

'I must speak,' Amy shouted, cursing herself for her wobbly voice.

'Your name?' the minister asked, adjusting his tie.

'Amy Weston. I'm an intern at the Foundation with Professor Harket.'

His fixed smile gave away nothing. 'You aren't on the speakers' list, but you clearly have something you want to say. Come up here.'

She took off the headphones and went to step round the professor. He grabbed her leg. 'Don't,' he warned. His hand was hooked round her thigh, his blue eyes locked on hers.

She tried to ignore the pulse in her stomach and prised his fingers off her. 'Don't get too cosy,' she mimicked his words back at him, and pushed past.

She concentrated on walking the long expanse to the stage as the lines of experts watched her. It would be just her luck if she stumbled now. Her heart raced as she reached the steps. Two men flanked the stairs leading to the podium, carrying guns in their belts.

She took her place at the lectern and blinked up at the bright spotlights in the ceiling. They were clustered around a large red star in the centre, which stared down at her like an eye. Sweat tickled the backs of her knees.

She wished she had written something down. 'Your cloud-seeding effort won't work,' she said. 'It's just a sticking plaster to the solution. It will help in the short term, yes, but you're forgetting what happens to the rainwater. You're not accounting for precipitation.' She turned to the girl with the neck scarf and held up her phone. 'Can I link this up for visual?'

'Use the lead under there.' The woman pointed to under the lectern.

The screen behind her lit up to show an image of a hillside and clouds, with circular arrows. 'Everyone knows how the water cycle works,' Amy said. 'Ocean water and moisture from the mainland evaporates and condenses in the atmosphere to form clouds. The rainwater becomes surface run-off and soaks into the ground, down to the ocean, and the process begins again.'

'Do we really need a primary school science lesson?' the bald man at the UN table asked.

She took a deep breath and carried on. 'Acid rain is caused by emissions of sulphur dioxide from power stations and nitrogen oxide from traffic pollution.'

'We know that,' he replied, drumming his fingers on the table. 'What's your point?'

'Acid rain is corrosive. Once it gets into the water supply, we have no control over it. When we drink water contaminated by acid rain, it can damage the brain.'

'You're scaremongering,' said Janice Barber. 'Tap water is perfectly safe to drink.'

'There was a case years ago in Sweden when the corrosion of copper pipes turned people's hair blue,' Amy said.

'I was thinking about going a different colour,' Janice said, preening her hair. Sniggers went round the room.

'It's affecting the trees. You live in London, don't you, Ms

Barber? All the leaves are falling off the trees. The ecosystem is screwed. And the buildings – several years ago, the Washington Monument in the US was closed off.'

'That was earthquake damage,' the US secretary general Carla Jenson spoke into the mike.

'Prove it, can you? Statues and stone engravings are losing their features. I was nearly crushed by a churchyard statue when it crumbled in front of me.' She took the thumb from her pocket and held it up. 'All that remained was this. How many historic buildings are there in the world? Hundreds of them metres high. What do you think would happen if the Tokyo Tower collapsed?' She threw the stone down over the stage and it shattered into dust.

'Don't be ridiculous, the tower is metal.' Carla smoothed her slicked-back bun. 'Acid rain can't affect metal.'

'Can't it? Have you seen the cars outside? Nearly all of them are riddled with rust,' Amy said. 'If it can do that to cars, what do you think it does when it gets into rivers?' She tried to concentrate, despite Janice being engrossed with her phone. 'This isn't going to just affect Asia. Air pollution can be carried on the winds. Up to sixty per cent of total acid deposit is caused by dry gases sticking to the ground and other surfaces.'

'There is nothing to worry about here,' Carla said, standing to address the hall.

'You're wrong. With the high toxic levels already established, it's only a matter of time before the acid gases will mix with nuclear waste in the ocean, the smog, and the volcanic ash in a concentrated form, of unprecedented levels. Once it rains, the poison balance will be tipped.'

'The what?' Carla asked.

Amy pointed at the screen behind her as it changed to the graphics of a chart. 'I've been doing some research on the Earth's temperature and the predicted forecast. If the temperature keeps rising, the trees will not be able to absorb the CO2 effectively and climate change will accelerate. As the weather cycles move around the globe, the effects will be international. It's all linked, don't you see? Drinking water will be contaminated as well as the soil. Once the poison gets into the brain—'

'Are you a doctor? Do you have evidence to back this up? A PhD, perhaps?' Janice asked.

'I wrote my thesis on it.'

'Can we read this thesis?'

'I... I didn't finish it,' Amy muttered.

'Why was that?' Janice stood up, looking at her phone. 'You flunked out, didn't you?'

'What the fuck? Have you been checking up on me?'

Janice looked thrilled at Amy's inability to control her temper, as though it was proof of her unreliability. 'You expect us to believe someone who hasn't completed a doctorate? I'm sorry,' she said, and gave her a patronising smile, 'we can't take the word of a failed student. It's time you left the stage.'

'No!' Amy banged her fist on the lectern. 'The wild dogs that killed those people in this country were poisoned by their water supply. It sent them crazy. It's going to keep happening, and it's getting worse. You need to do something—' She felt a hand grip her arm. She looked up to find Professor Harket standing over her, his eyes burning with anger.

'Shut up,' he spat, and dragged her away from the microphone.

'Thank you, Miss Weston,' said the minister, back at the lectern. 'Now, back to business.'

The professor pulled her hard and she stumbled down the steps after him.

'Sorry. I had to,' she said.

He stopped at their seats and picked up their bags. She waited for him to say something. In silence, he hauled her all the way out of the auditorium and did not let go.

CHAPTER SIX
Mei

Mei got up from her chair as the minister steered back to the agenda. No one noticed her pick up her bag and slink into the wings. She hurried along, hoping to catch them before they left. She need not have worried. She heard the shouting long before she found them in the lobby.

'You silly cow,' the professor yelled, pacing up and down. 'You've single-handedly made sure I never get into a place like this ever again.'

'What's the point?' the girl said. 'Those fucking guppies wouldn't listen. They only care about the money.'

'You made us look like lunatics. *Killer dogs*? How am I going to pitch to government now?'

Mei stood by the end of the lobby desk, feeling she was intruding on a lovers' tiff. She gave a little cough, hoping they would notice.

'I said what needed to be said,' the girl said, handing her visitor badge to the receptionist.

'You say whatever you like and bugger the consequences.' He ripped off his badge and slammed it on the desk. 'Daddy pays for everything, doesn't he? You throw a strop and he paints over the cracks with money.'

She pointed her finger at him. 'You don't know anything about me. Or my parents.'

'Yeah, thank God,' he said, and stared at her. It was as though the two of them froze in time at the crest of their argument. Then he tutted and started to walk away.

Mei darted after him. 'Professor, I've been following your work,' she called. She got in front of him and he stopped. 'I was most interested in the speeches you both gave.'

'Are you joking?' he snapped. 'We were laughed out the summit back there.'

'Don't mind him, he has no people skills,' the girl said, squeezing past him to shake Mei's hand. 'I'm Amy.'

'Mei. Please, professor.' She touched his arm, as he started to turn away. 'I have some findings that you may find relevant.'

'Thank you,' the professor replied, curtly. 'If you email my department, I'm sure someone will get back to you. If you don't mind, I'm off to get a drink.' He tried to walk off but she followed him.

'It's very important that you hear it – both of you – now. I wouldn't trouble you otherwise.'

Applause rang out from the auditorium. If Mei left the summit, the minister would be furious. Her job might be in the balance, but she had to risk it. 'Might I suggest we go somewhere else a little less prominent? I know a bar not far away,' Mei said.

'Deal,' he said, and slung his bag over his shoulder. 'Let's go.'

*

'This isn't the kind of bar I had in mind,' the professor muttered as they sat on bar stools.

Each of them had tubes running from their nostrils. The

intern sulked as she watched the acrobats on stage. They contorted themselves into the crab position, balancing drinks glasses on their stomachs and necks; trays with more glasses being held up by an outstretched foot.

Mei wished she could enjoy the lavender scent a little more. If Chen was right, they had no time, and the professor looked ready to leave at any moment. 'Thank you for coming,' she said.

'You've got five minutes,' he growled.

'For fuck's sake,' Amy told him. 'What did she ever do to you?' He glared at her. 'Come on, what bit of you doesn't believe the poison balance could happen?'

'You think it's going to happen like a tsunami, all at once, all over the world?' he shot back. 'This isn't Hollywood.'

'It already is happening,' Mei said.

Mid-argument, they stopped and stared at her. Jars of purple, green and pink liquids continued bubbling away.

Amy pulled the cannula from her nose. 'What?'

'It was something you said about the water being toxic,' Mei said. 'I've got a friend staying at my flat. He's a vet from the southern province. He gave me his research. He wanted me to pass it on to my boss. I didn't, and now I wish I had, as you two might've stood more of a chance in there.'

Amy rocked back on her stool, mouth open. 'You believe us?'

She nodded. 'Chen started to tell me about the water in the village, and something to do with wild dogs.'

'Dogs?' Amy asked. 'That killer dog attack?'

'You mentioned the drinking water can damage the brain,' Mei said. 'I think it's done something to them.'

Amy hopped down from the stool. 'I fucking knew it. The

food chain is poisoned – already.'

'Not necessarily,' Joel said. 'But we're going to need that document.'

'I don't live far away,' Mei replied, remembering Chen back at home as she said it. She could not bring them back there. She was not sure for definite whether he had a drug problem. If he did, he might be having withdrawal symptoms. Neither could she guarantee he would not sound crazy. She had to hope the research held up.

'Shall we wait for you?' the professor asked.

It was as though he sensed her discomfort, and she was secretly grateful. 'No, no, it's fine. Go back to your hotel, I'll meet you there.'

She had fitted her face mask by the time she got to the top of the stairs. The streetlights were on, even though it was midday. As she turned into an alley, she heard the scuff of a footstep behind her. She whirled round – no one. An ambulance screamed past in the distance. *City life as usual*, she assured herself. She quickened her pace along the darkened alley until she reached the streetlights of civilisation.

*

At the front door to the flats, she checked around her before getting her keys out. She had just got the key in the lock, when the door burst open. A man tore past her, lumping into her shoulder.

'Excuse me,' she shouted after him. He was already gone. She shook her head and grabbed the door before it closed.

She started to climb the stairwell. When she made it to the

second-floor landing, she heard another set of footsteps in the lobby below. She stopped to listen. They kept coming. She peered over the banister but could not see anyone. Silence, then a door closed. *Must be one of the neighbours coming home.* She hurried up the last flight of steps.

As she walked along the hallway to her flat, she found the front door wide open. He had gone, given in to go and get a fix. She blamed herself. She should have come back straight away, not gone to the oxygen bar with the others.

Flicking on the light, she found the sofa seats ripped open on the floor. Her fern was knocked over, magazines were everywhere, a vase smashed. She dumped her bag on the dining table and sighed. She had almost believed his story. Instead, he had betrayed her. Why come so far, just to steal from her?

The TV was untouched, and the stereo cast its gentle blue light over the chaos. The carriage clock ticked away on the bookshelf. Her grandfather had given her that when she turned twenty-one. Chen had been there, raised a glass with the family.

Nothing had been taken. If it was not theft, what was it? She rubbed her neck in frustration and frowned. Something was different: there was an empty space on the table. Chen's papers were missing. Why would he take them if it was all a lie?

A spluttering, burbling sound came from behind the sofa. She rushed over to find Chen sprawled on the floor, blood dribbling from his mouth. 'Oh, my god, no.' She scooted to the floor. 'Who did this to you?' Grabbing a cushion from the floor, she placed it under his head. A dark patch spread on the carpet by his ribs, as he laboured to breathe. 'Chen?' She got her mobile from her pocket to dial for an ambulance, but his bloodstained hand closed over hers.

'Don't. Police will come. It'll put you in danger too,' he whispered, and winced. 'The document is all that matters now.'

She pulled up his t-shirt to reveal an oozing wound. Finding another cushion, she pressed it firm against him. 'You were stabbed?'

'Quieter than a gunshot, isn't it?'

'I need to get help.'

'No, Mei. The best way you can help is get that document into the right hands.'

She pressed the cushion harder to his chest. 'I didn't read it. I'm so sorry. They've taken it, the ones who did this.'

'Don't drink the water. The wild dogs from the forest, they're diseased.' He struggled to speak. 'I tested the river water. There's all kinds of poison in there, from factory by-products, to the leftovers from the cocaine manufacturing. It's done something to their brains.'

'You rest now,' she said, stroking his head.

He pushed her hand away. His eyes were not focusing. 'No, you have to know. I cut open two of the dogs before I fled the village. Their brains looked like nothing I've ever seen before, in all my years as a vet.' He coughed hard. 'They both had the same symptoms.'

Blood was seeping through the cushion. She pressed harder onto the wound. 'I need to get you to hospital. Please.'

'The disease will come this way, like wildfire. You need to tell your boss, shut down the city. It's not safe here. The people who did this, they'll come for you. You have to go.'

She shook her head. 'I'm not leaving you here.'

He brushed her cheek. 'I shouldn't have waited until now to come back to you, but I'm glad I did.' Overcome by choking, he went limp.

She cradled him in her arms, stroking his clammy face. She pressed her fingers to his neck, feeling for a pulse, but there was none. 'I'm so sorry.' She kissed his hair and lowered him down to the pillow. 'I love you.'

Wiping tears from her face, she spied one page left of the dossier under the table. On her knees, she snatched it up and held it to her chest. City lights glared through the gaps in the curtains. Soon, the planes would fly over and the skies would rain poison. Chen was right: it was not safe there anymore.

Joel took a gulp of whisky and watched another tank roll along the now-empty street. From the hotel lobby window, he worried the unrest could cause some delays getting to the airport. After the summit debacle, all he wanted to do was get shot of the intern and salvage what was left of his career. The stupid girl had destroyed his reputation in minutes. Not to mention Ron's as well, after he had given her that chance. He chugged back another shot of whisky. Ice cubes bumped his lips, but the drink had yet to settle his nerves.

He wished the intern would stop twitching her feet. Her legs were crossed and she balanced one of her black ballet pumps by her toes as it fell loose from her heel.

'We need to get out of here,' he said.

She prodded the lemon in her Coke with a straw and sat back in her chair. 'Chill out. We said we'd wait and see her research. Otherwise, the entire UN will think we're raving lunatics.'

'Too late for that.'

Picking up her drink, she smiled. 'I'm proud of what I did. They needed to be told a few things. Why won't you believe it's possible?' she asked.

He sighed and rubbed his head. 'Because it isn't. It's like what-if times a thousand.'

She tucked her hair behind her ear. 'What do you think the

Big Bang was? And the *what-if* that killed the dinosaurs? If the poison balance tips, that is just what it will be. You know yourself that the ocean acidification is beyond control.'

'Tell you what,' he said, 'if it turns out you're right, I'll buy you dinner.' The words were out before he could stop himself. What made him say that? He had offered to spend more time with the most irritating person in his life right now – idiot.

It had shut her up though. She was staring at him, stuck for words for a change. He bit back a smile. The determination in her face was then replaced with a look of suspicion.

She folded her arms. 'What makes you think I'd want to?'

He tried to mask the pause in his bravado. Getting dates back in the day had never particularly been a problem for him. It was just the way things were. There was never much persuading to do, at any rate. After Lauren, he had given up any idea of dating. His mojo had all but abandoned him.

The girl had a point though. Why should she bother? He looked in the bottom of his empty glass, swirling the ice cubes round. 'Everyone's got to eat,' he said.

Christ, what was wrong with him? Eating on his own in silence was comfortable. Maybe not always preferable, but it was the way things had gone. Was there much point in changing it? He had the perfect chance to backtrack, and he did not. After all the hassle Lauren had caused him, he did not need another woman in his life again. It did not need to be a date, he reasoned. It did not need a label. They needed to discuss the summit, in any case. They would keep it professional, and that was it. He was worrying for nothing, of course. The dinner would never happen anyway. Her theory was crackers, and he had placed his bet.

Nothing wrong with having a gamble.

She squirmed a little in her seat and bit her thumbnail. 'I thought you hated me.'

He tilted the glass to watch the cubes dance in the glass. 'I never said that. You're a pain in the arse, for sure.'

'You really want to slum it with a pleb who lives in a rental above an Indian takeaway?'

He nodded. 'That decides on the food choice. And it saves on a taxi.'

'Skinflint.' She nudged him and they both gave a little smile.

'Are we on? If you're right, I pay. If I'm right, you pay.'

'Will there be afters?'

He frowned, not understanding her English colloquialism. 'What is "afters"?'

She leant her elbows on the armrests of her chair, rolling her shoulders forwards. 'Whatever you want it to be,' she whispered. 'You could go savoury or sweet. It could be cheesecake or chocolate mousse.'

He chugged back some more drink, trying to rein thoughts of what they could do together with a bowlful of chocolate mousse. She was just a kid, despite the sultry look that suggested otherwise. 'The best you'll get out of me is poppadoms,' he said.

'It's a shit deal, but if it shuts you up…' she said.

'Likewise, you're a mouth on legs.'

'And you've got no people skills.'

'Says the person who got us kicked out the UN summit,' he said. She bit her tongue and, for once, watched out of the window in silence. 'You live in London?' he asked.

She nodded. 'Penny Lane.'

'As in the song.' He loved that melody, from another time. Before life got too fast, too complicated. He settled back in his seat and glanced out at the black night. When she looked blankly at him, he sighed. '*The Beatles.*'

'Oh right, yeah,' she muttered.

All they had in common was science, and that was pushing it with her bonkers theory. He necked the last of the drink. Nope, it would never work, he told himself, even on a professional level. They were just too different.

He stared out the window for a while, glad to have a few minutes' silence. When he looked back, she was fully immersed in the sophomoric cocoon of her phone. He was right: they were way too different.

He turned round at the sound of clacking footsteps. The porter glided across the lobby. He bypassed the revolving doors, which were out of action. He went to the side entrance instead. In the short time the door had been open, the fetid air plumed into the lobby.

'Please let me in,' a girl murmured, her voice breaking.

The porter stared at the hunched girl as though she were a tramp. Joel could see Mei was covered in blood. The doorman shook his head and made to close the door on her.

Joel jumped up from his seat and managed to keep a relaxed demeanour as he walked across the tiles. He had to get her inside, had to be calm. He barged into the porter, choosing only to concentrate on the girl. 'Here you are, my dear.' He reached out and took her hand, leading her past the bemused doorman. 'It looks like you've taken a fall.'

'You know this person?' the doorman asked him.

'Yes.' Joel struggled to hold her up as she sagged against him. 'Let's get you fixed up right away. Those hooligans outside will be the death of us. Hardly good for tourism, is it, these riots? The least you can do is get us some water, don't you think?' he asked the porter, who nodded and scurried away. 'It's OK. I've got you,' he whispered to her, as he guided her to their table.

'What the fuck?' Amy looked up from her drink.

'Get her in the corner, quick.'

She moved aside and helped get her into the alcove. 'Are you hurt?' Amy asked.

Mei shook her head, on the verge of tears. For all he knew, she had killed someone. He did not know how to deal with these women. After Lauren, he was way out of practice.

The waiter arrived with a glass of water, bowed and left. Once he was out of earshot, Joel whispered close to her, 'What happened?'

'My apartment has been wrecked.' Her face screwed up in anguish. 'Chen came to me because he thought he was being followed. He wrote the papers. When I got back from the summit, the papers were gone.' Mei began to sob as the intern put her arm round her. 'Chen's dead. They killed him.' Water sloshed onto the table as Mei raised the tumbler to her lips.

Joel looked at the smear of red on her neck scarf. 'Did you call the police?'

'It's not safe here,' she murmured, and began to shake.

He could hear a phone beeping. It was coming from Mei's bag. He picked it out and checked the screen. 'It says Heng Chung,' he said.

Amy took the phone from him. 'It's her boss.' She rejected the call and turned the phone off.

Mei stood up and bit her lip, her red eyes wide. 'You shouldn't have done that. I have to get back to the office. I need to tell him.' She went limp and fell towards the glass table.

Joel kicked his chair away and caught her just in time.

'What do we do now?' Amy asked, giving him a strange look.

'Take her upstairs. Get some food into her,' he said, holding Mei up. 'We need to find out what she knows. Looks like we'll be getting a later flight home.'

Amy pretended to be busy, putting the cleared dinner plates back on the tray, as she listened in on the professor's conversation.

'I warned you, Ron. I said it'd be a car crash,' he spoke down the phone. 'They chucked us out after she swore at the UN members. Oh, you heard?' He threw her an accusing look.

She bit her lip and fought the urge to argue. Instead, she took the tray to the table by the door.

She went over to the bed and tucked the blankets tighter round Mei. Shouts came from the street. She went to the window and, pushing back the curtains, found it was dark. The room faced the glass of another high-rise. Blue lights rebounded off the buildings. She heard a bang outside.

'Anyway, I'm calling because we may have some new evidence,' the professor told Ron. 'They want to see us? See you back in London.' He hung up and put his phone back in his pocket.

'What's up?' Amy asked, feeling braver.

'The government panel want us to meet with them at their offices in Whitehall. Turns out they'd already rung Ron. Don't look too smug, they might just want to smack your legs for making us look like dicks.'

'Ron is free to fire me, if he wants.' She walked around the bed and over to the table to pick up the page from Mei's bag. 'I stand by what I said.'

'I suppose we should get on with it, then,' he said.

'Huh?'

He nodded to the page in her hands. 'I've packed my reading glasses. You'll have to read it.'

She swallowed and smoothed the page out on the table. 'Do us a favour and make the tea.' She read, hunched over the table, while he sorted out the mugs. Having expected him to moan or backchat, she was surprised that he carried on in silence. 'Looks like he wrote it in a hurry.'

'What does it say?'

'He'd seen a rise in admissions to his surgery, animals that had been bitten by something. This guy, Chen, did an autopsy back at his surgery on one of the forest dogs. He found unusual readings.'

'Meaning?' He put the mug of tea in front of her.

'There was significant scarring on the outside of the brain.'

'A trauma?' he asked, and sat opposite her.

'It couldn't be. He did a second autopsy on another. The findings were the same.'

He scratched his face in thought. 'OK, what else?'

'It says the dogs are usually scared of humans.'

'So?'

'They go from recluse, to suddenly targeting their predators. Why the change?

He leant back in his chair, hands clasped behind his head. 'You tell me.'

She scanned the page. 'The kidneys had a high level of toxicity, along with the liver. He tested the river water from the forests.'

She shifted to sit cross-legged on the chair. She tried to make sense of the document as it became more bunched up with technical jargon and words she could not pronounce. 'He mentions a word: eutrophication.'

'Oh.' The professor leaned back on his chair and rested his shoes up on the table.

She pushed his feet off. 'I've heard it somewhere. Remind me.'

His face was not giving much away, as though he was a doctor evaluating how much to tell a sick patient. 'It's what happens when there's too much nitrogen in the water. Algae blooms, and dominant plants take over and block the light for underwater plants. The algae dies and breaks down, and decomposing organisms use up all the oxygen.'

'The fish suffocated?' she asked.

'He took water samples, right?'

She nodded. 'It contained high readings of chemical residues and the pH levels, presumably including run-off from the illegal drug cartels a few miles upstream. The water was undrinkable.'

'Let me guess: it was the only water source nearby. So, then what?' he asked.

She rubbed her eyes. 'Fuck's sake, let me rest a little, will you? This is like the scientific equivalent of Shakespeare.'

'Come on, you want to be a scientist. You can do it.'

'I *am* a scientist.' She gulped her tea, reading fast as she swallowed. 'It says the dogs were showing group signs of a changed mentality. They attacked the settlement and started to hunt the villagers. The authorities turned up and barricaded the village.'

'Christ,' he breathed. 'Was it like rabies or something?'

'No. Look what he says about the autopsy.' She pointed to the page. 'He said the brain had scarring on it.'

'Well? What's the link?' he snapped.

'The only difference in the environment is their drinking water,' she said.

'Are you saying that it sent them crazy?'

She turned the cup in her palms, chancing a glance at him. 'I don't see what else it could be. If the water can do this to the dogs out in the sticks, what do you think forcing it to rain in a highly polluted area is going to do?' She picked up the paper and looked at him. 'Acid rain affects the brain. It's a fact. It takes just a small concentration to do the damage.'

Deep in thought as he looked at the paper, his tongue ran over the small gap between his two top teeth. 'This is what I'm talking about – brilliant.' He looked up at her and smiled without parting his lips. Amy wondered if he was self-conscious about his tooth gap. It was barely noticeable, but she suddenly longed to feel the gap with her own tongue. Blushing, she picked at her fingernail, hoping he would not notice.

'What are you staring at?' he asked, with an irritated edge to his voice.

'Nothing. Sorry, professor.' *Inappropriate.* He was hot, but it would be unprofessional to do anything about it. He was just a colleague, and he did not even want to be that. He hated her fucking guts. Plus, his wife was dead. Was he grieving still? He had offered to take her out on a date, but only as a bet. Did he wear a wedding ring? She had not noticed. Maybe there would be a tan line if he had taken it off recently. She could not look now; it would be obvious. For all she knew, he had a girlfriend. *Fuck, stop it.*

'Call me Joel, all right?'

His name repeated, screamed inside her mind, like it enjoyed hearing the informality of it: Joel, Joel, *Joel.*

Ignoring the cowed sensation within, she held out her hand. 'Hello, I'm Amy.'

He gave a shy smile and shook her hand. His grip was firm, with reassuring, broad palms. No ring mark on his wedding finger. As he sat back, his jacket fell open and she noticed a flash of something silver in the inside pocket. He covered it up when he saw her looking and went back to scowl. 'Come on, then,' he urged. 'It's proof that we need to take to Whitehall.'

Amy held up the paper. 'This is the only page we have. The rest was stolen from Mei's flat, remember? Who would do that?'

Joel thumbed the page. 'He was murdered.'

'If any dogs escaped and they're diseased, this thing will spread. Fuck me, it'll spread by itself anyway. God knows how far it's got. It won't be just dogs next time; it'll be people killing people. If everyone knew, there'd be wide-scale panic.'

He sat back and sighed. 'There's the motive: they wanted to shut him up.'

'Who did?'

'Where do you think we are? And guess who works for the government – our little friend.' He pointed to the sleeping figure on the bed.

'No,' said Amy. 'She couldn't be involved. She wouldn't kill him.'

'Why not? She's covered in blood.'

'Couldn't you tell? They were lovers. She wouldn't kill someone she loved.'

'You saw how keen she was to get back to her boss when we were downstairs. She must've worked hard at her job to get into the power corridors.'

'You think she snared Chen to Beijing and killed him before the secret could get out?' she whispered. 'Just to further her career?'

'Why not?'

'Why would she tell us about Chen in the first place?'

'You saw how desperate she was to stop us leaving,' Joel whispered. 'She fainted. Or we're made to think she did. Maybe she wanted to find out how much we knew, or keep us here until the big guns turned up.'

Amy got up and cricked her back. Unsure, she watched Mei sleep. 'No, she's not like that. She's nice.'

'How do you know?' He tilted back on his chair.

'She tried to help us.'

'That makes you her friend, does it? Christ, you're so naive.'

She put her hands on her hips and looked him up and down. 'I've known her about as long as I have you. In that case, why should I trust you?'

He stood up, taller than her. 'Really, kid? You really want to do this now?'

She fought her instinct to step back. 'I'm no kid, and I'm not scared of you. You could be a spy just as easily.'

'I've been working with Ron for years. We advise the British Government. What good would come of me being a double agent for the Chinese?'

'You tell me, Mr Greenpeace activist,' she said. He was so close she could smell whisky on his breath and a hint of mint.

'Did you Google me?'

'Your accent isn't British.'

'If you Googled me, then you'll know I'm from Norway. I've got nothing to hide.'

'Oh yeah?' She put her hands on her hips. 'I've been working in the lab for nearly six months. I've seen you once. Where have you been?' *Girlfriend – ask him if he's got a girlfriend. Go on.*

'I've been on a marine research trip.'

'On a boat? Where's your windburn tan? Your cracked lips?' She walked round him, relishing that she had the power for a change. 'I heard you came out of retirement. Bit young for retirement, aren't you? I think you've been living in the dark.'

He stepped away from her, his fists clenched. 'So what if I have? I've been getting over my wife.' His voice cracked and he bit his lip. His eyes red and watery again, she almost felt sorry for him. Just as fast, he clenched his jaw and poked her in the shoulder, making her jump. 'Let's look at you, shall we?'

'Me?'

He held his hands up in mock horror. 'Me? Just happened to turn up at the lab as an intern. Some bright young thing with all the right theories and no evidence to back it up. Where are *you* from, Amy?'

Red card – her past was none of his business. He would only use it as ammunition against her, anyway. For someone who hated her as readily as he did, he was always there, in her face. 'Do you know what? Fuck you.' She shoved her shoes on and made for the door. 'I don't have to put up with this bullshit, and I don't have to explain myself to you.'

'Oh no you don't.' He dashed ahead of her and blocked her way.

They were so close, their chests breathed against each other. Without her consent, her mind started to imagine her easing his shirt off, daydreaming what his unclothed torso might look like. From the feel of things, she bet he had a pretty ripped body under there – for an older bloke. She would get to see the tattoo on his arm in its full glory. Her brain could not control itself. What was wrong with her? She needed to get out. 'Move,' she said.

He pressed harder into her. 'What was it Janice Barber found out, eh?' he breathed. 'You're shaking.'

'No, I'm not. I said move.'

'No chance, spy.'

They tussled, she elbowed him in the stomach and reached for the doorhandle.

A voice behind them made them stop. 'Stay there. Both of you.' Mei had a steak knife in her hand, tipped at Joel's throat.

'What the—' Amy began.

'I don't know who you two are, talking about double agents and spies.' Mei's voice shook. She had the blade tip just below his ear.

Amy held her hands out. 'Please, let him go. We're just scientists.'

'We aren't spies,' Joel said, trying to turn round and look at Mei. 'Just put the knife down.'

Mei shook her head. 'Don't move... I don't understand you two. Why did he accuse you of being a spy? Why didn't you finish your thesis?'

Amy swallowed. 'I got kicked off my PhD, OK? Lockdown hit and I couldn't concentrate. I lost my scholarship. I got too far behind in my studies. I couldn't get another bursary to go back, and I never have.' She looked down at her hands rather than see their faces. She did not want to go into the whole thing. After all, they had only just met.

Joel strained to look round at Mei, still with the knife pressed to his neck. 'We need your help.'

'Me? Why?' Mei asked.

'You need to take the findings to your boss. Tell him why they mustn't do the cloud-seeding. We need the test results,' he said. 'This is only a report. We need stats.'

'If we can stop all this, Chen's death needn't have been in vain,' Amy said, getting closer to the bed. 'Come on, give me the knife.' She reached over Joel's shoulder. Her hands closed over Mei's, who relinquished. As Amy took the knife back, Joel flashed her a wink.

Well done, he mouthed.

Mei collapsed on the bed, crying. Amy put the knife on the table and knelt next to her, placing her hand on her shoulder. 'We'll sort this out.' She gave her a tissue. 'But we need to explain the findings to you first, because you're the one who'll have to explain it to your boss.'

Mei put a hand to her head. 'Oh no, he was trying to call me.' She stood up fast and looked about the room. 'Where is my phone?'

Amy held out her bag to her. 'Here.'

Mei snatched it and pulled out the phone. She put it to her ear. 'He's left a message for me.'

'Have you packed?' Joel asked Amy.

'Yes, why?' she whispered.

'Go and get your things and come back here quick as you can.'

Gunshots echoed in the distance. They all looked at each other. 'We need to get to a window. Now,' Amy said. 'Come on.'

They hurried out of Joel's room and down the corridor to the glass stairwell. Amy watched the human chain of riot police clustering around the main monument in the square.

In the night gloom it was difficult to make out what was going on. Scuffles of arms and legs; someone was dragged away under the armpits by police in crash-hats and they hauled them behind a tank; gunshots rang out. She tried to reassure herself that it was the riots, but what if it was more than that? What if the disease had already made it to Beijing?

'Hey, look,' Mei said, 'the fog has lifted.'

Amy pressed her hand against the cool glass of the window. 'Then it's too fucking late. The cloud-seeding – they've already done it.'

CHAPTER NINE
Mei

Mei stood looking at the luggage at their feet as she waited for Amy to zip up her bag. With a sadness, she realised she would be saying goodbye to them sooner than she expected. They were her friends, her only confidants in the madness that was unfolding.

'Where's the report?' Mei asked.

'In here,' Amy said, picking up her notebook from the table and waving it. 'I'm not letting it out of my sight.'

Mei nodded, looking at her two friends. 'It's time. If we want to get out of here, it's important we act like everything is normal, OK?'

Down in the hotel lobby, people kept glancing to the window, too scared to venture out. Mei watched a couple kissing as they sat on the leather couch in the bar area. A woman wearing a shawl gripped a fistful of the man's hair as he buried his head in her neck. They were too rigid, too tense for passion.

The woman had a stain of drink spilled down her top. The man pulled back and took a tendril of her red scarf with her. It was wet, shiny. Her neck was a fleshy red mess of chewed-out muscle and sinew. The woman dropped back, lifeless into the couch. He swept forwards to gorge on her once more.

Mei, Joel and Amy ran to the front door. From inside the lobby came an echoed scream.

'Where are the fucking taxis?' Amy asked, as they waited on the pavement.

Mei watched her. If humans were to stand a chance, the three of them had to survive. It was her job to ensure they did. She stopped and looked up. Snow rushed on the breeze. Red flags on the government buildings billowed proud. She jolted as a flake landed in her eye. Rubbing it simply made it burn more and more.

'What is it?' Amy asked.

'Nothing. This way.' Mei pushed past her, trying to ignore the agony searing across her face, and strode round the corner to the taxi rank. 'This one'll do.' She rapped hard on the window, startling a catatonic driver from his sleep.

'Open the boot,' Joel yelled.

As the driver popped it open and Joel loaded the bags, Mei checked around them for danger. It was too quiet. Where were all the cars?

'What happened to your eye? It's gone all red,' Amy said, having caught her up.

The pain in her left eye made it almost impossible to think. In the distance, she could hear a collective roar, like the chant of football hooligans. Then she saw them: people running in an un-coordinated swarm, swaying as though drunk, but determined. They were headed straight for them.

Mei turned and banged hard into Amy. The report slipped from her notebook and fluttered down to settle in the gutter.

'No,' Amy screamed, bending down to scoop up the already soggy paper.

Joel grabbed her wrist. 'Don't touch the water, remember?'

'Just leave it,' Mei said. 'Get in the car.'

Amy held her by the shoulders. 'We can't go without the research.'

'We need to get out of here,' Joel said. Not waiting for an answer, he shoulder-barged Amy into the back seat and climbed in after her.

'What's that noise?' Amy asked.

The sound of the infected herd was getting louder. Mei could see the faces, not vague and drowsy, but noses screwed up with hatred, eyes white with hunger and intent. They howled as they hunted the streets.

The infected people were less than a hundred metres away. Mei shut the boot. At the same time, she heard a bang and something whooshed past her ear. With her one good eye, she looked towards the hotel. An Asian guy in a dark suit stood on the front steps, aiming a gun at her. His face was hard. He was about to fire again. They had finally caught them up.

Instead of firing, he fell hard to the pavement, his skull cracking as it hit stone. The gun skidded away from his limp hand. The porter had his hands clamped on his legs, and sprawled his belly over the fallen gunman, coiling his hands over his shoulders. Baring his teeth, he swooped to the gunman's exposed neck and bit down to rip out flesh.

A strong arm whipped round Mei, winding her, as she was tackled backwards into the taxi by Joel. She screamed as she landed. The porter looked up from his feast and dragged himself upright. As though he could sense her, he stared at her. Anger and hunger were all that remained in his features. He started lumbering towards the taxi, and then stumbled over.

Joel got in and slammed the back door shut. 'Airport, fast as you can.'

'You, out of my car. You trouble, I want no more. Out, out,' the taxi driver shouted.

Mei gripped the front seat. 'No, please. We have to get out of here. You've no idea how important—'

'This city is going crazy. I need to find my family.' He started the engine.

Mei thrust her bank card at him. 'Have everything that's left on here. Believe me, it's a lot.'

He nodded and sped off past the hotel. She looked out the back window. Chen's murderer was a slumped mess by the front doors. The porter had given up on the departing taxi and had gone back to eating the gunman.

'Those fucking things,' Amy said. 'Is that what Chen's dogs were like in the village? Is that what people will become?'

'I guess so,' Mei whispered.

Turning away so Joel could not see, she pulled back a sleeve to reveal pinky-red blotches on her arm. She rubbed her eye as it watered down her cheek. She could not see out of it anymore, no matter how much she blinked.

The taxi was slowing. The police were putting up red and white striped roadblocks. 'There's no way through,' said the driver.

'Go round it,' Joel yelled.

'They will shoot at me.'

'Just do it. That gap, there,' said Mei.

Three blocks had been placed in the road, one space left at the side. The taxi was hurtling towards it. He swerved and drove the wrong side of the road around a traffic light. Policemen were carrying a blockade towards the gap. He beeped his horn and they looked up in surprise.

'You'll kill them,' Amy screamed.

'I can't,' he shouted.

'If you don't, we're all dead,' Mei said, gripping his arm.

The policemen dropped the block and levelled their guns. The gap was too narrow to pass but the taxi was going too fast to stop. The car jolted as it clipped the block and it went into a spin. Joel's head smacked into Mei's and her arm banged into Amy as the car stopped with a jolt.

The taxi was facing the soldiers, who were running at them. 'Get out, now,' one of them shouted.

'These people are important, aren't they?' the driver asked Mei.

'Very,' she said.

He gripped the gearstick, shoving it into reverse. He swung on the steering wheel and stamped on the accelerator as a bullet shattered the windscreen. Facing the road ahead, the taxi sped out of firing range, where the road merged into the main highway.

'Time to say goodbye to Beijing,' she said, and rubbed her eye.

Joel squeezed her hand. 'You'll come with us? To London?'

She nodded, looking away to the snowflakes melting on the car windscreen.

*

Mei noticed a plane soaring into the sky, its taillight flashing as it went higher. She sighed with relief, knowing that if flights were still on, they could get to safety. The taxi peeled off the roundabout to the approach road for the airport, and pulled up outside the entrance. Joel got out, with Mei close behind. She could not see any signs of the infected people. The temperature had dropped since the summit, when it had been in the mid-twenties. It must have dipped by half. The taxi driver got out and helped them unload their luggage.

While Amy and Joel sorted their bags, Mei took the driver aside. 'Wait at the taxi rank,' she told him. 'If I'm not back in twenty minutes, go without me.'

He nodded, shut the boot and got back in the car.

Outside the airport, people milled about, pushing trolleys piled high with luggage. 'It's just totally normal,' Amy said, her mouth open. 'You wouldn't have guessed that—'

'Shh.' Mei elbowed her. 'We need to get out of here, remember?' They hurried into the lobby. The ceiling was a huge, curved glass dome. 'This was built for the Olympics. A display of might,' she said, with a tone of sarcasm. 'For all the good it'll do us now.'

They passed a TV showing footage of the snow, people smiling. The picture changed to a soldier in camouflage stood bracing a green machine on a hillside. A rocket exploded from the machine, into the sky. They were showing a broadcast from a brightly lit studio. Smiling presenters and guests seemed to be heralding the smog eradication a success.

'I don't understand,' Amy said. 'Why aren't they showing the riots, the spread of the disease? Shouldn't they be warning people?'

'The media is state-run. They tell us what *they* want us to know.' Mei looked at her watch. 'We need to find the check-in desk.'

The sparkling white marble lobby, with its green copper dragon fountain, was a pocket of austere serenity. Through the doorway to check-in, the tone had changed to a hubbub of raised voices and metal scrapes as a crowd pushed against makeshift barriers.

Staff at the gates struggled to hide the panic in their gestures as they let through people one at a time.

'We'll never get through there,' Joel said.

Mei looked at her watch and then the screens above their heads. 'The check-in for the next flight ends in five minutes. Give me your passports and your government ID,' she told him. She turned round and began pushing through the people. 'Come with me.'

The man in a navy blue uniform and peaked hat stood at the barriers with the guards. 'We are letting nobody through now,' he said to Mei.

Mei stood tall and flashed her ID. 'I am secretary to the environment minister and I am under orders to get these two people on to their plane.' She showed him Joel's pass.

He nodded and stood back, the guards bracing themselves as the crowd surged.

She gestured to her friends. 'You have to go. Get on your plane.' She thrust their documents back into their hands.

Amy would not let go of her arm. 'You're coming with us.'

She shook her head. 'I haven't got my passport.'

Joel came forwards and pushed Amy through the barriers. 'Go on, I'll sort this,' he told her. He turned back to Mei. 'Why didn't you say? We could've gone back for it.'

'I need to get you two out. If we leave it any longer, you'll be stranded here.'

'You never had any intention of coming with us, did you?' he asked.

She shook her head. 'I can do some good here, I think. I'll find those stats you need, somehow.'

The checkpoint man encroached. 'I'm sorry to interrupt, but I really must insist—'

'It's OK, he's going,' she replied.

'Thank you, Mei – for believing us,' Joel said, holding her hand.

'Say goodbye to Amy for me.'

'Wait.' He pulled out his wallet and handed her a business card. 'It isn't goodbye, I hope.'

She smiled, and soon the view of her friends was lost as people jostled around her. With the back of her hand, she wiped tears away and walked back past the departure boards.

'Back up,' the guard shouted at the crowd as a gurgling roar emerged from the cluster. Heads sank, people fell and screams reverberated as they turned on one another. The disease had arrived.

On the fringes of the stampede, Mei turned and fled past glass windows and soaring metal girders. She ran to the exit as the snow continued to fall, praying the taxi had not left without her. All she could think of was the guard's last words: "Back up". The report might not be lost after all. Getting back to the city was all that mattered now.

Joel held onto Amy tight to stop her going back for Mei. The guards had put the barriers across and were locking the glass security doors behind them. They fired warning shots into the air. People ducked.

'No, we can't fucking leave her out there,' she cried.

'She's going to get the data we need.'

Amy was wriggling so much that he narrowly avoided being head-butted by accident.

'We have to go back,' she pleaded.

Joel looked at the people left behind at the departure doors. Those that stood wore faces of ravaged infection with sunken, wild eyes, and open hungry mouths. 'That's not an option. Amy, stop it. Mei wanted us to get out of China. If we don't, more people will die.'

She began to relax in his arms. He took hold of her face, damp where tears had pasted her wavy, blonde-streaked hair to her cheeks.

A stewardess stood in front of them, feigning ignorance to the horror beyond the glass. 'Excuse me, sir. Can I inquire which flight you are checking in on?'

Startled by her unerring politeness given the situation, Joel was thrown for a moment. Then he flashed his pass and their tickets. It was vital they got their flight. Death was certain if they did not.

'Check-in is due to finish shortly.' She read his pass. 'Ah, I see. Come with me.'

Everyone was in their seats when Joel and Amy got on the plane. People glared at the late arrivals. On board, it was a porthole of calm and normality. Nobody knew – yet. The only clue was the twitchy air stewards lingering by the blue curtains, rubbing their hands with alcohol gel and wipes. They had masks on. All the other passengers were settling down, stowing bags, getting books out and waiting for take-off. He read the numbers on the overhead storage compartments.

'It's these ones,' Amy said, pointing.

'Yes, I can see that.'

She swooped in next to the window and got her phone out to start texting. Joel sank into the chair as the plane engines started up.

'Can't you stay off bloody TickerTok for five minutes?' he grumbled.

She frowned at him. 'It's called TikTok, and I'm not messing about. I need to tell my sister I'm OK, in case that psychic link has bust between here and London.'

'Psychic? You're a twin?'

She nodded as she typed.

'There's two of you? God help us.'

The stewardess marched past. 'Phones away for take-off, please.'

The plane began creeping forward along the runway. He looked at Amy again. She stuffed her phone in her pocket and looked at the view of the airport. 'She ought to be with us – Mei.' She nodded to the window.

He reached out and squeezed her hand. 'I know.'

The engines roared and the plane launched forwards, as the snow began to fall more heavily. Picking up speed, there was the customary jolt as the aircraft flew up into the sky.

Amy looked out the window, unaware of Joel staring at her ringlets of hair. He wondered if anyone had ever cared for her, wanted her. As white wisps of clouds floated past the windows, he realised his fingers were interlinked with hers. He did not let go.

*

'Hey, look at that.' Amy's finger was pressed against the window, pointing down at the mountainous landscape.

Joel leaned over and wiped the fog from the spot where her finger had been. 'What am I looking at exactly?'

'You won't see from there.' She grabbed his arm and hauled him over her lap. 'See that?'

Nestled in the mountains was a huge lake. The water was a vibrant green, almost neon with its brightness. 'It's the eutrophication Chen was talking about in his document,' he muttered, feeling increasingly awkward at entering her personal space.

Aware that her perfume was all he could think about, he moved back to his seat. He covered himself by crossing his arms. He glanced up and, to his relief, saw a stewardess coming round with the drinks trolley.

'What do you fancy?' Amy asked.

'Sorry?'

'Oh, relax for fuck's sake,' she said, with a laugh. 'Gin and tonic, please. Double.'

'Ignore her. Two *single* shot G&Ts, please,' he asked the stewardess.

'All right, skinflint.' Amy looked vaguely disgusted. 'You're acting like you're my—' She stopped herself.

He tried to ignore the awkward silence. 'Can I get some peanuts too?'

'Does the budget stretch to a packet of ready salted?' Amy asked.

'Sorry, miss,' the stewardess said. 'We've only got smoky bacon crisps left.'

Amy made a face. 'Forget it,' she muttered as Joel handed over her drink.

'Got something against smoky bacon crisps?' he asked.

She pursed her lips as she busied herself with pouring her drink. 'I just don't like them.' She took a sip and looked out the window again. 'If the lake's bright green, surely the authorities must know something's up?' she asked.

He went with her abrupt change of subject. 'You're assuming they give a shit. They can see the damage for themselves.'

'Are you joking?'

'Come on,' he said, 'you did your thesis on acid rain effects. What about all the other lakes in Europe that are crystal clear? They are like that because nothing is able to live in them anymore.'

He ripped open a packet of peanuts, poured some out into his palm and started eating them. He did not eat peanuts much as a rule, but it was something for his hands to do, and it would stop him knocking back his drink too fast. 'Want some?' he asked.

She stared at him and held her hand out slowly. He smirked and dished some into her palm. She formed her mouth into an O and ate the whole handful. How the hell could she make something so simple look so...

'So unless they're presented with findings, the world will do nothing?' she asked, before taking a sip of her drink.

He hauled his brain out of the gutter and tried to keep up with the conversation. 'Exactly,' he replied.

'So it *is* up to me to make people listen?' she said with a smile.

He swallowed. '*Us*. Don't get too bolshy.'

'I can't believe I dropped the papers. Mei risked her life for nothing.'

'No. She saved our lives – got us out of China.' He brushed the salt from his hands. 'We've still got your phone and all the stuff at the lab. Mei's going to find the test results. We'll figure it out.'

'Harket, you old bastard.' A suited man with a gameshow-host tan stood in the aisle.

Joel clenched his jaw to stifle the profanities threatening to spill from his mouth. It was the one person he had hoped not to see on the trip. He put his drink by Amy. 'Don't drink it,' he muttered to her. 'Long time, no see, Nick.' He gripped hard handshakes with him.

'Bugger me. Nobody's called me that for years. It's Nicholas now.'

'You were at the summit?' Joel asked.

'Of course,' he said, with a conceited air. 'The paper's running a story on it. Green fear sells copies.'

It was worth finding out how much everyone knew about the disease. 'Will the paper be reporting on the riots?'

'The protests? They're blaming it on extremists. Nothing more,' Nicholas said, dismissing the idea with a twitch of the hand. 'Truth is, I wanted to see the Toki district for myself. Man, the girls are every bit as filthy as the rumours go. Makes the smog worth putting up with. I mean, if you're going to get filthy, go the whole hog, I say.' He let out a bray that the whole plane could hear.

Joel heard the chink of ice cubes knocking together. Amy had finished her drink already.

Nick noticed her, and he peered round Joel for a closer look. 'That's a right little spitfire you've got there, Joel mate.'

She looked up from the remnants of her drink. 'I do have a name, you know.'

'I bet. Along with a safe word, right?' He winked at her.

Joel put his arm across as she went to leap out her seat.

'What the fuck did you say?' she asked.

'It's all over the Internet,' Nick said.

'What is?' Joel asked.

He brayed again and slapped the back of Joel's headrest. 'Guilty conscience?'

'What are you talking about?' Joel asked in a level voice. This guy was going to be eating teeth soon, if he did not watch it.

'Someone put up a video of her speech. The conspiracy theorists are having a field day.'

'Oh,' Joel said, smiling.

'What'd you mean?' Amy asked.

Nick bounced on the balls of his feet. 'This is your fifteen minutes of fame, sweetness. No one's ever given the UN panel a bollocking like that before, let alone the Chinese Government. Man, I bet this one's a firecracker in bed, eh?'

Joel leant close to him, grabbing a fist-full of shirt as he did so. 'Shut up, or I'll bang you out.'

'Oh yeah?' Nick scoffed. 'You can't do bugger all.'

Joel stared him down, releasing his grip. 'I can't here, but there's nothing to stop me taking you down at baggage claim.'

Nick rearranged his collar. 'Lauren sends her best,' he said, with a grin.

'You're sick,' Amy said.

Nick turned back to her. 'What's that, sweet one?' he asked.

'Talking about the dead like that.'

'Is that what he told you to get you into bed?' He laughed and turned to Joel. 'Nice one, mate. Enjoy the rest of your flight,' he said, and scuttled off down the aisle.

He had almost made it to China and back without his past catching up with him, all thanks to Nick and his big mouth. He sat back down next to Amy.

'You were so calm,' she said. 'How did you not punch his smug face out?'

He turned to her. 'If I had, they'd have diverted the flight,' he whispered. 'I can't let that happen. We have to get back to London – now.' He took the drink from her table and downed it.

'Tell me you weren't willingly friends with that knob?' she asked.

'I was. We went to uni together. He's always been a bit of a dick, but he was my roommate.'

She folded the empty packet of nuts, not looking at him. 'What did he mean about your wife?'

He took the drink from her tray and gulped it down in one. 'She's not dead.'

Her mouth fell open. 'What?'

'You were right. I wasn't on a research trip. I was stuck in my flat drinking away my problems after she left me.' He turned the cup in circles, watching the ice slide around the bottom. 'I'm just a sad act, OK? I bet Google didn't tell you that.'

'But Ron sent you to the summit. He said you were brilliant.'

He shrugged. 'Maybe I used to be.'

'What happened with your wife?'

'It's a long story.'

'It's a long flight.'

The TVs flicked on and began rolling the titles for the beginning of the in-flight movie. 'We got married young,' he said, 'we were in the same class at college together. Then we were both busy trying to build our careers. When lockdown happened, we were shoved together and realised we'd drifted apart. She left me for Nick, left me in the flat, and that's where I stayed.' The stewardess was passing by, and he handed her his empty cup. 'Thanks, I'm done.' As he said it, he realised how final it felt. He had felt like the inside of a garbage bin for so long, all his hate and negativity festering within. Maybe Amy was right, and it was time to crawl out of it for good.

'I'm sorry,' she said, folding the peanut packet into a tiny square. 'No wonder you hate him. There's one thing I don't get. If you don't care what I think, why lie to me about your wife?'

'I'm a sad act, remember? It's a bit embarrassing to admit it to a total stranger.'

'It's not, I mean, we aren't—'

He had to stop her right there. This was exactly why he preferred working on his own. No misunderstandings, no having to explain himself. 'Look, there is no "we". I'm not into jailbait, in case you were wondering.'

She sighed. 'And I thought we were getting somewhere with the foul moods. I'm hardly jailbait. I'm twenty-five.' She dug into her bag and got her notebook out.

In the gloomy light of the cabin, he watched her. Half an eye on the film playing, he saw the way she absently flicked the end of her pen with her thumb as she read back her shorthand.

'You could have written anything there and I'd be none the wiser,' he said. 'What does that say?' he asked, pointing at a random scribble.

She looked up at him, her eyes sparkling. 'It says *Professor Harket is a skinflint.*'

'Very funny. How do you know shorthand?'

She sighed and closed her notebook. 'I did a year on a journalism course. I thought I wanted to be in the media for a while. But I never forgot.'

'Forgot what?'

She shook her head and turned away to look out the window. 'It doesn't matter.'

'Yes it does.'

She looked at him hard. 'I'm not a twin, I'm a triplet. We were put into care when we were just months old. My parents died. We got moved around a lot. I kicked off a lot. We never got homed with anyone, so we stayed stuck in the system. The longest place we stayed was a few years at a right old dump on the North Circular. That's when Aanya's breathing got bad. She'd always had asthma, but the attacks kept getting worse.

'Then she had a really bad attack and that was it – she died. Ten years old and I was burying my sister. A decade was all she got. The inquest said she died from the air pollution. If I'd not been such a little shit, we could've been adopted and got away from that hellhole.'

'That is not your fault,' he said.

'Yes, it is.' She put the pen in her notebook and slammed it shut. 'I promised her that one day I would do something about it. I guess that's why I followed science, and my other sister, Ash, went into medicine. We needed to do something or we'd go crazy. Me and Ash made sure we stuck together in our ratty old flat. So that's me.'

'I'm sorry,' he said and touched her arm.

'That's why I might come across as an obnoxious little bitch sometimes. I owe it to her to make a difference, but I keep fucking things up.'

'I'm sorry life has been so shit for you.'

'Shit? Nah, shit always has a habit of turning into roses.' She tossed her hair and grinned at him. 'Look at us, we're an Internet sensation.' She raised her empty glass.

*

Joel worked on his laptop as Amy slept curled up next to him. He felt more comfortable this way. When he was typing, it occupied his mind. He checked his emails and found one from Ron, who wanted the notes from Amy.

The cursor blinked on the empty space. Things were bad in Beijing, and if Amy's poison balance theory was right, trouble was going to spread on a global scale. Despite the fact that things were going to get bad, he realised he felt different inside. He was thinking clearer, as though a fog of anaesthetic had evaporated. He was feeling again. The things he was thinking about Amy, he had not thought like that in so long. All the while it was getting brighter, like the sun coming out.

She stirred in her seat. Maybe Ron was right, that spark he had the day when they met, she was the reason. Her sleeve had rucked up as her forearm dangled over the armrest, revealing a smattering of little pock-mark scars, too deliberate to be chicken pox.

He wondered what pain she had been through in care, with no parents, just her and her sisters, to be then left with only one sibling. It put his break-up with Lauren into perspective. She had not divulged how her parents had died, and he was not about to push it. If she wanted him to know, she would say. He knew he had not been particularly kind to her since they met, and the awful thought occurred to him that she was used to people treating her with callousness. Amy started to sit up and he looked away.

He went back to working on his laptop. There was nothing on the news sites about the China uprising, other than "several incidents of civil unrest". The white screen glowed, goading his inability to find the words. He had to start somewhere.

'Don't you ever stop working?' A bleary-eyed Amy asked him, her forehead poking out the top of the grey blanket.

'You sound like my wife.' He closed the lid on the laptop and stashed it back in his holdall.

'*Ex*-wife.'

'Mmm.'

She grabbed her bag from under the seat in front. She pulled out her bottle of water and took a swig. She stopped and looked up at him, concerned. 'Don't you have anyone to text? You got family?'

'Mum died from cancer years ago, and Dad during lockdown. We moved back to England from Norway when I was doing my exams. My dad was Norwegian and Mum was English. I was an only child. I've got some distant family out there, I daresay. Ron is probably the closest friend I have.'

'He's a good guy,' Amy said. 'He took me on, and he didn't have to.'

He looked at her. 'I guess some people come into our lives when we really need them to and maybe we didn't even know it.'

Her eyes, bleary from sleep, looked into his. She gave a curious smile. 'What do you mean?'

He had risked it and there was no taking it back. The fear crept in like a tide, filling his mouth and rendering him speechless.

She leant towards him and grabbed at his sleeve. 'You don't get to look at me like that and then turn away. Come on. What is it?'

Had he gone too far? Before either of them could act on the enormity of his words, a bang came from the wing by the window. The plane pitched and began to plummet towards the ground.

The plane jolted as it fell from the sky. Amy gripped onto the seat in front of her. Everybody gasped. She heard screams. Feeling Joel's warm, reassuring hand round hers, she hid in the crook of his shoulder, eyes shut and holding on tight to his neck.

Then nothing. The plane had levelled out. Amy looked through the window at the wing. It all looked normal, apart from the tiniest wisps of smoke.

'What was that?' she asked Joel.

'Put your seatbelt on.'

Her hands shook as she fumbled with the straps and clicked the buckle in place. When she gripped the armrest, her hands were shaking hard.

The passengers had taken on an eerie quiet. An announcement came over the tannoy. 'This is the captain. We have just lost one of our engines. Everything is under control. We are detouring to the Charles De Gaulle airport in France. Please take note of instructions from the cabin crew and we will keep you updated.' The radio clicked off.

'It's OK, they're trained for this,' Joel whispered. 'They've got one engine. It's flyable.'

The flight attendant stopped near Amy and Joel. She was talking to the man in the row in front. 'This is your door,' she told him, pointing to the exit hatch. 'When we land, you're in charge of getting the rows around you evacuated in ten seconds.'

He nodded but looked terrified. From then on, he did not stop reading the emergency card, as though it was his lifeline.

A few minutes later, the radio clicked on again. 'This is the captain, prepare for a crash landing. Brace for impact when the cabin crew gives the word *brace*.'

Amy looked up at Joel. 'I thought they'd only lost an engine.'

'It'll be fine.' He pulled the blanket around her. 'But just in case, I want you to do one thing for me. When we brace, put this blanket over your head.'

'Why?'

He reached into his bag and pulled out a hoodie. He put his arms into the top and stuffed his head through the top, over his shirt. 'Just make sure that as much of your body is covered up as possible,' he said.

'What for?'

'For once, don't ask.'

'Oh fuck, this is it,' she breathed.

He grasped her hand. 'We'll be OK.'

'You don't know that.'

'OK, suppose this is it.' He turned to her. 'Would it be such a bad thing?'

She gawped at him, wrapping the blanket round herself. She thought back to the first time she saw him in Ron's office, and he looked like he wanted to pitch out the window back then. 'Are you fucking kidding? I don't want to die.'

'Why not?'

'Because I, er,' she stammered, 'I never said sorry to my sister for being such a massive brat. All I do is drag her down with my problems. I never got to say goodbye.'

'Imagine her face. Tell her you're sorry.'

She shut her eyes and could see her sister's smile. Amy heard the creak of the bedroom door as she waited for yet another boy to come to her bed instead of her sister's.

A tear rolled down her cheek. She had never let them see her cry. From rough grasps of boys from the past, now Joel's hands brushed away the hair from her face. No one had ever been that gentle with her. She closed her eyes and turned into his touch.

'Amy?'

'Maybe I'll never be OK with it,' she said.

'With what?'

She looked at him. 'But if this is it, then there's one thing I want to do first.' She moved in and kissed him on the mouth. His lips were soft and warm, and as he kissed her back, heat pulsed through her.

His fingers slid across her scalp and he breathed into her ear. 'I don't know what to make of you, I really don't,' he whispered.

'Any regrets?' she asked.

He smiled a closed smile. 'Actually, no. Because it's led me here.'

She gave a nervous laugh. 'You're bonkers if you're happy about being on a crashing plane.'

'If we make it through, just let me try and figure you out, OK?'

She laughed and kissed him again. 'I'm not that easy.'

'Oh, I know. You're a pain in the arse.'

'Brace, brace,' the stewardesses shouted.

Joel pulled the blanket over her head, and they both bent over.

She concentrated on the scratchy fabric of the blanket on her fingers. She felt a jolt as the plane slammed on to the runway. There was a bang. She could smell burning machinery. The plane jarred and skidded along. The cabin tilted and the left wing smacked into the ground.

A white-hot ball of fire exploded through the door seal and hit the man sitting by the emergency exit. He screamed, flailing to get up. Amy grabbed at her seatbelt, even though the plane was still sliding across the runway.

'Don't,' Joel shouted.

She ducked, trying to shut her ears from the sizzling sound of burning skin. The plane bounced up, came back down on to its nose and began to spin round. Her head smacked into the window. Everything turned black.

*

All she could hear was silence, and she became aware that the plane had stopped. Joel, where was he? She was upright in her seat, but she could not turn her head. Her neck had seized. As the feeling came back, she began to moan, shouting for Joel.

The cabin had filled with an acrid smoke. It was dark, but for the flames licking the wing. She could smell blood and piss. She did not know how long they had been there. The exit door in front was a charred, mangled mess.

'Hey, it's OK,' Joel said. He was next to her. He leaned over her, to undo her seatbelt. Blood trickled down his temple from the cut on his eyebrow.

'Are you, you are—' She found it hard to speak.

'We need to get out of here. Can you wiggle your toes?'

She tried. 'Yes.'

Blue and orange lights flashed outside the window. She heard shouting and a low droning sound started up.

'Can you get to your feet?'

'I think so.'

People scrambled towards the emergency door. She could hear the slither as they went down the canvas slide. Joel ducked his head under her armpit and helped her to the end of the aisle. She looked back to where the man in front of them had been. A blanket covered the body.

'Come on,' Joel said, holding her arm. They were at the doorway. It was her turn. 'Don't worry. I'm right behind you.'

On that promise only, she crossed her arms, shut her eyes and jumped.

CHAPTER TWELVE
Mei

At the airport entrance, the automatic doors swished back and forth, smearing blood across the glass panels. Mei stood alone in the lobby, while the pavement outside was crawling with the diseased. Some had severed legs, others spilled entrails as they squelched across on their bellies.

What was in the water no longer mattered, there was no holding the contagion back, no segregation. Like water, it would find a way to seep through and take over. While she still lived, she could fight to survive as best she could. Only able to see out of one eye made things worse. She looked about her for a weapon. Opposite was an abandoned coffee stand and a luggage shop. From the belly of the terminal, the hooligan roar emanated, louder, nearer than she expected. It was a hunting call. She would be next if she did not do something.

She tried to think as the glass doors continued to open and close. The wounded and half-dead were between her and escape. Snowflakes made their lazy way to the ground. If she went out in that and got blinded in her other eye, she stood no chance.

The slapping of quick footsteps came from behind. Heads streamed past the back of the dragon fountain in a pack, spewing blood and bile into the water. They surged around the edge, the group fronted by a young teenage boy-howler. His eyes had clouded white, tears bled down his cheeks. Yellow-red pus billowed from his mouth down his turquoise t-shirt.

He staggered forwards, his eyes wanting Mei. His fingertips flexed in a pincer movement, as did his mouth. The group knocked into newspaper stands and bins, lumbering over, sprawling to the floor.

Scooting out the door, she pulled her neck scarf around her head to protect herself from the snow. She tiptoed over bags, suitcases and bodies in between. The breathy roar of a howler came from the floor. It was trapped underneath another body. Its teeth champed as it tried to get purchase on her ankle.

The herd from the terminal roared back, as though in reply to the grounded invalid. They piled out of the doors fast, making their way over and through the detritus on the pavement. A metallic, scraping sound accompanied the attempts of the howler at Mei's feet. It had a plaster cast on its foot and laid on top of something long and silver, with a grey handle pointing out at right angles – a hospital crutch.

Dodging its snapping teeth, she pulled hard on the crutch, but with two bodies piled on top, it was near impossible to extract. She looked up. The herd was gaining on her. She gave it one last haul, kicking the howler in the hip at the same time. The tilt of its pelvis gave her the wriggle room she needed to pull the crutch free. She climbed over the bodies, trying not to slip on the uneven surfaces. As heads and hands rose, she gripped the crutch and swung at them.

Jump, swing, hop, swing. It became a rhythm. She found clear tarmac, pitted from the toxic snow. With no bodies to climb over, she ran flat out, gaining ground all the time. The taxi rank was up ahead. Their car was at the front, complete with dents from the journey there. As she got nearer, relief was replaced by panic. The driver's seat was empty. Where was he?

She ran round to the driver's side. He was crouched over a body, chewing on its arm. He stopped and sniffed the air. He turned round to reveal his blood-stained face, tendrils of flesh hanging from his teeth. He made a throaty sound and dropped the limb. Intent etched on his face, he lunged at Mei. She threw herself into the driver's seat and slammed the door behind her, hitting the central locking. She slung the crutch in the passenger footwell.

Her hands grasped air as she searched for the key in the ignition. It was not there. The driver thumped his hands on the window, eager for his next meal. Light flashed off something at his trouser belt: the keys. Mei opened the door. Before she had time to prepare herself, he was on her. She slammed her hands against his clammy forehead. His eyes were bloodshot, his pupils dilated. As she fought him on her back, his hot breath smelled like old drains and rotting fruit. Pressed into the car seat, she could not hold him off much longer. The sheer force of holding him back was burning her arm muscles; her fingers sliding on his slimy skin.

A deep sound vibrated through the floor, the entire car and her. There was movement ahead. The howlers had found clear ground.

Kicking up with her legs, she pushed him back out of the car enough to get her feet on his shoulders. All the while his teeth snapped, and snotty blood oozed from his nose. She stretched her arm backwards and tried to feel around for the crutch. The daylight cut out as a howler landed on the windscreen, its eyes wide as it spotted her exposed belly. Its fists came down on the glass.

Her fingertips brushed the plastic armcuff of the crutch. Howler hands grabbed her ankles, pulling her away from the weapon. His body humped over her foot. He opened his mouth and a red-toothed smile sank towards her thigh.

A rumbling sound made him look up. Through the sunroof, she saw a plane soar into the sky. In her heart, she knew her friends were on it. They were depending on her to find the report. The bodies of the infected had surrounded the windows and bonnet, blocking out all the daylight.

His grip had lessened in surprise at the sight of the plane. Mei stretched further back and grasped the cool metal of the pole. She sat up and jousted the taxi driver in the chest with the end of it. As he staggered back, it gave her the chance to heave herself upright.

He was coming back. She held him off with her crutch in one hand and bent forward to grasp at the keys on his belt. Saliva dribbled onto her head from his jaws as she unclipped the keys.

The incessant thrumming of the howler on the windscreen was like a war drumbeat, bringing more of them to the vehicle. She threw the keys onto the passenger seat so she could grab the crutch with both hands. She jabbed the taxi driver's head and heard bones snap. She kicked out with both legs at his groin and he stumbled back into the howlers amassing behind him.

Teeth clamped onto the heel of her leather boot. As a howler made to clamber in at the bottom of the door, she lunged forwards, grabbed the driver's door and slammed it into its head. Its skull cracked against the metal and slid onto the floor. She shut the door and slapped the central locking on. Her relief was short-lived as others piled onto the crumpling bonnet. She shoved the keyfob into the slot and hit the start button.

She put her foot on the accelerator, but the wheels caught against the mass of bodies around the bonnet. Screaming in frustration, she got it into reverse as a bead of sweat trickled down her ribs.

The car flew backwards, and before she could get her foot on the brake, she slammed into the taxi behind. Putting it into first gear, she bumped the car over the kerb and sped past the howlers. Out onto the access road, the car span round on the settling snow. She took her foot off the accelerator. She had not driven for years, and certainly never on snow. Her heart was beating fast and she felt sick. She let herself sob a few times.

Fighting the urge to drive faster, she kept it steady, not wanting to risk a crash. For now, she was safe and wanted things to stay that way. But she was alone. The only thing for company and comfort was the metal crutch which rested in the footwell. Her empty stomach cramped with hunger, and her throat was dry.

On the other side of the motorway barrier, lines of cars jammed the road. She almost missed the turn-off for the motorway services and, turning the wheel hard, made the car spin round. The back clipped the central reservation and rammed hard into a pothole. The car stalled to a halt. Hot tears dribbled down Mei's face and she thought of the gunge that had oozed from the taxi driver's face. She checked herself. There was a large clear blob with congealed blood on her neck scarf. Her throat felt full. She reached for the door and vomited on the snowy road.

When she had finished, she checked herself in the rear-view mirror. The eyelids on her left eye were so swollen she could barely see that her eyeball was bloodshot. She cried out as she tried to open her eye wider. Blood-mingled tears had left a reddish scum on her cheek. She spat on her sleeve and tried to rub it off as best she could.

She started the car again and drove down the small side road towards the mini roundabout. She stopped at the entrance to the motorway services car park and watched for trouble. Apart from a few vehicles dotted about, it was empty. The glass panels of the main building, with potted plants by the steel structures, seemed too empty.

Her common sense screamed at her to avoid the place, while the devil in her whispered in delight at the thought of bottled water and a clean lavatory, snacks and supplies. She squinted. A dark shape moved in the restaurant. Was it a head? If it was danger, she could back out, leave the way she came.

Letting off the handbrake, she turned away from the main building and opted for the petrol station. She parked at the far end, away from the pumps, to give herself a clear view all around the area. The shop was dark. Tacked on to the side of the building was the plastic pod of a telephone kiosk. Her heart ached with the thought of home, her family. She picked up the crutch, opened the car door and ran across the forecourt, her feet crunching on snow as she went.

She grasped the handset and dialled, chewing her lip. The line made a clicking sound as it tried to connect. She prayed they would answer. Knowing they were OK would make everything all right. *Derrrr.* The line had gone dead.

'No, no, no.' She rapped the earpiece against the metal casing of the phone.

Leaving the handset swinging on the end of its cord, she crept towards the shop. She could see herself on the black and white CCTV monitor above the kiosk. The doors parted by themselves, making her heart leap.

Looking about the whole time, she edged past the doors and into the shop. Apart from the low whirr of the air conditioning above the doorway, it was silent in there. Peering past the ice cream freezer, she looked along the sweet aisle to the tills – no one. To her right, at the far end of the shop, the bright lights of the cold drinks cabinet beckoned. Checking each aisle was clear, she made her way to the glass doors. She pulled one door open and grabbed the biggest bottle of water she could find. Sinking onto her behind, she unscrewed the bottle top and swallowed back a large gulp of water. She straightened out her legs onto the cool tiles and drunk some more. There was a wooden door to the side, which read Staff Only and a white one in the corner with a sign: Toilet. She got to her feet. That was when she looked over at the counter and saw that both of the cash tills were open and empty. Someone or something had already been there before her. There was every chance they might still be there.

She tiptoed back towards the exit, clutching the bottle of water. Her eyes went to the crisp aisle. Not knowing what was behind any of those doors was making her want to leave.

When she got to the exit, she was glad to see it had stopped snowing. She had no choice but to break cover and dash back to the car. She opened the driver's door and dropped the water bottle on the other seat.

Waiting for as long as she could bear, nobody came out the shop. If she was on the start of a long journey, now was the time to relieve herself. She hitched up her skirt, pulled down her tights and underpants and began to pee in the snow.

Steam rose from the yellow patch, which trickled away down the slight incline. That was when she heard the bang. It came from the direction of the main glass building. She finished up and got down onto her knees to look under the door. It was people in baggy trousers, bomber jackets – alive people. Thanks to the gods, she was not alone. They had already seen her and were signalling something, waving baseball bats. It was difficult to tell what they wanted as they had scarves round their faces.

One of them stopped and held up something. Even from that distance she knew what it was. A bullet smashed out of the taxi's front lights. They shouted again and began running faster towards her. She tugged at her tights, snagging them as she half-pulled them up. She slammed the door, jabbed the start button and screeched the car round in a U-turn. Another bang and her back window shattered. The car slammed over the speed bumps as she sped out the car park, back onto the motorway.

Joel held his breath as he stood helpless at the doorway of the plane. All he had been thinking about when the plane went down was the next step to survive. This was it, the final straight to safety.

Amy was halfway down the canvas slide when her body went slack. Her limbs caught up and she tumbled towards the asphalt. He jumped out after her.

A paramedic caught her at the bottom and scooped her on to a stretcher. Joel kept his eyes on her as he went down the slide. They were strapping her in when he caught them up. 'Is she going to be all right?'

'I think she has just passed out,' one of the men said. 'Maybe a broken arm. We will check her over just to be safe. You will need that seeing to as well.' He pointed at Joel's head.

'Can I go with her in the ambulance?' he asked.

'Are you a family relative?'

'I'm her fiancé.'

They nodded and loaded her into the ambulance. He climbed in after them and sat down. He was surprised by his mouth moving of its own accord again. Why had he said fiancé and not something like brother-in-law? He did not have time to think, he reasoned. There was no logic to a reflex answer.

Amy laid on the stretcher, her eyes closed, but breathing. He found her hand under the blanket and laced his fingers through hers.

He looked out the open back doors at the broken plane, smoke curling up from the wing. Chunks were missing from the underside of the plane and the edges of the wings were curled like burnt plastic – as though it had been eaten away by disease. How long had the plane been on the runway at Beijing in the snow? He thought back to Mei, when she had been outside the taxi when the snow began. She had complained about her eye. Amy was right: the weather cycle had gone toxic. The doors of the ambulance slammed shut. The lights and sirens kicked in and they sped away from the wreckage.

*

While he waited to be patched up at the hospital, he could not stop worrying about Amy. Had she woken up yet? Would she be OK? Would they be able to get back to London before the acid storm caught them up? Would anyone believe them?

Then he thought of all the people on the plane. As the nurse wiped up the cut on his eyebrow, questions consumed him. What of the ones who did not make it? Was Nick dead? Was Lauren left all alone now? The break-up had not been pleasant and he could not risk doing that to Amy too. He was too old for her, anyway. Lauren had spent her life waiting for him; always waiting for him to come back from another research trip. She always seemed to want more from him than he could give. Did he want to risk Amy being reliant on him? If there was a time to get out, it was now.

Once the nurses had finished with him, he went to the nearest exit. The glass doors slid open before he got there. Another stretcher was wheeled through, only this one, this person, was covered with a blanket.

You're a long time dead, his father's words echoed round his head. He turned away from the door and raced back down the corridors to the reception desk. The foyer was rammed with people wrapped in foil blankets, black with dirt. There was a smell of diesel and blood. People were shouting, and phones rang unanswered behind the desks.

'I'm looking for Amy. Er, a woman called Amy Weston,' he told the nurse at the desk. 'She's British. We came in by ambulance from the plane crash.'

She tapped onto the keyboard and checked the screen. 'Second floor and to the left. Are you her next of kin?' she asked, but he was already off down the hallway.

He raced up the stairs two at a time, thinking the whole time about seeing her again, and how he would kiss her as soon as he saw her. He was gasping by the time he reached the ward reception. 'Hi, sorry, I'm looking for Amy. I was told she's up here.'

The matron smiled, looking over her glasses. 'So you're Joel, are you? She woke up just before she was about to go in for the X-ray. Was shouting your name. Had to really calm her down before she'd go in. Now I see what all the fuss was about.'

'Where is she?'

She pointed with her pencil to the doorway opposite. 'The last bed on the right, by the window.'

He strode across the ward and there she was. Her streaked hair was scraped back into a bun. Dressed in jeans and a hoodie, she looked out at the pale, early morning light. She was about to turn round, see him and beam. He reached the bed. 'Amy.'

'My arm's fine, just a sprain.' Her toneless voice stunned him. She turned round. All the joy had gone from her brown eyes. 'They said I can go.'

'That's a good thing, isn't it?' He pulled up a chair and sat down. 'We need to get to the meeting in London.'

'I'm not going.'

'What?'

'I can't do this anymore.'

He sat back and rested his boots on the edge of the bed. 'Yes, I can't be bothered either.'

'I know what you're trying to do, you know. Trouble keeps following us – death. Why me? Why am I alive and so many others dead?'

'Fate, destiny, karma, who knows? Maybe you were meant to do something amazing with your life.'

She folded her arms. 'What's the point? We told them and they didn't listen. Why should I have survived Beijing and the plane crash?'

'They call that survivor's guilt.'

She bit her lip in annoyance. 'I don't care what it's called,' she snapped. 'I'm a bad person, I don't deserve to get to live above other people. The thoughts I have in my head... I hate myself.' She hid her face in her hands.

He got up and rested his hand on her shoulder. 'It wasn't your fault. Any of this.'

'Then why does it feel like it is?'

'Oh boo-bloody-hoo. At least you're not in a body bag.'

She gawped up at him through fallen tendrils of hair and shrugged him off. 'You have no bedside manner at all. Why are you here?'

'I think the poison balance had something to do with the crash.'

She swung her legs over the side of the bed. 'You do?'

He got up and sat next to her so he could whisper. 'I saw the plane just before we left in the ambulance. I think the engine had melted.'

'Sorry?'

'Given the rough landing we had, I suspect the landing gear was affected too.'

'You've lost me.'

'Come on,' he said and nudged her, 'where's the scientist in you? You said at the summit that in high concentrates, the acid rain could affect buildings and metals.'

'Yes, but—'

'It was snowing before take-off, wasn't it? They had to wait for us to board the flight. The plane flew through the atmosphere.'

'Obviously.'

He shifted on the bed. 'Don't you see? The poison balance is in the weather cycle now. We can't let them cover this up. Everything we've been through now, it matters. We have to do something.'

Steeling herself, Amy nodded and picked up her hoodie from the bedside table. She put it on and stood looking up at him. 'Fucking right, we do.'

'By the way, if anyone asks, I'm your fiancé,' he muttered.

'I'm honoured.' She linked arms with him and they walked out the ward together.

'I'm fine, I promise,' Amy told her sister on the phone. The passengers were queued up to get off the ferry. As soon as she saw those white cliffs of Dover shrouded in mist, she realised how grateful she was to be back. It was not like the first time she had arrived on these shores, when only she and her two sisters made it. Luckily, she could not remember the awfulness of being plucked from the lorry surrounded by the corpses of her parents and others just looking for a safer, better place to live.

'Ash? You're breaking up. I'm coming straight back to London. I've got to go to a meeting, but I'll come home as soon as I can. OK, love you. Bye.' She blinked away tears and slung the rucksack on her shoulders.

Having stopped to make the call, Joel had gone on ahead of her. He was among the cluster of heads on the gangway leading down to the terminal. She saw him give his passport to the uniformed man at the turnstile into the building.

Two boys in front of her, computer nerd-types, were plugged in to their phones. One of them handed his pass to the man at the turnstile. 'The ferry company have got some cheek charging us for tickets. It's not our fault the flight was cancelled,' he said.

'All planes have been grounded internationally,' the man replied, checking their passports.

The second boy shrugged. 'Not our fault. These tickets

weren't cheap either for a poxy ride in an old tin can.'

'Welcome to Britain,' the man said to their backs as they stomped into the arrivals lobby. 'Good morning, miss.'

She flashed him her passport and he nodded. 'Did you say that all flights have been suspended?'

He nodded.

'Why?'

Someone knocked into her leg. The queue behind was backing up.

'I think it's to do with the volcanic ash cloud coming over from Asia,' he said. He reached past her to the next person. 'It's what they said on the TV. Good morning, sir.'

When she met up with Joel in the lobby, she slammed her bag down on the floor. He was smirking at her. 'What trouble are you causing now?'

'The plane crash. It's a cover-up. They're blaming it on some volcano.'

'Come on,' he said, heading for the exit. 'We need to get the next train to London.'

*

When they got out of the train station, a car was waiting for them on double yellow lines. The back windows were blacked out and the driver stared straight ahead.

The driver pressed a button to make the window slide down. 'Car for Harket and Weston?'

'That's us,' Amy said, and hauled on the back door, but it was locked.

'ID, please,' he replied. He nodded when Joel flashed his card, and the central locking clicked.

Once they were in the back, Amy settled into the seat, breathing in the beautiful smell of clean, new car. She was grateful when she saw the familiar London terrain once more of red buses, black taxis, and a constant torrent of people on grimy pavements.

'Ron set up the meeting, so I've no idea who will be there,' Joel told her. 'I've kept him up to date with what's happened since the summit. Whether they'll take it seriously, I don't know.'

'We haven't got the dossier, only our word.'

'Hmm,' he mumbled, looking at his phone with a faraway expression.

She wondered if he was thinking of Mei. She had to say something to fill the void of silence. 'How come you ended up working for Ron?'

'It was after I broke away from Greenpeace. I got arrested in Russia and Lauren suggested I take a back seat for a while.'

'What? Why?'

'We had our own research boat up near the Arctic Circle. We were taking water samples to check the oceanic acidification levels there. Next thing we knew, there were helicopters overhead, and people coming down on zip wires and boats drawing up with more people coming aboard. They seized all our data, smashed all our computers, beat up the skipper, and arrested us all.'

'How did you get away with that one?'

'We faked American accents. When they thought they'd arrested a boatload of boffins with close ties to the White House, they started to panic. Once we called in our lawyers, we were released within a week.'

'Wow, you make a habit of upsetting foreign countries, eh?'

'I wouldn't be doing my job if I wasn't upsetting people.'

The car halted in traffic. She groaned in longing, as they pulled up outside the white Portland stone frontage of a fashion shop. She looked down at her natty hooded top and cheap jeans. At least she still had her earrings. 'Couldn't we just stop really quickly?'

'No, we could not,' Joel said, his accent more clipped than ever. 'We haven't time for a shopping spree.'

'Pig. Then I'm going back after the meeting.'

'Good for you,' he said.

It was all right for him – he had managed to find a half-decent pair of trousers and top at the hospital, and they had cleaned up the cut on his face.

The car turned at the Centre Point building and wiggled along the narrow part of road where wooden hoarding marked the edge of the construction site. Realising what she had said, she fell silent. What would happen after the meeting? Would they go back to just being acquaintances? She realised they were only getting closer because of what happened in Beijing and on the plane. He had almost seemed pleased to see her at the hospital but she had another strop and fucked it up – again.

Looking out the windscreen, the cars in the distance had a distinct haze about them. Her tongue felt strange as she rubbed it against the roof of her mouth. Something was not right. 'What's with the fog?' she asked the driver.

'Don't know, miss. Been like this since this morning. Said on the news that it was dust coming up from the Sahara. Made my car filthy, it has. Had to wash it down before work. I'll need to do it again before tomorrow.'

He began to ramble. She sighed and titled her head to the side, secretly peeking at Joel. He was checking his phone. The car stopped at a red light. To the left, in between canopied shops, Amy spied the tall red lampposts and tasselled paper lanterns that marked the beginning of Chinatown. The car moved forwards and she spotted the sign for Leicester Square tube station. The car's windscreen wipers thunked their own beat. People hurried along and normal life continued. She felt disconnected from it all. Would life ever be as simple as that again?

She knew she ought to be happy. She was back in Britain, after they had survived several very close calls, and they were going to meet the head honchos at Whitehall. They wanted to hear what she and Joel had to say. Not bad for an intern who flunked the education system. Yet Joel seemed distant already, checking his emails, waiting for a message from Mei, no doubt. After the meeting, that would be it: no more Joel. She chewed the inside of her cheek, fighting the urge to glance at him again.

She craned her neck to look back at Trafalgar Square as the taxi turned at the lights. Beyond the tree skeletons that lined the streets, Nelson's Column stood proud in the murky air. The figure, propping himself up with his sword, looked out towards Big Ben and the Thames.

The car turned right onto a side street. Portland stone buildings towered each side of the road. They pulled up outside a building with a high wall and steps with golden rails leading up to the front doors. The driver held the door open for her.

'Thank you,' she said, embarrassed at how scruffy she looked. Her hands ached with nerves and she shook them out.

'Hey, Amy.' Joel was holding her bag for her. The driver shut the doors behind them and drove off back to the busy street.

Joel led the way up the steps. Taking a deep breath, she followed him up to the reception desk. As he spoke to the woman behind the counter, Amy noticed movement beyond the glass security doors. A suited, serious young man with spiky brown hair swiped a card at the panel and ushered through a stout, middle-aged man, wearing a tweed jacket and beige slacks.

Ron was walking straight towards them with a smile on his face. 'Amy. What have you been up to? You weren't meant to talk at the summit.'

'I know.' She looked at the floor in shame.

'Good job she did though,' Joel said. 'Or we wouldn't be here now.'

'Mate.' Ron gave him a hug. 'Change of plans. If you'll follow me, quick as you can.'

The wind rattled the windows and rain pelted down onto the pavement outside. They had missed it by minutes.

The young man who had accompanied Ron handed them visitor badges and led them towards the security doors. Amy struggled to keep up with the three of them and she got more and more disorientated as they weaved through endless corridors. She lost track of the number of keypad doors they had to go through. Finally, they halted at a side door.

The young man held out a clipboard to her. 'You will need to read and sign, before you can go in.'

'What is it?' she asked.

'Official Secrets Act.'

'I'm sorry?'

'It's all right,' Ron said, clasping his arm round her shoulder. 'This is COBRA, the cabinet office briefing room. Given everything that's happened since Beijing, the ministers thought it best. As we're an outside organisation, we'll all have to sign it. Joel and myself included.'

The man with the clipboard thrust a gold fountain pen under her nose. 'Here you are.'

She gave the page a scan and found the signature line at the bottom. As she signed, she noticed Joel look at his phone again and sigh. She desperately wanted to ask if it was good news, but something held her back. She handed over the clipboard, realising that her hands were clammy. She wiped them on her jeans. She could not help thinking that if only she were in a trouser suit, she might make a better impression.

Their chaperone knocked on the door and listened for an answer.

'They're ready for you.' He opened the door.

She hesitated on seeing Joel's concerned expression. 'What is it?' she asked.

'Not now,' he whispered.

'Come on, Amy,' Ron said, breezing past, followed by Joel.

She filed in behind and almost bumped into him. The room was tiny, long and narrow, with a huge table in the middle. The far wall was taken up with a whole bank of screens, showing graphs, surveillance photos and what appeared to be a live news feed.

'Please sit down.' A man in a midnight blue suit spoke. She would recognise that beak nose and floppy fringe anywhere. *Oh, my god, the prime minister*, the voice inside her screamed. She took the free chair opposite him and sneaked a look around the table. There was a man in full military uniform with medals and peaked cap, and various other suits. In a breath, her courage abandoned her as she stared back at the roomful of officials.

The wind whistled through the smashed-out back window of the taxi, and the early morning sun beat down on the glistening white carpet of snow, dazzling Mei's vision. Her face itched and she wiped her cheek with the back of her hand. She had not seen any howlers since leaving the airport. If they hated the sun and hid from daylight, that would suit her. It was the looters that concerned her and she would need to find food before too long.

She was left with another problem, if she counted the shot-out rear window. If she was surrounded by howlers again, the car would be as good as a windbreak. *Beep.* There was the third problem: the fuel gauge was just above the red empty line. She had to make it back to the city. What of her family? The line was dead, so they must be too. Maybe she would never know. With her mother on her own, she would be unable to fend off howlers. She was in remission, but very weak. Mei took a breath. She would try again on the phone as soon as she could.

Her stomach grumbled – back to problem number one. She should have had the guts to grab food at the garage. At least she had the water bottle. She looked at the glove box. Cursing her stupidity, she found the button to open it. She had not checked the taxi for provisions. The compartment fell open to reveal a lunch box.

'Yesssss.' She put it on her lap and managed to open the lid with one hand. Inside were pork balls, vegetable sticks and a long wheaten pancake. She gave a prayer of thanks to the taxi driver as she broke a piece off the pancake and shoved it in her mouth.

Her gaze went to the fare meter on the dash. Red numbers racked up credits payable as the seconds passed. She worked out that she owed approximately a month's wages.

*

Back on the smaller city roads, she soon came to the roadblocks. She spotted the one where they had broken through before on the way to the airport. She was getting closer to her flat.

Home was meant to be a place of sanctuary, safety. Instead, it housed the dead body of her ex. What was she meant to do with it?

Her eyes widened as she stared at the radio and stabbed the *on* button. How had she not thought of it before? If normality was out there, the media would be in operation. She flicked through the dials, listening out for something. All she got was dead noise.

She eased the car to a halt by the corner of her street and turned the engine off. Opening the door, she listened out for signs of trouble. Water trickled into the drains by the kerb. Most of the snow had melted now, except for where it had settled on cars and railings in front of peoples' houses.

She could just make out the front door to the flats. Every second she stayed there, she was wasting time and perhaps a window of safety. She hooked the bottle of water under her left arm and took the crutch with her.

Electric power lines overhead fizzed and sparked, as she snuck along by the line of cars. She listened to her footsteps – one-two-three, two-two-three, and three-two-three. All she wanted to hear was the sound of a human voice, something, someone normal.

At the door to the flats, she put down the water and patted herself down for her keys, which were still in her pocket. As soon as she unlocked it, she grabbed the water and tried to close the heavy door behind her as quietly as she could. At the bottom of the stairs, she looked up. The strip light on the top floor kept flickering. If the power went, she would be forced to stumble about in the dark. Holding the crutch out in front of her, she crept up the stairs. At the first floor, she listened at the door of the first flat.

'Hello,' she whispered. Nothing.

She kept going and up the second set of stairs. Now she could hear something else, as well as her footsteps. It was a scuttling sound, almost like mice. Passing the doors, she found the noise was coming from behind them. Things were scraping on them – fingernails – hands of howlers that had forgotten, through disease, how to open doors. She prayed they would not remember.

Finally, she was on her landing. On the floors below, she heard thumps as bodies lumped into the doors, desperate at the scent of living flesh. Back in her hallway, she double-locked her own door and hauled the side table against it.

The place was in darkness from the closed blinds and she remembered it was not the haven it used to be. The table and the mess of papers was as she had left it from the break-in.

Deliberately not looking the far side of the room where Chen's body was, she got her laptop out the cupboard, put it on the dining table and switched it on. She walked to the bathroom, wishing she could have a shower, but the face wipes in the cabinet would have to suffice.

She perched on the edge of the bath and unzipped her boots. The soles had almost completely worn away from the acid. She threw them in the bath. Peeling off her urine-soaked clothes, they went in the laundry bin.

A distant bang made her go still, listening, as she stood there nude. It was the pipes, she reassured herself. It was an old building and the pipes creaked and popped. It was an idiosyncrasy that she liked about the place. Usually, it made her feel secure and not so alone. It almost sounded as though she could hear the swishing of footsteps padding along the hallway. She peeked round the doorway – nothing. Getting a grip on things was paramount. Being on her own was sending her crazy.

In her bedroom, she stared at the clothes in her wardrobe. If fighting was to become a way of life, she could not go around in her work suits. Something comfortable and practical was required. She settled on another pair of leather boots, leggings and that leather jacket Chen had given her years ago, just before they broke up.

Now she was changed she needed a weapon, something better than a hospital-issue crutch. A search round her tiny kitchen and she found a few small knives which were barely sharp enough to cut through butter. There was her grandfather's old fishing knife, which had a sheath. That went into her pocket. What else? Nothing had the useful reach of the crutch. She picked it up from the kitchen counter and examined it as she thought.

If there was a way she could make it a bit more lethal, it might just work. The rubber stopper on the end had to go. She got out the knife and set to work trying to lever the blade underneath the covering. She worked until she was sweating, but it would not budge. Either it was secured with glue or just squeezed on too tight. The lights had been flickering more often since she got back. She got to cutting through the rubber with the blade and ripped off the excess. Now she had a solid metal edge to jab with. *It could do with being sharper*, she thought.

She reached round in the cutlery drawer, until her fingers closed around a small leather cover. She opened it to find the knife sharpener was in there. Sitting down, she worked until the edge was as sharp as she could get it.

The lights strained and went off, leaving her in darkness. Seconds ticked by and the power came back on. If she was ever to send the email to Joel, it had to be now. What if the very thing she counted on was not there? She went back into the living room and made herself walk towards the armchair. He was just as she had left him, surrounded by blood and the cushion behind his head. The other cushion was to the side, stained red where she had tried to stop the bleeding. She knelt next to him, trying to believe that it really was not him anymore. Her hands shook as she reached for the inside pocket of his jacket and undid the zip.

He had always been so organised at college with his revision timetables, books lined up, not a hair out of place. When her computer died, taking her assignment with it, he had been the one to chastise her.

'Only a stupid person wouldn't have a back-up copy,' he had said.

Those words might save them all. Her fingers gripped

something the size of a cigarette lighter. In her palm was a black memory stick.

She got up and went to the dining table. Slotting the pen into the laptop, she waited while it loaded. There were hundreds of files. Most of it looked like his ordinary vet work. She had no idea what the document would be called.

Several clicks into a folder and she was relieved that he was as methodical in his paperwork as he was his practical work. He had added medical notes into dated folders. Then she found a folder marked *for Mei*. She double clicked and the egg timer stalled as it turned, labouring to open the enormous document. The lights flickered, for longer this time. She needed the Internet connection.

The document loaded and page after page revealed itself. She worked quickly to open up Silverweasel and her own email. Reaching into her pocket, she retrieved the business card Joel had given her. She thumbed the print, wishing she could have left with them on the plane.

She typed in his email address in the top bar. What to write? How should she tell them the world was collapsing from Asia up?

Dear Joel,

Here is the complete version of Chen's dossier. The city has gone crazy and the people are infected. The disease is transmittable from person to person. The symptoms are the same as how Chen described the dogs. They attack to kill. I hope the document may be of some use in determining a cure.

I am in my flat, but I don't know how long the power will hold out. You have to hide out until the poison balance restores itself and your people have found a way to cure the "howlers", I call them. I pray for you and Amy's safety. If the power stays, I will try to keep in touch. Mei x

She hit send and watched the email sitting in her outbox. It was a big document. If the server was not up to it, she did not know what she would do. Then, the email sent. She sighed and sat back. As she did so, all the lights shut off, leaving her in darkness.

Shuddering, she felt more alone than ever. She went over to the blinds and opened them. She blinked at the daylight, only able to see now out of one eye.

The city was always so alive. Now it was dead with emptiness. She knew she could not stay holed up in her flat with her ex-boyfriend's dead body. Leaving was the only alternative. She needed to get her weapons, a backpack of food, and find her boss. There was one thing left to do in the flat before she could go.

She took the memory stick out of the laptop and gripped it in her palm. She picked up the blanket off the back of the sofa. Bundling the material into her arms, she went back over to Chen's body. She dropped the blanket by his side and pressed the memory stick under his hand.

'There you go, my darling. You have that back. You were so brave. Thank you.'

His leather jacket was smooth against her touch, as she went to hold his other hand. Her fingertips found bumpy skin on his wrist. She gasped. That part of him was warm, roasting, when the rest of him was not. It could not be. She pulled back his sleeve to reveal the semi-circular line of puncture wounds. Only teeth could have done that. If he had been bitten, in her experience of the last few hours, she knew the dead did not stay dead. It was impossible. She had seen him die. He passed away in her arms.

The disease had not killed him, the people following him had.

He was a mystery and always had been. Now in death, he still confused her. She stroked his face. He deserved a funeral and flowers, people to mourn his beautiful features. Those dark brown eyes that stared back at her now – those eyes rolled to look at her. His grey lips opened and stretched wide as he let out an unearthly roar.

Mei scrabbled away from him and got to her feet. Screams seeped through the apartment walls around her from the howlers contained within. Their reply energised him as he sat up, all the while staring right at her.

'Chen, no,' she said, backing away. She needed the crutch but it was in the kitchen. He circled her around the dining table.

'Please, stop,' she screamed.

Her voice seemed to be the catalyst as his hands went for her throat. He shrieked, and she reached sideways and picked up her laptop off the table. She heaved and smashed the machine against his head. Plastic exploded against bone into shards, black liquids arced across the room. He slumped to the floor.

She had failed Chen more times in one day than she dared think about. Looking at the shattered laptop, the letter keys were illegible, pebble-dashed with red. She dropped the computer on the table.

The pounding on front doors above and below her flat increased. She heard a bang as a door downstairs below burst open. Footsteps echoed in the stairwell.

Mei edged into the hallway. Shadows moved under the front door. A sniff and a low growl came from beyond the doorframe. Her neighbours who she used to ignore, only greeted when she had to wait for them to pass, were now hunting her.

Her only exit was blocked. Looking back to the lounge, she realised Chen's body was testament to his efforts to save her and the world. She could not let his life be a waste if she no longer tried to save hers. Thumps on the front door made her jump and look round. The keychain rattled against the wood. If she did nothing, this was her only future, and it was not one she wanted.

'Now, you may wonder why we summoned you here,' the prime minister continued. 'I have convened this COBRA meeting of the government's national emergencies committee.'

He pressed onto the table with his hands. 'Our official remit within this room is to co-ordinate the preparation of plans for ensuring, in an emergency, the supplies and services essential to the life of the community.'

'Are you aware of what happened to our plane on the way back here?' Joel asked.

'I have been fully briefed on what has happened to you and your colleague after the summit, although we have no footage at all from the disease outbreak in the city,' he replied. 'Officially, it is unconfirmed. The weather systems in Asia are causing much concern. We have blamed the sudden influx of smog on Saharan sand dust. But we believe that the winds from Asia may be here already. If I may pass over to Sylvia Linnet from the Met Office.' He gestured to the end of the table.

A woman with long black hair stood up and pointed the remote at the screens. A weather map of the world started running. 'We've been examining Miss Weston's theories and how it relates to the sudden precipitation in China. A large band of cloud has amassed and headed across Asia to India. It is what we call a retrograde weather pattern.

'While the effects of cloud-seeding don't last that long, we have noted the pressure system from China make its way to Delhi. As a city, it is in fact more polluted than Beijing, and has also been experiencing temperature inversion – where the pollution traps itself in a bubble, if you like.'

'I think we need to know what exactly is happening in Beijing.' A woman's voice came from the left end of the table. The pug face of Janice Barber was unsmiling.

Sylvia pressed the remote in her hand and the weather screen disappeared. 'It seems people have been using the Silverweasel network to release recordings on their phones.' She clicked the remote again and the screens showed riots, people attacking people, fire, and blood. 'It is the same in Delhi: reports of thousands dead, military chaos, hospitals overloaded with the sick and the dead.'

'We saw this in China,' Joel said. 'We have research proving a link between the poisoned water supply and damage to the brain in canines. It is causing human-on-human attacks.'

'A virus. Is it contagious?' the prime minister asked.

'We don't know.' The man sat next to the prime minister spoke. His name badge revealed he was from the World Health Organisation. 'It's too early to say.'

Sylvia looked at the map of the globe, tracing a finger around India and China. 'Given that the two pockets of polluted air have mixed, I believe it has increased in speed and made it to the UK. Think of it like those teacup rides at the funfair: the man doing the ride gives it an extra spin as he passes, and you go quicker.'

The prime minister rested his elbows on the table, looking at the raven-haired woman. 'If what Miss Weston is saying is correct, we have been experiencing the effects of the poison balance for some time.'

'What are the implications on people's health?' Janice asked.

'I have the proof right here, Ms Barber.' Joel got up from the table, holding up his phone. 'If I may, Prime Minister?' He waited until the prime minister nodded. Joel stood up and walked over to the bank of screens. 'I have a complete dossier emailed from a vet studying the effects of drinking water in China,' he said, and plugged his phone into the console. The monitor flashed up graphs and text.

As he spoke, every now and again he glanced at Amy. She would not give him eye contact. Was she upset with him? What had he done this time? He lost his train of thought. He had to stop thinking about women. They too, were an infection in his mind. He tried his best to concentrate on explaining Chen's research – the high readings of the pH levels in the drinking water, and the dogs' autopsies. He explained his own theories about the plane engine parts dissolving too. 'So, as you can see, it is far from coincidence.'

Janice shrugged. 'If it is rain, why don't we all stay indoors until it passes?'

Amy stood up and leant over the table. 'Because it isn't normal rain, you stupid woman. This is what we are trying to tell you. Even drinking the tap water would be foolish.'

Joel remembered how her rant had started at the summit. If she was not careful, she would undo all their hard work so far. 'Amy,' he warned.

'It's OK, professor,' the prime minister said. 'It's why she is here.'

Amy cleared her throat. 'It isn't a normal weather system. It could effectively dissolve the very structures we believe are safe. Limestone and marble are vulnerable to acid rain, let alone once it has mixed with toxic levels of pollution from two major cities. And there are plenty of buildings at risk in London – Buckingham Palace, for one, then there's the Tower of London, and don't forget, right here in Whitehall. Oh, and metal is affected too. When we were in Beijing, the cars there all had severe rust damage from prolonged exposure.'

Sylvia raised her hand. 'We have no way of predicting whether the "poison balance", as Miss Weston puts it, has dissipated with the rain.'

'What do you suggest?' the prime minister asked Amy.

'Me?' she asked, looking unsure.

'Yes.'

Joel noticed a bead of sweat at her hairline as she spoke. 'We can't assume buildings will be safe. I recommend, er, evacuation to underground bunkers until we can test the rainwater outside.'

Janice scoffed. 'That's your solution, is it? It must be wonderful being so sanctimonious all the time.'

'Hardly, Ms Barber,' Amy said. 'We are all guilty of using the sea as a toilet, but there's a difference between me and you. Money and policy were all you cared about when something could have actually been done to prevent this mess from happening.'

'We can't evacuate an entire country underground in just a few hours,' the prime minister said, with a frown. 'There aren't enough provisions. Chief Commissioner, what say you?'

The man sitting next to him sighed. 'We have to prioritise.

Evacuate schools and hospitals. Platinum Command.'

The prime minister coughed. Joel could not be sure, but was it a hint of embarrassment at the suggestion?

'What's Platinum Command?' Amy asked.

Before anyone could answer, a boom vibrated the building.

'What the hell was that?' Janice yelled.

The young suit scraped back his chair and stood up. 'Rat-run.'

People began to gather their belongings, getting out of their chairs. Amy turned to Joel as he picked up his bag.

'What is rat-run?' she asked.

He held his hands to her cheeks and her breath caught. He looked into her fearful eyes and tried to say it as gently as he could. 'We have to leave now. This is a code red evacuation. If we don't go now, we might not get a space.'

'A space where?'

'For once, just stop asking questions.' He took her hand, and they followed the line of people briskly moving down the corridors.

They spilled out of a narrow visitors' entrance onto a smaller side road. To the right, a small stone archway interconnected the two buildings. Already, cars were pulling up alongside and people from the COBRA meeting were piling in. He looked to his side. Amy was not there. Panic flushed through his veins.

'Amy,' he shouted. He caught a glimpse of curly hair zip round the corner, away from the cars. He pounded after her, grabbing hold of her wrist as she reached the front entrance. 'Where the hell are you going?'

She shrugged him off. 'I'm not running away like all of them. I have to know what that was.'

'Fine, we'll find out. But we have to go now.'

She looked past him, gawping at the sky. 'Oh, fuck.'

He followed her gaze as they stood at the corner of the junction onto Whitehall. A plume of smoke hung in the air. He could just about see the pillared façade of the National Gallery, and the metal pod of the BT Tower beyond it. Something was missing. All that remained of Nelson's Column was a huge pile of rubble surrounded by a grey-white dust cloud.

Cars, taxis and red buses had stopped and backed up either side of the statue of the horse and its rider. People were getting out of their vehicles, mouths open.

'I need to find my sister,' she whispered.

'Not now.'

She shook her head. 'I have to.'

The clouds above had turned a greeny yellow. 'It's happening now,' he shouted. 'The poison balance has tipped. It's really here. We have to go with the others.'

'Go without me.'

'No chance.' He bent down, seized her by the waist and threw her over his shoulder. She kicked and screamed as he carried her back to the side entrance. He did not care how cross she was, she was coming with him whether she liked it or not.

The line of cars reminded him of lifeboats on a sinking ship. When each car was full, they sped off towards the main road. He found Ron waiting by the kerb.

'Put me down right now, you fucking arsehole,' Amy screeched at Joel.

'Lover's tiff?' Ron asked, with a smile.

'Hardly,' she said upside down, through her hair.

Another car pulled up next to them, and when the door was open, Joel lowered her down with one arm, and slung her in the back. He got in next to her, blocking her exit.

'Let me the fuck out.' She pummelled him hard on the arm.

'This is the safest place for us right now,' Joel said. 'I'm not having you go off and—'

'Who do you think you are? You aren't my dad,' she said, sitting as far away from him as she could.

'Thank God.'

Ron got in next to him. 'Room for a little one?' He put his briefcase on his lap and slammed the door, oblivious to their fight.

The young suit got in the front passenger seat and the driver floored it to the main road. A siren started up, blue lights on the dashboard. He was fearless, mounting pavements, weaving past cars and motorbikes by the two sentry outposts of the Horse Guards building. He carried on, narrowly missing pedestrians, traffic cones and metal barricades by the Cenotaph.

A line of fire engines screamed past, heading back towards Trafalgar Square. A red police car followed behind it, lights going.

Amy got out her phone and put it to her ear. She stared at the display in disbelief as it failed to connect a call. Now it was the phone she directed her anger at, and he was momentarily relieved it was not him for a change.

'There's no signal,' she said to no one in particular. 'This is the middle of London, for fuck's sake.'

'I'm sorry.' Joel placed his hand on her leg.

She slapped it away, blinking back angry tears. 'I need to warn her. You have no right to decide for me. I'm no child.'

'I know you're not,' he said in all sincerity, for there was no child in the world who was as sassy and streetwise as her. The fire that flashed behind her dark eyes and streaked curls sparked the tinder lying dormant within him. Every time he looked at her, it burned.

She crossed her arms. The car swung into a narrow street, with columns and three archways. They drove through the middle archway and sped down another road, bookended with tall, ornate buildings. The driver pulled up at the back of the convoy of cars. People were joining the queue at the top of the steps.

Joel, Amy and Ron got out the car and walked over to the group. Joel noticed the suits around the edge of the crowd, watching for trouble. Amy stood close to Ron, looking back at the rising cloud of dust over the rooftops. Joel felt a pulse of anger. All he had done was try to save her from her own stubbornness, and in an instant, they were strangers again. He moved forwards in the crowd to try to stand the other side of her, but all she gave him was the back of her head.

The sky rumbled with thunder. If they got caught out in a deluge of acid rain, they stood no chance. He was just about to shout out, when the young suit walked calmly down the stone steps, gesturing people to follow. He turned a sharp left at the bottom of the steps, to a black pod nestled at the side.

Two security guards, on the inside of the glass doors, held them open for the crowd. The wind was picking up. It was about to rain again. The crowd surged from behind. Amy was by the doorframe, talking to Ron. If Joel did not hold them off, she would be crushed.

He turned round and slammed the man behind him full in the chest. 'Back off, buddy, OK?'

Amy glared at him. People piled into the small grey room, which was more of a landing. They filed down the stairs. By the time they reached the bottom, the air was cold and stale. The walls of the ticket lobby were the same shade of uniform grey. The monitors were turned off and everything had a layer of dust.

Amy stumbled. Joel grabbed her elbow, propping her up against the counter. 'Are you all right?'

She frowned at him. 'Get off.'

'What is your problem now? We're safe, aren't we?' he asked.

She flicked her hair back. 'Why didn't you tell me you've been emailing Mei?'

'You're not jealous, are you?' he said, and laughed.

'I've been worried about her. You should've told me she was OK.'

'Yes, I should have. I'm sorry.'

She turned her back on him again. He sighed. Things were never straightforward with women. Life must be a real disappointment with all their impossibly high standards. He jingled the change in his pocket and went back to standing on his own.

Amy returned to the ticket booth, with all kinds of profanity-laced retorts simmering within her as to where Joel could stick his apology. She looked round, but Ron had vanished.

The young suit at the front waved his arms for quiet. 'Right, I think we're all assembled. Please follow me and we will proceed.'

Amy followed the group down the grey corridors. She read the sign on the wall, below a missile bomb that hung from the ceiling:

This was the global hub of information on the war. The government's secret bomb shelter. An easy target that was never hit.

They turned the corner into a narrow area with white walls. To the right, instead of a wall, was a bank of glass. Beyond it was a small room with a huge black table, a thick red girder running along the ceiling. On the wall, behind the chairs, was a map of the world. To the side a male mannequin was posed, holding papers.

She pressed a finger against the glass. 'Wait a minute... This is Churchill War Rooms.'

'Didn't you ever come here on a school trip?' the dark-haired woman from the Met Office asked.

Amy shook her head. 'Why have we been evacuated to a museum?'

They went round another corner, past a big metal door with the word *cabinet* written in red above a small square window.

'You're Amy, aren't you?'

'Yes.' They shook hands as they walked down spot-lit corridors, filled with wooden lockers and wide desks. 'You?'

'Sylvia Linnet.'

'That's it.' Amy pumped her arm and made a victory fist. 'I thought I recognised you when we were in the meeting back there. You used to be the BBC TV weathergirl. Are you head of the Met Office now?'

'I'm a senior advisor.'

'Well, from doing that reality TV dance show, and going out with that weird politician, it's not bad going.'

'Not my better choices in either case.' Sylvia laughed. 'What's life without taking a few risks?' she said, and walked along, self-assured in her clingy pencil skirt and blazer.

She's the sort of "together" woman that Joel should be with, Amy's thoughts told her.

'I don't think I ought to be here,' Amy whispered.

'Why not?' Sylvia asked.

They passed another cell-like door and a portrait of Churchill. 'I'm not like everyone else here. You lot have all got your doctorates, your Nobel prizes.'

'Not me. People still don't take me seriously. I'm just the tits and hair off the TV to most people.'

'I'm only here because of Professor Harket.' Amy felt weird calling him that, an overly formal name. He was always going to see her as a stubborn child and no amount of flirting was going to change that.

Sylvia shook her head. 'I really doubt it. You see, this is Rat-run protocol. Government takes the crème de la crème of

COBRA and any other bright brains they think will help the national relief effort.'

'So, we're here to save the world?'

'Believe me, you're here for a reason, and quite what they expect from us, we'll find out soon enough. Oh, what do you think that is?'

They had entered another gallery-type room. This one had artefacts in glass boxes, including several typewriters on desks. Sylvia was pointing at something that looked like a cross between an old flashbulb camera and an open jewellery box. In the lid was a white box and wires curled out from the bit in the main portion of the box.

Amy read the label. 'It says it's a portable sunlamp. They must have needed it, being out the sun for so long during the war.'

They walked on and Amy began to feel a sense of unease. She had completely lost her bearings. 'Do you think we'll be down here for as long as that? To need a sunlamp?'

'To be honest, I have no idea. But equally, we don't know how bad it is up there. If the weather passes over, everything will be fine,' Sylvia said.

'The sun always shines on TV.'

'Doesn't it just?' Sylvia nudged her.

Amy looked behind her, at the long line of people. 'Do you know anyone here?'

'Not really. A few acquaintances. You two came together, didn't you? You and Professor Harket.'

'Well, yes and no,' Amy replied. 'We did, in the sense that we came back from the summit together. But that's it.'

Sylvia shook her head, and her sleek black hair went back into place perfectly. 'If you say so. Keep telling yourself that.'

Up ahead, the security guards were reaching up at glass doors in the narrow corridor and turning keys in the locks in the top corners.

They had come to a lobby at the end of the corridor, with a few chairs, a desk and two green leather armchairs.

The security guards huddled around another set of glass doors and unlocked them. They turned on the lights to reveal a long room. In this place, everything was painted magnolia, down to the girders and pipes in the ceiling. It reminded her of the COBRA room, with one long table filling the length of the room, expect this one was covered in a dark green tablecloth and white candles in holders.

'Right, here we are everyone.' The young suit raised his arms above everyone's head as he signalled for quiet. 'This is the old Chiefs of Staff Conference Room. We won't be able to fit everyone in here, but the extra space in the lobby means we can accommodate you all. Can the COBRA committee come through and take their seats, please? It'll be a few minutes before we can begin.'

Sylvia walked forwards and people made room for others passing in the crowded lobby. Amy shivered. She looked up at the snakes of wires leading to strip lights and fire exit signs next to old-style fans that hung from the ceiling.

'Are we waiting for a few more?' the suit asked.

Amy looked back to the assembled room. Ron, Joel and Sylvia were all looking at her, gesturing her to follow.

'Me? Oh,' she whispered, and began to weave through the people.

As everyone began to take their seats, she noticed that Joel had found a place at the end of the long table. There were no seats either side of him and he was avoiding eye contact with her.

Rejection stabbing at her heart, she walked past him and sat down a few seats away. Sylvia had got her laptop out, as had a few other people, and started furiously typing. Amy's gaze wandered to the lecherous grinning face of the man next to her: Nicholas Burn. *Oh, God, no,* she groaned to herself.

'It's my lucky week. First, I survive a plane crash and then I get to sit next to the firecracker.'

'What are the odds?' she said.

'They're calling me a hero, you know.' He smoothed back his greasy hair.

'Congratulations,' she said.

'I was sat at the front exit. Got a stewardess out.'

Amy picked at her fingernails. 'I bet she was grateful.'

'Nice outfit,' he sniggered.

She looked up, sharp. 'I haven't been home yet. That OK with you?'

'Just teasing you, hot stuff.'

She thought she saw Joel watching them out the corner of his eye. His expression did not change. She must have imagined it. 'What are you doing here anyway?' she asked Nicholas.

He flashed his badge. 'Press liaison. You two split up, then?' He looked at Joel.

She wondered how many people were listening in as they waited. 'We aren't together,' she said in a low voice, feeling her face flush.

'Glad to hear it. I like you.' His leg brushed against hers. 'A lot.'

She squeezed his thigh as hard as she could, making him wince. 'What about Lauren?'

'I, er, well...'

'That's what I thought.' She let him go. 'Don't touch me again.'

The door opened and the prime minister entered the room. Everyone sat a little straighter in their seats. In the lobby, heads bobbed to see the man himself. He edged past the ladders stacked against the wall and passed the portrait of King George VI on the wall.

'Right, everyone, sorry for the delay. A national state of emergency has been declared. Given the information and the high danger to buildings, we can only assume for the moment, that the poison balance is in effect. As a result, we decided to implement the Rat-run procedure.

'This is the Churchill War Rooms, a former museum to preserve the Second World War bunker of the former PM. It has been closed to the public for several years, to safeguard it for events such as these.

'We believe this is the best place to co-ordinate our efforts in safeguarding the nation. We've installed wi-fi, there's a full complement of catering facilities, water supplies and sleeping accommodation for everyone.'

'Why here?' Amy asked.

'We needed a quick retreat, and given this place is right under Whitehall, it would be silly not to take that advantage. This bunker covers three acres and the ceiling is over five feet thick, reinforced with concrete and steel. While it isn't that far from the surface, we'll be quite safe.'

'Sir,' the young suit nudged him.

'Sorry, getting back on track. Let's get you up to speed. Given the smog conditions, we are continuing to reiterate that people stay in their homes. The army is evacuating schools and hospitals, but we are keeping that on the QT. We have issued a press release to the media, thanks to Nicholas, advising the public not to drink any unfiltered water.'

Amy raised her hand. 'Have you explained why?'

'Excuse me?' he asked.

'The first thing people will do is ask questions, no matter how much danger they are in.'

'We are advising there is a threat to national security, and following the attack on Nelson's Column, people keep their windows and doors shut as a precaution against a chemical weapon attack.'

'It wasn't blown up,' she said. 'You're blaming it on terrorism, when it was the acid rain? To keep the masses quiet?'

'To keep them contained – *safe*,' the prime minister said, louder than he needed to. 'We are dealing with mass evacuation and a natural disaster on a scale never seen before.'

She folded her arms. 'Hardly a natural disaster,' she muttered, as he turned his attention back to the room. She chanced a look at Joel. He was glaring at her as though she had massively shown him up again.

'We need to know what we are dealing with here,' the prime minister said. 'Since the weather system began in China, it will have altered on its journey in the atmosphere and so will the make-up of the rain. Am I right, Miss Linnet?'

'Yes.' Sylvia nodded. 'We need to take samples of the rainwater and get them tested in a laboratory.'

'Good. Sort that out. Now, we need to find out about the virus, if that is what it is. Would vaccinations be possible?' he asked the man from the World Health Organisation.

'Maybe, but it could take a long time to find a cure or inoculation. Again, we would need a laboratory.'

He nodded. 'I'll sort that out for you. Right, everyone, this is Command Central. We work from here to co-ordinate and hold meetings. What I ask from each of you is to go away, work on your area of expertise and we will call you in when we need you. Right now, I need you people to stay behind.' The prime minister pointed at Sylvia, the army man, the chief of police, Nicholas and someone in the lobby Amy could not see.

People began to get up from their seats, wearing looks of uncertainty. 'If everyone could assemble in the Churchill Museum or the café, until we have your quarters ready, please,' the suit struggled to make himself heard. 'We will be sorting out some food as soon as we can. Please follow me.'

The clock above the door was at five o'clock. Amy struggled to think. She had no idea if it was early morning or evening. Down there, all sense of time had gone. Right then, she made a promise to herself: as soon as she possibly could, she was going back up to the surface. She had to find her sister.

CHAPTER EIGHTEEN
Mei

The architrave juddered as the howlers rammed into Mei's front door. She ran to the kitchen. Grabbing the crutch off the side, she dashed back to the lounge. The door had a big split down the edge where it was giving under the pressure.

Red-raw fingers wriggled through the fissure. Another thump and the table jolted. She sped to the bookcase and picked up her sunglasses, shoving them on. When she got to the window, she swung the crutch at the glass. The pane exploded, shards landing on the fire escape outside. She dropped the crutch on the metal grating and hauled herself over the window-frame, trying not to catch her legs on the broken edges. One leg was through, when she heard another bang. A section of door exploded into the hallway.

A howler, dripping blood from its gashed chest, lumbered behind it. It used to be a woman, long hair, matted with blood. It stopped and snapped its neck to look right at her. Its eyes were filled red. Screeching, it held out its gnawed hands, white knuckles showing through. It ran at her, with the others close behind.

Mei scrabbled to get out but it was too late. The howler had clamped down on her other leg and she could not shake it off. The angle that she was at, she was stuck. She looked on to the fire escape. The crutch was out of her reach. She swung her other leg back over, trying to ignore the pain from the splinters of glass. Raising her feet, she slammed them into its face. A crack of bone and it turned its face back to her, its jaw slack and dislocated, unable to gnash its teeth. She hauled herself out onto the fire escape.

Others massed at the window, arms out, trying to reach her, too stupid to think their way to a meal. Getting to her feet, she ran down the first set of steps, wondering if any of her neighbours had thought of the same thing. If someone, anyone, she knew could have made it, then it would be worth it.

Glancing in every window she passed, she saw a different scene of death: children devouring the innards of their parents; an elderly woman slumped on the floor in an empty room, face fixed mid-scream. She must have died from fright. Mei stopped looking. All those doors she heard being scraped when she returned home, every single one meant death.

Two floors up, she stopped and gripped the handrail. She cursed again. Howlers were milling in the main street, drawn to her car as though they could smell her scent on it. There was a handful of them. She might just be able to do it on her own. It was more than she had managed in one hit before. Squinting, she could see a figure inside the vehicle, gnawing at the driver's seat, the steering wheel. It must know her scent but be confused. If they were hungry enough to be mistaken like that, her actual body would emanate a smell stronger than a prime steak cooking.

Down on the street, more howlers were around the car. As one, they looked up, right at her. She hesitated. Should she go back up to her flat to certain death, or down with no escape route?

CHAPTER NINETEEN
Joel

Walking the shadowy corridors, things did not seem right without Amy, but he could not find her anywhere.

After going through what felt like miles of corridors, the hallway widened and he found himself in a large room, equally as dark as before. The room was more of a gallery, with glass artefact boxes and description plates on the sides. He passed dusty, blank video screens, not paying any attention to the exhibits on display.

He had almost gone round the whole place. Would she really have been stubborn enough to go after her sister, with all the dangers outside?

Passing round some thick pillars, he found the black monolith of the Number Ten door. Beside it, rousing words of the former prime minister were carved into a white stone wall. Sitting in a corner not far away, with her knees huddled up to her chest, was Amy.

'Here you are,' he said.

She did not answer, and her eyes would not meet his as she picked her fingernails.

He scooted down next to her. 'Are you going to talk to me?'

Glassy-eyed, she looked up at him. 'I don't see why I should apologise when I have done nothing wrong.' She flicked her hair away from her face. 'All I wanted to do was find my sister and you dragged me here.'

'I was trying to save your life.'

'I don't need saving,' she shouted, her words echoing round the room.

A man and woman who had stopped to look at the door exhibit, turned and walked away fast. Joel rubbed his eyes and face. Stubble bristled his fingers. How come they always ended up arguing in public?

'I can look after myself,' she added, not shouting this time. 'I always fucking have.'

He looked at the floor. 'I know and it's one of the things I admire about you. You fight for what you want. That's how you got to the summit. The lockdown has been implemented because of you. Don't you see? You probably saved a lot of lives with that big mouth of yours.'

She frowned at him. 'What are you trying to say?'

He slid down next to her, hoping she would look at him. 'You're right. I'm sorry.'

She slapped her hands on her lap. 'I don't get you. I tried to talk to you earlier and you wouldn't let me sit with you.'

'I had a reason...' His words trailed away. Thinking back, she had been distant with him since it all went crazy. It was further back than the Whitehall meeting. It was in the car, when he was checking his phone to see if Mei had emailed the dossier.

'I've had enough of this,' she said and went to get up.

'Wait.' He held on to her arm and pulled her back down. He quickly let go when he saw the anger in her eyes once more. 'I just want to know one thing.'

'What?' she snapped.

He took a deep breath and leant back against the wall. If he did not ask her now, maybe he never would. 'Why did you look at me like that when I was carrying Mei in the hotel lobby? And when you were reading Chen's research in my hotel room?'

'I don't know what you mean.' She chewed her thumb.

He pulled his phone out and pressed a few buttons. 'I need to show you something.' He thrust the phone at her. 'Just read it.'

Silence ensued as she read the email. 'No. Poor Mei. She calls them howlers?' she asked, handing the phone back to him.

'See? She's a good person. It wasn't a love note.'

She shrugged. 'Your love life is your own concern.'

'You don't understand,' he said, shaking his head. 'You kissed me on the plane. Why?'

She laughed. 'I thought we were going to die. I wanted my last moments to be something nicer than screaming in terror. Why are we even having this conversation?'

'I think we need to. It's like there's something we can't get past. I need to explain something.'

She covered her face in her hands. 'Oh, God. Can you just leave it? I'm not stupid.' She tucked her hair behind her ears. 'You look at me like you fucking hate me sometimes. You prefer women, *proper* women, like Mei and Sylvia. I'm just a kid to you. You even call me kid. I know what you're going to say, and I'd rather you didn't.' She scrambled onto her knees to get up.

He grabbed her by the wrist. 'Stay.'

'No. There's no point,' she said turning away.

'Yes, there is.' His hands slid through her hair as he pulled her towards him and kissed her. Half-expecting a slap round the face, he was glad when she began to kiss him back. He put his hand to her jaw, his eyes taking in all the contours of her face. 'Since the day we met, you're all I can think about,' he said.

Her brown eyes widened in expectation, and she pushed him back down onto the floor. Straddling him, she kissed him and traced her tongue along his lips. She began to ease herself against his hardening crotch, only a few layers of fabric between them. How his trousers did not combust right there, he did not know; he felt like he was on fire being pressed up against her.

Amy ran her hand along his chest and down to his belt. To his surprise, he found she was still propping herself up with one hand, and had expertly managed to undo his belt and unbutton his trousers with the other. She raised an eyebrow and grinned at him, as if she knew it was her party trick.

She gently tugged his zipper down – again, one-handed – and eased her hand in. His cock was magnetised to her fingers, as she stroked up and down, pausing briefly to glide her fingers across his pubes.

It had been a long time since he had last done it. God, was this the best place to do it? On a museum floor when anyone could walk past? Somehow, that did not seem to be the problem.

As amazing as it felt to have Amy's hands all over him, it felt all wrong, and he could not quite figure out why. He had no problem being aroused by her, clearly. She was stunning beyond measure, but what he had said earlier – it felt like there was something between them, a barrier of some kind. He distinctly got the impression that there were things both of them were not disclosing. He had to stop this before it went too far; the last thing he wanted was to end up ruining things and then regretting it.

As she moved in to kiss him, he pulled away. 'You aren't saying much,' he said.

'I'm kind of busy,' she said, leaning over him and looking confused. 'What do you want? Dirty talk?'

'No, wait a minute.' He took her hand out of his boxers. 'Since Lauren, I've felt nothing. But you, you've changed everything.' Amy watched him behind fallen tendrils of hair. 'You've never really talked about anyone from before,' he said.

She sat up, frowning at him. 'Well, I think we've established I'm not a virgin.'

'I don't mean that. You've had a boyfriend before though, right?'

She smoothed down her hoodie. 'No. I guess I have some trust issues. So?'

'Does it have anything to do with this?' he asked, and pulled up her sleeve to reveal the marks on her arm.

She recoiled as though he was the one who had burned her. She pulled the sleeve down. 'No. Look, I can't.' She got up and started to walk away.

'Amy, you need to trust me,' he shouted after her. She started to run. By the time he had done up his trousers and moved to follow her, she had gone. 'Amy!'

He shouted all the swear words he could think of in Norwegian. Why was he trying to pursue things with her, when he knew deep down he was probably no better than the other men who had clearly hurt her? Every now and again, he dared to imagine some kind of future with her. The dark voice in the inner recesses of his thoughts reminded him that he did not deserve her attention when he was so incapable of loving someone else.

He had the potential to hurt her badly with his own austerity. He knew he cared for her, but he did not dare give into emotion again when the one person he had married had gone. He felt like a foolish old man. If he could cut out his heart and leave it in a box there with all the other museum exhibits, then he would.

'Professor Harket?' A man's voice called out.

Footsteps clacked towards him. Joel wiped his mouth and turned round to find the young suit approaching. 'You must come with me, professor. Right away. Bring your phone with you.'

Joel obliged and followed the suit's brisk pace. 'So what's your name?' he panted.

'Tristan.'

'What is it that you do in Government, Tristan?'

He jutted his chin out, gripping his clipboard. 'I am the prime minister's personal secretary.' He unlocked the top corner of some glass doors with a thick key.

Despite being so slight, Tristan held himself tall, walking with confidence. 'Here we are. Although, you might want to zip up your flies before you go through.' Tristan winked.

The prime minister was sitting in the same seat as before. Joel got the feeling he was intruding on a private conversation; he noticed Marcus Caines, the government's senior energy advisor at the table. There was also a woman from the World Health Organisation, with another man he did not recognise.

Tristan busied himself at the end of the room, turning on a large, wall-mounted TV, then strode up to him. 'Your phone, if I may?'

'Um, sure.' Joel handed it over.

'I'm sure you can appreciate that we need to understand what is going on out there, professor,' the prime minister said. 'So, we need to examine the evidence we already have from your friends in China.'

As they all re-examined the dossier, he sat there, fidgeting. While he never really minded being in small spaces, it was the idea of all that concrete, and bricks and mortar above him, that unnerved him. It felt like a colossal coffin lid. He never wanted to be buried, to rot in a box. He would rather burn. Now, with the world as it was, he might not have the luxury of choice.

The poker-faced WHO woman pointed at the TV, where the pages of the dossier were displayed. 'We need to know if the attacks that are happening in Asia will happen here.'

'The research is only based on the dogs,' Joel said, shuffling in his chair. 'We don't know what the effect is on people.' He thought of Mei's eye, from when she had been out in the first flitters of snow.

'All we know of the poison balance is what Amy – Miss Weston – has told us,' said the prime minister.

'That is just the thing, isn't it?' Marcus said, leaning forwards. 'We are relying on an unqualified girl. We cannot take action if we can't be sure of the danger.'

Joel's chest tightened. 'What are you saying? That you don't believe her now?'

The WHO woman coughed. 'Air pollution causes all kinds of respiratory problems. One thing people often don't know is that pollution can be carcinogenic.'

'You mean cancer?' Joel asked. 'What's that got to do with what's happening in China?'

'Carcinogens can cause side effects within themselves. Our organisation must look at health as a whole, just as scientists look at the problems of the environment. We only need to look back in history of previous disease to learn about ourselves. In medieval times, outbreaks of the disease ergotism were common. It was known as Saint Anthony's fire because of the severe burning sensations in the limbs caused by restricted blood circulation. People lost limbs, contracted gangrene.'

'The cause?' Joel asked.

'A toxin called ergot, which is produced when mould infects rye and other grains. The neurological symptoms of the infection included hallucinations and irrational behaviour, convulsions, and death,' said Tristan with pride in his voice.

'So, you see,' the prime minister said, kneading his hands, 'the Chinese with their rice-based diet, most likely have succumbed to ergotism, nothing more. The smog and acid rain issue is no more than coincidence. The howlers simply have a sort of food poisoning.'

Joel laughed. 'You aren't serious.' When he saw they were, he stood up quickly and his chair banged into the wall. 'You're being brainwashed.'

'If I may?' Tristan walked up to him. 'We believe the problem is your intern. *You* are the one being brainwashed. We know you two are close and, if I may say, your relationship is a little inappropriate.'

Joel stared back at him and around the room. Back in the lobby, he spied a little black camera up in the corner. He realised the prime minister had used Mei's name for the infected: howlers. There was only one way he could know about that.

'You've been going through my emails?'

'Sit down, please,' Tristan said, adjusting his cufflinks.

Joel snorted. 'Mate, I could knock you out with a flick.'

Tristan puffed his chest out. 'You forget who you are in a meeting with. There are several armed guards outside this room. Just one word from me...'

The prime minister massaged his temples and sighed. 'Let's all calm down. Tristan, a drink please.'

He nodded and swept away to the side table and began to fill up a glass of whisky. He opened another jar and plopped several ice cubes in the drink. As he served him the glass, the little weasel practically bowed before going back to the TV.

Joel rubbed his eyes with the heel of his palm and sat down again. 'I still don't understand what this has to do with Amy.'

'It has everything to do with her family connections, in actual fact.' Tristan said. 'One of triplets, she grew up in care.'

'I know that,' Joel said.

'And of her parents? Did she tell you about them? They came over illegally in a lorry with the children. The mother was from Morocco, we believe. Father possibly from India. Both dead on arrival. The children were brought up in care. So, you see, she will have grown up resentful about her lot. Doesn't she fit the bill of an angry young rebel?'

Joel said nothing, stunned that he had not asked about her parents. He had no clue her trauma went further back than the care home.

Tristan skirted round him, his back to the lobby. 'You also provided your own historical backdrop. A Greenpeace turncoat, or so you would have us all believe. You're a dual national too. British-Norwegian, aren't you?'

'I've been advising Government for years.'

'Not since my party came to power,' the prime minister said. 'Where've you been?'

'Look, this is ridiculous. I'm just a scientist.'

'A scientist with knowledge,' Tristan replied. 'And knowledge is power. Power is money.'

'I don't care about money,' Joel said.

'Is that so? Your account has been in the red for the past five years,' Tristan said, undoing the buttons on his blazer. 'Your wife left you.'

'You aren't really the PM's private secretary, are you?'

He shook his head, smiling. 'I'm one of many aides, as it were – an investigator. You two are a dream team of an asylum seeker's revenge and an eco-warrior's terrorism plot. There is no apocalypse. You're having a mid-life crisis and that girl has got her claws into you good and proper. You two are just a modern-day Bonnie and Clyde, with plenty of brushes with the law between you. And now, we've got you.' He perched on the edge of the table, with triumph written all over his face.

The prime minister took a sip from his glass. 'As it is, we have averted a disaster, but we do not believe you two were working alone.'

'So, Nelson's Column?' Joel pointed to the ceiling. 'That just collapsed of its own accord?'

The prime minister shook his head. 'We believe it was blown up. It wouldn't have been too difficult to fit a device to the landmark.'

'By us? That's impossible. We were with you when it collapsed.'

Tristan sneered. 'Oh yes, you both have the perfect alibi.

Nicely planned. Therefore, you cannot have been working alone. You have accomplices. Ron Dean, for one.'

Joel rested his palms on the table. He had to appeal to the prime minister's better nature. 'You have got this completely wrong.'

The prime minister stood up. 'We will get the truth soon enough from your little girlfriend.'

'Where is she?' Joel asked, trying to remain calm.

Tristan moved nearer. 'She'll give us everything we need.'

Joel wanted to throw him across the table. Tristan seemed to be revelling in having the prime minister's complete attention. He took that moment to elbow the prime minister in the cheek and sucker-punch Tristan. He bounced into the wall and fell hard to the floor. As the prime minister shouted for backup, Joel leapt over Tristan's slack body and dashed out through the lobby.

He heard shouts from behind and he ran as fast as he could down the corridors. A thundering of boots told him the guards were right on his tail.

He ran though down the hallways, shouting for Amy. He had no chance of finding her in that massive place.

He thought back to the CCTV camera he had seen. He ran back through the wide room where the glass-encased exhibits were, along with the old typewriters. He went back on himself and soon enough, he was back at the grey walls of the ticket office. He vaulted over the counter where the audio-phones hung on the walls, and into the back hallway. There was a bank of about twenty screens, all showing black and white images of people milling about the Churchill Museum, and waiting for food in the café.

How was he supposed to find her like this? The pictures kept changing to different cameras within the complex. In one room, with more glass cases and bookshelves, was a girl with curly hair, holding a t-shirt up to herself as though on a shopping trip. Another woman with long, dark hair nodded with her choice. That was her, but where the hell was she?

'Oi, you. Stop.' A guard was pointing a gun at him. He was young and looked more scared than he did. *Bang*. The shot exploded brick dust into Joel's face. 'I said stop.'

Joel ran away from the screens and heaved a locker across to block the guards' exit. His back twinged, but he ignored the pain to sprint round into the alcoves of the ticket desk. An arrow sign on the wall pointed the way to the museum shop. He just prayed he could get to her before they did.

CHAPTER TWENTY
Amy

'Thanks for helping me with this,' Amy said, holding up a t-shirt against her chest. 'I just had to get out of those natty charity clothes.'

Sylvia was leafing through one of the books from the shelves. 'Every tourist trap has a shop. Who is going to miss a few clothes?'

'Do you think the weather cycle can ever go back to normal?' Amy asked, picking out an armful of clothes. She bent down and pulled off her jeans.

Putting the book back, Sylvia sighed. 'If it hasn't made people ill, then we stand a chance of normality. Sure, we would have to wait it out until the weather cycles calmed down.'

'How long would that take?' Amy asked as she pulled on a pair of tight, black combat trousers.

'Hard to say. We'd have to take lots of air and water samples. What concerns me is the water supply down here.'

Amy got to her feet and buttoned up her trousers. 'Isn't everything stockpiled down here?'

'I suppose so.'

Amy looked at herself in the mirror, wearing a black t-shirt, along with the new trousers. It was nice in the shop, away from all those arsey politicians and civil servants. Even Joel looked at her with the distain one would give an errant child sometimes. Sylvia just spoke to her like a friend. It was nice to have an ally down there in an otherwise gloomy place. The last time she had thought like that was about Mei.

'Hey, are you OK?' Sylvia put a hand on Amy's shoulder.

'Sorry, it's just that I lost a friend in Beijing. To the infection. That's why I know it's real.'

Sylvia gave her a squeeze. 'It's OK. I believe you.'

'I'm sorry,' she said, blinking back tears. 'I'm knackered and I'm worried about my sister. She's up there, in London. And I, I—'

'Tell you what,' she said, picking some fluff from Amy's top, 'once we've had something to eat, we'll go back up to the front doors and see what we can see. How's that sound?'

Amy smiled. 'Yeah, it's a deal.' She shook herself off. 'No, you're right.' She looked at her new friend in her fitted skirt and blazer. 'Aren't you going to change?'

'This is a man's world, Amy. They won't take me seriously if I'm not in a suit.'

They both jumped as the shop doors banged open. Joel came flying through, knocking over stands as he raced over to Amy.

'Go. Now,' he shouted.

'What are you talking about?'

'They think we're turncoats.' He panted and grabbed her wrists.

'Who do?' she asked.

'*We* do,' said a voice from the doorway.

Amy looked past Joel to find a group of suited men, aiming pistols at the trio.

'Now wait just a second,' Sylvia said, walking towards them. 'I think there's been some kind of mistake here.'

'Stay where you are,' one of them shouted.

She retained a serene air. 'On what grounds?'

'Aiding and abetting enemies of the Crown.' The guards stepped aside to reveal the voice from the back. The young suit strode past her to take Amy by the arm.

'Leave her alone, Tristan,' Joel said.

'This is fucking bullshit,' Amy spat. 'I haven't done anything.' She smiled. It looked from the blood trail from his nose and the lump on his cheek that Joel had smacked him one. Probably the one he was saving up for Nicholas.

'I see you've been helping yourself to government property,' Tristan said, looking at her outfit as he dug the end of a gun into her shoulder blade.

'You're arresting me over shoplifting?'

'It's a bit more serious than that, Miss Weston.'

He marched her out the shop. She looked back over her shoulder to see more suits grab the others. 'Joel,' she shouted.

'Just tell them the truth and everything will be fine,' he yelled back. One of the men raised his arm and smashed the pistol across his face.

'Don't,' Amy cried as she was dragged through the doorway.

'Shut up and keep walking,' Tristan said, shoving her in the back.

They marched her through the ticket office. 'Where are you taking me?' she asked.

'Interrogation. Standard procedure for suspected terrorists.'

'What? I'm not a terrorist.'

'I'll take it from here,' he told the other suits.

He pulled her round a corner and shoved her up against a wall, knocking her into a wooden desk. 'When I say shut it, you might want to obey me, or my finger might just slip on this trigger by accident. You get me?'

The cold metal of the gun pressed on her temple. 'Fine,' she said through gritted teeth.

He pulled her along the hallway with the red painted girders going across the ceiling, when she stopped.

'What now?' he snapped.

She cupped her hand to her ear. 'You hear that?'

'If you're playing any silly little games,' he said, giving her a shake.

'I'm not. It sounds like bangs.'

He gripped her arm harder. 'I don't hear anything.'

There it was – a thump – except it sounded soft, like a fist against a door. 'That. Tell me you didn't hear that.'

'Nope.'

They were walking again. At the end of the hall was a black metal door with a small window. It reminded her of a cell.

'Who's in there?' she asked, craning her neck.

'No one.'

'Let me out. There's nothing wrong with me,' a man shouted from inside.

'What the fuck?' Amy gawped as Tristan yanked her away down the corridor to the sleeping quarters.

'Do you remember what I said about shutting up?'

'You can't keep him locked up like that. What did he do?' she asked.

'He's ill. We're running tests on him. Now shut up.' He pushed her along and through into the meeting room. She stumbled and slammed her hands into the table to stop herself from falling.

The prime minister's mouth was open as he sat at the table, his hand in mid-swill of his whisky and ice. Sweat beaded his forehead. His skin had a distinct pallor about it. Maybe his constitution disagreed with life underground. 'Please sit down, Miss Weston.'

Tristan pocketed the gun, eyeing Amy. She stared him out and then took up a chair. 'What exactly is it I am meant to have done?' she asked the prime minister.

'I'll be asking the questions from here on in.' The prime minister interlocked his hands on the desk. 'When did you see your mother last?'

'Sorry?'

'Just answer the question. I'd rather we sorted this out sooner rather than later.'

'I, um—'

'Speak up, please,' Tristan said.

Amy took a deep breath. She had never expected to need to justify her family. 'She died when I was a baby. I don't remember her.'

'And your father?' the prime minister asked. 'From India, yes? And your mother, Moroccan. See, we know all about you, *Amal*.'

Her face flushed. They had done their research. It did not make it any of their business, however. 'Don't call me that.'

'It's your name, isn't it?' Tristan sneered.

She folded her arms and looked away. She had not gone by that name in a long time. It simply reminded her of what she had lost and how she and her sisters had been left to rot in the care system. Now it was being rubbed in her face.

'You're an orphan refugee,' the prime minister said.

She clenched her jaw. 'So? I don't really see what that's got to do with what's happening now.'

Tristan clapped slowly and smirked. 'Oh, that's very good. I love the way you're feigning complete ignorance.'

The prime minister shook his head at him. 'I'll handle this.'

'You think I'm here illegally? Is that why I was dragged here by gunpoint?' Disbelief flooded through her.

The prime minister shifted on his elbows. 'Look, we know the Foundation is in financial trouble. We believe Ron Dean was heavily involved in the energy sharing agreement with the Chinese.'

'What? No.'

'Then you just so happen to apply to be an intern at the advocacy group. Oh, and you got the job, despite your thesis being unfinished.'

It could not be true. He would not have set her up. He was the only one who had read it, and believed her. 'Ron wouldn't do that.'

'You're so sure, are you?' Tristan walked round the desk. He rubbed his punched nose gingerly. It looked puffy and red, with a black eye forming. Despite her predicament, it gave her some comfort to know Joel was fighting for her. 'We needed to know what you knew, so we let you in close enough. Then the unrest in China and India kicked off, followed by the explosion in Trafalgar Square.'

'Explosion?' she cried.

The prime minister slapped his hands onto the table, his face reddening. 'How did you do it? Tell me who else is involved.'

She banged her fist on the table back at him. 'You are wrong. The toxic weather cycle is strong enough to kill and destroy buildings. People have died. Why will no one listen?'

He stabbed a finger in her direction. 'Stop lying. You and lover-boy are in collusion with Ron, and you will tell me who else is involved.'

'Get fucking stuffed,' she screamed. 'We've risked our lives to get the information back here, and this is the thanks we get?'

The prime minister stood up and ran a hand through his greying hair. He swayed a little. 'Take her away. Maybe she'll tell us what she needs to, after she's had time to think on it.'

'I'll do it, sir.' Tristan grinned and hauled her out her chair by the scruff. 'I know just the place.' He pulled her out the room and along the empty corridors, not saying anything.

'Where are we going?' she asked, as they rounded a corner.

'Somewhere fun.'

He walked her round a red display board into a smaller corridor. Lurking in the shadows was the old security guard, fumbling with a set of keys.

'Come on. I haven't got all day here,' Tristan said, giving Amy a shake.

'Would you like a slap to go with that shiner?' she asked.

'Shut up, you.'

If she went any further through those doors, she knew something bad was going to happen. Fighting would not do any good as he was armed and she had nothing. She had to try to reason with him. 'You don't need to do this,' she said, desperately trying to dig her heels in.

'Nice try.'

The guard heaved the door open. All she could see was darkness beyond. She was shoved hard in the back. Her head clipped the doorframe and she fell onto the damp floor of a tiny room.

'This is your new abode. Enjoy.' Tristan was rubbing his hands together as he stood in the doorway. His face was shadowed, the only light coming from behind him in the hallway.

'This isn't legal. You can't do this,' she said.

Tristan stepped nearer, keeping his voice low so the guard would not hear. 'We know all about your family. What would you do to see your sister again?'

'You stay away from her,' she warned from the cold floor.

'You know,' he said, 'when the Second World War was over, the staff here just flicked off the lights and left. Nobody ever came back. You'd better hope we don't leave you down here to rot.'

'You should be ashamed of yourselves. This place used to represent bravery, courage. Churchill would be turning in his grave.'

Tristan stepped back to the doorway. 'If you want out, you'd better start telling us the truth.'

'I am. You can't just lock me up like this.'

'What are you going to do? Phone Amnesty?' He laughed and slammed the door. The metal thump echoed round the walls of her new cell. He grinned through the tiny window in the door. 'By the way, there's a chamber pot in the corner if you need to answer the call of nature. We thought we'd be kind.' He laughed and walked off, his shoes clacking as he went.

When Mei got to the roof of her apartment block, she fought to get her breath. She had no choice but to go back up, past the howlers at her windowsill, to the flat roof. Skyscrapers were empty monoliths, unlit against the indigo sky. The brown haze of streetlights had been replaced by twinkling stars and a full moon.

Now that Amy and Joel were safe, it was time to go back to her original plan. She had to get back to work. Peering over the edge, she saw even more howlers on the streets. She crouched back down and tiptoed over to the other side of the roof. She looked over. It was a smaller service road, only accessed by delivery vehicles to the shops. Only a few howlers could be seen milling about, bumping into bins and parked cars. Scrambling over the wall, she dropped down onto the fire escape.

Going as quietly as she could, she pulled the last ladder out to street level and climbed down. By the time her feet reached the floor, a howler came close by, its head down as though hibernating while walking. It looked up and spread its lips, about to roar its hunting signal. Mei swung the crutch and the howler's skull cracked against the wall. It slumped to the floor.

Mei crossed over to a side road and headed down the back streets. By the time she reached the edge of Tiananmen Square, it looked like a war zone. Smoke billowed from buildings, soldiers ran around shooting at whatever moved, and there were plenty of targets. The howlers had swarmed to the open space. A roar told her more were approaching from behind. She hid in the alcove of a shop doorway and crouched down. More gunfire rang out from the Great Hall of the People.

Howlers surged past her and others wandered just metres from her hiding place. The street was full and she was hemmed in, but so far unseen. A car alarm started up in the distance and the howlers turned to stare at the signal of the living. They plodded away, blocking her route to the office. She ran away from the square and down into the narrower alleys. The smell of smoke was replaced by urine and rotting garbage. Grotty takeaways abutted neon backlit strip joints. At the windows, semi-clad howlers clawed at the glass, desperate to get to Mei. Their teeth scraped at the windows, red lipstick smeared the glass and black saliva dribbled down.

The next street was empty. The manhole was up ahead, next to the apartment block with the blue front door. She crouched down and placed the crutch next to her. She wiggled her fingers into the holes and heaved the metal cover up, ready to place on the tarmac. It slipped from her grasp and landed with a clatter. Straight away, she heard a roar. She looked up to find two howlers lumbering round the corner at the end of the street.

She grabbed the crutch and hurled it down the hole. Her pursuers had spotted her and wailed, running fast. She got her feet on the rungs that led down the well and reached over for the manhole cover. It scraped on the road as she pulled it nearer. She managed to get down a few more rungs, and was hauling the disc into place when a howler landed on it. She cried out in frustration, unable to pull it across any further. A grey mottled hand grasped through, bloodied fingers searching for her. She hauled again on the holes, trying not to poke her fingers through too far in case they bit her.

The pain from her eye had now spread to her forehead and her neck. As quick as the arm had appeared, it retracted. The howlers fought amongst themselves like two wild beasts scrapping over a carcass. She hooked her fingers into the holes and scraped the cover into place. With no light at all, she felt her way down the rungs to the sploshy floor.

*

The back door to the bar clunked as she opened it. She struggled to make out the shadowy shapes of the recliners and tables. There was barely a hint of the heavenly scents that used to cloud the room. Behind the bar, she stepped up to the counter. She held the phone up and shone it around the room. A cloth was on the side of the bar, along with half-empty glasses.

She walked along to the end of the counter. She spied a silver pod on the table at her usual place. The tube was trailing on the floor. Over at the chair, she sat down and picked up the cannula. She attached it to her nose and turned the wheel on the canister. The familiar hiss made her happy. The oxygen was cool in her nostrils. She took a deep breath and the scent of peppermint made her relax. She let her eyes close. If this was all she had left in the world, before she ran out of food and water, then so be it.

Her muscles tingled, grateful for the sit down. Her eye did not hurt as much with her eyelids shut. *A sleep would not be such a bad thing.*

Unaware of how much time had passed, she woke with a desire for food gnawing away at her insides. The smell of peppermint from the beaker had been replaced with an even richer smell: someone was cooking meat.

A hand clamped on her mouth. Unable to breathe, she thrashed about in her chair as she tried to wriggle free. All she could think of was the crutch out of her reach on the floor.

'I'll let you go, but you have to promise not to scream,' a man said.

She nodded, unable to see her attacker. He sounded familiar. There was only one person she knew in this place who had an Australian accent.

A tall man with brown spiky hair stood over her, arms crossed. 'Have you been bitten?'

A young woman rushed in from the side, armed with a golf club. She was all long red hair and spray-tanned legs. The look on her face was ferocious. 'He said "have you been bitten"?'

'No.' Pulling the tube from her nose, Mei blushed as they witnessed her guilty pleasure.

'You look like shit,' the woman said with a sniff. 'You've got blood all over your face.'

Mei self-consciously put her hand to her eye. 'I hurt myself escaping from the airport.'

'Where do you come from?' the girl asked with a sneer.

'Don't be like that, Kirsty.' The man pushed her aside. 'Go get some water for her.'

'Another mouth to feed,' she muttered, and slunk back behind the bar.

'You're a regular here, right? I recognise you,' he whispered as he crouched down next to her. 'I'm Dan. I work here – used to, that is.' The cooking smells emanated from him. He must have been the one in the kitchens.

'Yes. I'm Mei,' was all she could think of to say.

'How did you get away?' he asked.

She knew what he meant. How many undead people had she fought off to escape? How many loved ones had she seen turn? Nothing they did now would be of any use.

'I don't know.' She covered her face with her hands.

'Hey, it's OK. You're safe here.' His hand on her shoulder was almost too hot to bear.

Kirsty slammed the bottle of water onto the table in front of them. 'Yes, how fortunate that you found us. How was that, by the way?'

'It was through the old tunnels, am I right?' Dan asked.

Mei nodded.

'Has anyone bothered to check if she locked the door after herself? The biters could have followed her,' the girl said.

'Go check, then,' he said. The door to the kitchens banged as Kirsty left. 'Sorry about her. This is a shit day for everyone.'

Mei shuddered. 'How many of you are there here?' she asked.

'Three. There were four of us, but a little boy turned,' Dan said.

'Good job I found this, wasn't it?' Kirsty said, coming back into the room, holding up the golf club.

'Introductions,' he said and held out his hand, helping Mei up. 'This is my girlfriend, Kirsty.'

'G-day.' She gave a sarcastic, over-cheery wave.

'Over there in the corner is old Mrs Onion.' He walked over

to the alcove and shone the torch over a bundle of clothes. He bent down and rubbed the pile. It began to emanate a high-pitched squeal. 'It's all right, it's me.'

'Her name is Mrs Onion?' Mei looked closer. The old lady had a very short haircut and her face was covered in wrinkles. She looked vacant, yet troubled.

He shook his head. 'She won't talk. She only screams when we come near her, so we have no idea what her name is. She holds that bag of groceries like an oracle, so the name stuck.' He returned to the counter and angled the torch on it so a half-light spread around the room.

A beeping startled them all. 'What is that?' Kirsty asked.

It was Mei's phone – Joel's number was on the screen. 'Oh, Joel,' she cried, 'you got through. Are you all right?'

'My name is Sylvia Linnet. I work for the Met Office,' a calm woman's voice spoke.

Dan and Kirsty eyed Mei with suspicion. She got up and walked to the opposite end of the counter. 'Where's Joel?'

'He's OK, but in a spot of bother. Our government is trying to discredit the poison balance theory. They're accusing him and Amy of terrorism.'

'That's not true.'

'Where are you?'

Mei looked around at the silver pods on the bar, the jars on the shelves. 'Beijing.'

'We haven't got long. I need you to do me a favour: I need you to go out there and collect some more water samples. Get them tested.'

Mei gripped the edge of the bar counter. 'I don't know how.

It could take days.'

'As soon as you have the details, you send it back to this phone, right?'

'How do I collect them? Hello?' Mei looked at the screen. The signal had gone.

'Hey, you didn't tell us you had a phone,' Kirsty said, folding her arms.

Mei gawped at her. She had forgotten they had been listening. 'I haven't had signal for ages. I don't know how it got through.'

'Ain't that lucky. Give it.' Kirsty sniffed and walked towards her.

Mei took a step back, knocking into a bar stool. 'Excuse me?'

'Don't bother being all polite. I need to make some calls.'

Mei held it tight in her grasp. 'I can't let you do that.'

The girl laughed. 'Are you serious? You're a guest here. This is our place.'

'I've got work to do for the government. They need me to do some research and I need to keep the battery on this.'

'What else have you got that you're not telling us about?'

'Nothing.'

'Just your crutch?' Kirsty sniggered.

Mei wanted to throw the phone at her stupid head, but she needed it if she was to save her friends.

'Woah there, you two,' said Dan in a soothing tone, and stood between the two women. 'Let's not have any fighting. We've all done enough of that to last a lifetime.'

'I'm not fighting,' Mei said, putting her phone in her pocket. 'There are slightly more pressing things going on than some high school catfight.'

Kirsty rolled the golf club round in her grip. 'She needs to start telling us the truth. Like what is up with her gammy eye for starters?'

'Stop it,' he said, in a stronger voice.

Mei had never wanted to pick a fight with someone before – until now. Her stomach clenched with hunger. Mei touched her eye socket and found it no longer hurt. She picked up the crutch from the floor. 'I shouldn't have come.'

'You can't leave,' Dan said.

'Why not?'

'We're barricaded in,' he said. 'When all this first happened, I was on my way to work, but I dropped my keys. I had to smash the lock on the front door.'

'We'll have to come with you,' Kirsty said in a tiny voice. She was sitting on the bar counter, swinging her legs, head down.

'No, you won't,' Mei said.

'We can't stay here.'

'Why not?' Mei asked.

Dan sighed. 'No food. Sure, we've got all the drink in the world. But without food, we're screwed.'

Mei was confused. She had smelled food earlier. 'There's a kitchen.'

Dan chewed his thumbnail. 'This place used to be a restaurant, years ago, when the tourists came. Not been serving food for years; only air to commuters.'

She realised that smell was the scent of the living. She raced behind a recliner and threw up on the floor.

'Oh man,' Kirsty said. 'Shotgun not clearing that up.'

Mei had no idea how long she had before she would turn into one of those salivating cannibals. Chen must have turned after a few days, but he had been bitten. All it took to infect her was one snowflake – just one.

'How are you feeling?' Dan asked, as she came back from the toilets.

'Fine,' she lied.

Kirsty jumped down off the bar. 'So, what's the plan?'

'We need to get somewhere safe, right?' Dan asked.

'You aren't coming with me,' Mei said.

Kirsty watched her as she picked up the crutch from the bar. 'We are. You're a bloody hero, don't you see? You got here on your own from the airport.'

Mei's leggings clung damp to her. She looked down at her hands to see her fingernails were beginning to turn blue. 'You don't understand.'

'Were you bitten?' Kirsty asked.

'No. But—'

A bang came from upstairs. 'The door has been breached. They're here,' Mei said.

'But how?' Kirsty asked.

'They can smell us.'

Kirsty picked up her golf club and hopped down from the counter. 'We're coming with you.'

'You do realise I'm not going anywhere remotely safe?' Mei asked.

'In any case, we can't stay here.' Dan went over to the corner.

'Come on, Mrs Onion.' He tried to get his hands under her armpits to pick her up. She squealed and bashed him hard over the head with her string shopping bag. 'Ow. I think she's got a tin of beans in there. Help me, will you?'

'We haven't got time. Come on,' Kirsty said, heading for the back door.

'Please,' Dan cried.

Seeing the helpless look on his face, Mei went over to him and put the crutch down. Despite Mrs Onion's screams, they hauled her up, but the old lady backed into the corner and kept swinging her bag at them.

They heard another bang and Mei looked up to see a howler tumbling down the stairs. It rolled over and screeched at her. More followed behind. She picked up her crutch and jabbed hard, aiming at its forehead. With a crunch, the pole speared through bone. She felt more than heard it reach the squishy brain matter. She managed to stamp her foot against its head to pull out the crutch.

'Oh, shit,' Dan mumbled.

She adjusted her grip on the crutch. The sound of footsteps filled the stairwell. 'Leave her.' Mei grabbed his hand and hauled him behind the counter. 'We need water. Where is it?'

Dan pointed. 'The fridge cabinets. Over there.'

She raced over and pulled out two bottles. She spotted a rucksack on the side and stuffed the bottles into them. The howlers spilled into the entranceway and she pulled Dan along with her. Looking back, she saw bodies dive onto Mrs Onion.

Kirsty was standing by the door to the tunnels, not wanting to take the lead. 'It's going to be dark in there, right?'

Mei ran to her and hauled the door open, throwing the bag through the gap. 'You go first, we'll catch you up. Take my phone. Turn the torch app on.'

Going back into the bar, Mei could hear the crunching sounds of Mrs Onion being eaten. Dan was just standing there, watching. 'Dan, come on,' she whispered.

'I can't.'

She grabbed a fistful of his shirt and hauled him backwards. 'Why?'

'Because this door only locks from the inside. If we all leave, they'll eat us one by one.' He held up the knife. 'If I stay behind—'

'You can't. You mustn't.'

One by one, the howlers looked up from the remnants of their meal and started to show an interest in Dan and Mei.

'I have to,' he said, jutting his chin out. 'Go now. It's the only way.' He shoved her into the tunnels and heaved the door shut to slide the bolt across.

'What's going on?' Kirsty's eyes widened in recognition and she tried to fight her way past Mei. 'Don't you dare, you little bastard,' she screamed at him through the door. 'Don't you leave me like this.'

'I love you, Kirsty,' he cried.

Mei heard scuffling and Dan's screams mixed with the roars and gnashing sounds of the howlers as they decimated his body.

Mei watched as Kirsty put her hand to the door. Mei stared at the white fleshy nape of her neck. She shook away the thought. She had no idea how long had passed before Kirsty shoved her aside, saying flatly, 'Let's go.'

As they scuttled along the tunnel, Kirsty kept at the front, holding the phone for light in one hand, the golf club in the other, while weeping quietly. Mei was at the back with the crutch. They took a few turns, passing lines of cables and pipes along the brick walls. Mei prayed she had taken them the right way.

'You said back there, those things can smell us,' Kirsty said, her voice croaky from crying.

'Yes.'

'How can they do that? I mean, they're kinda dead, right?'

Mei thought back to the autopsy report Chen had done on the dogs. The only thing that had truly killed them was the gunshot. Chen had died, or so she thought. She had to smash his brains out with the computer to truly make certain. 'I'm not sure. If they're dead, how can they walk and run?'

'Whatever it is, it's effed up,' Kirsty said. 'First, I thought it was a riot, some extremists from the protests at that summit. But people killing people? The police shot at them, body shots, you know, and they just kept coming. I started running to find Dan. I knew he had gone to work. We were saving up to get back to Australia.' She sniffed. 'I guess that won't be happening now.'

'I'm sorry about Dan.'

Kirsty swung round, glaring at her. 'Are you, though? I bet you've lost people, family. Why would you care about my boyfriend?'

'He died to save us.'

Kirsty sat down on the floor and jabbed the golf club at the floor. 'What for? What's the point when all those things are out there?'

'Everyone who died has made a sacrifice to save the rest of us,'

Mei said, leaning back against the wall. 'It has to be for something. Everyone is precious and we must honour that.'

Mei's words seemed to resonate in Kirsty, as she shook herself off and stood up. 'You're right. Let's get the hell out of this pisspot. I'm not dying down here.'

Mei knew what was coming for her and it was slowly taking over her bit by bit. She had to make sure she got Kirsty to safety and the water analysis sent to England before it arrived.

The moon cast a silvery glow over the huge dome structure of the performing arts centre as Mei and Kirsty hid in the shadows. It took longer than Mei expected to go the long way round the square, in order to get to the back of the Hall of the People. A security door was wide open, blood trailed across the gravel.

Mei sniffed. The stench of death was ripe. Past the trees were lumbering figures. She bit her lip and looked back at Kirsty. 'You shouldn't be here. You ought to find somewhere safe.'

'I am safe. I'm with you.'

It was no use arguing with her. There was no time. 'We need to collect the water samples.'

'What with?' Kirsty asked.

Mei took the bag off her shoulders and unzipped it. She pulled out a bottle of water, unscrewed the cap and poured the water onto the floor.

'What are you doing? We need that,' Kirsty said, crouching down next to her.

'Keep your voice down. We need to find some groundwater. Start looking.'

Kirsty pointed to a pavement kerb. 'What about over there?'

In the gulley, a puddle had formed. 'That'll have to do,' Mei said. 'Stay here and keep quiet. If anything happens, do not try and help me, OK?'

Kirsty nodded and kept tight to the shadows of the building. Mei crept across the open ground and over to the puddle. As she knelt on the floor, she checked to see if there were any howlers about, while the bottle filled. There was one not far from her, oblivious as it gnawed on a leg, with the shoe still attached. As though it knew it was being watched, it stopped and looked right at her. Curious, the howler sniffed the air. She waited for the screech, to see its glinting teeth. Its face was nonchalant at her presence, and it went back to eating its find.

She screwed the bottle top on and crept back to Kirsty, who was holding the bag tight, fear on her face. Mei could smell her the whole time she was gone. She was a promise of food and sweat, making her stomach squirm with hunger.

'Follow me and stay quiet,' Mei said. She took the phone out, turned the torch on and stepped through the doorway. All inside was dark and quiet. Soon they were in the ceremonial chambers. She side-stepped a fallen pot plant and a crumpled rug. The rotting stench of howlers filled her nose. They were near – too near.

'Keep behind me,' Mei murmured.

All the lights flicked on. At the end of the marble hallway, a drooling figure came round the corner. It stopped and looked their way. Kirsty gasped and Mei stood in front of her, blocking her from its view.

Mei knew she was in a biological limbo, partway between human and howler. The anger burned inside her. All she wanted to do was rush at it and kill the howler. It would feel almost worth it to kill every single one she came across between now and the end of the world.

Its jaw slackened and it grunted disinterest at her. It turned away and lumbered off back the way it came. 'Come on,' she whispered to Kirsty.

She had never gone higher up than the second floor, where her admin department was. The labs were on the top floor. They found a side door that led to some stairs. Once they got to the next level, it led onto an atrium. All the rooms around the edge had walls of glass. Beyond, workbenches were filled with computers and microscopes. The walls were covered with shelves lined with test tubes, books, folders, more equipment. Mei pressed her face to the glass. She could not see anyone in the nearest room.

Kirsty nudged her. 'Look up there.'

A body lay sprawled on the floor. As they got nearer, Mei found it was a woman on her front. Her black hair splayed out on the floor, blood smattered across her white lab coat. As Mei lifted the girl's head, her long hair fell forwards, revealing her eaten-away face. Mei tried not to look as she took the security pass from round her neck. They went back to the lab door and Kirsty grabbed hold of the wall. She doubled over, dry-retching.

'What is it?' Mei asked, rubbing her back.

Kirsty leant back against the wall and took some deep breaths. 'I'll be OK in a minute,' she breathed. 'Don't look so agonised,' she said, with a slight smile. 'I haven't been bitten. It's morning sickness. It'll pass in a minute.'

Mei gawped at her. 'You're pregnant?'

'Uh-huh. Only two months or so.' Kirsty took the office pass from her and swiped it across the pad. The door swung open and she went ahead, armed with the golf club.

It made sense now, why the smell was so strong. It was the

extra hormones; the extra life Kirsty was carrying inside her. It was why Dan had sacrificed himself so readily: he was trying to save them all.

The place was empty and papers littered the tables and floor. 'What is this stuff?' Kirsty asked, leafing through some pages she had found. 'I mean, it's all squiggles to me. What's wrong?'

'Our department,' Mei said, reading the pages. 'They've already done the tests. They just abandoned it.' Mei wiped sweat from her head. The hot flushes and the shivers were coming more often. Her insides felt as though they were on fire, while her hands ached with cold. She sat down and read more. Although it was a brief email, there was no doubt they had known danger was coming. There were several references to Chen's dossier and "subduing the threat". He had been their immediate risk and they had tried to kill him for it.

'Seen a ghost?' Kirsty asked.

The smell of her was too much. Saliva collected under Mei's tongue. She shot up from the chair and moved away from her. 'It's er, they've already done tests. They knew an infection was coming.'

'Now it's too late.' Kirsty shook her head. 'Stupid bastards.'

'Not for everyone. If we can get the results.'

'Where are they?' Kirsty threw up her hands. 'They're hardly going to miraculously fall from the skies.'

'They're in the computer,' a voice came from the back of the lab.

Together, Mei and Kirsty grabbed their weapons from the desks and held them up. 'Who's there?' Mei said.

A man stood up from the benches, his hands up in the air. 'I'm not armed, I'm not infected. You have nothing to fear,' he whispered.

Mei's breath caught as she stared at her boss. Fear and fatigue made him look years older than when she last saw him. 'Heng? What're you doing here?'

'Is that you, Mei?' He squinted, gawping at her clothes.

She looked down at herself. Clad in a leather jacket, leggings, and sporting a sharp weapon, her Girl Friday days were long gone. 'It sure is. What are you doing up here?'

'Who is he?' Kirsty asked.

'My former boss.' She thought back to the men with guns she had seen at the square. They had shot at her when she got the snow in her eye. They were working for the government. She strode over to him where he cowered and pointed the crutch at his face. 'You knew about all this, didn't you?'

He stared at the end of it, his eyes wide. 'We couldn't risk the information leaking out on Silverweasel. It would've caused a riot.'

'It already has. A fatal one,' she shouted. 'I've been out there. The city is a mess.' She flung the crutch aside and gripped the whimpering man by the lapels. 'Everyone is dead because of you.'

'We'd only known for a few days.'

'Can we cure them? Can you tell me that much?' If she bit him now, she knew she would feel no guilt at all. He was the one who could have prevented it all from happening, but pride had stopped him.

'I knew they were doing the tests, but I don't know if they managed to find anything out before all this. I was looking when you arrived.'

'It'll be here somewhere. I just need to think.' She let him go and he slithered to the ground. Her thoughts were jumbled. It all depended on her, but she struggled to think.

'Er, Mei?' Kirsty asked.

'Not now.' *Back up.* If the research was going to be anywhere, it would be on the computer. She aimed the crutch at her boss again. 'Who was working on the tests?' she asked Heng.

'Guiren.'

'Where did he sit?'

'Right there.'

She reached under the desk and turned on the machine nearest to her.

'Mei, we've got company,' Kirsty said, pointing to the stairwell.

Her boss raised his hand. 'Maybe I should—'

Kirsty pointed her club at him. 'You stay right there.' She looked at Mei for approval, who nodded.

'I'll go.' Mei picked up the crutch and went to peer over the balcony. A group of howlers wandered around the ground floor, getting nearer to the stairs. When she got back to the computer, she found it was on the log-in screen. She grabbed her boss and hauled him up. 'You've got clearance, right? On the system?'

'Yes.'

'Good. Log in.' She pushed him up to the keyboard.

He started typing. 'The folder is here, but it's huge.'

Mei nudged him aside. There were hundreds of folders the scientists had produced. It would take ages to go through them.

'Let me,' Kirsty offered and hit the icons at the top of the page. It had assembled into date order.

'Now just scroll to the bottom and we'll find the last thing he uploaded.'

'Hurry up,' Heng said. 'Those biters are on the stairs.'

'I'm going as fast as I can,' she said, and double-clicked on a document.

He snatched a clipboard from the desk and hurled it over the balcony.

'What're you doing?' Mei asked.

'Trying to buy us some time.' He snuck into the hall and peered over the edge. The tense expression on his face said it all. 'They're still coming.'

Mei wiped sweat from her forehead. 'How many?'

'Enough. A dozen maybe.'

'They can smell us, can't they?' Kirsty asked.

'Yes.' Mei stared at the screen, willing it to speed up. 'How long will this take to load?'

'I don't know. It's fairly big. Ah, here we are.' As Kirsty scrolled down, there were pages of graphs, pie charts, colour bands and reams of code.

'Oh.' Mei's voice fell.

'What? That's it?' Kirsty asked. 'There's nothing at the end. They should've written a conclusion.' She turned to Mei, who wrung her hands. 'They can't have had time to analyse all the data, before all this happened.'

'We need to find another way out,' Heng said.

She hit the desk with her fist. 'Do you think the email system works?' she asked Heng.

Kirsty hopped out the way and pulled Mei's boss into the hotseat. 'Do your stuff.'

'Pardon?' he asked.

'Send the document to my email,' Mei said. 'Be quick.'

He nodded and typed fast. 'It's done.'

'What now?' Kirsty picked up her golf club.

Mei's phone pinged. 'I need to get online.'

The others kept a look out while she hurriedly tapped out an email:

I hope this gets to the right person. I have emailed details of the water samples collected in Beijing. This should corroborate Joel and Amy's theory. The city is overrun. Please make sure this information gets to my friends, and let them go. Tell them I miss them. Mei.

At the lab doors, Mei looked beyond the body on the floor wearing the lab coat. In the far corner, she spotted the lift. 'Come on.'

'I'm staying,' Heng said.

'If you come with us, at least you'll stand a chance.'

'This was my fault, and I'm trying to do something about it.' He drew a gun from his pocket.

'Suits us.' Kirsty jogged up the corridor.

Mei looked back to see the howlers race up around the corner, stumbling on the carpet, as they eyed up their next meals. 'No,' she told Heng.

'I'm not hanging out to be a shrimp on the barbie for those suckers,' Kirsty said, and sprinted off to hit the lift button.

Heng took Mei's hands. 'I am your boss and you do as I say. Go, now.'

She squeezed his fingers back and gave a small bow. 'Thank you.'

'Go.'

She nodded and ran as the howlers' snarls and shrieks got closer. Sprinting hard, she scrabbled around the corner, the crutch hitting the wall.

'Hurry up,' Kirsty screamed.

The lift doors were beginning to close. Mei pounded her legs for all she could and threw herself into the lift, glancing off the doors and sprawling onto the floor. She got up to see her boss knife a howler square between the eyes. Another bit into his outstretched arm. His screams echoed around the atrium as the lift doors closed.

Kirsty covered her ears, the golf club nestled in the crook of her arms. Mei rubbed her good eye, which was throbbing. She did not know how much more pain or running she could handle. She wondered if she should say something but there was not anything she could think of that would make it better.

The lights dimmed inside the elevator. Mei almost willed the power to go out. If it did, they would be confined in there for ever. She would have her feast – two meals for the price of one. She shuddered and looked to the console. The lights flashed each time they descended a floor.

As they went down and down, she realised she had no plan at all now. Yet, she had these two relying on her to keep them safe. All she wanted to do was lie down and close her eyes, to avoid the incessant hunger that twisted her gut. If she did not, she feared relenting to the urge to sink her teeth into her friend's neck.

The lift juddered to a stop and the two of them held their

breath. Mei stepped out first and inhaled. The dead odour lingered above their heads.

'Is it safe?' Kirsty asked.

'As safe as it'll ever be right now. Let's go, quick.'

She took them back the way they came. The corridors were silent but for the breathing Mei could hear behind her, and the thumping of the two heartbeats.

'Follow me close,' she whispered as they ventured out under a sky of stars. Only a few howlers staggered along the wide, straight road. To the right, she could just make out the red walls of the Forbidden City. It would be a perfect fortress. It was surrounded by water and, hopefully, other people had thought of the same thing: food, flesh, running blood; warmth in the darkness.

'Mei?'

She opened her eyes to find she was sitting back against the wall. Kirsty watched her with a face of worry and touched her hand. 'You're freezing.'

'I'm fine,' she said, pushing her off and getting to her feet. Her vision pitched as though she were at sea in choppy waters. Pain gripped at her ribs. She leaned against the wall.

'You're not,' Kirsty said.

The girl was too close. That cooking smell – it was overpowering. Mei wanted to throw her to the floor and crunch into muscle and bone. It would make everything all right again. The need would abate for a while at least. Mei screwed her eyes shut and turned away.

Kirsty held her shoulders. 'You're ill. Where are you taking us?'

She pushed her to the edge and pointed across the square. 'See that? The Forbidden City. That's where we're going. Do you think you can run that far without stopping?'

'I'm not exactly a gym bunny.'

'There's no time left,' Mei said, feeling a tear roll down her cheek. 'It has to be now.'

They pelted along the street together, passing the oxygen bar, but kept on sprinting. The door flew open and out spilled a bundle of howlers.

'Keep going,' she screamed to Kirsty.

They looked back and, mouths open, realised the danger. They ran harder, past the square, towards the humped bridges leading to the Forbidden City.

Mei's legs gave out and she bowled over into the dirt. The howlers kept running, their gaze on Kirsty who was further away. Mei had to make them see she was a viable feast. She bit down onto her own forearm until it bled, squeezing hard so the blood dripped down her wrist. 'Hey, I'm human. Come and get me.'

As they veered her way, she clenched her teeth and held onto the crutch with both hands. 'That's it, right here,' she shouted. She managed to bat a few and slice through one's mouth. The collective weight of their bodies was too much as she fell to the pavement.

She managed to see the bouncing red hair of Kirsty as she ran over the bridge to the fortress. The searing pain as they ripped into Mei's stomach made her cry out. She could feel teeth biting into her scalp as the howlers devoured her. Closing her eyes, she remembered the glorious scent of mandarins, of home.

Sat in the dark confines of his cell, Joel had never imagined he would be banged up again, not when he was on the right side of the law. He and Amy must be doing something right if they had them that rattled. He smiled. It was almost like the good old days at Greenpeace. He felt more his old self now than he had in ages. They were trying to make a difference, make people listen. He knew he would not be there at all if it was not for Amy. Having propped himself in the farthest corner from the door, he drifted in and out of sleep. Guilt touched on him and he wondered if she was all right.

'Joel, are you there?' A woman's voice was at his cell door.

His heart thumped. 'Amy?'

'It's Sylvia. Are you OK? Have they hurt you?'

He could see the silhouette of her head in the viewing pane of the door. 'I'm fine. How did you get away?' He got to his feet and groaned, his back clicking as he stretched up.

'They had nothing on me, so they let me go.' She looked at the floor. Bad news hung heavily in the silence.

'Where's Amy?'

Just inches from her, he could see the anguish in her face. 'I don't know. All I know is that they put her in a cell too. They are getting ready to stand down, let people back up outside.'

'But it's not safe,' he said.

She looked over her shoulder and whispered to him. 'They're waiting for the lab test analysis, but the food supplies are running low. I think they'd rather let people go than starve down here.'

'That's suicide.'

'The meetings I've sat in on, they've told the public that they can go about their business again.'

He rubbed his face. 'How long have I been here?'

'A couple of days. Enough time for me to sneak upstairs a few times, to the front doors.'

'What did you see?'

'They've barricaded the doors with anything you can think of: lockers, desks, benches. Both times I got headed off by security, so I only got a glimpse.'

'Of what?'

'Nothing.' Sylvia shook her head. 'There's no one out there that I could see, despite being given the all-clear. I looked out to the park and couldn't see anyone. When I looked out at night, it was pitch black. No streetlights, no planes going over. There's nothing. It's not right. The Internet went down a few days ago. The mobile networks are down as well.'

He was so close to the glass that his breath fogged up his view of Sylvia. 'You need to get me out of here.'

She flinched, looking to her side. 'Someone's coming,' she whispered. 'I have to go. I'll figure something out,' she said, and ran off as the footsteps got louder.

'We haven't got time,' he muttered to himself and sank back down into the shadows.

CHAPTER TWENTY-FOUR
Amy

Amy paced her tiny cell. Self-pity had soon been replaced by anger. No one had come for her since they abandoned her there. It could be the end of the world above ground, and she would be none the wiser. What if the place was empty? What about Joel? Last seen, he was putting up a fight, but he was easily outnumbered.

'Hey, you bunch of bastards,' she shouted at the door, 'you can't keep me in here. Is anyone listening?' She screamed and kicked the door until her toes hurt. The glow from a fire exit sign was the only indication of life outside her cell.

She heard a bang down the corridor. The sound of clicking heels made her groan.

With a clunk, the cell door opened and Tristan stood in the doorway. 'How is our guest? Sleep well?'

'Get fucked,' she spat. 'You can't keep me here.'

'You're coming out, on one condition.' He was rolling something silver in his hands. 'The prime minister wishes to see you but is very keen that you do not escape. We'll be putting these on you.' He dangled a set of handcuffs from his fingers as he smirked.

She huffed back against the wall. 'No chance.'

He shrugged. 'Then you stay here. Although I can't guarantee when anyone will be back for prison visits. What is that smell?'

His face wrinkled.

She glanced over at the almost-full chamber pot. There were wet patches on the floor where she had missed in the dark.

'Have it your way, then.' The sound of his clipped footsteps brought her back. He was walking out of the cell. 'Door please, Martin.'

'Wait,' she yelled. Humility upon her, she held out her wrists. 'I'll do it.'

He swivelled on the spot. 'There's a good girl.' He sidled up to her and slapped the cuffs on her. They were cold and rather too tight, pinching her skin. He grabbed her by the elbow and dug his fingers into her forearm. 'Come on.'

With that, she braced herself as she was hauled from her confines. The pain from the bright corridor lights on her eyes made her blink. She had to jog to keep up with him as he paced along the corridor. Martin followed close behind, his keys jingling in his pocket. The further along the halls they went, the more silent the whole place seemed.

'Where is everyone? It seems a bit quiet,' she muttered.

They came to another narrow lobby-type area. Instead of the metal girders she had seen before, thick wooden posts went down the room in two avenues. They led to a closed wooden door. Painted white, it had racks of keys on it. Martin bustled ahead and opened the door for them.

Through a long tunnel, they passed another glass-lined room which was crammed full of white, black, green and red telephones. Display mannequins had been propped up against the walls, their costumes covered in grey dust.

Ahead, people were bustling in the corridor. As they got

closer, she could see their faces were full of concern. They were looking into a room at the side. The glass doors were open. They turned round at the sound of Tristan's clacking shoes and spotted Amy.

'She's here,' one of the suits said.

'Bring her through,' answered a weak voice.

Nicholas came jogging out and grabbed her by the handcuffs. She had expected a lewd remark or catcalling of some sort.

'What's going on?' she asked, but he did not answer. His face was serious and straight.

The metal cuffs pinched as he tugged her into a room. There was a desk at the back. Maps covered the wall and a mirror hung on a white pillar.

People clustered around the bed, fussing over an invalid. The man was pale, his greying hair slick with sweat. It was only by the hair that she recognised it was the prime minister. The sharp smell of vomit was almost too much to bear. His eyes were flitting, not focusing on those who were trying to mop his brow. Recognising Amy, he attempted to bat them away with a feeble arm.

'You, come here.' His voice was rasped and thin. Nicholas pushed her forwards. As she got down on her knees next to the bed, he had a coughing fit. 'I need to know how you did it.'

'Did what?'

He gripped her hands. 'You've poisoned me.'

All of the suits pulled their guns out at her.

'No, no,' she shrieked. 'I swear, I haven't.'

His nails dug into her and veins around his temples stood out as he watched her closely. 'You've been locked up for days. You must have another accomplice down here. Who is it?' He fell back onto the bed, eyes shut.

Tristan shoved the gun in her face. 'If he dies, you'll hang for this.'

'I swear it wasn't me.' Her eyes were drawn to the bedside table. On it, was a whisky glass with ice in the bottom. She pointed at it. 'What was in this?' she asked Tristan.

'What do you mean?' he asked.

'What has he been drinking?'

Tristan was near-hysterical now, his face flushed. 'Nothing. Just whisky on the rocks. It's his favourite drink.'

She stared at the two half-melted ice cubes at the bottom. 'The ice – where did it come from?'

'The ice bucket in the meeting room.'

'And he's the only one who has had some?'

He checked the faces around the room. 'Yes.'

She set the glass down on the table. 'Don't you see? It's the water.'

'Everyone's been drinking bottled water since the explosion.'

'And the ice? Did you make it yourself?'

'Yes.'

'From the tap?'

'Yes. What does it matter?'

The prime minister roused, his eyes fixed on Amy. 'I'm sorry,' he whispered. His eyes met hers with sincerity.

'For what?'

'We should have believed you,' he said.

His lips were turning blue. He murmured something she could not hear. She leant close to him. 'Sir?'

'The dossier. It said don't drink the water.' He pointed to

Joel's phone on the bedside table. Amy's was right next to it. 'The girl, the Chinese girl. She knew.'

'Mei? You spoke to her?' Amy snatched the phones from the side.

'She emailed Professor Harket before the Internet went down. The Chinese had taken water samples from the city. All the findings are on that phone.' He pointed with a shaking hand at the mobile in her grip. 'You need to take that data to Professor Malrose. It's our best bet.'

'Why can't one of your lot do it?' she asked.

'You two are the only ones who know the current research inside out. No point sending in one of our grunts.'

Tristan made to calm him, dabbing at his head with a wet cloth. 'But, sir—' he began.

The prime minister dismissed him with a pathetic wave of the hand, focussing his fading energy on Amy instead. 'I shouldn't have dismissed it. I thought your friend was a fantasist. I did nothing.' His eyes bulged and his pupils rolled up to reveal the whites of his eyes. He shrieked and began to convulse. Just as quickly, his body went limp.

'Do something. Someone, anyone,' Tristan squealed. 'We can't just let him die.'

Nicholas ripped his blazer off and dove down onto his knees. He locked his fingers together and began to do chest compressions on the prime minister.

Amy got up and slowly backed away. 'We all need to get out of this room now,' she said.

They were all transfixed, watching Nicholas's efforts to save the prime minister. Now he had his nose pinched and was giving him mouth-to-mouth.

'You aren't going anywhere.' Tristan pressed the gun into her side.

'You don't understand.' She wriggled away from Tristan and tried to get round the side of the bed to Nicholas. 'It's happening.'

Nicholas had stopped. He held the prime minister's wrist. 'He's dead. There's no pulse.'

'He's not dead,' Amy said. 'The toxic water – it causes brain damage, it makes them change,' she said, yanking Tristan back to the glass doors.

The prime minister's torso arched on the bed. His eyeballs were wide open, revealing grey veins and milky irises. His mouth peeled back into a screech. Black vomit spurted from his mouth, covering the bed. He flung himself forwards and sank his teeth into Nicholas's neck. Blood fountained across the map above the bedstead. Nicholas screamed as the prime minister pulled a chunk of flesh from his neck.

'Kill him,' someone shouted.

The prime minister chomped again and this time, more flesh and entrails came from his neck. Nicholas slumped onto the bed. The black eyes of the prime minister then spotted Tristan and he leapt from the blankets to sink his teeth into his shoulder. Tristan cried out in pain, dropping the gun as his arms flailed. Nicholas retched clots of blood onto the bedspread.

Amy looked to the other suits. 'Shoot them.'

They raised their guns, all except one. 'We can't shoot the prime minister,' he cried, and stepped backwards.

The movement alerted the still-vomiting Nicholas, who tackled a suit by the legs and jumped on him before he could escape. Amy fled into the hallway. She made it to the tunnel, when gunfire and screams sounded out from the prime minister's bedroom. Then it was silent. She stopped and caught her breath as she looked back. She heard running and then a suit came flying round the corner.

'Run, for God's sake,' he yelled.

She took off ahead of him. It was not easy running with her wrists cuffed in front of her. Stabbing pains gripped her shins and her lungs burned as she ran along the tunnel, heading for the white door. Then she was there. She held it open and looked back for the suit. He stumbled into the tunnel, clutching his arm.

'Hurry up,' Amy shouted.

By the time he was halfway through, there was a figure behind him. The spiky hair was the only thing that defined what used to be Tristan. As a howler, he was fast, faster than the suit, who was nearly at the end of the tunnel.

He ran out, and under the light. Amy could see blood at his elbow as he came towards her. Two of them – if he was bitten, that was two howlers. She had no choice. Her hand gripped the bolt. She looked back at the suit, and his eyes flashed with fear.

'It's a gunshot wound. I'm not bitten,' he shouted.

'I'm sorry.' She put her weight into the door and heaved. Hooks and sharp edges of keys jabbed into her side as she hurried to close it. Her fingers fumbled to push the bolt across. She tugged on it hard, but it stuck in place. Sweating in panic, she wiggled it again. It freed up and shot into place, making her stumble back. Just then, hands slapped onto the other side of the door.

'Let me in.' He kicked and banged on the wood. His final

words were muffled by the hunting cry of the howler. Together, they fell against the door.

Her ears filled with the suit's screams and the howler's roars. Two sets of hands thumped against the door, mouths screeching at the gap under the door. There had to be another way back. She had to warn people, get them to safety, wherever that was. She needed to get out of the handcuffs.

Keys jingled on the rack as they swung from the thumps at the door. More howlers had joined the fight. There was just an inch or so between her and infection. If the door gave in, she was royally screwed.

She needed to get out of the cuffs if she stood a chance of saving herself and the others. She scanned the keys. They were all big, old-fashioned-looking, not small ones that might fit the lock on her cuffs. Then she thought of Martin, the guard. If anyone would have a set of keys, it would be him. He had fled, right at the start. He could be anywhere by now. She turned and ran.

CHAPTER TWENTY-FIVE
Amy

As Amy ran, a deafening sound rang out through the speakers. The air raid sirens – someone had started up the PA system. She needed to find Joel and Sylvia. Reaching the café, she found the place was empty. Gunfire came from down the hallway. She kept close to the walls, crouching for cover. She peeked round the corner. Ahead was the door that led to the restaurant.

'Is there anyone here?' she whispered into the dark room.

A head popped up from behind the long table. 'Amy, over here.'

Her heart leapt. It was Sylvia. She ran over and joined her behind the draping tablecloth.

'I'm so glad you're OK,' Amy said. 'The prime minister has turned into one of those things. He was the first, I think. Before he turned, he wanted me to find this professor who he knows. We're going to get out of here and find a cure.'

Sylvia gave her a brave smile. 'You need to go and find Joel. He's in a cell just down to the left from where you were held.'

A door in the far corner opened. A man in black and white chequered trousers and a white buttoned jacket crept across the floor to them. In his hands was a shiny kitchen knife. 'I thought I heard voices. Alive ones, that is,' he whispered, struggling for breath.

'Who are you?' Sylvia asked.

'I work in the kitchens.'

Amy could see movement in the corner of her eye. The trio fell silent and ducked lower behind the table. A howler stood in the doorway, its hair flopping about as it sniffed the air, drooling black gunge onto the floor. Its shoes clacked as it ventured into the room and Amy realised it was Tristan, infected.

'Anyone got any guns?' the chef whispered. They both shook their heads. He flashed the knife. 'I think I can take that one.'

Amy sensed danger in his enthusiasm. 'Wait a minute,' she said.

He leapt up and banged into a chair, knocking it over. The howler screeched as it leapt towards him, its eyes burning with fury. They sprawled to the floor. He plunged the blade into its stomach. It did not flinch, but as way of a comeback it sunk its teeth into his neck. He screamed out and grappled it around the head. Soon, he stopped fighting and it continued to eat him.

She knew as soon as it was finished with him, it would be after them next. The knife was protruding from the howler's stomach. If she could retrieve it without being eaten herself, then she would have a means to truly finish it off.

'Stay here,' Amy said.

'What are you going to do?' Sylvia asked.

The howler looked up at them hiding behind the table. White lumps of fat spilled from between its blue lips. The howler rolled over onto its knees.

'Hey, fuckface. Come and get me,' Amy screamed at it and ran round the table, diverting the howler's attention away from Sylvia.

It made a clumsy run for Amy and tumbled backwards,

skewering itself onto one of the upturned chair legs. The pole stuck out through its stomach and its entrails squelched as it flailed its arms and legs. The knife clattered to the floor.

As she marched up to the howler that used to be Tristan, its hands clawed for her. She pressed a boot on its throat and its screeches turned into gurgles. Its eyes were wild with a need for her.

'If only you'd listened,' she told him, awkwardly picking up the knife and unclipping the gun from his belt. 'Things could have been so different.'

With her hands cuffed, Amy pressed her fingers to what remained of the chef's neck – no pulse. She said a quick apology in her head and brought the knife down onto his temple. She looked away as she tried to pull the knife from his head. It was stuck in there.

'Shit.'

It always looked so easy when they did it in films. Pressing her foot against his head, she pulled again and seesawed the blade. It came free.

'It's time we went,' Sylvia whispered.

Amy felt wretched, but it was not the time for wallowing. If they were to survive, they needed a plan; she would find Joel and Ash, and then go and find the prime minister's professor to create an antidote. She knew her way would be blocked by hundreds of howlers, but she was not about to give up now.

Joel took a sip of water from the bottle they had given him, as he sat on the floor. No one had been to visit him since before the sirens started. Was it a fire, or worse, had the infection spread underground?

The politicians had distrusted them again and it would be their downfall. There was no way Amy could be a honeytrap. They had been through the plane crash and the escape from Beijing and Whitehall. No one could be that brilliant at acting. He had read the research himself from Chen. Unless it was a big con and the findings were just an inconvenient truth. His fingernails dug into his scalp as he scratched his head. He had no idea what was real now. He had been in there so long that he had forgotten how it was to just have a normal day. Time had turned into waiting with no end. Apart from the lack of a sofa, it was not much different from when he was stuck in the flat for all those months, though back then he could have left whenever he wanted to.

He was aware of a pleasant sensation. Then it dawned on him what it was: his ears were no longer being subjected to that awful siren whine. He opened his eyes, but it was dark in his cell. He closed his eyes with the hope some sleep may make him feel a bit better. The silence was replaced by the sound of footsteps.

'This one? Are you sure?' someone whispered.

'Yes, quickly.'

'OK, stand back!' a familiar voice warned.

Joel was unsure whether they were referring to their companion or him, so he pressed himself against the back wall, just in case, and closed his eyes. A gunshot, followed by the door thunking open, prompted him open his eyes. Light filled the room and he blinked. Amy stood before him, with defiance and blood on her face. In her cuffed hands was a gun. She strode up to him and put the barrel end to his head.

He looked up at her and smirked. 'I knew you'd end up in cuffs one day.'

'You're hilarious.' She lowered the gun, but seemed no less annoyed. 'I had to be sure you hadn't turned into a howler.'

Sylvia had a knife in her hands. It was stained red, already used. 'The disease is here, in the War Rooms.'

'Right,' he said, and groaned as he got to his feet.

Amy looked at him as though they were strangers, with several tablespoons of sulk. *Old times. Brilliant*, he thought.

He had wanted nothing more than to see her again, but he thought back to what the prime minister had said about her. 'Do you know what they're saying about us?' he asked her. 'That we're spies. You are a refugee spy in league with Ron and the Chinese, and I'm a rogue Greenpeace eco-warrior.'

Hurt replaced the bravado in her eyes. 'They aren't saying fuck all anymore. They're turning into howlers left, right and centre now, so we're free to leave any time we want. As long as they don't eat us first.'

There was panic in Sylvia's face. Her top was drenched in sweat.

As he took a step towards Sylvia, she took a step backwards. 'Are you sure you're OK?' he asked.

She would not look at him. 'I haven't got long,' she told Amy. 'Please, just tell him what you told me.'

Amy scuffed her feet and looked at the ground. The handcuffs were still round her wrists, cutting red marks into her skin. 'The PM gave me back your phone. Before he turned, he gave me – *us* – a task.'

'The PM is a howler?' he asked.

Amy nodded. 'Him and about twenty of his minions down here. He got an email from Mei,' Amy said. 'It was meant for us. We need to take Mei's data to some old professor the PM knows.'

Sylvia stepped forwards. 'You need to take this,' she said, holding out the knife to Joel. She dropped it before he could take it. She staggered back to the wall and slithered down to the floor.

He picked her up.

'You two have got to make it up,' she murmured, as she fought to keep her eyes open.

He spotted a soggy bloodstained napkin she held against her wrist.

Amy scooted down next to them and stroked her head. 'Why didn't you say?'

'We've had a lot on, haven't we?' Sylvia's face screwed up and she put a hand to her temple. 'God, it's really hot isn't it?'

Amy hugged her. 'I'm here.'

'*We're* here,' Joel said.

Amy glared at him, before tending to Sylvia again.

Sylvia was crying. 'I can't see.'

Amy took her hand. 'You need to hold on.'

She gave a little laugh. 'Do you know who it was who got me? Ron. Little bastard.'

A stab of mourning hit Joel's chest as he thought of his friend. Sylvia's sweat seeped warm into his own clothes. Her hair was damp and the whites of her eyes had turned grey.

Amy stroked her hair again. 'We're going to find the cure. We can make you better.'

'Don't waste time on me,' Sylvia whispered. 'Remember what Winston said: "If you're going through hell, keep going".'

'You need to hold on,' Amy said.

Sylvia rocked into Joel's grip as she began convulsing. Amy stepped back, gawping as her friend turned into their nemesis.

'Come on,' he said, and took Amy by the arm.

'We can't leave her, not like we left Mei. I won't do it again.'

He grabbed the knife and helped Amy up as she watched her friend dying on the floor. 'You already know what happens next and it's going to happen very soon.'

Amy wiped her cheeks awkwardly, pointing the gun away from her face. 'I, I couldn't save her.'

'You can't save everyone. If we don't get out of here now, we'll both end up like that too. Is that what you want?'

He shoved her out into the corridor. Holding the knife in front of him, aimed at the slumped body, he hesitated.

Amy looked at the gun in her hands. Sylvia's ribcage rose and fell with a raspy gasp. She rolled over onto her front and sprang up onto all fours. Black tendrils of hair were matted to her grey face. Her black eyes were wide with a mad hunger.

'Decide now or I'll choose for you,' Joel said, pointing the knife at what was left of Sylvia.

'You aren't killing our friend,' she said.

He slammed the door and watched through the glass as Sylvia hurled herself against the cell door. 'Is this what you want? Your friend stuck like that for ever?'

She shut her eyes. 'No.'

'You need to start facing up to life, Amy,' he said, over Sylvia's shrieks.

'I always have. Don't you dare tell me that I don't.'

'Then talk to me. Why won't you trust me?' he asked.

Amy pushed him aside, wrangled open the cell door and, raising the gun, she blasted Sylvia in the head. On her way back out, she shoved the gun into his hand. 'There. Happy now?' She strode off down the corridor.

'No, not really.'

'What's new?'

Every time he thought she might fall to pieces, she found steel girders and welded them to her defences. Was there any chance he could ever chisel down to the real Amy, the one who was not always fighting her own corner? Had he any right to when he had his own shipwreck of a past that trawled behind him under the surface? Slowly it was breaking up, stormy waters were eating and dissolving it, but one only had to dive down to the seabed, and it was waiting to be discovered – in plain sight.

He shook the thought away and jogged to catch her up. 'Where did you get this?' he asked, gesturing with the gun she had given him.

'Off that little prick Tristan,' she said.

'What did he do to you?'

She stopped and whirled round to face him. 'I had to piss in a pot in the dark. Stop hassling me, OK?'

'Did he *do* anything to you?'

She shook her head. 'As if I'd let him.' She tried getting the hair out of her eyes with the backs of her hands. 'Fuck, these are annoying,' she said, holding up her handcuffs.

'They rather suit you.'

She glared at him. 'Not funny. How come you didn't get cuffed?'

'I expect I put up less of a fight.'

Their faces were inches apart as he ran his fingers down her arms to where her wrists were shackled by the cuffs. Was there ever a time when they were not fighting? In all his years of marriage, he never fought with Lauren. Yet they never talked about anything, either. Amy made him feel different; she made him want to be the man he was before he hung up his boots at Greenpeace. He had to tell her everything.

'If we're going to survive this, you need to trust me,' he whispered.

She draped her arms over his head, so her cuffed hands cupped round his neck. 'I'm stood here in cuffs and you've got a knife and a gun. If that isn't trust, what is it?' she asked, her eyes searching his.

'Prove it,' he said.

She moved forwards, her lips just inches from his. 'You wish,' she said with a smirk. 'We keep ending up like this, don't we?'

It took everything he had not to kiss her as she looked deep into his eyes. 'I'm not going to lie, the cuffs are an interesting addition,' he said, grazing his nose along her neck, her skin soft with a hint of perfume.

'Probably not the time or the place,' she said.

'It never is with us, is it?' He slid out from under her arms and placed the knife and gun on the floor. Standing up, he turned away from her, taking the opportunity to rearrange his tackle, which was straining against his trousers. Since Amy had come along, his sexual appetite was that of a mountain lion. Probably heightened by the fact they had not actually consummated anything.

But there was something he needed to do for her first. He crossed his arms over his front and started removing his top.

'Joel... what—?' Amy half-coughed, half-laughed in bewilderment, brazenly eyeing him up and down.

He tried not to let her obvious appraisal distract him but *Christ* he wished the circumstances were different right now. He took her cuffed hands in his and eased her down to the ground. Laying her hands palm up on the floor, he released her.

As she knelt there on all fours, she gave him one of her sultry looks that were impossible to ignore. 'I think you'd better explain yourself, before I start overthinking my position here.'

He nodded, knowing that he might start imagining certain scenarios too pretty soon. He shook the thought away – it was all about survival now. 'I need to shoot through the chain, and I'm not doing that without something to dampen the blast.'

'But, you might...'

'I know,' he said. Carefully wrapping his t-shirt around the chain and Amy's wrists, Joel positioned the gun just above the covered chain. He looked up at her, a question in his gaze.

'This is completely fucking nuts,' she said, gawping as her hair fell down over her face. 'But seeing as we're embracing the whole trust thing, you may as well get on with it.'

He thought back to the day they first met in Ron's office, when she had held her wrists out to him before. It was all a bit too real now. He didn't want to think about what could happen if he screwed it up. Taking a deep breath, he pulled the trigger.

Amy flinched as the gunshot shuddered through the metal of the handcuffs, and he looked up in concern, quickly unwrapping the t-shirt and clasping her hands in his. *No lasting damage, thank God*, Joel thought with relief, and he released her hands.

'It's OK,' she whispered, putting her fingertips to his chest. 'I'm OK.' She pressed her lips to his cheek. 'Thank you for not killing me off.'

He bit back a smile as Amy busied herself with removing the remaining metal, rubbing at where the cuffs had dug into her skin while he took some deep breaths to recover.

He shook out his top and shrugged it back on, despite the holes. 'Come on, we need to go. If there's any howlers nearby, they'll have heard that for sure.' He knew they had to come up with a plan to leave right away. 'What's the name of this professor?' he asked.

She closed her eyes. 'I don't know.'

He held her hands. 'Think, Amy. It's important.'

She nodded. 'Professor Malrose. But I don't know where he is.'

Before he realised what he had done, he had dropped her hands. He chewed his lip and sighed. 'I do. We go way back.'

'Old friends?' she asked. 'That's good, isn't it?'

Joel shook his head. 'We need to get down to the Solent. It's not going to be easy.'

'Look around. None of this is exactly a breeze, is it?'

A shriek came from down the hallway behind them. 'Let's go,' he said.

They started walking towards the door of the main corridor. The hard expression on Amy's face told him she had a plan and the best he could do was back her up and go with it. He had not expected to hear Malrose's name coming from Amy's lips. His past was soon to become his present and he had to face it, even if it meant going underwater once more.

Amy went to open the door, but Joel touched her arm. 'What is it?' she asked.

'Which one do you want?' He held up the gun and the knife.

'As if you need to ask.' She smiled and took the gun from him.

Joel opened the door and went into the corridor. 'Jeez, it stinks out here,' he said, pulling up his top again to cover his nose.

Is he trying to torture me? Amy wondered. There was only so much exposure to Joel's naked torso she could take before she caved completely. Seeing his tattoo earlier, the intricate design begging her to trace it with her fingers, had been an exercise in self-restraint.

'It's clear,' he whispered. 'Come on.'

She followed him into the stink of stale blood, piss and decay. They walked softly along the corridors, back towards the museum entrance. They passed the meeting room with the green table, where they had the first conference after Rat-run. As they came to the hallway where the VIP bedrooms were, he checked each of the rooms.

He came back out, frowning. 'I don't get it. If the place was overrun, where the hell is everyone?' he whispered.

'I don't know. I think they had been getting ready to head back up to the surface when the prime minister turned. I had only been let out to go and see him.'

They edged along the corridors. 'It's not going to be much of a haven up there either,' he said.

'What do you mean?'

'Wait.' He crouched down and held the knife out.

Up ahead, a figure laid out on the floor. Amy gripped the gun tightly with both hands. If that thing so much as moved, she would have it.

They moved slowly up to it. Joel winced. 'Oh, shit. Don't look.'

Before she registered what he had said, she saw the body was completely disjointed from the head. Something had eaten away all the neck and shoulders, leaving only the white knobs of the spine. It was a woman. Looking closer, she recognised the pug face of Janice Barber.

Amy looked at Joel. 'It's only going to get worse from here on in, isn't it?'

'She had the same idea as us.'

She frowned at him. 'What?'

He picked up the rucksack next to the body and unzipped it. 'She wanted to get out too. There's water in here, food.' He zipped up the bag and hoisted it onto his shoulders. 'It's going to be a long way to the coast. This might be all we have to rely on.'

'Don't be daft. My flat is bound to be stocked.'

'Could be.'

'What do you mean *could be*?' she asked, as he got up.

'The food might have gone off by now.'

'You think my sister's dead, don't you?'

'I didn't say that.'

'No, but you're thinking it.'

'Don't start,' he warned.

She pointed the gun at him. 'You were never keen on finding her, were you? Why don't you want me to care about my family? Is it because you don't have any?'

'Don't be a bitch.'

'Why not? You're being a cold-hearted twat.'

'Stop it,' he growled.

'Look, if you want to be with me, accept the fact that I have baggage. I'm not abandoning my sister if there's a chance she's alive. And she's a doctor. The world is going to need doctors, now more than ever. If you don't care about that, then go find the professor on your own.'

'OK, you win. We need to leave.' His voice sounded weird, but she did not care.

'I know.'

'No, I'm serious.' He stared past Amy, over her shoulder, down the corridor. 'Come towards me, now. Slowly.'

She looked round to see the howler scuffing along the floor. It banged on the glass of the bedroom doors, looking for its next victim. A waft of gone-off eggs crossed with blocked drains drifted along the hallway.

'It hasn't spotted us yet,' he whispered. 'Keep going slow.'

She tiptoed, following him. She stepped across Janice's body, and looked up to see Joel about to bang into an A-frame. Grabbing onto his shirt, she pulled him away. *Thanks*, he mouthed. Hanging onto each other, they sidestepped until they were safely round the corner.

'Christ, that was close,' he murmured.

'You're telling me.'

'Don't fire the gun unless you absolutely have to.'

She bit her lip, annoyed he was telling her what to do again. 'Why?'

'Once the bullets are gone, that's it. I haven't got an arsenal down my trousers.'

She struggled to keep up with his fast pace. 'You shouldn't admit to that, my sweet.'

'Shh.'

'Don't fucking shush me,' she said.

'Just listen.'

She could hear echoed, fast footsteps. 'That spells trouble.'

They ran past the glass panels of the old cabinet room to find the place was in darkness. The occupant roused at their presence; white palms slammed against the windows and gnashing teeth sought for a way through. Then they were at the ticket desks and the exit signs. Joel stopped. He snatched the gun from Amy's hands as he ran back.

'What are you doing?' she screamed. 'If you're thinking about doing something heroic, then don't.'

The howler was closing in. It was snorting, sniffing them out. Amy bit her fingernail. Joel had the gun aimed at the entranceway, waiting for it to come.

'Get to the exit,' he told her.

She looked at the glass door – it was wide open. Odd bits of furniture lay strewn about the floor, as if thrown away from the door. She could not just leave him, there was no way. The howler tumbled round the corner. This one was in a suit, shirt wet with blood, drool and black goo. It was the prime minister.

'Sorry, buddy,' Joel said, raised the gun and fired.

A neat hole appeared in its forehead. It stumbled back against the wall and slid down into the corner.

'What should we do?' she asked, as they stood over him. 'Cover him with a blanket or something? I mean, he was the country's leader.'

'Best not. We aren't exactly being quiet down here. We really need to go,' he said, flicking the safety back on.

'So long then, sir.' Amy gave him a salute. On to the exit, she found a curved staircase leading upwards around Portland stone walls. Daylight spilled into the alcove. Everything glistened and water dripped to the floor. The clouds sped along overhead.

'Looks like we just missed the rain,' he said. 'Let's see what's out there.'

Together, they climbed the steps and, despite the danger of outside, she was grateful to be above ground once more.

CHAPTER TWENTY-EIGHT
Joel

Joel led the way up the stairs and kept the gun ready. The exit brought them to street level, just above the black pod of the museum entrance. He blinked from the daylight hurting his eyes, which he had not seen in days. Or was it weeks? It was hard to keep track of time after being locked down below for so long. But where were they?

Down to the left, the red tarmac road bordered St James's Park. Along the avenue, he could almost make out Horse Guards Parade. He could not see any howlers around. Judging by the long shadows cast by the leafless trees, he deduced it was early evening.

'What are you waiting for?' Amy asked. She went to push past, but he held her back.

'I don't think we've got long before sunset.'

'It's half an hour or so to the flat, if we walk fast.'

He chewed in the inside of his cheek. 'We have to get inside before it gets dark.'

'I can get us there. Don't worry.'

They headed along the road where the car had dropped them off all that time ago. The façade with the three archways was up ahead. Amy glanced round the whole time and gripped the knife handle so hard that her fingertips went white.

'We'll be all right, you know,' he said, touching her forearm.

They had made it to the metal barriers the other side of the façade. To the left, down the wide street, he spied the poppy-laden Cenotaph. In the other direction, he could make out one of the golden towers of the Houses of Parliament and opposite it, the sloping rooftops of Westminster Abbey. Days ago, the road was clogged with cars, red buses, black taxis, bike couriers and vans. The pavements bustled with people and the air was a lifeblood of beeping horns, shrieking sirens and the constant drone of engines. Now the silence was filled with an eerie anticipation, as though the air was itching for something to happen.

'Fuck, this is weird. It's so empty,' Amy said, glancing around. 'It's like I'm waiting for more of those things to just swarm out of the shadows.'

'Try and not let it freak you out. Let's just go, OK?'

'Hang on a minute,' she whispered, grabbing his elbow. 'Westminster tube station is just over there.' She pointed to the right. 'If we went below ground—'

'No. If those things prefer the dark, we're screwed. Are you expecting the trains to be running?'

'All right, grumpy.'

'I'm trying to be logical,' he said. 'The only chance we stand against the howlers is to do what they can't: think.'

As they began to walk back along past the Cenotaph, only now did its engraved words *The Glorious Dead* mean something completely different to Joel. The flags billowed in the breeze.

Amy's stomach rumbled and she pulled on his wrist. 'Is there any food in that bag?'

He felt a bit lightheaded himself. He pulled her in next to a building and shrugged the bag off his shoulders. 'Not much,' he said, peering inside. 'We've got to make it last. Some squares of chocolate?' He broke a piece off from the bar and handed it to her.

'You sure know how to treat a lady, don't you?' she said. They munched on the chocolate as they passed the tall black memorial to the women of the Second World War.

'We ought to cross over,' he said.

'Why?'

He pointed over to the Horse Guards building. The sentry outposts were empty. Black doors barred the way and the railings were locked. Guards in red jackets and gold helmets clawed their white-gloved hands through the bars, growling and dribbling in desperation to get at Joel and Amy. Beyond, the bodies of gutted horses were strewn out on the gravel, picked clean. The rounded white ribs reminded Joel of an apple core.

'Shiiiiit,' she breathed. 'That's sick. They're eating animals now?' She held the knife up as they crossed the road. 'Do you think they can get out?'

'Doubt it. It's designed like a fortress.'

'Hey, if the prime minister is dead, who the hell is in charge now?' she asked. 'If this is Whitehall, shouldn't we be looking for them?'

He looked up at the white stone building with the blue plaque on the outside. 'I think anyone who was important came with us on Rat-run.'

'And the royal family?'

'I don't know, Amy,' he hissed. 'You want to go gallivanting all over London now?'

'All right. Sorry. Jeez.'

The light was fading fast. 'Come on,' he said. 'We need to run if we're going to get there before dark.'

By the time they reached the next junction, Amy was gasping, and stopped to clutch her side. 'I can't run all that way. How the fuck are you so fit?'

'I've got a gym in my flat.'

She snorted. 'All right for some.'

'These should help.' He grinned as he picked up two bicycles that had been abandoned on the pavement.

'Boris Bikes? Are you serious?'

He swung his leg over the blue bike. 'We'll get there a hell of a lot quicker.'

'OK.' She sighed and got on the yellow bike.

They came to another junction, back to another wide road; tall buildings with arched windows and balustrades above the doors. They cycled down the wrong side of the road, veering past empty buses and trucks. She stopped just after a set of traffic lights.

'What is it?' he asked.

'Nothing. It's just, if we keep going that way, it'll bring us to Charing Cross Station. I think we need to go a bit more north.' The knife almost slipped from her hand. She pumped the pedals again and wove down a side street, past an olde worlde pub, with wilting hanging baskets. He yearned for a cold bottled beer in a place like that, maybe with the sport on in the background. Surprised, he realised he had not thought about alcohol in a while, despite the world being as it was.

They slowed as, to the left, nearer than they hoped was Trafalgar Square. The fountains were still, the water brown with dust. All that remained of the column was a stub – rubble from the fallen structure laid everywhere.

Amy stopped. The street was empty except for a group of howlers huddled around something in the middle of the road to the right. She swore under her breath. 'We can't.'

'Nah, we can take them. All we need to do is ride round them.'

'It's not them I'm worried about.' She nodded towards the square.

About fifty howlers were swarming over the rubble, headed straight for them. He hauled his bike round. 'We need to outrun them. Well, out-peddle them.'

'Are you mad?'

'Would you rather stay here and die?'

They kicked off and started cycling for the smaller group of howlers. By now, they had spotted them and forgotten their previous scavenge.

'This is a better option, is it?' she asked.

As they cycled harder, the wind roared in their ears. 'Keep the line until I say,' he said. 'If you go too early, they'll mob us against the walls. Keep with me and then go hard left around. I'll go right.'

'This is fucking nuts,' she screamed.

The howlers ran down the middle of the road, arms wide and mouths gaping. If he got this wrong, it would kill them both.

'OK, now.'

They peeled away from the crowd, swerving hard. The howlers were too tightly packed together to change direction and surge at them. By the time Joel got round, he saw Amy's yellow bike headed up a narrower pedestrian street, flanked by iron railings and a tall, stone church. He pumped hard to try to catch her up; by then, she had reached a crossroad of smaller streets.

'This is too dangerous. They're everywhere,' she breathed.

'Just keep going.'

He followed her as she took a few turns, leaving the grandiose of Whitehall behind them. Orange-red brick offices and glass-fronted buildings lined the streets. They found a lorry abandoned at an angle in the middle of the road. The windscreen was covered in dust and a front tyre was flat. The cab door was open.

They came to a T-junction onto a street lined with shops. It was only wide enough for one car and was paved with bricks. Bollards and black lampposts led the way. Amy turned left, and at the end of the road they found a building opposite with a scrolled, ornate façade of the Noel Coward Theatre.

'Are we going the right way?' he asked.

She struggled to get her breath. 'OK. No, wait a minute. The sun is going down over there. I think we need to head north for a bit longer. So, it should be this way.'

They turned right, and Joel felt vulnerable as they rode through a wide crossroads. It felt weird cycling the wrong way up a one-way street. Like it mattered these days. They were hardly going to be hit by a bus. Was life going to be this surreal from now on? Would they ever have schools or hospitals again? He felt sorry for any children that were living now or born into this chaos. How would they learn to read? It certainly would not help them fight off a howler. Though at least they would not have to deal with the toxic disillusionment of bloody social media.

Amy had stopped. The road had forked into several smaller roads, one with brightly coloured shop windows, cheerful flapping bunting overhead and a cobbled pavement below.

He dared not ask where they should go next. Her face was tense, and he realised the burden he had put on her. She had not asked for any of this. All she wanted was to find her sister, and he could not deny her that. What was left was precious. What was Amy to him? She had been meaning more to him for some time now, he realised. Definitely since before they left Beijing and the airport, but after the summit. Still, he knew now was not the time for taking stock of his feelings.

'Shall we try this way?' he asked, nodding to the street festooned with the billowing bunting.

The shops were quaint in their way, cafes with pastel awnings, and another old pub with a Union Jack flag hanging from the wall. Another time, he would have liked to go for a stroll with Amy around here, milling in the crowds, being happy.

They slowed up again as the road ended at a mini roundabout. In the centre was a concrete-type spire with a blue sphere near the top and ending in a point. They glanced up the road – it was clear. He followed her down a street to the left. They passed a grey-painted building with a CCTV unit mounted above the door. Howlers beat against the glass panels of the door, desperate to get to their newly-sighted prey.

'Oh,' Amy said when they got to the next junction, looking at the Odeon building with dismay.

'What is it?'

'This isn't Charing Cross Road.' Tears welled in her eyes. 'Fuck. I've got us lost.'

Joel knew it was the worst time to be checking fingerposts, as the sun sank down behind the skeleton trees and lonely rooftops.

Amy beat her fist on the bike handlebars, blinking away angry tears. 'I've probably got us killed because I don't know my way round my own bloody city. Fuck's sake.'

'We have to keep going, right?' he asked. 'For your sister.'

She nodded and wiped her nose on her sleeve. 'Sorry.'

'Come on, we'll figure it out. Let's go down here.'

She followed him down an alleyway alongside the theatre to pull up at another junction. A natty-looking park sat behind red railings. Construction cranes stretched into the skyline in the distance, along with another tall building. There was only one building around there that looked like a large block of council flats: the Centre Point building.

She squealed. 'Yes! We're on track. Come on.'

They pedalled faster, steering around manhole covers and pitted tarmac. The further they sped through the city, the more she wondered how much further she could go. Her calf muscles burned, and her throat was so dry it hurt. Joel braked ahead of her.

'What?' she asked, pulling up next to him.

He gripped her hand. 'They're here.'

Voices echoed around the grey city streets. It sounded like howlers, but different. It was more sing-song, higher pitched. She listened closer, able to pick out snatches of sentences.

'No – people,' she said. 'It's people.' She grinned and saw that up at the crossroads there was a blockade of tanks. They had been parked nose-to-tail across the street. She parked her bike up to find Joel still sitting astride his.

'Soldiers,' he said, with dread in his voice.

'How is that bad? You want to turn down the offer of help?'

'I thought you wanted to find your sister.'

'I do, but if there's a refugee point or something, we won't be the only ones left. Surely that's a good thing? Once we've been to the flat, we can come back with Ash.'

He looked back the way they came. 'We're meant to be looking for Malrose.'

'These are the first survivors we've found. We may as well try and find out what's going on.'

'Fine, we'll play it your way,' he said, and dumped the bike with a clatter. 'But when we meet the soldiers, keep quiet, right? Hide your knife. If they see us with weapons, they might not take kindly.'

'Sure.'

'I mean it. They mustn't know about Malrose, right?'

'I said "sure".'

As they reached the tanks, there was a sign high on the Portland stone building that read New Oxford Street. Soldiers spilled out from between the caterpillar-tracked wheels, holding their guns on their forearms. The men watched them, waiting.

'Can we come past?' Joel asked.

'You here for the rescue point?' one grunted back.

'What else?'

The soldier jostled his gun in the affirmative and spat on the floor. 'Best you go to the northern containment, er, muster point.'

'Thank you.' Joel turned towards the tank and the soldiers moved aside.

Amy said nothing, aware of eyes on her. Joel pushed her on ahead of him. She squeezed through the tiny gap between the tank and the brick wall of a coffee shop. When she was through the gap, the sheer noise hit her. She looked up to find the entire street full of jostling people.

She had seen this before. The soldiers had blocked every exit, using the old street system. She knew of the May Day protests on TV, when the police had taken advantage of the wide, straight avenues to pen in any protestors and make them sit it out. That was what it was designed for. This was different; nobody was looting the shop fronts. The faces she saw looked anxious, ready to lash out through fear alone.

'What do you think he meant by *containment*?' she asked when Joel came through from behind.

'We need to get out of here,' he whispered.

'You're being paranoid.'

He leant close, so only she could hear. 'You think they're going to find homes for all of these people? Where? There are oceans of bunkers to go around, right?'

She frowned. 'I don't know. There must be old military bases they don't use anymore.'

'How will they transport all these people?'

She ground her boot into the tarmac. 'I don't know. Why are you asking me?'

'This isn't the solution you think it is. We are walking into a trap.'

'Why would they want to trap us?'

'They're going by protocols – doing what they have to – though there's barely a dozen of them.' At each avenue there were, at the most, three soldiers brandishing guns. 'They don't look like they're evacuating anyone, do they?'

'Right then,' she said, with her hand on her hip, 'if you think you know it all, what do you suggest?'

'We need to stick to the plan – *our* plan: get your sister and leave the city.'

She was glad he was on board. 'How are we meant to get through that lot?' She nodded at the mass of people.

'Pretend it's a game of football.'

He dove in and she followed, careful to keep the blade of her knife pointed downwards. People swore and shoved back. Soon they were in the middle and could not go any further. They were running out of time. The howlers would be there soon if they had followed the scent. The smell of a concentrated pack of the living would be a powerful stink to the hungry.

'Oi, you bastards. We can't just stay here,' a man shouted at the soldiers. They stared back at him, their guns nestled in their arms.

'We need to get to the evac point. Why are you just standing there?' another person yelled.

People whistled and booed the soldiers, who simply chewed gum like cows chomping cud.

Thunder rumbled and feather-edged clouds, which were an ominous shade of yellow-grey, loomed overhead. 'We need to leave,' she whispered to Joel. 'Let's get back to the bikes.'

He looked at the skies. 'No. We need to find shelter – now. We can't be out here when it rains.'

'Now listen,' a soldier shouted at the crowd, 'central London is under quarantine. You are advised to go to the evac point in King's Cross and find a way out of the city.'

'That's miles away. It'll be dark soon,' a man yelled back.

'There's a convoy ready at the top of the street,' the soldier said, pointing up one of the roads heading north.

'That's where we just came from. There's bugger all there,' someone else shouted.

'We need to get off the street,' Joel whispered to Amy. 'Get under the cover of those shops.'

She nodded and they started to edge through the crowd.

A man clamoured at one of the soldiers. 'We need food. You have to help us, or we'll die.'

'Get back.' The soldier opened fire and the man was blasted into the people behind him.

People panicked and surged backwards. Amy was shoved and she fell to her knees. By the time she had got to her feet, she could not see Joel anywhere.

'No,' she screamed, but it was too late. The momentum of the crowd pushing into the road was too strong.

Above all that, she could hear a sound like a car driving over gravel. Sheets of rain pummelled the tarmac in the roads ahead, coming towards them fast.

An arm clamped around her waist and dragged her sideways. 'Get off,' Amy cried. 'Where's Joel?'

'We need to be quick-smart,' the boy said, and pulled her into the alcove of a boarded-up shop, as the rain drummed down on the roads and windows.

People began to scream and cower from the deluge, as it began to fizzle and burn their faces and hands. A woman fell to the pavement, inches from Amy.

'Come on.' Amy held her hand out to her.

The boy pulled Amy back. All she could do was watch the woman's skin bubbling under her fingers as she clutched at her forehead, the rain beating down on her.

Amy sobbed. 'We need to do something. We need to help them.'

The boy adjusted the head torch he was wearing. His wiry black hair stuck up in clumps either side of the straps. 'Go out there and you're a gonner.'

'Fuck's sake,' she cried. 'Joel is out there. I need to help him.'

'Too late. I've seen this before. Ain't no going out there – not now.'

Someone in the horde began to make an unearthly whooping sound, like a wounded animal. It had begun: the infection had reached the streets.

The yelping sound was getting louder. More and more people joined in, so it seemed more like a hunting call. Surrounded by tall buildings, the sound of the approaching howlers echoed off the structures. It sounded as though it came from everywhere all at once.

Howlers spilled over the top of the tanks and dropped down the other side. The soldiers clustered together and fired their guns. Someone next to her got hit in the shoulder and went down.

'Joel,' Amy cried to herself, as the boy held her tighter against him. He could only have been about fourteen or fifteen. He was as tall as her, yet stronger. She could not free her arms enough to use the knife. 'Get off.'

'It's decision time,' he said. 'Time is money and it's a-wasting.'

'What?'

'I don't fancy being eaten next and I'm only a chicken nugget. But I got some skills. You want my help?' he asked.

The howlers had started to pick off people at the edges of the crowd. Amy looked past people running, screaming, falling to the floor, being eaten. She could not see Joel anywhere. 'Yes, I do. You'll help us?'

'Where you need to go?'

'Liverpool Street.'

He pursed his lips, then nodded. 'I can get you there, Ma Chere. Totes safe.'

'How? We can't go out there. You said so.'

He stood a bit taller. 'Got a better plan, Stan. I'll need payment, though.' He stared at her gold anklet.

'But it was my mother's.'

'We ain't got time for this, chica. You want my help or not? Cos we going nowhere until you pay me. I want your bag too, and the knife.'

'I can't do that,' she whispered.

'Must be a pretty important journey, is all,' he said with a shrug.

'You promise you can get us there?'

'I'd stake my reputation on it. Can we hurry things along now? The mothers are looking pretty eager today.'

Sentimentality would not save her life now. 'Fine.' She bent down and unclasped the chain. She gave it one final look before he whipped it away and stashed it in his combats.

'And the rest.'

She chewed her cheek in defiance but handed over the knife and the bag. People close to her screamed as they were felled by howlers.

'Right, stage two of the plan is about to commence,' he said.

'You're going to help me find Joel?' she asked.

'He's gone.'

She felt a blow to the back of her head and the heavy motion of going down, her legs collapsing beneath her. Someone had hold of her, helping break her fall. Opening her eyes, she had a blurry view of boarded-up windows. The pavement was cold against her side. All she could see was a bright red door in front of her. Then it was opened to a dark space within. The boy had her by the wrists, dragging her through on her stomach. The concrete was cold and gritty against her skin. This was not what she had in mind. She tried to talk.

'Shh. None of the mothers have seen us. Let's keep it that way, eh?' Upside down, she saw the bright head torch on his head. He grinned. 'I'm Dex.'

A million questions were going through her mind. She wanted to scream, to get back outside. She could not form the words. She felt sick, it hurt to breathe. There was no holding back the blackness that enveloped her vision. Then, there was nothing.

CHAPTER THIRTY
Joel

Elbows dug in Joel's ribs as he tried to get away from the stampede. Someone trod on his foot. People yelled and the soldiers fired shots. He had lost Amy, but amid all the chaos he could hear another sound above the others: the pelting of rain. The street ahead was white with sheets of it coming down. He dropped to his knees and rolled under a parked car. Rain slashed hard onto the tarmac. Agonised shrieks and chorused yelps were all he could hear.

He watched from the ground, desperately hoping Amy had got away to safety. A woman staggered across the wide street. Her hair was greasy and lank, her skin all blotchy. As she put her hands to her head, Joel saw she had red sores at her temple. Her shirt was plastered to her chest, showing the white bra straps. Yellow, burning flesh spread across her shoulder blades.

The more he looked round the crowd for Amy, the more people chorused with yelps. It was their instinct to do it, to connect with the other ones coming this way. They were guiding them to find their prey.

Soldiers fell, their guns going off as they convulsed against the tanks. Others collapsed around him, while people shoved on past, eager to get to safety. The howlers had arrived from the south, teeth bared, arms reaching for people at the edges, the ones not fast enough. Their long hunt from the square had driven them into a frenzy.

The woman who had been near the pavement thrashed around, black saliva spraying from her mouth. She turned and sunk her teeth into the arm of a soldier who was trying to keep the crowds back. He cried out and smashed her with the butt of his weapon. She chomped at his neck and they both fell to the ground.

Then Joel spotted Amy through a gap of the stumbling, walking wounded. She was over to the east side, under a shop canopy with a young boy. Relief that she was safe was short-lived. The boy seemed to be holding her back. She handed him something. Was she making a deal of some kind? He looked up and spotted Joel watching him under the car. Then he swung his fist at the side of her head. She slumped down out of sight.

Joel's shouts were drowned out among the screams of the crowd and the roar of the infected. The rain was beginning to trickle under the car, towards him. There was nowhere left to go. The howlers pushed forwards into the throng. The soldiers fired at them, and a few went down before they too were overpowered. The infected swarmed over the tanks. This was an invasion, a victory.

CHAPTER THIRTY-ONE

Amy

When she woke, Amy was aware of a stabbing pain in her ribs. She grimaced as she moved and bedsprings creaked. Every bit of her felt as though she had aged by fifty years. She sat up with a groan and found she was on a bare mattress on the floor. Her head was heavy and she could not move her legs.

Memories, snapshots of the hideous scene in the street, thundered back into her mind. The screams of terror, the pap-pap of spraying bullets, people stampeding over each other to flee. She stared up at the greeny-black patches of mould on the ceiling, barely caring where she was. Joel was gone. If he had survived the rain, there was no chance against the howlers. The whole thing was her fault. If they had just gone south, like he wanted, not right into the nest of the infected, he might still be with her.

Would the prime minister have expected her to go to Malrose on her own?

'Wakey-wakey.' Dex pushed back colourful silk drapes, which bordered the makeshift bedroom. He came over to the bed and held out a small bottle of water.

She grappled around, looking for her knife. She could not remember how she got there, or how long she had been there. Why was her head banging as though she had the worst hangover ever?

'Get the fuck back,' she yelled. 'What have you done to me?'

She wriggled back against the wall.

'I needed to give you a little something to calm you down when we told you about your friend. Do you remember?' he asked.

She bit her lip and shook her head. 'How long have I been here?'

Dex scratched his nose. 'A day or so.'

'I need to get back outside.'

'I've already been out there looking for your friend. It's a mess. It's nothing but dead bodies and mothers. I'm paid to keep you safe, right? Up there is anything but.'

Amy bit her lip and covered her face. 'He can't be.' She sobbed into her palms, kneading the wet tears into her skin. 'No, please, no.'

He sat down next to her and put his arm round her shoulders. 'Sorry, chica.'

If she sat there and listened to it, it would be true. It could not be… the thought of another man touching her, not Joel, felt wrong. She pushed him off and got up. She groaned, her head swimming. 'I need to get out.'

He looked up at her with a commiserating expression. 'Ain't no doing. It's brutal out there. You ain't well, neither. Just stop a sec and drink this.' He offered her the water again.

'Have you kidnapped me?'

He laughed. 'Nope on a rope – you paid me. This is a pit-stop at my digs. You weren't fit to go anywhere, so here's as good as any place. Drink.'

'Is it bottled?'

'Yeah. There's no running water here, I'm afraid,' he said as he sat down next to her and stretched his legs. His skate trainers scuffed on the concrete.

She took the bottle from him and sipped the water. 'Where are we?'

'It was a bare hurry to get you in. I couldn't risk anyone seeing. It's on the hush-hush here. It's how we've survived for this long.'

'What is this place?'

'All in good time. Drink some more water.'

She took a sip. She would just have to trust he was not going to poison her after she had paid him in jewellery and provisions. She looked round the room. By the head of the bed, there was a stack of skating magazines. A bulging black bin liner was in the corner with a Sudoku book on top of it.

'I need to go back out there. I need to get back to my flat, to my sister,' she said.

'No can do. It's a bit hairy-scary on the level right now. And I'm sorry, but it's a no-return policy of ours. Only leaving from the back door. House rules.'

'This is ridiculous.'

'You get the knife back when we're through, OK? I'm keeping it safe for you.'

She said nothing, but took sips of water, looking round the room uneasily.

'Where did you come from,' he asked, 'when this all hit?'

It all came back in flashes: the plane crash, the War Rooms, Beijing. If anyone knew she was working with the government, it might put her in more danger. She did not even know where she was. 'I'm trying to find my sister. When Nelson's Column fell, I holed up in a mall for a few days – with Joel. We only came out above ground about an hour ago.' It hurt just to say his name. He could not be dead, not him. They had survived so much together. Yet, he was gone, just as simply as that.

All she wanted to do was run and hide from her thoughts, but there was Ash. She had to be strong for her sake. If she wanted to get out of this place, she had to stay calm. She thought back to the barricade and vaguely recollected handing over her anklet to Dex. She rubbed a sore spot on the back of her head. 'Did you hit me?'

'Sorry.' He looked at the ground and scuffed his trainers. 'I needed to get you in quick without a hussy fuss.'

'I don't get it. You said you were going to get us to Liverpool Street. I need to go.' She managed to get herself to her feet. She wobbled a bit and Dex caught her.

'Just sit tight for a bit. You eaten?' he asked, sitting her back down again.

'We, er, I had a few squares of chocolate.' She placed the empty glass on the magazine stack.

'Nah, I'm talking actual proper food. That's just sugar shit. You're not going anywhere until we get you something in that belly-belly of yours. Part of the payment, all right, chica? No arguments.' His wristwatch beeped. 'Hmm, sunset. Darky-dark from here on in.'

'Why are you waiting? Won't those things be hunting at night?'

He tapped his nose. 'Not where we're going.'

Whoops echoed round the place. She sat up fast. 'What is that?'

'It's OK. There are loads of us here. This end of the building is mine. Perks of the job, you see.'

'Job?'

'I make myself indispensable; favours here and there, errands and that. I'm a scurrier, not a worrier. I'm one of the lucky ones. At least I got a bed. Most have to lie on crap, old newspapers and the like. Apart from me and Napalm.'

'Who?'

'He's the head honcho, my hombres. Founded this place. Without him, we'd all be dead. He's the dude with the food. Let's on go a magical mystery tour.'

He opened the drapes and she followed him out into a large open-plan space. Room dividers created little spaces and old heaters sat underneath a wall of windows. A green fire exit sign was above a doorway to the right. Broken tiles and random bits of wood littered the floor; an upturned chair had been abandoned at the far end of the room and grubby strip-lights hung from the ceiling, redundant.

'We think this floor used to be the offices,' he said. 'This one and the one below. Got the best views in London. See?' He led her to the windows.

She looked at the panoramic view of the city below. Not far away was the tall structure of the BT Tower, with its pod on the top. It always kind of reminded her of a washing machine cylinder, gone wrong. Around here too, cranes rose into the sky.

'That's Bloomsbury,' he said.

'Do you know this building isn't safe?'

'It's as safe as it gets. Where else can you look at the city and not be at risk from the mothers? That's why I like it here. Tickedy boo, peachy as a new shoe.'

She frowned at him. He seemed to be convincing himself.

Surely being somewhere safe was as good as it got these days?

'You good?' Dex asked, too close to her, shining the head torch light on and off in her face.

His breath did not smell too great. Neither did hers, she reckoned. Teeth-brushing came a long way down the line from keeping alive. 'Don't you ever take that thing off?' she asked, taking a step back.

'Nah, it's well useful. I'm in the dark more than the light these days. I'll probably turn into Gollum soon. I only take it off when I'm in bed. On my lonely lonesome, I might add.'

She said nothing. Whether it was a hint or not, she did not want to know. She was fed up of him being cryptic. 'Is there a loo here? I'm desperate.'

'No probs, chica. This way.'

He took her along some smaller corridors and then opened a door to reveal a room with more broken windows and a single yellow bucket in the corner. It was not a toilet, but another office, a much smaller one. From this window, she could see the glass pyramid of the Shard to the left, and the very top of the London Eye. She tried to look down, but they were so high up she could not see.

'I wouldn't look if I were you,' he said. 'As I said, we ain't got running water. Once you've done your bizz, lob it out the window.'

'There's no sink. What about my hands?'

'Ah, now,' he said, patting down his pockets. He pulled out a pack of baby wipes and handed them to her. 'Here.'

'Thanks.'

'Now I want the packet back, mind.' He pointed at her.

'Boots is a no-go now too. Man, those mothers... I'll be just down the hall.'

When she caught up with him, he tutted and shoved his phone back in his pocket. 'What a moment. That was the last of the charge gone. I'll never get a text never again.'

'Are you so sure that's it? The world's ended?' she asked.

He shrugged. 'Meh. I kinda hope so, to be fair. I never really fitted in the old world. Here, we don't need jobs. I can do what I like now.'

Amy realised that between Rat-run and getting out after the prime minister turned, was when the world they knew had ended. She and Joel had entered a no-man's land, and Dex had been there all the time. 'What happened, after Nelson's Column fell?' she asked.

'Well, the city went into lockdown,' he said. 'We all thought it was a new Ground Zero or something. The news channels began to go down and nobody knew anything. Everyone was told to go home. Two days later, they had created an exclusion zone around the square. We came back into work. I used to work in the bookshop on Charing Cross Road on weekends and after school.

'Only a few people made it in. Some phoned in sick. We assumed it was a bug going about. But that day, we kept having, er, incidents, with the shoppers downstairs. We figured out pretty soon what caused the transformation.'

He turned on his head torch as they entered the gloomy stairwell. 'Watch out for the dead pigeons. This place has been empty for years,' he said, his voice echoing as they went down the steps. 'Except for the birds. We've managed to get rid of most of the nests, but they keep getting in through the broken windows.'

'So, go on,' she said, 'what happened?'

'We got holed up for a few days in the bookshop and people kept getting ill, puking up black stuff and trying to bite us, like we were the biggest burger they'd ever seen.'

They made it into the light of the landing and down another corridor. 'We had to narrow down the possibilities of why people had become ill,' he said. 'So we looked closer at the survivors, the staff we had here. Only the people who drank from the water cooler were fine and dandy. That's when we figured it out. Anyone who went out in the rain never made it back.' His stomach rumbled. 'Hmm, dinner should be on the go by now. Come on, part two of the mystery tour is about to commence.'

'You still haven't said where we are.'

The first room they came to was double height and looked more like a warehouse or factory, with yellow metal structuring like scaffolding or racking suspended from the ceiling. To the left, a blue spiral fed down through the floor.

'Why the big secret?' she asked. 'Why can't you just tell me what this place is?'

He sighed. 'Have you heard of the Post Office Railway? The Mail Rail?'

'No,' she replied, feeling stupid.

'Back in the day, Royal Mail used to use a network of tunnels to transport post around the city. Kinda like a mini Tube network. They had little trains and everything. But they closed the network some time back in the eighties. Thing is, it still exists down there – a whole access route across bits of London. Nicey-nice for me as I can go about my business without risk of being attacked.'

'There are no howlers down there?'

He grinned. 'That's the beauty of it. The whole system is sealed off, ever since the shutdown years back. So, no waggly-stragglers. No one could get down there, anyways.'

A conveyor belt led down from the ceiling to a landing point. The door of a grey panel box beneath was left open, revealing buttons and a key-turn. Round the corner, the room got even taller. The top half was separated into a giant, yellow carousel-type structure.

'This is the West Central District Post Office,' he said. 'It was a sorting office. The mail would go down the shafts and onto the mail rail network. It got too expensive to run as a system and they shut it down just after the millennium.' He took his glasses off and wiped them on his t-shirt. 'This place got forgotten. Before the outbreak, they sometimes used the ground floor for arty farty-type events, but apart from that, it's been left to rot.'

'How come you know so much about it?

He put his glasses back on. 'My dad used to work here. Maybe that's why I don't mind coming back here. A nice little hidey hole for Dex.'

Further along, near another doorway, they passed more drapes, but these were grey and tatty, and not drawn. She looked to see a guy kneeling on a mattress with his butt pulsing. The legs of a girl flailed around. She made moaning sounds. Another boy held her down, his trousers bulging as he waited his turn.

'Oh shit,' Amy whispered. 'Is this a brothel?'

She watched the girl, unsure if she needed rescuing. The girl saw her and gave a slight shake of her head. She reached her arms up to the boy standing over her head. The two boys, realising they had an audience, broke into laughter.

'I should, we should…' Amy muttered.

'Come on, I don't get involved in all that,' said Dex, pulling Amy away. 'We all have to pay our way round here. I pay in favours and supply runs. Some people have nothing else to give but themselves.'

They passed on, stepping around dead pigeons. She wrapped her arms tight around her. There was a smell of stale ale and strong urine. Not everyone had been using the bucket upstairs. 'She's paying to stay in this dive? What makes this place so special?'

'I told you: no one knows it exists. The mothers can't get in neither.' Dex stopped and pulled her close. 'Just need to give you a little worm in your ear,' he whispered. 'You need to know something about Napalm before you meet him. He's dangerous, you get me? In a crazy-dangerous, probably-needs-to-be-smothered-in-his-sleep kinda way. So, just mind your manners, OK?'

She followed him as he climbed a set of stairs. 'It doesn't matter, I'm not staying,' she said. She was not about to be intimidated by some budget gangster who had got lucky by breaking into an old museum piece when the world went to shit.

Out of the shadows, a stocky man seized her round her neck and pulled her close in front of him. All of a sudden, the repugnant stench of BO and smoky bacon crisps filled her senses.

'Hello, Amy,' the familiar voice said. 'I'd recognise that sweet behind anywhere.'

CHAPTER THIRTY-TWO
Amy

The man spun Amy round to face him. He still had a muscly neck, but now it was tattooed. His smile revealed some gold teeth on the top and some black rotten ones on the bottom.

'Nathan? I thought you'd be in prison by now.' She tried her best to keep her voice level as revulsion pooled like acid in her stomach.

She had not forgotten the searing pain of being held down and the sizzle as the cigarette tip was stubbed out on her arm each time he forced himself on her.

He grabbed her by the hair and pressed the cold barrel of a gun into her ribs. 'I ain't gone by that name in a long time. My name is Napalm, and you'd do to remember that since you came blundering into my crib.'

'I'm not—'

'You're not staying. I heard you.' He looked past her. 'Dex, man, is she packing?'

Dex replied from the top of the stairs. 'Nope, I picked her clean. Her bag's in my hidey hole.'

Napalm's teeth grazed her earlobe and she shuddered. 'Tell anyone that we were in the home together,' he whispered, 'and you'll wish you hadn't.'

'Like I want anyone knowing about that.' She tried to inch away from him.

'Shit, it's fucking awesome making you squirm. I've missed it,' he said. 'Plenty of time for that.'

She could not hide her frustration now. 'What do you want? I've made my payment.'

'Your payment was with Dex for the journey. You owe me an entrance fee for this place. I've got some questions. Come with me,' he said, and shoved her in front of him up the stairs. 'Here, brethren, we have a visitor.'

They neared a cluster of youths seated on old chairs and tables. Most of them looked either miserable, or out of it. Some looked up blearily from the floor as they dragged on fags or drank from bottles.

'This is Amy. She'll be staying for dinner,' he said.

A skinny white girl with dark hair, wearing a crop top, tiny skirt and clumpy heels, whispered to her friends and threw Amy a filthy look. 'Fucking chancer,' she said, loud enough for her to hear. 'I thought we were closed doors. What's for dinner?'

Napalm marched up to her and slapped her round the face, making her fall off the chair. 'Go wait for me over there,' he bellowed, as she struggled to sit up. 'Just you remember who gave you digs here,' he addressed the room with his arms wide. 'You lot get food when I say.'

Tears glassing in her eyes, the girl stormed off, her white platforms crunching over broken glass. Her hair billowed as she passed the shattered windows, swearing under her breath.

'You mind your manners. No food for you tonight,' he said. 'Gordon, what we got?'

A mousy-looking boy with spots shuffled up to him. 'I've got rice, beans and soup. Found a packet of Smash in Dex's delivery, but we need more water for that.'

'I'll sort that on the next run,' Dex said.

Napalm nodded. 'Start dishing it out, then. Need our strength for partying later. Any luck with that camping shop yet?'

Dex shook his head. 'Heading out that way tomorrow.'

'Fancy taking Shannon with you?' He looked to the girl sulking by the window. 'She's starting to get right on my pecs.'

Dex shot an unconvinced glance at her. 'I think she'll slow little Dexy down.'

Napalm nodded and swiped a mess tin from the food station. He handed the steaming tin to Amy. 'For our esteemed guest. Sit.'

He had never been this nice to her before – ever. What did he want and what would the price be? She was aware of all the eyes boring into them, as she, Napalm and Dex tucked into the food, balanced on their knees. 'You can have yours when we have finished ours. Drink your beer,' Napalm told the group.

She thought back to Joel and missed him so much it made her heart hurt. He was everything they were not. He looked after her, cared for her. These pigs only looked out for themselves. If Dex had not held her back, she could have at least tried to go and save Joel. Now he was dead while they were alive, spreading their own bile and STDs among each other. The only thing keeping her going was the thought of Ash.

'Why you here?' Napalm asked Amy as they ate.

She took a bite and chewed longer than she needed to. The place stank of danger. She was eating, and food was currency. She had to give them something and would rather it not be sexual favours.

'I, er, was in a shopping mall. Our place got overrun by the infected. We got separated and Dex brought me here.' She snuck a look at Dex. He was picking a scab on his hand. She wondered who else he had helped like her, taken payment for. Then came the horrible thought that Dex could have been "saving" girls and bringing them straight to Napalm for his own pleasure.

'Who is "we"? Boyfriend?' he asked, shovelling food into his mouth without much care.

'He's dead,' Dex piped up.

Napalm grinned. 'What about that hot sister of yours? She—'

'Dead,' Amy cut him off.

He laughed. 'So, you're all on your own, eh? Your pussy boyfriend wasn't much good, then.'

Amy gritted her teeth, fighting back her anger. How dare he speak about Joel like that? She thought back to the vision of that girl on the bed. She did not want to end up like that.

She felt Dex's hand slide across her thigh. She was just about to punch him when he pushed something cold and bulky into her pocket. She gasped in surprise and Napalm frowned at her. She spotted a huge speaker on a ledge.

'What's with that?' she asked, trying to divert his attention away from Dex's retracting arm.

'That has a little story behind it, doesn't it Hans Christian?' Napalm looked at Dex.

He nodded. 'A few years back, an anarchy group broke in and had a rave, got down onto the lines. The police busted the joint but all that gear got left behind.'

'We got some power in here, thanks to Dex and the car battery delivery,' Napalm said. 'Have a bit of a party, you get me?'

The boys laughed, all except Dex. The girls swigged from their bottles. Some of the boys were staring at Amy's chest.

'So where were you when this all hit?' she asked Napalm.

'We from the streets, my sweet.' He had moved on to drinking a can of lager. 'The ghetto. We owned the south estate, until the mothers hit. Lost a lot of my crew. Lucky for me and my top men, we are tooled up.' He jigged his leg to reveal the gun in his low-slung jeans. 'Me and Hans are blood, yeah? Cousins. So happens he had some free-running skills to outwit those mothers, and with us lot armed we got here no sweat.' The group murmured in approval. Napalm stared at her. 'So, those mothers – what do you know about them?' he asked. 'What is the secret?'

Luckily, Amy was mid-way through another forkful of rice. She measured up how much she should let on. If she let slip about being a scientist, there was no way they would let her leave. 'They, er, rely on their sense of smell. They hunt as a pack or if on their own, they send out signals to each other.'

'What kinda signals?' he asked.

'Like yelps I suppose,' she said, digging her fork around the bottom of the tin.

'What they afraid of?'

'Nothing that I know of,' she said. 'Fire might work, I don't know. I was busy trying to get the hell away.'

'We had a drought for a month before all this began,' a voice behind them drawled. Shannon was at the window, gripping onto the sill. 'Then it pissed it down. When the rains fell, the world burned.' With that, she swung her legs over the ledge and plunged out the window.

Amy gasped, but the others barely registered emotion, their

faces a drug-fuelled blank.

'Fucking cokehead,' Napalm said and took another sip from his can. 'No great loss.'

'But she just, went—' Amy stammered.

'Yeah, you're right. We'll get someone on cleaning detail. Otherwise, the mothers will get a whiff of the mess.'

'She was a gobby cow, anyway,' one of the boys sitting on the floor said.

'Drink?' Napalm held out a can to Amy.

It could be spiked with anything. 'I'm fine, thanks.' She was far from fine. She had just witnessed a suicide, the final words from a desperate soul. If Amy stayed, she knew her fate would be a long way from cosy. She handed back her tin to the food station and grabbed Dex by the lapels. 'I need a word,' she said and pulled him away to the wall.

She could not stop wondering what Shannon's poor body looked like, spread all over the pavement. Growls and roars of the howlers below drifted up the concrete walls. It was dark out there now. They must be braver, hungrier. She gripped his elbow tighter. 'We're going – now.'

He winced and wriggled from her grip. 'If that's what you want.'

She spotted a youngish girl with a peroxide bob, eyes vacant as she stared out the window at the chaos below. She twisted her hair through her fingers. Amy walked over to her. 'Hey, you OK?'

'Oh sure, kettle's on. Tea's gonna be chips and beans.' Her face dreamy, she quickly changed to anger. 'How the fuck can everything be OK?'

'What's your name?'

She tucked her hair behind her ear. 'Blondie.'

'How old are you?'

'What? This ain't no nightclub or anything. And you ain't no pig neither.' She prodded her in the shoulder.

Amy took a step back. 'No, sorry. It's just if they're hurting you, if you have to pay your way, well, you don't have to. You can come with me.'

The girl's face changed from anger to surprise and uncertainty. Was that hope she saw in the youngster's eyes?

'What's going on?' Napalm asked, striding over, swinging his arms.

Amy dared not flinch. If she showed she was scared, it might be the end for her. 'What you're doing to these girls is disgusting and degrading.'

'I ain't forcing no one.'

'They aren't disposable, they're people.'

'Oi, you. Shut your face.' Blondie pulled up her red bra strap. 'You want to get us all kicked out, you stupid cunt?'

Dex walked over, puffing out his chest. 'Let's all just calm it down, eh? Happy shiny people all around.'

Napalm shoved him away. 'Acting the big man? Do me a favour. Fuck off and grow a pair. You is lucky we're blood. Anyone else do that and you'll get a bullet up your arse.' He turned back to Amy. 'Look, we ain't into anything funny. I'm no nonce, you know. It's just a little bit of fun. That's where you come in.'

She clenched her jaw. 'I told you, I'm not staying.'

He backed her up against the wall. 'I own this gaffe and I say who comes and goes.'

Dex tried to pull his arm away from her. 'She's my fare.'

Napalm threw him off, pulled out his gun and nudged it into Amy's ribs. 'So, what you say? I ain't begging.'

She shoved Napalm back, telling herself to not be scared by the fire-anger in his eyes. She was not about to let him rule her destiny again. 'I'm not staying here, it's fucking disgusting. Anyone who doesn't want to be raped anymore is welcome to come with me.'

'You what?' His forearm bulged and he swayed towards her, reeking of beer and old fags.

'You heard.' She walked away into the stairwell, not a clue where the exit was, but knew she had to leave.

He grabbed her by the hair and pulled her round. She stared into the wide, blazing eyes of Napalm.

'Stay the hell where you are,' he said, jabbing the gun against her head.

'I hate to disappoint you, *Nathan*,' she whispered into his ear, 'but I'm not scared of you. I never was.'

'You're shaking,' he said, victoriously looking her up and down.

'I'm trying not to be sick from remembering all the things you used to do to me.'

He grinned, his gold teeth flashing. 'Yeah, I owned your arse.'

'You did,' she said, with no emotion in her voice.

He frowned, but quickly covered his annoyance. 'I loved it every time. Doesn't that piss you off?'

'Nope. Because I won. Doing what I did, you never got to touch my sister – not once. I protected her and I won. I'm going to win this time too.' She smiled.

'If you call winning being banged 'til you bleed, then congratulations. It didn't have to be this way, it still doesn't. Come willingly and you can be my queen.'

Amy laughed. She had a vision of sitting on a throne, wearing shimmering robes like fancy curtains. 'How romantic of you. But I've got places to be. And I'm not walking away from this place so you can ruin more girls' lives. I was going to, but how could I live with myself? This ends here.'

'Oh, yeah? You're forgetting who has the power here.'

'No, I'm not,' she said. In one movement, she elbowed his palm, knocking the gun from his grip, and took the knife from her pocket, holding the blade to his crotch.

'Fuck you,' he spat.

'No thanks.' She pressed the blade harder against him.

'Whatever plan you got, you ain't got the bollocks.'

Amy snorted. 'Very ironic. You might not soon. So my dilemma is, do I take off your balls so you don't have any urges at all, or your dick so that you'll have to piss like a girl? Maybe I could feed it to the howlers afterwards?'

'You know, I remember how little you were back then. How I broke you in.'

'Am I supposed to be enjoying this trip down memory lane?' She saw movement from the side and looked round to see all the group standing in the doorway, faces of shock.

'Us two,' he said to her, 'we know each other in here like no one else does.'

'I don't want to know you. You raped me – a lot, and it's time you paid for that.'

'Is this what it's all about? You want an apology?'

She edged the blade harder against him and he winced. 'I'm not interested in your apology.'

'Ow, you mental bitch! Fucking stop right now.'

'Take your trousers down,' she said.

'What?' His face screwed up. 'You ain't serious.'

She jabbed harder. 'I am. Trousers down now. It's either this or I kill you.'

He squirmed and looked to his crew. 'Someone help me, for fuck's sake,' he shouted, but they just stared back, waiting for events to play out.

'See? That's what happens when you treat people like animals. And now I'm turning on you, Nathan,' she said, pressing the knife until she felt the material give.

'No, please.' He sunk to the floor, sobbing. A dark stain of urine spread across his trousers.

Then, Amy heard the clack of heels, and turned round to see Blondie standing behind her, holding the gun.

'I'm taking over now,' Blondie said, and fired at Napalm. Red splattered from his head, onto the wall behind. His body arced backwards and he lay twitching on the ground. 'Don't feel sorry for him,' she said. 'Feel sorry for the bastards who have to clear that mess up. Come with me,' she said, walking back into the main room. 'Now, listen up, everyone. This is the day everything around here changes.' She stood up on top of a wooden pallet and put her hands on her hips. 'Who run the world?' she shouted. 'It's time we found our voices. It's our time now. Who run the world, I said?'

'Girls,' all the females shouted back, scarcely believing what was happening. Amy could not figure out whether to be happy, proud or terrified. If Blondie took exception to her being there, she could very well go the same way as Napalm. She stayed very quiet next to her.

'What is this?' one of the boys squared up to her. 'A fucking lesbo takeover? Do me a favour.'

Blondie pistol-whipped him across the cheekbone, and he staggered back. 'Napalm is dead. We run this mother now. We've put up with this for too long. If you've got a pussy, you are part of the ruling matriarchy. Sex is no longer currency here. If you want food, you earn it. I will keep you safe.

'Boys, if you have a gun I suggest handing it the fuck over now. Girls, you all know which boys are packing.' When all the boys had handed over their weapons, she smiled in victory and flicked her hair back. 'If you don't like it,' she whispered to the boy she stood over, 'pack up your shit and leave. But you ain't welcome back. What about you, Dex? Are you staying?'

'I've got a fare to make,' he said, nodding at Amy. 'But you know me, I like my hidey hole.'

'Then you have a place here, if you do me a favour and come back with some intel, OK? I need to know what it's like out there.'

'Indeedy, my queen.'

Blondie nodded at Amy, as if giving permission for her to leave. Amy nodded back, unsure what to do next. She knew she was leaving the place in good hands. Before she realised it, Blondie swept her into a hug. 'Thank you for having our back. You always have a place here if you change your mind.'

'Thanks, but I need to get back to my sister,' Amy said, putting her knife back in her pocket.

Her stare hardened and Amy knew it was time to go. 'Let's get our victory party started,' Blondie proclaimed to the room as she strutted across the floor. 'You,' she said, to the boy on the floor, 'get me a drink. Get all of us one. Turn on the tunes, girls.'

Loud music thumped out the huge speakers as Amy and Dex made for the door. Amy took a final look back to see the girls dancing and high-fiving each other. Blondie blew her a kiss and Amy saluted, smiling back.

All the while Dex led her down the stairs, Amy could not fathom why he had put up with Napalm's bullying. Then she realised: he did not have a choice. They were family and it was all he had. She got the odd logic. Getting back to her sister had become the only thing she was living for. She wondered what Dex was thinking, now that his only "sibling" was dead. She had gotten her revenge and played a part in Napalm's downfall, his death. Hopefully Dex did not see it that way, for he was the only one who could get her back to the surface. Keeping silent seemed like the best option for the time being.

The only light came from Dex's head torch. The snatched illuminations from it showed her they were in a tiled corridor. He took something from his own backpack and it made a whizzing sound as he wound it up. He pressed a button and light shot from the end of it. He handed her the torch. 'No batteries, uh? Part of the service. You're welcome.'

'Thanks,' she muttered.

'No probs.' He pulled his bag onto his shoulders. 'You ready?'

She did not feel all that strong in herself but took a breath. 'Let's do it.'

Despite the big empty space and not knowing what was ahead, it was a comfort to have her own light. She held the torch in her left hand, gripping the knife in the other. He had promised to give it back, but only after they left, so why had he given it to her early? Did he sense what was about to happen and wanted her to be able to defend herself? In any case, he had saved her from Nathan – *Napalm*.

Industrial pipes led along the walls, loose cables wound upwards. Strips of peeling paint hung from the ceiling and there was a musty smell in the air.

They passed a lift shaft door. On the wall opposite was a huge, blue map. The white diagram looked like a spaghetti junction.

'What's this?' she asked.

'It's the map of the rail network. The whole line is over six miles long, but there's over twenty-three miles of actual track. They made this place into a museum so people could ride the lines.

'You know the funny thing?' he said as they carried on down the corridor. 'Loads of artefacts were moved away from London during the Second World War to keep them safe from the bombings. They brought the Rosetta Stone down here from the National Museum until the war was won. It became a museum before it really was one. So trust me, it's safer than the streets right now. Gets bare bad up there when Mr Sun goes to bed. Here we are. Ta-da.' He led her from the hall into what was much like an ordinary tube platform. It was relatively clean, despite the grimy hall behind them. The steel girder walls were white and a stopped clock hung from the ceiling. Yet it all seemed too small, like she was walking in a model railway.

'It's like I've grown two metres,' she said, aiming the torch around. The platform drop was only knee-high, to narrow rail tracks. 'Aren't the rails live?' she asked, as he hopped down onto the track.

'No power, so the trains don't run either, I'm afraid.'

She climbed down and followed him over to a tiny red train with open carriages, no bigger than a rollercoaster. 'It's like a model train set,' Amy said.

'Yeah, a dead one,' he said. 'I think they are powered by batteries, big ones like. But still needs power to charge. I ain't got a clue how. Stupid, ain't it? We needed electric like it was life-support, and now we're screwed cos most of us we don't know how to start a fire without a lighter. Wish I was a twisted firestarter.'

He launched into a rendition of the Prodigy song, complete with jerky dance moves. Her voice sounded alien to her as she laughed. She could not remember the last time she had done that. Biting down on her lip, she stopped. When there was so much shit going on, she did not deserve to be happy. It was impossible to know what the right thing was anymore. Losing Joel had happened too soon, and now he was gone. The more she tried to not think about him, the more he kept coming into her mind.

They were approaching a tunnel, but it was much smaller than regular ones on the Underground. Dex looked back at her. 'It's a bit parky in there. The tunnels were designed for parcels, not people.'

'I'm sure I'll cope.'

Soon though, she was beginning to regret her optimism. She could not get used to being only a few inches from the cocoon-like walls. After stumbling a few times, she had steadied herself on the grimy walls, to find her hands covered black. Yellowy, limescale stalactites hung from the roof. She fell into a few and they snapped off and crumbled in her hair.

He strode ahead and she struggled to keep up. All she could see was his big hair and the occasional flash of his white trainers in her torchlight. If she could just stop and stand up straight, her muscles might not feel like they were about to seize. All they had for company was the rhythmical clunking sound of their footsteps as they tramped along the tunnel.

Dex kept asking if she was OK in a kind of sing-song voice, as though he expected everything to be fine. He almost seemed to thrive on it. She was not going to admit her fears to him. The further they went along the never-ending tunnel, the more she felt claustrophobic. If trouble hit now and they came under attack from howlers, there was no way out.

She tripped over the rail tracks and caught her elbow on the tunnel wall as she steadied herself. When he asked again, she bit her lip to stop herself from snapping at him. Then the thought occurred that his own knowledge could be invaluable. Surely there was something he would know to help her survive out there, on her own. 'Dex, tell me this: how do you get away from the howlers – sorry, mothers – if they can smell you, hunt you?'

'I'm quick, baby. Simple as. You gotta outrun them. Be lickedy-split quicker than Speedy Gonzales. Or he'll eat you for his tea.'

'What?'

He stopped and turned round, blinding her with his head torch light. 'I just leg it at the first sign of trouble. Always have done.' He turned back and kept on walking.

She wondered if that was how he put up with Napalm

throwing his weight around: just ran away. She could not fault it, really. If it got him somewhere to live and avoid the howlers at the same time, it was a blinder of a strategy. 'Why do they call you Hans Christian?' she asked.

'Always got a tale to tell, me. I worked at the bookshop and I can recite stories.'

'Are you glad he's dead?' she asked, surprised by the audacity of her own question.

He stopped again and faced her with a sigh. 'He was my blood so I'll mourn that. But I wasn't there much, if I could help it. We weren't two-for-tea, if that's what you mean. That's why I go on hauling detail. I just find the depot a bit—'

'Seedy?' she asked as they trudged further into the intestines of the rail network.

'I ain't like them. Never paid for it before and I won't now. I make my living as a kind of, er, what are those guides who go up the Himalayas? Sherpas. I'm a bit like a Sherpa. Go all the other places most sensible people wouldn't.'

Progress was slow and it was impossible to tell how far they had gone. Had they missed a turning? Gone the wrong way? Or was he leading her somewhere more dangerous, taking her off on her own to do with as he wished? Right now, he was the only one who could help her. She had to trust him.

After a while, Dex's head torch no longer bounced off circular walls. He was entering a bigger, longer space. 'This is Mount Pleasant, the central hub of what used to be the Mail Rail,' he said.

The tunnel opened into a wide platform. She stopped as soon as she could to stretch her back out. Her bones clicked and she groaned.

'You sound like an old lady,' he laughed.

'And this old lady has got to rest for a bit,' she said, heading for a stack of pallets on the platform.

He looked disappointed, but she did not care. After the day she'd had, she needed to sit for a minute. 'This place is like the Tube, isn't it?' she asked.

He nodded and wiped his mouth with the back of his hand. 'The tunnels pass right by each other on occasion. Won't catch me going in there, though.'

'The Tube? Why not? You could go wherever you wanted to in the city.'

He shook his head. 'Nah, not worth the risk. Even for a Sherpa like me. The Tube is riddled with mothers.'

'Haven't you ever seen one on its own down here?'

He sat down cross-legged on the platform. 'They ain't never on their own. They're hungry. They're like rats. If there's one, there's plenty more nearby.'

'That's instilling me with confidence, thanks.'

'Not here, chica. People were using the Tube all the time. When the infection broke, there was no one left to shut down the system. The fuckers are wandering around all over the place down there.'

'So how do you outrun them?' she asked. 'I barely managed it and we had bikes.'

'I got skills.' He got to his feet and ran along the platform. He turned in to the wall and ran up it and back-flipped over. In a second, he had hopped over a mini train on the tracks, jumped a chair and was back at her side.

'Wow,' she said.

'Used to be a champion free runner, before the mothers invaded. I was gonna represent the national team before this all hit. My skills come in useful if I'm out getting some UV on my skin. Never go up on the street if I can help it.'

'You were out on New Oxford Street? Why?'

'I moonlight, OK? I'm a bit like a taxi driver doing jobs on the side. Money goes straight in my pocket. Not Napalm's.'

'A private fare?'

'Yeah.'

'Me? I was the fare?' she asked, as the realisation sank in and he just stared at her. 'You engineered it so that I would need your help?'

His head dropped in shame. 'I've got a living to make. I'm not proud of it, chica.'

She jumped down off the pallet and punched him in the face. 'You did it just for money? I will never see him again. If you hadn't done that, I could've gone after Joel.' She shoved him so hard, the breath knocked out of him as he hit the wall.

'No, chica. The rain would've skinned you alive.'

Her fingers stung and she rubbed her knuckles. 'You cheated me. You said you'd help but you let him die.'

He rubbed his jaw and looked at her with regret. 'I did what I promised: I got you here. Safe as houses.' He tugged his lapels with pride. 'You will not find a single mother down here. I know it.' He dipped his head. 'If I'd let you go, you'd have died too. Your sister wouldn't want you dead. I'm sorry about your lover-boy, I really am.'

'You didn't know. He wasn't really my boyfriend. I suppose I thought one day he might be, could be. We barely kissed.' She was just starting to trust Joel though, maybe even love him (when she was not furious with him). She had never loved anyone before. Now he was gone, and she wanted him with an ache that would never leave her.

If she'd had the chance to tell Joel she loved him, who knows if he would have said it back? It was clear there was an age gap. She did not care, but she could tell he did. He had come looking for her in the War Rooms and somehow they ended up together on the floor. He had wanted her to trust him. Why say that if he was not interested in her? Wiping away an itchy tear, she knew she had to pull herself together. Being strong for her sister was what had to count now, for her own sanity if nothing else.

The old saying went that if you could survive something bad, you could survive anything. Not in this case. Joel did not have that chance and now she would never know what she could have had. The world had turned into something else. It did not deserve to be called a world anymore. The name Planet Earth was too good for something so shit. That was what it should be called – Shit. Welcome to Planet Shit, population 5,000. If that many were left, if it was worldwide. How to find out? Surely there were clever people out there with radios, radar. Down there, scuttling along the Mail Rail like rats, she was useless. She knew no more than a rat, looking out for danger and wondering when she would next find food.

'Can we go?' she asked with a croaky voice.
'Good idea.'

Beyond the end of the platform, the track meandered and split off into two directions, with a dividing wall down the middle.

'Mind your step,' he said, passing a reel of thick wires propped up against the wall.

'I can't wait,' she replied as they entered the narrow tunnels once more.

*

Going up the metal, spiral staircase seemed to take hours and was making her dizzy. She kept reminding herself that she would feel so much better when they got above ground. When they reached the top, he stopped by a door and turned to her.

'Got your knife ready?' he asked.

'Always.'

'Then let's go.'

He opened the door, led them through another set of concrete steps and up to another door. They pushed through. She gasped from the cold of the night air. It was dark, but the night sky was ablaze with thousands of stars. She stared up at the sheer beauty of the atmosphere above the crumbling buildings. She had only ever seen the night sky with a dim orange glaze to it from the streetlights. She had never been away from the city, away from the light pollution, to see the stars like that; only in books, but this was far more mesmerising.

Forgetting all the dangers, she was unable to look away from the sparkling canvas; different sizes, some twinkling, others whooshing through the atmosphere. Then she saw it – a shooting star. She wished her greatest wish on it. If there was only a chance, it was worth a childish habit.

'That's all then, folks,' Dex said, leaning against the door.

'Aren't you going to take me home?'

He shrugged. 'You said nothing about home. You said Liverpool Street, so here it is.'

'But, I—'

'Take this, cheeky chica,' he said, pressing something into her palm. 'I'm sorry for the joss-stick jostling.' He pushed her forwards and was already closing the door.

'Dex?'

'I ain't no fighter. I'll see you around, you naughty girlie whirlie.' The door shut and he pulled the bolt across before she could stop him.

'Bastard,' she muttered. She opened her hand to find her mother's anklet. Gawping at it, she did not know what to think. She fastened the chain back on her ankle, wondering why he had given the payment back. Was it guilt? Or sympathy, having realised what she had lost? Another person who had left her and she would never know. Could it be that he was grateful she had a hand in ridding the world of Napalm?

She found herself on a main road where glass buildings stretched into the inky sky. She needed to get to the quieter back streets as soon as she could.

A hacking, choking sound brought her back to ground level. Footsteps slapped hard behind her. She spun round to find a howler-man running at her. It was naked, but for a pair of grubby, grey boxer shorts. She stared at its ulcer-ridden torso as it raced at her. It sprayed saliva as it opened its mouth, ready to bite her. She jabbed the knife hard at its temple and it fell to the floor.

She struggled to seesaw the blade out from bone and sinew. Then a hacking sound began again. This time another one appeared from the side. It was a skinny howler-woman in a pinstripe trouser suit. It was missing some buttons from its shirt, revealing a strange growth, like a bulbous storm cloud. Blacky-red liquid poured from its mouth and it rasped.

She pulled the knife from the fallen howler, while the other one half-heartedly lunged at her. Losing her focus, she dropped the knife and it clattered across the tarmac. She kicked it in its stomach. Pus and guts released from the thin membrane over its belly. It looked down in surprise as its innards spilled onto the floor. It locked eyes with her, renewed with anger. It tackled her and they both went down, tumbling over one another.

It had her tight. Amy could feel cold, bulgy intestines pressed against her as they wrestled. The howler's straggly, long hair fell in her face. She managed to scrabble back, giving her enough room to get onto her side and ram her elbow into its face. It screeched and she wriggled back as the howler crawled towards her.

She slapped her hand against the road, desperately trying to find the knife, while keeping her sights on the howler. All she could find was the grit of crumbled tarmac. She felt clammy fingers on her leg. Somehow, it had pulled up the bottom of her leggings to find flesh. Its mouth split open to reveal white teeth.

'I don't think so, you mother.' Her fingers gripped round the knife handle and she rammed the blade into its eye socket. It went still. She scrabbled to her feet and wiped herself off with her hands.

She heard a roar, not that far away. Moonlight glinted on an open glass door of a high-rise building. More of the infected spilled out into the road. Keeping low, she crept to the corner of the street and once she found the way ahead was empty, she sprinted hard towards home.

She did not stop until she reached the end of her road. Crouching behind a red telephone box, she scanned the street for trouble. There was nothing that she could see. She ran up to the front door and tried to hide from view in the doorway. It was only as she stared at the intercom buttons, that she realised she did not have her keys on her.

'Shit.'

It must have been with all her things in the suitcase, the one she had lost in the plane crash. When she thought about it, it was a pure miracle she had made it that far at all. She pressed the intercom for *Weston*. It did not buzz; must have been hooked up to the mains power.

All she had left was a shit plan B. She jogged past the empty takeaway to the corner and down the back alleyway. There it was – the back of her old flat, the same as it ever was, with its yellow ochre London brick walls smeared with black, the flat roof extension of the Indian below. The kitchen window was dark, with no signs of life.

The gate creaked as she opened it, and she tiptoed into the gravel backyard. The smell of rotting rubbish was overpowering and the taste crawled over her tongue. She kept her blade ready.

The bins stacked up against the wall moved and some fell to the floor. Now she had both hands tightly holding the knife. Something small and scraggy darted out from under the pile. It stopped and measured her up with its big eyes. The fox's bottlebrush tail stood up straight, the white tip flicking. Red fur was matted with black. Unimpressed, it turned and slunk through the gap of the open gateway. It looked as wretched as she felt.

Looking up at the kitchen window, she guessed it would be a difficult climb onto the flat roof, but possible. The window was open a crack. It was all she needed. She scooped up a bit of gravel and lobbed it up at the kitchen window. It bounced off the wall, falling short of her target. It was too high and she was a lousy shot. She thought she saw something behind the glass, a glint of something white. A face? Ash? She gave a wave, but feeling stupid, she stopped. There was nothing there. It was the moonlight playing tricks on her.

The howlers were on their way. She could hear them, smell them. This was her only option. She locked the gate behind her and began to climb up the pile of garbage in the corner. The smell of decomposing refuse was too much to bear. She tried to scramble up the bags to reach the top of the brick wall. The bags slid beneath her feet, making it difficult to haul herself onto the ledge. She kept pushing up, her boots scuffing on the bricks. All the time she wondered, if she fell, there would be nobody to save her from being eaten alive.

CHAPTER THIRTY-FOUR
Amy

Amy jumped and made a grab for the wall but missed and slithered back down into the pile of stinky black bags.

The howlers were almost on her; she could hear their moans carrying on the wind. The gate flew off its hinges, and the creatures burst through the gap like water. Her fingers found the ledge. She pushed up hard, scuffing her feet up the wall and managed to swing her legs up onto the ledge. The first howler had scrabbled up the mound of bags and its black teeth made for her foot.

'Ash, help,' she shouted up at the window.

She kicked it hard in the face and the howler screeched in fury as it slid down the plastic. She balanced on the top of the wall, trying not to focus on the howlers packing into the yard just a few feet below. She edged along, doing her best to keep her breathing slow and not rush. Then darkness; the moonlight obscured by the clouds. It was only a metre or so to safety. She had to do it. She jumped over to the edge of the roof. Her hands gripped the rough grit of the felt and she hauled herself up.

She sat cross-legged on the flat roof, feeling sick as she got her breath back. There were about a dozen howlers in the yard, all snarling up at her and yearning for her flesh.

The kitchen window was open as usual, just a few centimetres to let a breeze in. Her heart soared. Ash had to be there. It would be shut if she had gone out. She got her fingers underneath the frame and eased it up. She climbed through into the kitchen and tried the light switch – nothing. She got the torch out from her pocket, the one Dex gave her, and wound it up to create a charge. Turning it on, she stepped forward into the hallway, shining the torch around.

'Ash,' she called. 'Are you here?'

She could hear a splashing sound coming from somewhere in the flat. She went deeper into the dark musty innards of the hallway, gripping the knife for courage. Stopping at the closed bathroom door, she could hear the splashing sound beyond it. Pushing on the handle, she found the door locked. The water sound got worse.

'It's OK, Ash. I'll get you out.'

Fearing she could be drowning, Amy shoulder-barged the door but it did not budge. She steeled herself and kicked the door. On the third strike, the door flew open to reveal a naked howler thrashing in the bath. The body was a mass of angry sores and white, shrivelled skin. Fury on its face, arms grasping, it flailed helpless in the bath.

Dark scuff marks dappled the body, reminding her of a banana that had been in the bottom of a bag for too long. *It can't be her.* As water sloshed onto the soggy bathmat, she realised she had to check for sure. It was wearing the silver star earrings Amy had given Ash for Christmas.

She dropped the torch and it skidded round in a circle. 'No, no. Not you.'

Ash lashed her limbs against the bath, scrabbling to sit up and claw at her as Amy stood in the doorway. There were no obvious bites on her skin, only the sores. The bath water – it had to be that. Amy remembered Mei's red, swollen eye, and the prime minister's ice in the whisky glass. The rain at the tank barricade made all those people turn.

She had lost Joel. She had endangered their lives to get to the flat and now she had nothing and no one to show for it.

She staggered backwards, bumping against the toilet. She slumped down on the lid, thinking about how she had to kill Sylvia. She was not sure she had it in her to finish off her sister too.

'I'm sorry,' she sobbed, covering her face. 'I should have protected you. I'm your big sister and I wasn't there. When I was, all I did was make my problems your problems. You're better off without me.'

She had a vision of a skeleton thrashing around in slimy green bathwater, entrapped forever by its dumb inability to rescue itself. Once more, she had to be the big sister. She was a protector, too late. She stood up and walked over to the bath.

'Forgive me,' she whispered and raised the knife, plunging it down into her sister's skull.

Water rolled back and forth the length of the bath over the slumped body. Waves turned black and green as liquid oozed from the slash along its head. She wrenched the blade out. Seeing her reflection in the mirror, Amy screamed long and hard back at it, until her voice cracked and her vision swam.

From then on, her brain could not keep a grip on the awfulness of it. She could see things happening as she took short panic breaths. She saw the long blade being wiped across the towel on the rail; the clatter of the knife across the bathroom floor; the torchlight bouncing off the hallway and her feet walking along the carpet to the kitchen. Her hand opened the top cupboard and unscrewed the bottle of vodka. The liquid burned her throat as she swallowed it. Her hands found the medicine box in the drawer and she took out a bottle. She thumbed the handful of white pills in her palm. She stuffed as many as she could in her mouth at once, downing them with another slug of vodka.

*

Laid in the dark of the hallway, curled up against the closed bathroom door, she had no sense of time as she came to. She felt wretched – her mouth was dry and her head hurt. What point was there in doing anything else than just staying there? She did not know how to get down to the Solent, let alone find Malrose. Joel had known. An Internet search would have probably got her the information she needed, but that had stopped working before Rat-run.

She was aware, for the first time in a while, that she could hear the howlers again. Then she heard the creak of the kitchen window being opened. She sat up and shone the torch down the hallway.

Through the gloom, came the figure of someone tall; dirty blond hair, grey stubble and Viking cheekbones that she longed to see just one more time. She pushed away any hopeful, happy thoughts. She could not bear the idea of believing, only to find it was just a fantasy.

'I don't believe in ghosts,' she murmured. 'Go away.'

'It's me,' Joel said, crouching down next to her.

'I've taken a lot of pills and most of this bottle.' She held up the vodka as proof, then skittled it across the carpet. 'So, I'm tripping my bollocks off right now. You're just a daydream.' She shut her eyes and rested her head back against the wall. She was not going to allow herself the possibility of hope, to just be hurt again.

'How much have you taken?'

'Oh relax,' she slurred. 'Just a few to take the edge off.'

'Why would you do that?'

Even in her muddled state, her delusion was skilfully managing to annoy her. 'I've never had to tell a hallucination to do one before, but there's a first time for everything.'

'Ever known a hallucination do this?' He cupped her face in his hands and kissed her on the lips.

She got up onto her knees and kissed him back, pulling his hips against hers. She did not want it to end, with the joyful realisation he was in her embrace once more.

'You came back,' she gasped when they broke apart for breath. 'How did you? How can you?' she asked. Her head was churning with questions that her mouth could not form, and her stomach was whirling.

'I came back for you. You know, you don't look so good.'

The walls lurched and the floor seesawed back and forth as she got to her feet and pushed the bathroom door open. She scooted to the toilet just in time to throw up.

Retching into the bowl, she knew Joel must have seen Ash's body and the knife on the floor. He held her hair off her face with one hand and rubbed her back with the other. He did not say a word, and she was grateful for that.

'Don't look at me,' she said, dragging herself away from the toilet and closing the lid.

He folded over some toilet tissue and handed it to her. 'Bit late for that.'

She wiped her mouth and chucked the tissue in the bin. 'Keep your judgement to yourself, OK? I've had a rough day.'

His strong arms enveloped her as she tried not to look at herself in the mirror. She drank in his reassuring smell and hugged him back tightly.

'Come on,' he said, taking her hand. 'You need some rest.'

*

She awoke to find herself laid on her bed. It was dark outside. Had she dreamt it all, Joel coming back? She called his name and she heard him reply from the kitchen. She walked through to find the window open and his silhouette outside.

'How you feeling?' he asked, looking round.

'A bit better,' she croaked. 'Still a bit groggy.'

She joined him on the flat roof outside the kitchen, under the stars. Joel took the last bite of a breakfast biscuit bar and put the crumpled packet in his pocket. He had found a bottle of water from the kitchen and handed it to her when she sat down next to him. She took a few sips, and some deep breaths.

She frowned. 'Hang on, how did you know where I live?'

'Penny Lane, right? You told me about it in Beijing.'

'I did? And you listened?'

His face gave nothing away as he looked up at the stars. 'Stranger things have happened.'

She smiled, secretly chuffed that he had retained a small detail about her life. She shivered. It was colder outside than she had expected. She edged up next to him, and he placed his arm around her shoulders, pulling her close. The instant warmth of him was heavenly.

'Are you going to tell me how you came back from the dead?' she asked.

'I was lucky,' he said, stretching his legs out in front of him. 'I had the gun and rolled under a car when it started raining. When I spotted you with that guy, he saw me and then whacked you over the head.'

Her stomach plummeted. 'He saw you?'

He nodded. 'People were turning into howlers all around me. I couldn't leave while it was still raining, but the water was starting to come under the car. When the rain stopped, I saw my chance. I rolled out again and when I got up, I couldn't see you anywhere. I knew where you'd go, so I got here as soon as I could. Basically the city is as full of people as it ever was, it's just now they're howlers. If I wasn't running, I was hiding.'

Amy took a sip of water, seething inside. Dex, the little bastard, had lied to her. Joel had been right there, metres away the whole time and he had let her think the worst. Yet, something had changed in Dex. In the end he had given back her fare payment: the anklet.

'I fought my way out the barricade, shot my gun a few times and ran,' he said. 'I didn't know how to find your street, so I went to a corner shop,' he said, holding her hand, 'to get a street map of London. You know, us old people had to map-read before the days of sat nav. That was when I found the alcohol at the tills.

And I—' His voice trailed off.

She held her hands up. 'Hey, this is a judgement-free zone. You saw the fall-out of what I did earlier.'

'I left it there. I had the chance to drink it and I didn't, because of you. I wanted to get back here, for you.'

'For me?' She looked up at him. Was he saying what she thought he was saying?

'I knew that boy had whacked you pretty hard. I didn't want to think about what he had done to you. But I knew that I had to find you if we stood a chance of getting to Malrose.'

Amy hid her disappointment by taking a sip of water. Of course, it was not for his love for her that brought his return – it was their mission. 'Right.'

'What happened to you? Who was that guy?'

'Dex? He showed me a safe way back.' She hesitated about whether to tell him more. If she told him about the depot, she would need to tell him about Nathan and what had happened before and after. She was not sure if she was ready for that conversation.

He did not seem to notice her deep in thought. 'We ought to get some sleep, we've got an early start tomorrow.'

'What for?' She gawped at him. The vision of them having a cosy lie-in together between the sheets was flushed away as quickly as it had appeared in her mind.

'What do you think?' he asked, gesturing up at the sky. 'We aren't safe here,' he said. 'The buildings aren't meant to withstand acidic levels like that. We can't just sit around waiting while the food runs out and the building falls down round our arses.'

'You think leaving here is any safer? You saw what happened

in the rainstorm,' she said.

'We'll be in a vehicle. We'll find a car or something.'

She shook her head. 'I don't like it.'

'Me neither, but if we want to try and stop all this, we have to leave at first light.'

'Can we do something with Ash's body before we go? I can't face leaving it there. If we could just bury it…'

'I'm sorry, Amy. That bath is full of water. If we get as much as a drop in our eyes, mouth or on our skin… We can't risk moving her.'

She pulled away from him and stood up. 'Of all the people to get left with, it had to be you, didn't it?'

'I am trying to keep us alive.'

'Oh, lucky me. Fuck's sake.' She climbed over the windowsill into the kitchen. Storming off to Ash's room, she slammed the door behind her. She laid down on the bed, wishing she could silence the sounds of the howlers in the streets below and the angry voices in her head.

CHAPTER THIRTY-FIVE
Amy

The sheets smelt of Ash, her perfume and the posh shampoo she guarded so much. She stared at the paint cracks running along the ceiling, too wired to sleep. The floorboards creaked as she heard Joel go into her bedroom, next door. Why did he always have to argue everything? Why did he always insist on being right about everything?

She should be happy. She had thought he was dead, but he came across the city in the night to find her. Why did they not have the Hollywood homecoming they should have had? He had kissed her. Even with all the booze and pills she had taken, in her befuddled state, it felt like it had meant something – to her and him. Could she dare pretend that he had searched the whole of the city for her and her alone?

It would be everything to her, knowing that she was all he needed. It looked less likely the more time she spent with him. He needed a companion to go on a road trip with. That was all she was to him. They really were just co-workers, after all.

The fetid, humid air in the room was making her skin sticky. She got up and went over to the window. She opened it up and looked down at the main street below. Howlers milled about, probably the ones from the yard which had got bored and wandered off. A few spotted her and began moaning and howling. More looked up and joined in when they saw her, smelled her.

She wanted to scream at them, go down there and slice them up for ruining the world. It was people who had tipped the poison balance in the first place, abusing the world to the point it decided to fight back. The infected were a danger but they all looked slightly different. They still had their own faces, their own clothes. They were throwbacks to a time when they had identities and people who loved them. The world could recover some day. It was up to her, Joel and Professor Malrose to ensure that it would.

She was never going to sleep unless she attempted to resolve the argument that hung over the flat like a toxic cloud. She closed the window and went down the hallway to her own bedroom. She tapped lightly on the door. 'Can I come in?' she asked.

'Yes.'

She opened the door and hovered with her fingers on the handle. It was surreal to see him laid on her bed, fully clothed, on top of her covers. He had found one of her candles in a glass jar and lit it. He had laid his boots on the floor, at the foot of the bed. The shadows flitted across his face as he half sat up, leaning on his elbows.

'The howlers are out the front,' she said.

'There'll be less of them by morning.'

'Yeah.' She twisted her hands. 'Er, can I sit down?'

'It's your bed.'

'I know it is. I just thought you might want some space.' She clambered onto the bed and slid down next to him. 'Can we start over, properly?'

'Yes,' he said simply, and turned onto his side to face her. The candle he had put on her bedside table illuminated his stubble and floppy fringe.

She took a breath. 'I just wanted to say thank you, for coming back for me.' She waited for him to say something, but he did not. She saw no reason to apologise for what she said about Ash, but they needed to resolve things somehow. 'Can we just forget about this shit situation for a while? Pretend we've gone out for a coffee or something?'

'Coffee?'

'Or a date?' she chanced, blushing at her words. She had never really been on a date before. The type of guys she hooked up with were not the sort to go bowling or to the cinema. She liked to go to a club and get fucked up in more ways than one.

'A what?' he asked. His clipped accent made him sound so abrupt sometimes. She never knew if he was joking or not.

Her heart was pounding. If she backed down now, she might never know how he felt. 'A date. You promised me one, remember? In Beijing you said if I was right about the poison balance—'

'I promised dinner. I never mentioned a date.'

'Humour me.' She stared him out and a smile flickered at the corner of his mouth.

'The takeaway is shut.'

She nudged him. 'Skinflint.'

'If we're going on a date, we really should dress up,' he said.

She grinned and jumped off the bed. The hurt of losing Ash threatened to invade her thoughts, but she shut it down. She just wanted to feel something else other than fear and grief for a while.

She opened her wardrobe and found her pink feather boa. Draping it round her shoulders, she put her hands on her hips. 'This'll have to do for now.'

She grabbed her aviator glasses from the dresser and put them on him. Her heart panged. He looked impossibly gorgeous, as though he belonged on an 80s pop video. He gave a little smile, almost as if he knew it too. Could he know how she felt about him just from a look?

'Hey, come here,' he called, and grabbed her trilby hat from the bedpost, popping it on her head. He laid back down on the bed and watched her, drumming his fingers on his chest. 'Cute.'

'No one has ever called me cute before.'

'There's a first time for everything.'

She reached into her back pocket and pulled out her phone. As she hit play, loud beats and the high notes of her dance album came belting out of her wireless speakers.

'What – is – this?' he asked, with a hint of disgust.

She laughed. 'Something made this century.' She danced around the room, loving how music instantly managed to cheer her up and revitalise her. 'Come on, grumpy,' she said, hauling him up. 'If we're on a date, you owe me a dance.'

He held up her hand and twirled her round on the carpet. She got fully into the rhythm of the song, and he stood for a while watching her as she paced round him to the beat. She was not sure if it was the remnants of the booze and pills that had given her the confidence to dance like that around him, or if it was the chance to start over again that made her feel ready to let him in.

It was hard to read his expression with the aviators on, but he wore a half-amused half-intrigued smile. 'The lyrics are quite in your face, aren't they?' he said.

Amy shrugged and whispered in his ear, 'I guess she knows what she wants.'

Joel took her hands and put them round his neck, as they danced together. She pretended the dark of her bedroom was a nightclub dancefloor, and the candles were strobe lights as they flickered in their jars. She imagined people giving them furtive glances as they wondered who the man was with the strong cheekbones and pale blue eyes. And she was the one he had chosen to be with.

'What're you thinking about?' he asked.

She opened her eyes and looked up at him. 'I'm just imagining we're in a nightclub on our date.'

'Sticky carpets and sweaty bodies? We're better off here.'

She laughed a little and he did too. He grinned a wide grin, showing his teeth gap as they kept on dancing, giggling into each other's shoulders.

The song soon finished, and he pulled away from her. 'I get to choose the next one.'

'Do your worst.'

He picked up her phone off the side. 'Let me have a look. Ah, now this is a good one.' As he put the phone back, Elbow's *One Day Like This* started playing.

Amy loved the violins and slow melody on that song. He slid his hands round her waist, and she swayed in time to the music and closed her eyes as the vocals began. She rested her head on his chest, listening to the lyrics.

After a while, Joel pulled away. He put the sunglasses on top of his head and stared back at her. Her insides surged with nerves.

How did he have such a strong effect on her?

The music was still on, but she realised they had stopped dancing. 'What?' she asked, dropping her hands to her sides.

He laced his fingers through hers and pulled her down next to him. 'Sit with me,' he said. He stretched out on her bed as she eased herself down next to him. 'I want to ask you something.' He took the sunglasses off his head and put them on the side table. When he looked back at her, his eyes burned ice-cold into her. 'If this is a date, isn't it time you followed through on your promise?'

She swallowed, trying to hide her flustered emotions. 'What promise?'

'When the plane was going down, I said that if we survived you should let me get to know you more.'

She took a slow breath. He was right: it was time to be brave. She had never really let anyone in. She let go of his hands and turned her palms up to reveal the scars on her arms. 'You want to know about these, don't you?'

He shrugged. 'That's up to you.'

'I got them when I was in care.'

'You did it to yourself?'

She shook her head. 'A boy called Nathan took a fancy to me and my sister. But I always made sure he came to me and not her. Word got round to some of the other boys, and they did it too – for a while.' She could not stop talking so fast, now she had sobered up and the nervous adrenaline had kicked in. 'He did this to me. I guess he enjoyed hurting me while he was, you know... Then I found him again at the depot, when you and I were separated in the rain. At the end of the world, it had to be him, didn't it?'

Joel cuddled into her as she explained what happened at the depot with Dex and Napalm, and how she was only one slice away from ridding him of his manhood for ever. She told him about how she left the place in Blondie's more than capable control. She smiled, thinking that, as she spoke, Blondie was probably busting out some Beyonce-style moves.

Joel held her hand gently and kissed her palm. 'You've never told anyone this, have you?'

She shook her head. 'I couldn't. Who would believe a care home kid? When I saw him again at the depot, and I realised that he was only going to keep on doing it to other kids, I had to stop him. I had a second chance to put things right.' She had been so close to dismembering him, she would never know if she could have actually gone through with it. Blondie put pay to that. But she had finally stood up to him and that was enough to be getting on with in her journey of healing. The past needed to be left where it was, so that she could move on.

'It's OK. I get it.' He brought her inner arm up to his lips and kissed her scars one by one.

'Don't,' she breathed. 'I don't like them.'

'You shouldn't be ashamed.' He looked up at her. 'They make you who you are.'

She crossed her legs on the bed, unsure what to say. 'I don't like me. I don't know who I am anymore. I don't even know where I'm from.'

'It doesn't matter where you're from. All that matters is that you're here, and so am I. Have you forgotten the feisty girl I met in Ron's office? She's still in there, you know, and there's a lot to like.' His hand went to her heart and she gasped. 'Sometimes it takes someone else to see what you are, even if you've forgotten.'

She bit her lip. 'How?'

He traced his fingertips over the lines on her palm. 'What did you want when we were going down on that plane?'

'I just wanted Ash to forgive me.'

'The only person you need forgiveness from is yourself. You are... you're amazing. I just wish you could see what I see.'

Her mouth quivered, thinking about how losing Ash meant she had no family left. 'My sister is dead. She was the only one... who have I got left now?'

'Me.' His hands slid to the nape of her neck, and he brushed her tears away with his thumbs. He slung her hat across the room.

They both moved in at the same time and their lips met. Neither of them pulled away, but he pressed in harder so his bristles grazed her chin. His lips were warm and soft, his kiss delicate. No boys had ever kissed her with the same tenderness Joel had. She had lost him once before and now she had another chance. Her heart had been Joel's for some time now, but it was another thing telling him that.

She wrapped her leg around his hip and rolled him onto his back. Pulling her top off, she threw it onto the floor and watched the way he drank in the view of her in her black lace bra. Her hair fell round his ears as she bent down and kissed him again. She reached for the buckle on his trousers.

His hands closed over hers, stopping her. 'It's OK. You don't have to,' he said.

She sat up, feeling hurt at his sudden rejection. 'I brushed my teeth.'

'It's not that.'

'I've had my jabs.'

'Have you sobered up?'

'Yes.' Fear and shame had taken over any heady feelings she had left. She had gambled on the chance of telling him about her past, and he was seeing her differently already. She shuffled back on his thighs, feeling the need to run away.

'Amy,' he took her hand and held it tight, 'you aren't like any of my previous... well, if we're using the word: girlfriends.' Her face must have given her away, as he quickly backtracked. 'I mean, you're not my girlfriend.'

'Oh, thanks a bunch.' She felt her cheeks going hot. He was bound to be looking for someone more mature. He needed someone with a successful career, their own house and car. She tried to take her hand back, but he held on.

'No, no. You don't understand. I can't call you a girlfriend because you aren't a girl. You're a woman, and you're more than a friend.'

She made a face. 'Partner?'

'We aren't cowboys.'

She ran her hands through her hair as she thought. 'I don't know. A date?'

He ran his tongue over the gap between his top teeth. 'We aren't going to a prom, either.'

She laughed. 'I think you're overthinking it. I'm here, you're here, and we both want it. Do we have to put a label on it?'

'You're the one who loves labels. I, um—' His voice trailed off as she took his hand and placed it on her breast.

She kissed him some more, daring to slip her tongue in this time. When he joined in, she shut her eyes with pleasure, warmth pulsing through her. She had the power and was leading him astray in her dance of temptation.

He pulled away and had hold of her wrists; the restraint showing on his face was almost revulsion.

'What have I done now?' she groaned plaintively, trying to wriggle off the bed.

'Amy, stop. Christ, you drive me crazy.'

She frowned at him. 'What're you trying to say?'

He rubbed his face. 'We don't have to just "do it" for the sake of it.'

'That's sweet, but that's something you'd say to a drunk virgin. I already told you, I don't need babying.' She felt stupid, straddling him now. Rolling away, she laid on her back and stared up at the ceiling. 'If you don't want me, just say.'

'It's not that. I'm just a bit long in the tooth for all this dating thing. Ever since Lauren...'

Her stomach burned for him as he rested his hand on her waist. 'I didn't realise. I thought that when you'd been drinking, you'd been out in bars and met people. I mean, have you *seen* you?'

'OK, there were one or two hook-ups, but nothing special. I mean, my heart wasn't really in it. When I married, I never imagined I'd be with anyone else again.'

She decided to take a risk and reached out to stroke her thumb across his defined cheekbones. 'I think I get it. You haven't used it in a while. It still works, right?'

He dragged his gaze back to her. 'What do you think?' He took her hand and pressed it to the hard bulge in his trousers.

'I don't think you've got anything to worry about.' She kissed him gently on the lips. 'But we can take it slow. I'd like it slow.'

'Sounds fine to me,' he said, and his fingers stroked round her ears.

She could hardly believe he was there. That childish wish on the star had come true. She had another chance to say and do all the things she thought had been taken away from her. If they were taking it slow and did not have a label, then baby steps it was.

'I love you being in my bed,' she whispered.

'I love being in your bed, with you,' he replied, and peeled her bra strap down to kiss her shoulder.

She stroked his hair and smiled with bliss. He was part of her life now and it scared her a little how much she had come to need him.

She took his hand and lifted it up to the smooth black silk and lace of her bra and guided his hand inside it. He soon found the hard nub of her erect nipple and circled over and around it with his thumb. He bent down, at the same time easing her bra down further to reveal her bare breast.

As he placed his mouth over her, he swirled his tongue over her nipple and she gasped with pleasure, gripping the edge of the headboard.

He brought his head back up, level with hers and watched her with those ice-blue eyes of his. 'I want every bit of you, Amy. I just can't help it.'

'What happened to going slow?' she asked, with a smile.

'I know, I know,' he groaned. 'You're right.'

'Why don't you let me steer for a bit? What else do you want?' she asked, running her hands through his hair and playing with the ends.

'What we didn't get to finish in the War Rooms.'

'Which bit?'

'*This* bit,' he said, taking her hand and placing it on his belt.

'Oh,' she replied, understanding and obliging by starting to unfasten it.

'Just promise you won't dismember *me*, OK?'

'If we're going to survive this, you need to trust me,' she said, mimicking his words in a high-pitched tone.

He grabbed her by the waist and wrestled her down. 'Don't think you're too old for a smacked bottom, kid.'

'I'm counting on it,' she breathed and kissed him into silence.

The early morning sunlight had turned the clouds a pale gold as Joel did an inventory of the kitchen by candlelight. He hoped it would not rain, at least for a few days. If the customary weather held true and it rained incessantly, they would have to stay longer and more howlers might come in the meantime.

Seeing Amy's peaceful face in sleep, he had left her in bed. He was up far earlier than he would have been normally. Being the wrong side of forty and one marriage down, he had never imagined being in someone else's bed again, doing all the things they had done the night before. He almost could not contemplate how fulfilled he felt, despite them having done little more than explore and taste one another's bodies. It had been refreshing to take it slow; to discover all the ways he could bring Amy pleasure without every orgasm being a prelude to full-on sex.

It was nothing like the few soulless, mechanical shags he'd had post-Lauren. Every touch brought them closer in more ways than one; his feelings grew stronger for Amy all the more. They were a team and they had one another's back.

He had been surprised by how easily he had fallen asleep afterwards. Usually, his night-time routine involved passing out in the early hours after drinking too much, just to get into some kind of sleep-state, but with Amy in his arms, he had not felt the need. He had been comfortable, asleep in her embrace, and had been surprised to find himself waking at dawn, rather than dragging himself into the land of the living in the early afternoon, still half-drunk. He had not slept that well in years.

He could barely remember the two women he had met up with not long after Lauren left, let alone their names. He had hoped they would help him move on from her adultery, but the emotionless sex had only served to plunge him deeper into self-pity and isolation, making him want to hide away from everyone and everything. Until that day when Ron had brought him back into the lab and he had met Amy.

Now, he was more awake and refreshed than he had ever been, as though he had slept solidly for a week. Finding himself in the quiet window of daybreak, with memories from the previous night that only he and Amy knew about, was worth getting up early for.

'Fuck, that feels better,' she exclaimed, standing in the doorway wearing her hoop earrings, yoga leggings and baggy green t-shirt. 'Nothing like being in your own clothes again.'

'Morning. Are you OK?' he asked, seeing the uncertainty on her face.

For all her feistiness, her eyes gave away a fragility he doubted she showed often. 'I'm just checking that *we're* OK? You weren't there when I woke up.'

'I thought you could use a sleep in your own bed.'

She ran her fingers through her hair, leaning against the doorframe. 'What we did last night – it hasn't changed anything has it?'

He put a tin down on the table. 'Yes, of course it has.' He walked over to her and took her hands. Reaching round her waist, he pulled her close to him, and kissed her. 'It was amazing,' he said, rubbing his nose against the soft skin behind her ear. He had never noticed the heart tattoo outline she had there until last night.

'We didn't even do it,' she said, as she nestled her head in his chest.

'But we're—' He went to jokingly finger-wag at her.

'Taking it slow, I know.'

'At your own volition, I might add,' he said.

'There's a first time for everything.'

Amy seemed lost in her own world, gazing out the window at the city skyline. He was about to ask where she had gone, when she stepped back to look at the kitchen table.

'What are you doing?' she asked.

'An inventory of all the food we can take with us. I don't know how long it will take us to get to the coast, or what stocks they'll have when we get there.'

'Hold that thought, I need to pee,' she said, and headed off to the bathroom.

He carried on searching through cupboards and putting tins and food packets on the table. At the back of the tea and coffee jars, he found a small jar of self-heating instant coffee. He turned it upside down and removed a ring pull. Back up the right way, he shook it hard. Finding two cups, he had just finished pouring them when Amy came back into the kitchen, pale-faced.

'Thank you,' she said. 'I saw what you did, putting the blanket over Ash in the bath. I went to go to the loo, and almost forgot about—'

'I should have warned you,' he said, pushing her wavy hair

back from her face.

She shook her head and squeezed his hand. 'No, it's not your fault. I guess waking up in my own bed, I kind of expected everything to be normal again,' she said, absently running her fingers over his chest. Squeezing him tighter as he held her close, she looked up at him. 'We shouldn't have come here.' Her eyes full of guilt, she broke away from him and flopped down at the table, with her head in her hands.

'If you hadn't, you would have always wondered. You had to, I get it. I can't make it all go away, but here,' he said, handing her a cup of coffee in an orange cup.

'How did you... there's no power for the kettle,' she said, staring at the cup as if it was the stuff of sorcery.

'Found it at the back of the cupboard. It was a self-heating packet.'

'I guess miracles do happen.' She nodded to the window. 'Are those things still out there?'

He looked out over the flat roof, beyond the yard to the access road. 'They're thinning out now it's getting lighter.'

'Good. Bastards.' She drank her coffee and looked at the stuff he had assembled on the table. 'How much of this are you thinking of bringing?'

He frowned. 'All of it. Actually, can you find me a few things? We'll need a first aid kit, painkillers, toothbrushes, toiletries. Antibiotics, if you've got any. We don't know if, or when, all this is going back to normal and we don't want to die from something stupid like toothache in the interim. Have you got any men's clothes here? I could do with a change.'

She nodded. 'Try Ash's room. Her ex-boyfriend used to stay

over sometimes. But don't you want to go back to your flat for anything?'

He took a sip of coffee and breathed through his nostrils. 'If I never go back there, it'll be too soon.'

'Would it be so bad?'

'Why would I want to go back to all that again?'

She smiled. 'What about your pipe and slippers?'

'Very funny.' He slung a carton of instant noodles at her. She gave him the middle finger.

'How're we going to get there? I haven't got a car.'

He rubbed his stubble and held his coffee cup tight. 'We'll figure it out.'

'No, that,' Amy squealed with excitement, pointing her finger to the window. 'It has to be that.'

He looked down at the street, then shot a look at her. 'Fine, if that's what you want. It'll be tricky though. Trust you to be stubborn.'

She kissed him on the bridge of his nose. 'At least I'm consistent.'

*

All of the bags were stashed by the window on the flat roof. The early morning air was cool on Joel's face. Despite the danger, it felt good to be outside again.

'Are you sure about this?' Amy asked, handing him her knife and the gun.

He put them in his pockets. 'Just stick to the plan, OK?' He could feel her eyes on his back and he tried not to think too hard about what was he was actually doing. Once he had got himself perched on the edge of the flat roof, his feet found the narrow brick wall. Looking out across the yard and down the alleyway, he could see no sign of howlers – for now. That did not mean they might not burst out from a side road or behind a bin. That was why Amy was stationed up at the window. They both had work to do.

He edged along the wall. As soon as he could, he climbed onto the garbage pile. The smell that exploded up from the black sacks was as bad the second time, if not worse. The sooner they were away from the city, the better. He looked up to Amy. Her hair blazed in the sunlight as she watched him from the window, worry on her face. He gave the best mustering smile he could, gripped the gate and stepped into the street.

Holding the knife tight, he crept down the road, past bins and human carcasses picked clean from the hoards. The occasional piece of clothing remained, maybe a shoe or jewellery. If it had not been for the bright sunlight, he might not have seen it. Glinting on the pavement was a gold ring, the diamonds clustered, goading him. His thoughts shot back to Lauren and he shut his eyes from the sudden epiphany. He picked up the ring and rolled it around in his fingers.

Not so long ago, it would have hurt him to remember his loss. He had already spiralled downwards before Lauren dumped him. That left him on his backside for far too long. Amy had brought him above water to find the sunlight once more. She was at his side and that alone should give him hope. Now it was dread he felt, for he knew what was coming and the fallout was not going to be pretty. How could he begin to explain it to her, make her understand, if he could not to himself?

A howler plodded down the main street in the distance. It lifted its chin in his direction. He spotted black drool fall onto its white football top. He heard a plate smash: Amy's diversion. The thought of her flinging old china from the kitchen window onto the road below would have been funny, had it not meant the worst. She was to keep watch and if there were more howlers coming, she was to sling plates on the main street to draw them away from the alleyway.

He stuffed the ring in his pocket. He could hear her shouts on the breeze. The plan had already gone wrong.

'Hurry up,' he heard Amy shout. 'I'm running out of plates here.'

As he approached the police car, he found the driver's side door was open. 'Shit.' There were no keys in the ignition. A perfect getaway made redundant. He looked up and down the road.

Slumped against a wilted tree was a body clad in police uniform. Joel edged nearer. It was facing the wall so he could not tell if it was dead or turned. It stunk, either way. He prodded its back with his boot and stepped back. It remained still.

He looked back to the group of howlers devouring the fat man up the road. None of them had spotted him yet. He rolled the body over with his foot to find the guy had a blue-grey puffy face, eyes closed. His stomach was a gaping hole, his innards eaten out long ago. Maggots wriggled around the inside of the guy's jacket. Joel held his breath and searched all the pockets but found no keys. He swore under his breath. Then he noticed the guy's black fingernails were bunched into a tight fist. He tried in vain to prise the cold and stiff fingers back. He could just see the keyring poking out. Pretty soon, those howlers would have finished their meal and be hunting for the next – him.

More plates smashed in the distance. He stood up and stamped on the copper's hand. Bones crunched under his boot. From the misshapen digits he grabbed the keys from the bloodless palm. He noticed one of the howlers turn its attention on him. It was busy chewing as he jogged back to the police car. It stared at him, then threw its head back and roared. The others sat up from devouring the meat and sniffed.

They ran towards him in a torrent of hunger and fury. He fumbled with the keys and stuffed them in the ignition. As the engine struggled to turn over, there was no point in running now, there were too many of them and they were too near. He said a prayer, turned the key again and the car started up.

The howler that had first seen him had broken away from the pack and was just metres away when Joel slammed the door and sped away. The howler grabbed onto the back of the car, making Joel swerve. It was struggling to hang on by its fingertips, so he snaked the steering, trying to shake it off. At the junction, he jerked the steering wheel round into a doughnut. The howler slid sideways across the tarmac and slapped into a car, setting off its alarm.

After some grinding of the gearstick, he found reverse and trundled the vehicle up to the back gate of Amy's flat. As he pulled up, a straggler was at his door, mouth open to gnash at his throat. Joel opened the door and stabbed it hard through the skull with the knife. It staggered back into a wheelie-bin. When he was satisfied it was not getting up again, he ran to the yard, and shouted for Amy.

'What the fuck were you doing?' she hissed at the window. 'I'm down to cutlery.'

'Throw the bags down.' He dashed back to the car doors and hauled them open. He came back to see a bag sailing in mid-air to land at his feet. He propped the gate open with a black sack and began to load up the car.

'How many more?' he called to her.

'Just this one,' she said, throwing down a rucksack.

She climbed down from the flat roof while he kept a watch on the gate. Somehow, it was worse to see someone else tackling heights than doing it himself. He sighed with relief when they had both got in and locked the doors. As howlers clawed at the windows, he remembered he did not know where he was going.

'Well, this is new,' Amy breathed. 'I've only ever sat in the back of one of these before.'

'There's a first time for everything,' he said. 'Can you get my bag? The green one.'

'What for?'

'I need the map.' Inching the car forwards, he could feel the burden of responsibility. Right now, it was up to him to keep them safe. So far, they had managed to outrun most of the howlers but he did not know what the rest of the streets had to offer. He pulled up to the main street and made to turn right.

'I wouldn't go that way,' she said. 'The contents of my entire kitchen is all over the tarmac.'

He looked to see a toaster and kettle laid among the shattered porcelain. 'Good work. Put your seatbelt on.'

'Put yours on,' she grumbled.

He threw her a dark look. 'I'm trying to get us the hell out of here. Don't backseat drive.'

'I'm not in the back,' she muttered and folded her arms.

'That can be arranged. Navigate and stop arguing with me.'

Some streets looked as though the outbreak had never happened. It was simply devoid of people, a typical Sunday in the square mile. Other roads were crammed with the dead and the walking infected. He had to drive around more and more pile-ups and soon they found road signs for Tower Bridge.

'Turn right,' she said, not looking up from the map.

Instead, he pulled the car to a halt and hauled up the handbrake. 'Houston, we have a mother of a problem.'

Amy jolted from the sudden stop. She looked up from the map and gasped. One of the gothic turrets of Tower Bridge had crumbled to a stump. The middle strut joining the two uprights had vanished into the river, along with the road. On the other side of bridge, howlers swarmed along the wharf-side apartments, while others stood staring ahead on the sandy shores at the water.

'Fuck it,' she said. 'What now?'

Joel had already started a three-point turn. He dinked a couple of empty cars on the otherwise desolate approach road and headed back past the steeples and battlements of the Tower of London.

'We need another bridge,' he said as they approached the next intersection. 'Preferably one that was built this century.'

'I don't know. They're all old, way old. Except for one.'

'Yes?'

'Go left,' she said.

He did not question her, keeping the Tower and the dead trees at the railings on their left. Brown leaf mulch carpeted the pavements and large puddles had formed in the clogged gutters. Oily water stretched out halfway across the road at some points. The black dome of the Gherkin leered over the buildings.

'You haven't even told me where we're going,' she said. 'Where does Malrose live?'

He altered his grip on the steering wheel and clenched his jaw. 'Stewart Castle, on the coast. Head for Portsmouth.'

They passed some road signs with big red Cs written on them, which marked the start of the congestion charging zone.

'Sorry? *Castle?*' she spluttered. 'How fucking loaded is your friend?'

'It's a military virology research base.'

'Riiight. I won't ask any more in case you have to kill me or something.'

The awkward silence was almost too much to bear, so she looked out at the view of the city instead. The glass pod of the entrance to the Tower Gateway railway station was nested in between tall buildings over the street to the right. Joel drove the car alongside the walls of the Tower.

She could not help wondering if they would be better off in there, where there might be other survivors. She knew better than to make him stop again, just for her. He did not go on about it. She knew they had been lucky to survive, after she insisted on looking for Ash. All the same, she kept a look out, just in case she could see signs of people at the windows or on the roofs, but she saw nothing.

They had passed beyond the Tower walls and a large glass building, to an ancient-looking church. Masonry from above had crushed some of the metal road barriers onto the pavement.

She checked the map. 'Keep on this road for now. We'll go over London Bridge. I think it was built in the seventies.'

His mouth twitched a smile. 'It might hold out better than Tower Bridge did.'

'Either that, or we can go to the south by going through the city centre and cross the river at Kew,' she said, flicking through the road map book. 'But I don't know how old that bridge is there.'

Joel shook his head. 'If we have to go back through the centre and they've put more roadblocks up, we'll never get through. No, we'll go to London Bridge.'

All Amy could think about was that every option they had contained its own risks. If they stayed in London, more howlers would come. The rains would continue to destroy buildings and infect people until the poison balance dropped, if it recovered at all. Leaving the city for the castle was an unknown. What if the professor was not there, or had turned? Was there a safe way out of the city? They were driving blind.

She reached forwards and turned on the radio. She was not expecting travel updates, but maybe there was someone out there. She kept turning the dial. The slightest change in static made her hold her breath. If only she could just hear a voice. After a few frustrating minutes of hearing nothing, she flicked it off and looked out the window.

Joel weaved past more empty vehicles. The street enclosed as they drove past high-rise pebble-dashed office blocks. A grey walkway linked the buildings above the road. Something white had been attached to the railings and flapped in the breeze. Amy read the large red-painted letters: Alive inside. She gasped and looked at Joel. His face was hard, concentrating on the road.

'I know what you're thinking, and no, we can't,' he said.

'We haven't seen any howlers for a while,' she pleaded.

'Let's keep it that way,' he said. 'Where are we now?'

She glanced at the map. 'Lower Thames Street. We should

make a left fairly soon here.'

He slowed the car and bumped up the kerb to avoid a bus that was skewed across two lanes. Amy looked past him to see a tall obelisk between the buildings. On the top of the column was a globe-like shape, dripping in gold. It was the monument to the Great Fire. London always survived in some shape or form, be it the plague, fire or floods – even howlers. The city still stood – for now.

They passed through a long, dark tunnel. She felt sick as she realised they were driving under the bridge itself. 'That's where we need to be,' she said, pointing above them. 'I thought this road would get us there. I'm sorry.' She fumbled with the map, trying to find the right page. 'Keep going. We'll find a way up. There, go up there,' she shouted, pointing to a road on the right, with a no entry sign.

He hauled on the steering wheel and the car slid sideways across the yellow hatched grid on the tarmac. Soon they were speeding up a smaller road and he only slowed when they reached a junction and an array of no entry signs and traffic lights. The golden monument was directly in front of them. He swung the car round to the right and they drove over painted arrows going in the other direction.

The road straightened out and she knew by the uniform streetlights down the middle of the reservation where they were.

The buildings either side cleared to reveal the vast expanse of the Thames. The shiny structure of the Shard glimmered as they drove onto the bridge.

'We did it,' he said, and smiled at the view and then her. 'You did it.'

To the left, she saw the crumbling turrets of Tower Bridge. To the right and disappearing from view, was the grey dome of St Paul's Cathedral. River boats twirled aimlessly in the middle of the waters. Sadness weighed on her chest. She knew she would never be coming back to this city again.

Joel rested back in the passenger seat, grateful for the driving break. The further they had got into the suburbs, the more vehicles they had found blocking the road. He lost count of the amount of times one of them had to get out and push the cars out the way.

They were on country back roads, having found the motorway impassable with huge sinkholes, some spanning the entire road. A few holes had swallowed up cars, leaving just the bonnets and boots tilted at the sky, broken and lost. Howlers that had fallen in flapped their shredded limbs at the lip of the hole.

The rest of the road space was choked with the milling infected and parked-up cars. It was clear what had happened: the disease took hold while everyone was busy fleeing the cities. In one mass traffic jam, they had no chance of escaping death.

With the map, Amy and Joel had managed to find another way round. The detour would take them longer, and he knew they might not make the coast by dusk.

Amy seemed unfazed. Her face was determined, ready for danger, yet she seemed at ease, with her elbow resting on the doorframe. She was even humming a tune. Once she had got used to the controls, her computer game face went on. She was focused. Maybe it was her young years, and she was more adaptable than he was. Having been brought up in care and losing the parents she never knew, confusion was standard. She was used to danger and chaos being the way of things. He had never really thought about it, but in this new world she was probably the best person to have his back.

They passed a road sign so pock-marked with rust bubbles he could not read the place name. As he checked the map, Amy gasped as they topped the brow of a hill. Below them, open countryside stretched all around them. Instead of green fields and crowned trees, the yellow and orange patches of deadness went on for miles. Leafless trees stuck out of the landscape like ugly pylons without power cables.

'What a mess,' he said, shaking his head.

'It's still beautiful. Look, the sea,' she exclaimed with child-like excitement.

Way off in the distance, he could just make out the white glimmer of water, a sliver on the horizon. He was glad they had nearly made it, but with a dread he knew once they got there it would change everything. He could feel her watching him, so he went back to checking the map.

She sighed. 'Be a bit more fucking chuffed about it then, eh? We're nearly there.'

He dropped the map in his lap and looked up. They were losing the light fast. He could just make out the outskirts of a town down in the valley. He shook his head. 'This isn't a picnic, Amy. And sorry, but we aren't slightly there yet.'

She slammed on the brakes and turned to look at him. 'Yes, we are. The coast is right there.'

'We can't travel in the dark, it's too risky,' he said as he folded the map up and looked at her.

'So what's your grand plan?'

'We hole up here for the night.' He stretched his legs out as best he could in the cramped space of the footwell. 'You know it's not like before. How many times have we had to go the long way round? Why are we arguing about this?' he asked.

She glared out her window, not answering. 'What exactly do you expect me to say? You've already decided for us.'

'I'm trying to keep us alive.'

'So you keep saying,' she snapped, her eyes wide with anger. For a second, she looked like a howler. 'Do this, don't do that. Go here, don't help anyone alive. Drive, sleep. Is it all right if I take a piss as well?'

'We are on a mission. The PM asked us. No one else – *us*. We're the only ones who stand a chance of helping everyone else. How can we do that if we're dead?'

'Sometimes I forget what a prick you are.'

'Yeah? And you're a pain in the arse.'

Her stomach rumbled. 'Well, if we're doing things the slow way.' She turned off the ignition.

'What now?'

'I'm going to take a piss.' She opened the door. 'Unless I really do need permission to do that too?'

He buried his attention in the map. 'Be careful,' he muttered.

Out the corner of his eye, he saw her pick up the knife. All the while she was gone, he checked the side mirrors and out the front windscreen for trouble. He really wanted to go with her, to be sure she would be OK, but he knew that would only incense her further.

The wind whipped up round her hair as she returned to the

car. She skulked round to the driver's door. Once she got in, she dropped the knife back into the central compartment and reached into the bag on the back seat. With a tin of spaghetti in her hands, she sat back round and frowned at him. 'What?'

'Nothing.'

He reached into the bag and found an all-day breakfast can, with mini sausages and spaghetti in it. He handed Amy a fork and they ate in silence, watching the view of the coast.

After a while he twiddled with the radio again and then tried the police radio – nothing. 'I'm sorry,' he said.

Glancing at him, she carried on digging into the tin with a fork. 'For being a prick?'

'I'm not doing all this to deliberately be a bastard, OK?'

She looked up with hurt in her eyes. 'You treat me like I'm some five-year-old who doesn't know shit. I told you, I'm not—'

'A kid, I know.' He nodded. 'I'm not used to—'

'Compromise?'

He laughed, and to his relief, so did she. Since he started winning awards, people pandered to his reputation. Lauren had pussy-footed around him, but not her. She just acted like he was normal. He knew she deserved the truth. It had to be now. 'There's something I need to tell you,' he said, 'about Malrose.'

She finished off her last forkful of spaghetti and wiped her mouth with the back of her hand. 'I know the calibre of your "old friends". If he's anything like Nick the Prick, I really don't need to know about tales of strip clubs and drinking games. We've all got a past, right?'

'Yeah, but—'

'You haven't judged me by my past, and I won't judge you on

yours.' She slung her can in the footwell and reclined her seat back. 'I'm going to try and get some sleep. So should you. Goodnight.' She kissed him on the temple and rolled over onto her side, facing away from him. In those seconds, the moment to tell her was gone.

Amy yawned as Joel pulled the car up at the entrance to the castle grounds. A chrome and glass curved building sat past the chain-link fence, a clubhouse of some sort. White yachts, big and small, bobbed up and down along the decking at the shore. Howlers had noticed the car and were massing inside the boundary fence. The big wooden doors of the castle were further ahead. The turrets and battlements stood proud, overlooking the shore.

'I need you to be awake now,' Joel said.

'I need caffeine,' she moaned, peering through the windscreen.

'Yeah? I want to see U2 at Wembley but that's not going to happen either.'

'Who?' she asked, and readjusted the sunglasses on the bridge of her nose.

'Never mind. We've got work to do, and this isn't going to be easy.' He gripped the steering wheel and looked straight ahead. 'Look.'

Fuck, she mouthed, taking off her glasses. Looking closer at the howlers massed at the fence, she could see their faces looked normal, but their necks and arms were ringed with deep red bites. Wide eyes sought out sources of food to tear and crunch into. The yellow lifejackets of the infected juveniles were smeared with grime and old blood. Some donned equally bright crash helmets and wetsuits. With the sheer amount of bodies pressing against the chain-link fence, she did not know if it would hold out much longer.

'There's no way to get the security gates open,' he said.

'Those howlers are about to do our dirty work for us.'

'That's great until we need to get through the main gates further up.'

She gawped at him. 'You have a plan?'

The fence gave way and the howlers spilled across the wreckage. He gave her a wink, opened the car door and picked up the gun. 'There's a marina down there, I'll divert them.' With that, he was gone.

She got out the car to go round to the driver's side, when a scraping sound made her look back. A squat, female howler emerged from behind a shipping container. Its brown hair was straggled into rat-tails, framing its boil-covered face. It came too fast, reaching for her throat. She screamed and fumbled to bring up her knife. She was too close and the howler had hold of her too tight. It belched garbage breath over her as it opened its mouth. The knife slipped from her sweaty fingers and clattered to the ground.

The howler pressed its cold, slimy fingers into her neck. She pulled back and they both fell. As it landed on her, the weight jabbed sharp stones into her legs. With the momentum, it rolled off her, just long enough for her to sit up and punch it. An arc of pus sprayed from its nose across the floor. It lay wriggling on its back, stuck, as though it had forgotten how to get up again by itself.

Dusting herself off, she noticed the puddle of blood she was sitting in and the knife sticking out the back of her leg. She cried out as she tried to pull the blade out, but it was embedded sideways. She looked for Joel but could not see him anywhere.

Amy held her breath and pulled the knife back hard out of her leg. It came away and she fell onto her side. The howler staggered and hungrily swiped at her, tripping over its own withered limbs. Amy twisted round and plunged the knife up at its neck as it glanced off her shoulder.

The pain from her leg was causing her to breathe shallow and fast. She bent over on all fours, unsure what the best thing to do was. The blood was running down her trousers and into her shoe. Why did she get out the stupid car in the first place? The choice was to get up in pain, or wait for Joel. As the conundrum whirled around her head, she heard a long, whining sound coming from the open door of the shipping container.

Sweat dripped from Amy's face on to the ground. The knife was implanted in the woman howler and out of reach. A mass of matted fur appeared at the doorway and the small, frightened face of a cat popped out into the daylight.

Amy nearly laughed in delight. When it saw her, its eyes widened further and it looked about to bolt.

'Hey, wait,' she panted. Her heart was racing and she struggled to think. She held out her hand. If she could just save someone, something, from the world before. She could not save her sister, Mei, Sylvia. It was only a stupid cat, but it was alive.

She breathed against the seizing pain spreading up her thigh. 'Don't be silly. Come here.' She could not believe it. All this way and she had managed to find a survivor.

Pain shot through her leg as she took a step forward to coax the animal. The pool of blood around her had grown in just a few minutes. There was a first aid kit in the car. It was only a few metres away, but it felt like miles.

She heard a hiss and turned to see the rat-tailed howler with its mouth clamped round the cat's leg. It ripped tendrils taut and chomped on sinew. Amy hurled herself forwards, just as the cat crumpled into a ball.

The howler had switched to the cat's jugular. It was too busy tucking into it to notice Amy wrench out the knife that stuck in its neck. She slashed at its head until it stopped moving.

'You fucker,' she screeched, blood all over her arms. She dropped the knife and crouched over the cat. Tears glassed her vision as she stroked its face. 'I'm so sorry,' she said and cradled it.

Fingers grappled at her arms, scratching and pulling at her. Teeth snapped as a howler tried to bite her hands. She kicked it and scrabbled away to find more trudging up the driveway. *Where the hell is Joel?*

She dropped the cat and picked up her knife. Stumbling back to the car, she shut herself in. Bright sunlight dazzled her bleary vision. Figures danced in the distance through the shimmering heat coming off the asphalt road down by the marina. Joel dashed back and forth from the boathouses as the howlers staggered towards him.

With a clanging sound, cylinders rolled away from him down the road towards the howlers. He fired his gun. A bright fireball mushroomed up and out. Her eyes burned. She opened the car door and could not see him anywhere. It was happening again. Before she could do anything, her own body felt too heavy to hold up anymore.

Her cheek was against something hard and gritty. She opened her eyes to find stones in front of her. Lifting her head from the floor took more effort than she had expected. Her whole body felt as though it weighed a tonne.

'Amy?'

Happiness from hearing Joel's voice was replaced by pain as he hauled her into the police car and sped up the driveway. She breathed in a glorious salty sea smell. Gulls called. She could hear him shouting in the distance.

A voice came over on the tannoy. 'Who are you?'

'It's me,' Joel shouted. 'Open the gate.'

'You need to show me the girl first.'

'She's injured.'

'She might be infected,' the voice replied.

'You have to let us in,' he shouted. 'It's a knife wound. She hasn't been bitten.' Joel opened Amy's door and helped her to her feet. 'You need to stay awake. Tell them your name.'

Nausea snuck up on her and before she could stop it, she had vomited over her legs. She swayed into nothingness as sunlight descended to blackness.

Amy came to as someone pressed their thumb against her eyelids. She tried to move away. Her vision was blurry and pitching. She felt light, for the first time in ages. Then she was gliding along as though she was flying. Seagulls called out. Her fingers and toes hurt with cold. Next thing she knew, she was lifted again into strong arms.

'Here we go,' Joel said, and placed her gently onto cool, crisp sheets.

She felt his stubble against her temple as he kissed her face.

'Her pulse is very weak,' a woman said.

Amy opened her eyes to see a red-haired woman watching her with concern.

'Come on, Amy,' Joel coaxed as he stroked her forehead.

Footsteps retreated and she was left in silence. She had moments of coming to, seeing gulls flit past the window in front of her; blue curtains, grey skies.

She woke to the sound of raised voices, yet could not make sense of the words. It was Joel and the woman again, and he was giving her grief about something.

'You must be able to do something. Please,' he said.

'This isn't a hospital. I'm not a doctor. She's suffering from severe blood loss. I have no blood stores here. All we can do is pump her full of saline and vitamins, and hope that she pulls through.'

*

It was the tugging on her arm that woke her from the dead sleep. She looked down to see a drip poking out of her, attached to a bag on a hook. She looked to her other side to find a little girl with blonde ringlets watching her. Her expression did not change as Amy came to, but kept her thumb in her mouth, her eyes unapologetically staring.

Amy tried to sit up so she could look at her visitor properly. As she groaned, the little girl sprang forwards, a pen-knife in her hand, and pressed it to her throat.

'What has four corners and four sides, but isn't a square?' the girl shouted.

'Huh?' she asked.

'Tell me or you're dead,' the girl said, all softness gone from her face.

Amy struggled against the pillows as she tried to wriggle back from her. 'W-what?'

'What shape has four corners, but isn't a square?' she demanded.

Amy's head hurt. She knew her life depended on an answer. 'I don't know. A pyramid. Can you get off now?'

The girl sat back, pleased with herself, and dropped the knife on the edge of the bed. She took a sheet of paper from her pocket and picked at it with her nails. She peeled off something small, reached forwards and patted it onto Amy's nightshirt. 'Gold star for you. I had to be sure, what with the biters. Mummy says never trust strangers.'

'That's some good advice,' Amy said, her heart racing.

The little girl got up, walked over to a window. Her footsteps echoed round the room. Light burned through a gap in the curtain. She thought they had come to a research base so the last thing she had expected was to be threatened by a psychotic primary school kid.

'Where am I?' Amy asked.

'You mean, where are *we*? You want the curtains open? It's a great view,' the girl said, and flung the drapes aside.

The sunlight hurt her eyes and she blinked. Her eyes slowly adjusted and she could make out the soupy brown-blue of sea.

'This,' the girl said, flinging out her arms, 'is Stewart's Castle.'

Amy remembered the boathouses and the fireball, Joel speeding the car towards the castle gates. 'Joel. Where is he?'

The girl had turned to the instruments on the table and idly turned them over on the white cloth. 'He's with Mummy.'

Amy thought back to the woman who had talked about blood. 'Is she the doctor?'

The girl twirled a ringlet of hair round her finger. 'Mummy's a scientist.'

The door opened and the red-headed woman came bustling in. Her eyes fell to the knife on the bed. 'Morgan, what have you done?'

'It's OK,' Amy said, trying and failing to sit up against the pillows. 'I'm fine.'

'I thought that maybe she had turned,' the girl said to her mother. 'So I tested her with the pyramid question. I've been watching her, like you asked. She's all pale. Just like—'

'Never mind that now,' the woman replied, folding the blade and putting it in her pocket.

'That's mine,' Morgan whined.

'The knife is for defence only. You know that.'

The door banged open again and Joel came striding through. 'Why didn't you tell me she was awake?' He approached the bedside and held her shoulders. 'How're you feeling?'

'My leg kills.' She tried to prop herself up, but Joel eased her back down. He looked different somehow, but she could not figure out what it was.

'It's a miracle you got this far to be honest,' said the woman. 'That's it, just lie down for now. I'm Professor Malrose, and this is my daughter, Morgan. Go and play in the games room please, honey.'

The girl huffed. 'I want to stay.'

'We've got things to discuss. Be a good girl, eh?'

The child got up and sloped off towards the door. As the woman set about attaching a bag of clear liquid to a hook above the bed, so many questions were flying through Amy's head. She could not hold onto one long enough to get her mouth around the words.

Malrose was a woman, the woman who was now saving her life. Of all the times she had spoken with Joel, had he ever said the professor was a woman? It should not matter, she reasoned, but it was not sexism that grated at the back of her head. It was something else she could not define, as she looked out at the blue sky.

The effort from constantly fighting to survive exhausted her.

She did not understand anything and the despair made her start to cry.

'Shh,' Joel said, stroking her forehead. 'It's all right.'

Her face screwed up and she fisted tears away. 'I can't remember.'

'We've got time,' he said.

She could not help but notice the tense looks exchanged between him and the red-head. The room was clean. The surfaces were white and there was a big silver refrigerator in the corner. 'Is this a hospital?' she asked.

Her leg was agony. She wriggled to get more comfy, but every movement was an effort. The bed springs creaked and the mattress poked into her shoulders.

'Medi-bay. Sorry, it's the best we could do under the circumstances,' the professor said.

Amy looked down, realising it was not a hospital bed at all, but a camp bed. Joel stood up. 'Where are you going?' she asked, worried.

'We've got work to do,' he said, glancing at the woman.

'Of course,' Amy said, trying to get the covers off her. 'The cure.' She felt a gust and realised she was only wearing a nightie and had heavy bandages on her lower leg.

Joel put his hand to her shoulder and eased her back to the pillows. 'No, you don't. You nearly died.'

'But I have to help.'

'You aren't well,' the woman said, putting a stethoscope back in her pocket.

Joel kissed Amy's hand. 'You lost a lot of blood. Just promise me you'll stay there and get the hell better.'

Then she realised why he looked so different. Had it really been so long? 'You've grown a beard,' she said.

As he tucked her back into the covers again, he gave her a smile. 'I guess so.'

She could not help but feel that there was something else that had changed as well. Joel seemed on edge. *Shouldn't he be relieved to see his old friend*?

'What's wrong?' she asked.

He stroked her face and sighed. 'Nothing. We'll be back later to check on you.'

'I'm not a baby,' she muttered.

Her eyelids closed as he reached the hallway, and she fell asleep to the sound of waves lapping against the rocks.

CHAPTER FORTY-ONE
Amy

Amy woke up with a jolt. She was alone in the room. Light peeped through the crack in the curtain. Somewhere far off, she could hear a man's voice, and someone crying far away.

The little girl was asleep in the chair. Her legs ached and she realised she needed the toilet. She had managed to use the bowl a few times to go to the toilet, but a bit of privacy and normality would be nice. How to move with the drip? Should she take it off? Maybe she could just carry the bag.

She peeled back the sheets. She knocked into the drip stand as she looked at the clear bag of liquid.

'Hey, no. Don't do that,' Morgan said, leaping round to the edge of the bed.

'I need to get up.'

Morgan shook her head and blocked her way. 'Mummy says you're too weak.'

'Where is your mummy?'

'Busy with the man.'

All they were doing was work, but jealousy twinged at her before she could stop it. Her legs aching, she sat back down on the bed. 'How long have I been asleep?'

The girl shrugged. 'A day or so, I guess.'

'It's Morgan, isn't it?'

She twined her hair round her fingers. 'Yeah. You?'

'I'm Amy. How old are you?'

She stood proud. 'Seven. It's my birthday soon. You?'

'Twenty-five.'

Morgan screwed up her face. 'You're old.'

'Thanks a bunch. Look, I really need the toilet.'

Morgan bent over to pick up the bowl. 'You have to use this.'

She spotted a wheelchair in the corner. 'Tell you what, I bet you know every single room in this castle, don't you?'

She nodded.

'If you take me for a tour of this place, I promise to stay in that wheelchair.'

Morgan looked unsure. 'Mummy said—'

'I'll take the drip with me. How's that? I bet you've got some cool stuff here, eh?'

Morgan grinned. 'I do, actually.' Her smile faded. 'We aren't allowed to leave this room.'

'You do everything you're told to? I don't. If your mum finds out, you can just say you were trying to stop me. I'll take the wrap, I promise.'

'Brownie promise?'

'Deal.' Amy shook her hand. 'Let's get a wriggle on, eh? I'm about to pee my pants.'

*

After the trip to the loo, she found her bag and picked a short khaki dress and her ankle boots to wear. It felt good to be in her own clothes again, instead of a nightie. She was fed up with feeling like an invalid. She picked out her gold hoops and put them back on too. With help from Morgan, she changed the bandage on her leg. They had given her stitches, just a few, but they were neat. It did not hurt too badly, as long as she did not overdo it.

Morgan insisted on taking her in the wheelchair to the staff wing. She opened a door and with it, wafted a smell of hot straw and the musty aroma of animals. A few cages sat on the shelves and single countertop in the tiny cabin. Most of them were empty, except for a couple which contained some fluffy brown rabbits.

'Where did you get those?' Amy asked from the doorway.

Morgan squeezed past and checked the water bottles. 'I did have four.' Tears pooled in her eyes and she closed the door of the hutch. 'I don't like it,' she said and chewed her lip.

'Don't like what?'

The little girl touched the cage with her fingertips. Her concerned eyes looked as if they wanted to tell Amy something. Then she walked behind the wheelchair. 'Nothing. Come on. I've got something else to show you.'

They went on and pushed through a set of double doors. Here, they came to plush carpets, gold-gilded mirrors and leather sofas of a lounge area.

'This is a bit plush for a research base isn't it?' Amy asked.

'It used to be a hotel but it closed in lockdown. The government bought it and Mummy has been working here since then.' Morgan grunted with the effort of pushing the wheelchair over the deep pile of the carpet.

'Take this instead,' Amy said, handing out the drip stand. 'I'll push myself for a while.'

As she stared at the bronze merman statue in the middle of the room, she thought she could hear people talking. Morgan started to drag the wheelchair backwards and Amy grabbed the drip stand just in time.

'Hey, what is it?' Amy asked.

'We shouldn't be out here,' Morgan whispered. Her voice was wobbly, as though she were about to cry. 'Let's go. Please.'

Amy turned as best she could in the chair to look at her. 'We aren't prisoners.'

Morgan shook her head, her ringlets flinging about her face. 'You don't understand.'

'Do you hear that?' She could hear someone crying again. Despite Morgan's protests, Amy wheeled round a corner to find Malrose's head dipped in mid-sob and Joel's hands on her shoulders.

'I'm so sorry about Nick,' he said, as she wiped her face. 'Have you told Morgan yet?'

She shook her head. 'It's going to hit her really hard.'

As old friends, Amy realised, they must all know each other. Probably went to the same wanky public school together.

'You've had a lucky escape, if you ask me,' he said.

'Have a heart, will you? I actually loved him, you know.' She flicked her hair back and batted her eyelashes at him. 'You never said you loved me, not even on our wedding day.'

'Lauren, don't.'

'Speaking of which, have you told the poor girl we never got divorced?'

Joel's hands slid up her neck and into her hair. 'It's none of her business.' He tilted his head and kissed her full on the mouth.

Amy gasped and the two of them turned to her, equally in shock. 'Lauren? *This* is Lauren?'

He stepped back from the red-head and rubbed his beard. 'I can explain.'

Amy shook her head. 'Oh, please. Don't let me interrupt your tête-à-tête, Professor Harket. It's *none of my business.*'

Amy tried to spin the wheelchair around, but it was stuck on the plush carpet. She got up and made to stride off down the corridor, and the drip stand clattered over. She bit back tears and ripped the drip from her arm and went as fast as she could in the opposite direction. Her paranoia was dancing on the tables in victory. It had tried to tell her, and she had refused to listen. She burst through a set of double doors and passed the bronze merman statue.

Joel's fingers curled round her shoulder. 'Wait,' he said.

She turned back and slapped him across the face – hard. 'How fucking dare you?' she screamed. 'You lied to me.'

He rubbed his cheek, his expression straight. 'I have never lied to you, not once,' he said.

'You never told me the truth, either. First you told me she was dead—'

'That was before.'

She was pacing the floor with anger. 'Before what? It doesn't matter, anyway. You had the actual cheek to ask me to trust you when you had this massive omission stashed in your back pocket? After I told you everything?'

'I tried to tell you.'

'But it was easier not to, right? I've told you everything about me. I let you in my fucking flat, sleep with me in my bed.'

'We haven't made love, though.'

She felt like she had been kicked in the heart. Was he really justifying his deceit because they had not done it? 'I didn't realise I meant that little to you.' She turned and walked further away from him.

'Please, don't do this. Please,' he said as he followed her. 'I've been waiting for you a long time and I think you have been too. If you're anything like me, you've never said the words to anyone either.'

She spun round, surprised to see tears in his eyes. 'Don't twist this round on to me. I thought I was beginning to understand what this was, you and me. How wrong I was. You weren't going to tell me about Lauren. Is that all you think I am, your bit on the side?'

'Of course not.'

'You haven't even said sorry.'

'I've got my reasons.'

'I suppose those reasons are none of my fucking business either?' she asked. It was hurting her too much to listen to anymore. Her inner critic would not stop goading her, telling her she was not good enough, she was not his type, only good for a good time. It was stupid to think either one of them was capable of love.

Remembering when they danced together in her room, she had been so happy. Now that memory was tainted. All the time, he had a wife stashed away by the sea. She went to walk off again, but he grabbed her by the wrists.

'Then I'll say it. Amy, I lo—'

'Don't say it now,' she snapped. 'It doesn't mean fuck all if you say it now. I don't need it by way of an apology. Actually, I'll look after Morgan while you and the missus have a cosy catch up.' The world stopped once more as she realised another gut-wrenching truth. 'Morgan's yours, isn't she?'

How could she not be his child? The same blonde hair and blue eyes. He stared back and let go of her wrists. All of her ached. Her face felt like it was curling in on itself and tears rolled down her cheeks.

All she could think of was the secret little looks Joel had been giving Malrose – the wife. She must have been using her maiden name. At the end of everything, he had come back to his family and Amy had been flicked off as a nuisance.

Just as she was expecting a denial or an apology to come from his lips, his eyes turned cold once more. 'Would it matter if she was mine?' he asked.

She did not know what to say. *Of course it would*, she wanted to scream, but the words would not come. How could he be so blasé about a child that may or may not be his?

'I'm older than you, Amy. And no, I can't remember every woman I've slept with. She might be mine, I don't know. I was married.'

'You still are,' she said, struggling to get the words out. She looked down to see blood had dripped down her arm and onto the carpet. It did not matter when the deceit stung like venom, slowly poisoning her.

'You're hurt,' he said, holding out his hand.

She slapped it away. 'You've done enough.'

'I don't love her.'

'You just fucking kissed her,' she shrieked.

He sighed. 'I wanted to prove to myself that I didn't love her anymore.'

'Nicely handled.' She applauded with slow sarcasm as she turned and then shouldered the door open. Heading for the medi-bay, she desperately hoped he would not follow her.

She limped through the castle, hating every inch of the place. She had not gone far before she heard a commotion behind her. Looking back, she saw Joel dragging a rather confused and upset Lauren down the room towards her.

'Tell her what you told me,' he said, pushing his wife forwards.

Lauren bit back tears. 'Morgan isn't Joel's. She is Nicholas's child. That's why I left. I was seeing Nicholas when I got pregnant and realised I had to leave. I never told Joel.'

'Well, lucky you,' Amy spat at him. 'You've sidestepped a hefty child maintenance bill there.'

He gave her a sheet of paper. 'Will you shut up and just read this?'

She scrunched it up without looking at it. 'There isn't anything you can give me that will change what's happened.'

'Is that it?' he asked, glaring at her.

'It's not all about you, Joel. Look at her.' She nodded at Lauren, who wiped her nose with the back of her hand. 'She's grieving. Why do you think it's OK to treat people like this? Is your ego too big to understand?'

All her sudden hatred of Lauren had evaporated like that, when she realised how in pieces she was over Nick. She had lost someone she loved. Amy knew what that felt like.

His cavalier demeanour had deflated and now he looked

uncertain, fearful. 'I thought that once you knew—'

'Did you expect me to fall into your arms after I learned that your estranged wife's child is not yours? Thank you sooo much.'

He ranted to himself in what she could only assume to be Norwegian. Eventually when he addressed her in English, he was no less angry. 'Do you know what? You're right,' he said, throwing his arms up. 'You and me is a stupid idea. I've been trying to ignore the fact all along that I'm too old and you're too flaky.'

'And I've been ignoring the fact that I actually fucking hate you. Don't follow me.' She turned on her heel and, pushing through the pain, attempted a dignified walk out the room.

*

She managed to clean her arm up and stick a plaster over it in the sanctuary of the medi-bay. She stood at the window, deep in thought. She was furious and had nowhere to run and no one to turn to. Could she stay here anymore? It would be too painful living with the three of them, watching them play happy families. Anything was better than this. Maybe she could return to London, she thought. If she returned to the depot, she could help Blondie rebuild it. Perhaps they could try and take back the War Rooms from the howlers.

There was a soft knock at the door. She was half-tempted to swear at the visitor, but she knew it could not be Joel. He would not have had the manners. He would have just barged in, with his ego following closely behind. She took a breath to compose herself. 'Come in.'

The door opened and Lauren edged in. 'I'm sorry to interrupt, it's just, um, we need to... I wanted to speak to you before we leave.'

Amy stared at the rucksack on her back. 'Aww, are you planning a second honeymoon? How sweet,' she said, through gritted teeth. 'I hope you have a lovely time.'

'The infection could have mutated since the first outbreak. We need to gather some more evidence for the vaccine. Joel didn't tell you?'

'What do you think? He doesn't tell me anything – clearly.' She tried to keep her voice level. He was pushing her out now he had his wife back again. It showed how little he thought of her to not even tell her what they were planning.

Lauren shifted, adjusting the strap on her shoulder. 'We need to bring back some live test subjects.'

Amy snorted. 'They were testing people at the War Rooms. You know how that played out.'

'As soon as we've collected the data we need,' she said, 'we'll put them out of their misery.'

Amy could not help herself and laughed as she chucked the plaster tabs in the bin. 'That's not what I meant. Have you been out there since all this started? I have. It's not the world you once knew. It's fucking vile. I can hold my own out there, I can—'

Lauren smoothed her hair down. 'I wish you could come, but you're far too ill.' She blushed. 'Look, the thing is, can you keep an eye on Morgan for me? I haven't been able to leave here with just us two. It'd be too dangerous.'

Amy got it; she was asking as a mother. It did not make it hurt any less. Joel had left it to his spouse to tell her what they were planning. She mocked herself up into a façade of nonchalance. 'Whatever, if that's all you're after – a free babysitter.'

Lauren shook her head. 'It really wouldn't be like that. She's my only child and all I have left in the world. We aren't palming you off.'

Amy plumped down on the bed and crossed her arms.

'We haven't seen each other in years, you know,' Lauren said.

'And that kiss brought all the happy times skipping back, didn't it?' Amy asked, her voice wavering.

Lauren sighed. 'It's fairly obvious Joel doesn't have any feelings for me. You can see that, right?' She inched a little closer to Amy, but looked concerned, maybe fearing a slap like the one she gave Joel. Amy said nothing. 'When he brought you into this place, bleeding in his arms, he looked at you like he couldn't bear to lose you. In all the time we were together, he never looked at me like that.'

Amy screwed her eyes shut. 'Just fuck off, will you?'

'OK. But just think on this: he's stubborn when he knows what he wants.'

Amy frowned, occupying herself by pouring a drink from the jug of water on her bedside table. Two things troubled her. She did not know what Joel wanted at all. One minute she thought he had hunted across London to find her, the next he was snogging his wife – in front of her. The second thing on her mind was that his stubbornness mirrored her own. They were just too similar in their negative traits to work.

She was so busy in her thoughts, she barely heard Lauren shut the door as she left. It helped to calm her, having a plan. She was going to leave as soon as they came back – if they made it back at all. She could not leave Morgan on her own.

They needed live test samples to work on, if they wanted to find a cure. That involved bringing a fully biting howler into the castle. She almost did not care. She *had* to not care. Caring for people only brought her more hurt. She was not going to be a part of Joel's games anymore.

Biting back tears again, she only had herself to rely on and she had to be strong. She watched the waves crashing over the rocky headland near the shore as she told herself she was stupid to let him in. She did not need him. She was fine before he came along and she knew she would be fine without him. They had not even had sex. Why was she getting so hung up over someone who could not decide what they were to each other?

She remembered what a mess she was when she thought he was dead. Life simply was not worth it without him. Then she remembered her own words, that he had not judged her past and she would not judge his. She stared at the balled-up sheet of paper on the counter. What could be so important that he thought it could change her mind? She strode over and smoothed out the paper. It was blank, except for two signatures on it – his and Lauren's. Underneath, it read: "This document terminates the marriage of the persons signed above".

'Oh, fuck,' she breathed and dashed out of the room. By the time she got to the cobbled courtyard, it was empty. No police car, no Joel and Lauren. She climbed the steps up to the battlement perimeter walls, wincing every time she put her weight on her bad leg. The driveway to the security gates and shipping container was cloudy with dust, kicked up from the car that had only just left.

Joel gripped the steering wheel, trying to ignore the silently crying Lauren. She had given Morgan a series of instructions, which included checking the radio every two hours and getting some more fluids into Amy.

He looked in the rear-view mirror, almost expecting to see Amy running after them. Was there ever a day when she was not the most stubborn creature on the planet? Was there ever a day they were not arguing?

God knows how far they would have to go before they found more howlers. He had blown up all the ones down by the marina. He caught a glimpse of himself in the mirror. His hair had grown longer and he was not sure about the beard, but so far, there had not been time to shave.

Lauren sniffed and wiped her arm on her sleeve.

'Maybe I should've gone on my own,' he grumbled.

'No, I'm OK,' she whispered. 'I just worry about Morgan.'

He realised this must be the first time she had left her child since the outbreak began. 'Have you got the guts to do this?' he snapped at Lauren. 'Because it's bloody risky.'

She wiped her face. 'We could've stayed for a few more days,' she said. 'We didn't have to leave with things the way they are.'

He knew what she was trying to say. If he had not left straight away and waited instead for Amy's leg to heal, they could have gone as a trio. Dear sweet Lauren, always trying to keep everyone happy.

If Amy was there, she would be giving him shit about something or other. In a weird way, he missed the sparring, but it was best they end it now. He had lied to her in the worst way possible. He had put her through enough. He should spare her any more hurt because he could not give Amy what she wanted. She needed someone reliable, dependable; that was not him.

'Why are you running away?' Lauren blurted out.

Joel pulled the car to a halt and turned to her. 'Don't make out like you know me inside out, just because we got married.'

'I'm not. But I've known you since college.'

'People change.'

'What are you so scared of? She's just a kid.'

'Exactly. I've got enough problems without making her another one.' He thought of that hip-flask that used to bang against his ribs. After Lauren left him, it became his only companion. He could not let himself lose control like that again.

She shook her head. 'Don't do that. It's more than that. This isn't just fooling around, is it?'

He pulled the handbrake off and accelerated again. 'I am not having this conversation with you.'

'The reason we broke up is because we never faced up to all this stuff. We never spoke about our feelings and if we had admitted we never loved each other, it might've saved us a lot of pain.'

'What're you saying?' he asked.

'I'm saying I think it's the complete opposite with you two. You never looked at me the way you look at her; like she's your whole world. That's worth fighting for. You need to tell her how you feel.'

'I told you, I'm not talking about this with you,' Joel said, driving round a pothole.

'Bloody hell. You make out like you're the adult and she's the child, but you need to grow up and embrace how you really feel. Otherwise, what's the point? You may as well be a howler if you're dead inside.'

He kept driving, keeping his focus on the horizon, but could not forget the fear he felt when Amy was bleeding out in his arms as he tried to get her into the castle. After travelling halfway across London to find her, he had told her it was because he needed her for the mission. Lauren was right: it was more than that. If they survived this trip, he would have to find a way to articulate his feelings. Amy meant more to him than he dared let on, particularly to his now ex-wife.

Amy's heart pounded with fury as she lay on the bed. How could he put her through all that when he knew her past? He knew everything. She was exhausted but could not sleep. She had cried angry, guilty tears. He had left because of her, she knew it. She cried with her hands over her face and sobbed, wishing her sister were alive to confide in her confused feelings. All she wanted to do was block out her emotions for a while, but she was unable to as she was in charge of Morgan.

He had gone, but he was still in her mind. Furious as she was, she missed him and wanted him with everything she had. Yet he had the capacity to be so cruel to her. She had never seen him that pissed off before. Was that him breaking up with her? Was there anything to break up in the first place? He knew she had not read the divorce papers, so how could he give up on them when she did not know all the facts? It made her brain spin too fast.

He had left so quickly and coldly. He was a Viking invasion that had stormed into her life and vanished with no regard for the mess left behind. Worst of all, he had left with Lauren, the woman he had just kissed, and she had not stopped him. Fucking *kissed* him. Saying he did not love her was no justification or comfort at all.

Truth was, Amy was terrified. She was scared of him leaving and not coming back. If those two did not make it, it would be just her and Morgan forever alone in the big, draughty old castle.

There was a knock at her door. 'Can I come in? It's Morgan.'

Amy tried to pull her thoughts together. 'Sure,' she said, trying to sound upbeat.

The door opened and the girl poked her head round. She looked a little scared of her, probably remembering how cross Amy was during the argument.

Amy felt embarrassed, wondering how much she had heard or witnessed. She had been so furious, she could barely recount what she had said.

'I'm sure he'll say sorry when they come back,' Morgan said.

If they come back alive, Amy thought to herself. How could she forgive him when he had not explained it to her? It made no sense. He had been the one pushing to come on the mission. Why, when he was so keen to end it with Lauren? Why risk coming to the castle at all, if his secret would come out eventually? The only reason could be, was that they *had* to come here. He took the risk so they could find a cure, despite what he might lose. Now he had gone without a chance to make things up with her.

Lauren had no idea what it was like out there. She had been safe with Morgan behind the battlements since it all started. Did she know how to fight? What if Joel went to her rescue, in that heroic way he often did, and paid the price with his life?

Morgan was carrying a tray, which she put on the bedside table. There was a packet of biscuits, a glass of squash and a cup of tea. Without waiting, Morgan started eating a biscuit, instantly getting smeared chocolate round her face.

'You're a star,' Amy exclaimed and grabbed the mug of tea.

She could not remember the last time she had a proper

caffeinated drink. A bit of normality was more than welcome in a place and time so utterly alien. They sat in silence as they ate. It was a pleasant surprise to her that she felt so relaxed in the little girl's company.

'I'd better go,' Morgan said, when she finished her drink. 'I've got things to do.'

The idea of being left alone in that cold, austere place did not thrill her. 'Can I come?'

'Sure.' Morgan's curls bounced around her shoulders as she nodded. Then she looked unsure. 'Only, I said I'd look after you. You still look pale.'

Amy bit back a moan as she swung her legs over the bed. 'Then I'll use the wheelchair, OK?'

Morgan pursed her lips, stern as a matron. 'I'm not sure.'

'Oh, come on. Live a little. You didn't get a chance to finish your tour of the fort last time,' Amy said.

Morgan's face lit up. 'All right, come on. I've got some cool stuff to show you.'

*

The lift doors creaked open to reveal a dark corridor in the basement. The air was dank and Amy could hear dripping water somewhere.

Strip lights flicked on automatically as they went along the hallway. Pipes fed along the walls and metal casings ran along the ceiling, reminding Amy of the War Rooms. It had that same empty, forgotten smell to it.

'This is the lowest floor in the fort,' Morgan said. 'The old heating systems are down here, along with the food storage areas for the kitchens – when it was a hotel, that is. It gives us enough room, just about.' Morgan puffed as she pushed Amy along.

'Here, I can push myself, it's OK.'

'We're here.' Morgan stopped by a large silver door. She slipped a security card through a slot on the wall. 'All the doors open by these.' She hauled on the handle and slid the door sideways on its casters.

Amy could see nothing except darkness. As her eyes adjusted, she noticed a faint red and blue light, fuzzy at the edges. A curtain of plastic sheeting hung in front of it. They went in and Amy found rows and rows of foliage. They stood in front of what looked like cucumbers. This was where the dripping sound was coming from.

'Hydroponics,' she said, more to herself than anything. This place was more than a research station: it was a survival base. Amy knew it would have taken ages to set this all up. 'Morgan, when you came here, was this place already planted?'

The little girl screwed her face up in thought. 'Um, yeah. The old man, the caretaker, was here.'

Morgan tried to push her forwards, but Amy held onto the wheels. 'Where is he now?'

'Gone,' was all she said in a matter-of-fact way. She hauled the door shut behind them.

Morgan wheeled her in, past the rows of salad and broccoli, as she explained the set-up of the cavernous room. The room would have been far too cold on its own, with its bare walls. Morgan explained the LED lights gave off enough heat to take it up to a perfect growing temperature. The fort had its own water supply that could be recycled and tested, and be used for the plants. She pointed to the dehumidifiers around the room. 'These take the water, produced by the plants, to put back into the system. It's kind of like they feed themselves.'

'That's cool.' Amy kept feeling a thud through the floor. 'Is that the sea?'

Morgan nodded. 'We're down at water level.'

Amy pushed away nasty visions of the seawater eating through the foundations and swallowing them up. 'What else have you got growing here?' she asked.

'In the next room, we've got some mushrooms growing. That's it so far. We want to get some chickens at some point, but we haven't been able to go to the mainland with just the two of us. Now you're here, we might be able to.' She looked at her pink wristwatch. 'We'd better go.'

Back upstairs, Amy felt a bit better being able to see out the windows, towards the mainland. Clouds wisped on the horizon. Morgan took her into a closed, wood-panelled corridor.

'These rooms are the old guest rooms,' Morgan said. She held up a small card. 'They all use key cards. We will sort your room when you're better. Unless you want to share with Joel?'

Amy gave a non-committal grunt and looked away. They pulled up at another lobby area. This one had a reception desk with an alcove leading to a small room at the back. Amy reached up and flicked on the light. Laid out on a table was a set of headphones and what looked like an amplifier covered in knobs and buttons.

'Is that a radio?' Amy asked.

Morgan sat down at the table and nodded. She put on the

headphones. 'We have to check in every couple of hours.'

'To who?'

'Anyone who's there.'

Amy bit the skin around her thumbnail. 'And *is* there anyone?'

Morgan turned the knobs and ticked off a checklist with a serious expression. 'Shh.'

Every now and again, rain spat at the window. Luckily, Morgan had not noticed.

'OK. Done,' the girl said and took the headphones off.

'What are you listening for?'

'Anything. Anyone.' Morgan turned the radio off and swung round on the swivel chair to face her. 'There was the same government announcement that ran on a loop. Then it stopped. Since then, nothing.'

Amy kneaded her hands. 'So, what next?'

'Ha.' She clapped her hands and beamed. 'My favourite place in the whole fort. Come on.'

*

The music blared through the sound system as Amy and Morgan danced on the carpet in the games room.

'Mummy never lets me have the music this loud,' Morgan yelled as she spun around in delight.

Amy twirled her round by the hand. 'You haven't lived. Throw me some moves.'

Morgan did a funny little shuffle-type dance, which gave them the giggles for the rest of the song. The room was stocked full with one-armed bandits and arcade machines. Morgan chose to do air hockey next and she went over to plug it in at the wall.

'Are they going to be all right?' Morgan asked.

She had been glancing at the window every time they started a new game. Clouds had rolled in since Joel and Lauren had left. The wind whistled at the windows and white-crowned waves surged at the bottom of the tower.

'They know what they're doing,' Amy said. 'Come on, how about a few games before dinner?'

Morgan gave a dramatic big sigh and got the game ready. Despite feeling tired, Amy carried on. They both needed to think of something else other than worrying about Joel and Lauren. As they played on, the rain threw harder against the windows.

Morgan stopped and looked out to sea. 'I don't like it,' she said.

The sun was setting over the coast in the distance. If they were not back soon, they would not be back at all. At least not that night.

Amy put the paddle down on the table. 'Your mum wouldn't want you to worry.'

'What if it gets dark and they don't get back in time?'

'Then they'll find somewhere safe for the night. Anyway, I think I'm getting my appetite back. Where's this kitchen of yours?'

After they had eaten their fill of chips and beans, Morgan pushed back her plate and put her elbows on the kitchen counter. She stifled a yawn. Amy could not help but laugh at the irony. She had gone from defender of the earth, to babysitter. 'You ready for bedtime?'

'Nope,' Morgan said and pursed her lips.

There was silence as Amy watched her for signs of fibbing. The girl stared her out, elbows on the table. 'Hmm, OK. Do you, er, want a story or something?'

'I'm not a baby.'

'What do you usually do in the evenings?'

'We read or play cards. I tell you my favourite though: hide and seek,' Morgan said.

Amy was not sure whether she had the energy for traipsing around the castle. 'What about watching a film?'

'Nah, I've seen them all already. Come on, hide and seek. You'll really get to know your way around then.'

'Wait a minute – what about these plates?' Amy asked.

Morgan waved her arm. 'Just shove them over on the side. We do the washing up in the mornings.'

Amy did not know her well enough to know if she was trying to get out of chores, but she let it slide. As they searched the fort, she realised Morgan was right. There was plenty of the complex she had not yet seen and she had to keep checking the maps at each landing to figure out where they were. The fort was laid out in a hexagon. Somewhere above her was the helipad and rooftop pool. If the weather had cleared in the morning, she would take a walk outside with the binoculars to keep an eye for the others returning.

Rain pelted against the porthole window and her breath fogged up the glass. It was pitch black out there. Wherever they were, Joel and Lauren were out for the night.

Amy pushed open the swing doors into reception. As she did so, the leaves of a pot plant swayed and Morgan sprang from her hiding place.

'Can't catch me,' she squealed and legged it down the corridor.

'Cheeky little whatsit.' Amy put her water bottle down on a table and began to wheel after her. She was soon disorientated as Morgan led her through the maze of hallways. It was when she had a long stretch of straight, past the games room, that Amy was able to make ground on her. Morgan was a dash of happy curls as she hurtled round the corner and down the stairwell to the basement levels. The automatic lights flickered on. Already, the sound of Morgan's footsteps were faint. She was too fast for her. Amy got out of the wheelchair and stopped halfway down the steps as a head rush invaded. She grabbed the handrail and sucked in air until it passed.

She took up the search again, this time at a slower pace, looking behind tins of food stacked on pallets and wheelie-bins. From what she had found so far, the whole of the bottom level was the service area. She found a room that appeared to once belong to the caretaker, full of cleaning provisions and a camp bed in the corner.

Another door led to the plant room, where she found the boiler system and electrics fuse system. The lights flickered and then cut out. Morgan cried out in the darkness.

'It's all right,' Amy called back. 'Stay there. I'll see if I can sort it. It's just a power cut.'

Amy reached along the rough breeze block walls until she found the cold, metal door of the plant room. All the boilers had fallen silent. She kept going until she found the smooth, wooden door of the caretaker's room. He had left the flashlight on his desk. She grabbed it and headed back to the plant room.

She opened the electric box, and stared at all the wires and fuses, with no clue how to fix it. She flicked a few switches on and off, but it made no difference. It was blowing quite a storm outside. If she could hear the wind from down there, maybe water had got in somehow and blown the electrics. It looked like they would be on candle-power until morning. Maybe that caretaker had some for such emergencies.

Sighing, she looked once more at the circuit box. There was one button she had not tried: the big, red one with an override sticker above it. She slammed her palm onto it and the lights came back on straight away. A heartbeat later and the boilers began to hum into life once more.

'Fucking yes,' she whispered to herself and did a little victory dance, punching the torch in the air. 'Who needs men?'

She headed to the stairwell, but Morgan was nowhere to be seen.

'Morgan, are you OK?'

'Come on,' she shouted. 'You haven't caught me yet.'

With a clatter, Amy backed against a bucket of sand that sat under a fire hose. She rubbed her ankle, where she had banged it. 'Right, the gloves are off now.'

The lights flickered, so she went every few steps in the dark.

Just then, she heard Morgan scream. *She's probably just being dramatic as only kids can*, she thought. Around the corner, she saw the scene in strobing lights, of a figure laid over Morgan, mouth open, about to bite.

She would not let it happen – not again. She fought the pain in her leg and bowled into the grown-up. The howler-man sprawled onto his back, snapping his white teeth.

Thinking they had been in a safe haven, Amy had no weapons to hold the creature back. She kicked it hard in the head, sending out a spurt of black goo from its nose.

Morgan was curled up on the floor, staring at the scene in shock.

'We have to go right now,' Amy shouted at her and shook her shoulders.

The howler dragged itself upright. Amy grabbed her hand and they hurried away. They were only a few metres away from another stairwell. She pulled Morgan up the steps as the howler roared at them.

Amy only had time for a cursory glance on the landing to make sure there were no howlers nearby. The howler was already screaming its way up the stairs behind them. She slammed the door on it, but there was no lock. They had to keep going.

'The safest place – where is it?' Amy asked her while they ran.

Morgan wiped her nose with her palm, wet curls stuck to her face. 'I don't know.'

All the lounge areas looked the same. Then they passed the pot plant Morgan had knocked over earlier. That meant they were near the games room. It would have to do.

Amy grabbed her hand and yanked her along as she tripped up over her own feet. As they headed down a smaller hallway, the door to the basement level smashed open. Howlers roared back and forth at each other. One was bad enough, but she had no idea how many others there were, or where they had come from. All she knew was they were not far behind.

Amy peeked her head round the corner to check the way ahead. The gap across the hall to the door opposite was clear. Then she saw movement further up. The shadowy figure of a howler paced up and down, as though it were on guard.

There was no way those howlers had come from outside the gates. The wall was solid and the gates were over twelve-foot high. No, they were already within the walls, locked up somewhere, and had got out when she had overridden the electrics. Most of the doors had electronic locks on them, to be opened with the cards. It used to be a hotel, after all. The power cut must have let them out; *she* let them out.

She turned back to Morgan, who was close behind and had not seen the extra howler. 'How many are there?'

'What?'

'Howlers – the undead.'

She shook her head. 'I don't know. Maybe three, I think. We were keeping them for—'

Amy grabbed her hand tight. 'We need to make a run for it to the games room. There's another howler over there, but we can do it if we're fast.'

Morgan's face flushed in panic. 'It'll see us.'

Amy thumbed Morgan's soft knuckles. 'I know,' she whispered. She heard a thump from back down the corridor and more roars. 'We have to be brave. Hold onto me and don't let go. Come on.'

Amy legged it across the hall and flung Morgan into the room, slamming the door behind them. She ran behind the fruit machine next to the door and shoved hard into it. It did not budge.

'Morgan,' she shrieked.

By the time she came to help, Amy had got the machine into a tilting rhythm. The door thumped as the howlers lumped into it.

'Keep going,' Amy yelled. It reached its apex and they tipped it over across the doorway. It was over – for now.

Amy staggered backwards and gripped onto the air hockey table to steady herself. Her head was heavy, and she watched the blinds on the back of the door shimmy as the howlers pummelled their fists against the door, screeching into the wood.

Once the dizziness passed, she opened her eyes to find Morgan knelt on the floor, hands to her face. She crouched down next to her. 'Are you all right? Did it hurt you?'

Morgan shook her head and covered her face again. The scratchy carpet dug into her knees as Amy held her close to her chest. The little girl's body trembled as she cried, and she rocked her. For once, she was grateful for the rain thrashing hard on the windows, partly drowning out the sound of their attackers.

It was the guttural, hoarse sounds of the howlers calling to each other before giving chase that she could not get out her head. If they were getting organised, the two of them were in more danger than ever. Joel and Lauren were out there defenceless and there was no way to warn them of what was waiting on their return.

CHAPTER FORTY-FOUR

Joel

Joel's muscles ached from being tense for the whole car journey as he sat on top of the bound and gagged howler on the back seat. All the time he kept hold of his knife, ready to use if it managed to wriggle free. It never took its eyes from him, its nearest meal.

'How's it doing back there?' Lauren yelled to him as she drove.

'It's pretty pissed off.'

They had only driven a few miles when it started to rain, and did not stop until the following day. Having found a lock-up garage to shelter in, they had to wait it out in the police car when the clouds finally cleared. They had to travel to the outskirts of Portsmouth to find some howlers, and now they had two: the one in the back and another in the boot, trussed up tight. Joel had to use his gun and only had one bullet left. He was anxious to get back to Amy and Morgan before anything else happened.

Returning to the castle proved much trickier than leaving. The relentless rain and the strengthening wind brought more howlers than they had seen in a while. Lauren had to adapt to driving round howlers in the road at speed. There were more stragglers on the driveway leading up to the castle.

Lauren pulled up short, by the shipping container. 'It's too quiet,' she whispered. 'Morgan knows the plan. She should've been ready on the gates.' She sped up, smashing into any howlers that got in her way as she drove up to the castle. She honked the horn.

'Don't,' Joel said, grabbing at her arm. 'It'll attract more of them.'

She weaved round potholes on the round, not slowing down. 'If something's wrong, Amy and Morgan are in danger. We were stupid to leave them.'

She skidded the car to a halt and sprinted up to the gates. As she hauled them open, the burnt figure of a howler staggered towards her from the rocky outcrop. Its skin was blackened and cratered, its hands reaching out for Lauren. She turned and screamed. Joel threw open the car door and shot the howler in the head. He got in the driver's seat and floored it through the open gates.

He turned the car off and got out, holding onto the gun in his pocket, despite it being now devoid of bullets.

'This isn't right,' Lauren said as they pushed the gates shut.

'We need to do a sweep.'

'I have to go,' she said, grabbing a knife from the bag in the car. 'You've got it covered here.'

'Splitting up is a shitty idea,' he said, giving her a dirty look. 'You know what happens in horror films.'

'My daughter is in there. I have to go and check.'

The look on her face was so fierce, he dared not challenge her. 'Just wait for me,' he said and picked a knife out, then shut the car door behind him. 'Where should we start?'

'The staff quarters. That's where the—' She looked away and ran a hand through her hair.

'Go on.'

She sighed. 'We've kept some of the infected from our party who turned in there.'

'What?'

'We needed some viable test subjects for when we had developed a suitable vaccine.'

Joel tried to ignore the pummelling from the howlers inside the car. 'Are you joking? You let us go and leave a sick woman and a child on their own with howlers in there? Why the hell didn't you say?'

'They're locked up. We feed them, look after them. It's not as sick as it sounds.' She turned and ran up the steps.

He looked back at the howler in the car, its eyes watching him through the back window.

Despite calling out for them both, he heard no sounds from within the fort. Eventually, he found a key, and went the way Lauren had told him, where the other howlers were locked up in the staff quarters. At the corner, he stopped and swore. All the doors were wide open, and empty.

CHAPTER FORTY-FIVE
Amy

Amy was dreaming of a woman's voice. She sounded happy, relieved, and made Amy want to stay half-asleep. It was how she had always imagined what having a mother would be like: safety and love.

'It's OK. I'm here now.'

'I know I should've kept to the plan, Mummy,' Morgan said. 'But all the lights went out.'

'The power? Everything?'

'I'm just so glad you're back.'

Amy sat up and saw they were hugging. 'No, wait.' She had to warn her. They broke off and stared at her. 'The howlers, they—'

A figure darted into the games room and dived onto Lauren's back, biting at her shoulder. She screamed, scrabbling for her knife on the floor. Amy threw her arms round Morgan and pulled her back as she cried out for her mum.

The howler slumped to the floor, a knife in the back of its head. Behind it, Joel pulled the blade back out. 'Are you all right? Did it get you?' He bent down and looked at Lauren. She shook her head. 'Are there more?' he asked.

'There's three,' Amy said, relieved at his return. A look from him was all it would take to know that everything was OK between them. Her breath caught in her chest; every cell in her body was waiting, wanting him to acknowledge her by sliding his hands round her waist or holding her face in his strong hands.

Instead, he stood up and looked back to the doorway.

'I got one in the first stairwell,' Lauren said.

He nodded, blanking Amy. 'Then there's one more. Shut this door behind you.' With that, he left.

By the time Amy had got to her feet and over to the doorway, he was long gone, but she could hear him whistling and yelling, trying to lure out the remaining howler.

'Give me that,' she snapped at Lauren, snatching the knife from beside her.

She made her way through the castle, anger making her almost forget about the pain in her calf. The further she went, the more fucking fuming she got with him for ignoring her on his return. He had been all she could think about, and kissing him had figured high up in the plan. Now, she just wanted to punch him in the face.

Far off, she heard the familiar screech of a howler. The door to the boundary wall staircase banged shut in the distance. With an uneven jog down the hall, she threw open the door and found Joel's knife on the floor. *Shit*, she thought. Maybe he needed her help after all. Retrieving the knife, she hopped up the stairs as fast as she could. Throwing the rooftop door open, the sea wind slapped her in the face, and she found Joel stood on the parapet, trying to hold back a howler with his bare hands. He punched it in the face and it fell to its knees.

'Stay back,' Joel called to Amy. He looked over the edge. 'If I take it with me, you'll all be safe.'

The howler sprung up and launched itself at his waist. Joel lost his footing and toppled backwards over the edge.

'Noooooo!' Amy screamed.

The dribbling howler turned in mid-air at the sound of her voice. A pendulum of bloody drool swung from its mouth as it observed her.

Then, they were gone.

She ran to the battlements and looked over the edge. Joel was a metre or so down from the roof, hanging onto an overflow pipe with the howler clinging onto his boot. Waves crashed onto the rocks below, flinging up sea spray in their wake.

Thank fuck, she thought. *He's alive.*

'Joel! Are you OK?' she cried out.

'Oh, sure. Having a lovely day out,' he replied, struggling to hold his grip.

His eyes widened as she held the knife up and threw it at the howler. It glanced off its head, making only a slice across its temple.

She looked around her, but there was nothing else to use and there was no time to find an alternative. She bent down and unzipped her boot. She threw it down and it bounced off the howler's shoulder.

'Come on, Amy,' Joel said. 'Imagine it's *my* head.'

There was an ominous creaking sound and the pipe bent. He scrabbled to hold on and the howler swung out in circles as it tried to bite his leg. Amy took off her other boot and chucked it hard. It landed square in the howler's face. Joel kicked out and the howler lost its grip. Its arms windmilled in a futile desire for flesh as it plummeted to the rocks below.

Amy reached over the edge and held her arm out. Joel's feet

found purchase in the brickwork and with her help, he got back onto the rooftop.

'Looks like that was the motivation you needed,' Joel said as he dusted himself down and looked at her.

In that glance, she saw a million things: relief that he was safe and relief that he was still alive for Lauren and Morgan; the family he had been denied. The cold look was one she had seen many times before. He had given up on her. He really had broken up with her, label or no label.

Amy swallowed back the lump in her throat. She did not know if her imminent meltdown was going to involve screams of rage or tears of heartbreak, but she was not prepared to let him see the fallout. The last thing she wanted was to be vulnerable in his presence.

'Look, I, er—' he started to say.

'Don't bother,' she croaked. Giving him her best unfeeling stare, she walked away along the battlements.

'Where are you going?' he called after her.

'I'm leaving and I'm not coming back,' she shouted over her shoulder.

'Really? Where?'

She spun round. 'London.'

He snorted. 'Like that's any safer.'

'Anything's better than being here with you.'

Blindly striding off, she found herself approaching a turret with no idea where it led. She jumped in surprise as Joel grabbed her wrist and pulled her back. Pushing her against the stone wall, he kissed her, hard and longing. She could not help but kiss him back, their tongues finding one another's. Her hands ran along his muscular back and down his shoulders as they reunited. *So, I do exist*, she thought. He was everything she wanted and everything she despised all at once.

'Stop,' she breathed, pushing him back. 'Don't.'

'You're really leaving? I've only just come back.'

'What were you expecting? Three cheers and the red carpet being rolled out?'

Absently, he rubbed his chest where she had shoved him. 'What have I done now?'

'You wouldn't even look at me when you came back with Lauren. What the fuck was that?'

He clenched his jaw. 'I needed to find that howler. I was trying to keep everyone safe. I didn't have time to tell you how gorgeous you look in that dress.' He smiled at her, then his face fell when she would not return one. 'Did you mean it before? When you said that you hated me?' he asked.

She bit her lip and could not meet his eyes when she remembered all the awful things they had said to each other before he left with Lauren. Fuck knows what he had said when he swore at her in his native tongue.

For everything he had put her through, she knew she ought to hate him, and there was no doubting he annoyed the fuck out of her a lot of the time, but her heart knew no logic. Despite everything that had happened, she longed to have him near. When he had left, it almost ripped her apart, and having him back gave her more joy than her pride could risk verbalising.

He moaned in exasperation. 'Talk to me.'

'OK, have it your way.' She pulled her dress straight. 'You kiss your wife right in front of me; you then divorce her, but instead of telling me, you piss off with said ex-wife and leave a still-injured me to look after a child in a castle full of fucking howlers,' she shouted. 'Even for you, that's cold.'

'You told me not to follow you. Bloody hell.' He threw up his arms. 'I wanted to give you a choice.' He looked at the floor and ground his boot into the flagstones.

Out of breath, she bit her thumbnail, confused at his words. 'A choice?'

'I can't give you much, other than what you see here. I'm not perfect and neither are you. This is our lives now: surviving. You didn't think that it would all be over once we got here, did you? Find salvation, make babies and everything be all cushy?' He leant back on the opposite wall and rubbed his neck.

'No.' Embarrassed at the thought, she ran her fingers through her hair, hoping her cheeks had not gone red. It was a silly schoolgirl whim and she felt like an idiot for fancying the idea, just for a moment. 'Forget it.' She went to push past him but he blocked her way.

'Don't go. I didn't mean what I said, about giving up on us.' He sighed. 'I didn't know the howlers were being kept here.'

'Sure you didn't.'

'I've only just found out myself. I *have*.' He paused, his eyes full of uncertainty. 'You read the paper I gave you.'

Amy thought back to the two signatures. 'Yes.' It was time she threw back some closed statements. His hands balled into fists and he sighed. She got the reaction she wanted but it did not give her the satisfaction she had hoped for.

'What else do I have to do?' he asked, sliding his hands round her waist.

She unhooked his fingers, staring him dead in the face. 'You know, for all the vile things Nathan did to me, at least I knew where I stood with him.'

He looked incredulously at her. 'Are you serious? He hurt you. I would never hurt you like that.'

'You did hurt me. In here,' she whispered, putting her hand on her heart.

'I'm sorry. I don't mean to.' He touched her cheek gently and she closed her eyes, drinking in his touch. 'I haven't felt the way you make me feel before. I don't think you have either. I'm not very good at this, I know, but we could figure it out together. I can't lose you.'

'Why couldn't you just tell me you weren't divorced?'

'Because of how I feel.'

She pushed his hand away in anger and stepped back. 'You still love Lauren. I fucking knew it. God, I was so stupid.'

'Will you just shut up for once?' He grabbed her by the wrists. 'It's because of how I feel about you. How I've always felt about you. I was scared that if you knew I was still married, you wouldn't want to be with me. And I do – I want to be with you.'

She could not bear the pain of getting her heart ripped to pieces so often. A tear rolled down her face and she felt ashamed of it, as though it had stripped her naked in front of him. 'It's all just words, Joel.'

'No, I need to explain.' He held her hands tighter. 'I'm sorry for not telling you about Lauren.'

Amy shifted her weight to her good leg. 'If you want your wife back, don't let me stop you.'

He shook his head. 'I had some unfinished business with her.

We didn't get divorced when she left me, because I wouldn't sign the papers. I wanted revenge for what Lauren and Nick did behind my back. I hid away in my flat, sulking like a petulant child.'

Amy glanced towards the rooftop door. 'That's all very well, but—'

'Doing all this means nothing without you. You mean something to me. A lot. More than a lot.'

'OK,' she said, still not really convinced.

He took her hands and put them on his shoulders. 'Amy, that day we met in Ron's office changed me. Don't you see? That hermit in the flat... that's not who I am anymore. I want something else now.'

'What's that?'

'Isn't it obvious? I want this... what we have. I need you, Amy. I love you, and I want you to love me back.' His blue eyes looked for affirmation; reassurance. For the first time, he was completely vulnerable in front of her.

'I love you too,' she breathed, reaching up to kiss him, hard.

Her fingers found his belt and she backed up against the wall, pulling him towards her. He ran his hands down her waist and up under her dress. His warm fingers rubbed over the fabric of her underwear, and she relaxed into his touch. He hooked her knickers to the side, and he slid a digit inside her, kissing her at the same time.

'Tell me what you need, Amy.'

She ran both her thumbs along his cheekbones and smiled. 'You. I love you and I want you. Now.'

He nodded and undid his buckle and unzipped his trousers.

'I'm not going slow this time.'

'Good,' she replied, breathing into his neck.

His strong arms lifted her up and pressed her against the wall. He took her thighs and pulled them round his middle. Laughing in pleasure, she draped her arms round his neck. He angled his cock and guided it into her. He moaned into her hair as they got a bouncing rhythm going. They looked deep in each other's eyes while they were entwined.

'Don't stop,' she gasped.

Buoyed on by her words, he grasped her bum and thrust even deeper. After all their arguments, and their passion, they had still not decided what it was "they" had. When it felt as good as this, she did not care. He said he loved her, and that was enough for her. All she wanted was him.

'Make me come,' she breathed.

He adjusted his stance and drove against her faster, harder. She dropped her head back as she came, and Joel climaxed not long after. He gave a breathless laugh and she put her forehead to his.

'Are you OK?' he asked when he had guided her back down to the floor.

She smiled up at him. 'Oh yeah, better than OK.'

He lifted her chin with his finger and kissed her gently on the lips. 'You're amazing, you know? How could I not love you?'

She shrugged and rearranged her dress. 'Because I'm a pain in the arse.'

'Well, that's true. But nobody's perfect,' he said, doing up his trousers.

'I guess so.' She stepped forwards and leant her elbows on the high stone window ledge, to look out at the view. Joel came up behind her and wrapped his forearms round her, linking his fingers with hers.

He held her to his chest as they both stared out over the sea. 'Life can be pretty beautiful in its imperfection.'

Amy thought about the poison that flowed through the sea and the clouds overhead, and realised how true his words were.

'I'm sorry for slapping you,' she said.

'You were right to be angry. I've been a dick.'

'I'm still sorry.'

'That's OK. Are you still planning on leaving?' he asked.

'Nope. But you do owe me a pair of shoes.' She kissed his arm, the golden hairs tickling her face. A seagull called out as it soared over the castle and Amy shut her eyes, leaning back against the warmth of Joel's chest. For now, it was the only place she wanted to be.

CHAPTER FORTY-SIX
Joel

When they got into the medi-bay, Joel was shocked to find Lauren laid back with restraints at her wrists and ankles. Her skin had a greenish pallor to it.

'You were bitten?' he asked in horror. 'You said you were OK.'

He felt sick with guilt when he realised what she and Morgan must have been going through while he was on the roof with Amy.

Lauren nodded. 'I'll be fine. We need to do the injection as soon as possible.'

Amy pulled up a chair, watching Morgan getting the syringes ready. 'But vaccines can take months, years even. It's barely been a week and there's only three of us.'

Lauren swallowed and grimaced. 'It's like any vaccine – we use some of the disease to become the cure. We'll need to get the dose right, but we've got to start somewhere. That involves us looking at the blood from the infected. Then we extract and use a single virus protein to stimulate an immune response.'

Morgan brought the syringes over and put them on the side. 'It's ready,' she said.

'What is?' Joel asked, standing there feeling useless.

'I want to see if we can use blood from a previously infected and cured person. It was beginning to work with the Ebola outbreak, years ago,' Lauren said. 'I've spent years working on this and now we can actually see it in action.'

'On you? Now?' Joel asked in a high-pitched voice. 'No. It's too risky.'

'Look at me,' Lauren replied. 'I've already been bitten. It *has* to work.' She looked at Morgan and smiled.

Joel frowned. 'You said about a cured person. You don't mean—'

Lauren nodded. 'Morgan was bitten a few weeks ago. By her uncle, my brother. He was in our team here. When he turned, it was important we didn't kill him.'

'Why?' Amy asked, watching the little girl sort out medical instruments on the table.

Lauren's cheeks flushed and she kneaded her hands. 'I thought that a similar genetic link might help the experiment somehow. I've been testing her every day. She's fine; she's resistant to it.'

'And you didn't think to say?' Amy asked, scratching her cheek. 'Whatever. It's done now. The longer we leave it, the less chance we have of it working at all.'

'Hang on,' Joel said.

Lauren looked up at them as a bead of sweat trickled down her forehead. 'I'll need to be in here for a while, under surveillance of course. I'm sorry to turf you out like this, Amy. Your bag's over there.' She was so calm, so trusting the plan would work. The ultimate faith a mother had in her child's genetic capabilities was amazing to him. 'You two can have the honeymoon suite,' she said, without a hint of a joke, or anything.

Joel stiffened and Amy frowned.

'The what?' she asked.

Lauren interrupted her. 'Will you do it for me?' She looked up at Joel and then at the medical equipment laid out.

It was all on him if it went wrong. 'I'm sorry, I can't,' he said.

Lauren gawped at him. 'I can't very well do it myself. I can't expect Morgan to.'

Amy stood up. 'I'll do it. Where's the syringe?'

Joel grabbed her by the shoulder and said in a hushed tone, 'You do realise if she dies or turns, that leaves Morgan without a mum?'

'That's the risk we've got to take,' she hissed back. 'If we do nothing, she'll turn anyway.'

'Who says she will?' he asked. 'Morgan didn't.'

Morgan held out the needle for Amy. 'It's this one.'

Joel shook his head. 'It's not even been tested,' he told Amy.

'There's no time,' Lauren said.

'If you're not going to help, just get out,' Amy snapped, with a dogged intention in her eyes.

Joel sighed. Deep down, he knew she was right. 'Come on, Morgan.' He led her out of the room so Amy could do the injection in peace.

They went to check the radio and Morgan gave him a tour of the castle. By the time they got back to the medi-bay, Lauren was peacefully sleeping, but there was no sign of Amy. Her bag was gone. He walked the hallways, getting more and more panicked the longer he was unable to find her. He eventually found her in the guests' lounge, opposite the merman statue. She was sitting on a leather couch with her feet curled up underneath her, a book on her lap, and her bag on the floor.

'Here you are,' he said, unable to disguise the relief in his voice.

She swivelled round and looked up from the book she was reading. 'Where the fuck did you think I'd be?'

'Honestly, I still wasn't sure if you meant it about leaving.'

She gazed out the window across the bay. In the distance, he could see the charred remains of the marina he had torched on their arrival. The storm clouds had closed in again and the wind whistled round the fort.

Annoyance flickered across her face. 'It's not always about you, OK? I'm looking for new digs anyway, since I got kicked out of the medi-bay.' She gave her bag a nudge with the toe of her ankle boot.

He perched on the armrest next to her. 'I'm glad you aren't leaving.'

She turned a page in her book. 'That's just as well since you're stuck with me now.'

'Have you done it? Lauren's vaccine?' he asked.

'Yes. She didn't react to it, not yet anyway.' She closed the book and looked up at him. 'Are you pissed off with me?'

He reached out for her hand, interlacing their fingers, and gave her a serious expression. 'You stepped up,' he said.

'I did it for Morgan.' Amy picked at her thumbnail. 'She's a good kid. She doesn't deserve this. She deserves to have a mother.'

He raised her hand to his mouth and kissed her knuckles. It did not need saying; he knew why now. She wanted Morgan to have what she never did.

His stomach growled. He could not remember the last time he had eaten properly. 'You hungry? I can make us coffee and bacon rolls.'

'Sure. You can test out your cooking skills on me.'

He held his hands out to her and pulled her up. He slid his arm round her shoulders as they headed to the kitchens.

Joel spent some time that morning getting the medi-bay kitted out as a little snug for Lauren and Morgan, so they could stay together. He got a TV rigged up in there with a games console and another camp bed for Morgan.

After lunch, he checked on Lauren. She was sleeping while Morgan watched a film. He agreed to take the restraints off, but kept the main door locked. Morgan had the walkie-talkie if she needed them for anything.

He found Amy back at her favourite sofa by the merman statue, reading the book she had found in the library corner.

'Come on,' he said, leading her by the hand. 'I've got something to show you.'

In the castle restaurant, they walked past empty tables to a set dinner by the window, overlooking the marina. On the white tablecloth, Joel had set out cooked crab cakes, salad and chips.

He pulled back her chair and helped her to sit down, while a rosy-cheeked Amy gawped at him.

'All this? Why are you—' she began to say.

'A long time ago, I bet you dinner about the poison balance theory. It turned out you were right,' he said, sitting down opposite her. 'You never once said I told you so.'

'Did you make this?' she asked.

He nodded. 'The chips and crab were already in the freezer.

But I made the mix.'

She took a bite of the crab cakes and closed her eyes in bliss. 'It's really nice,' she mumbled through her mouthful.

'You're welcome.' He enjoyed cooking and it had been so long since he'd had the chance to share a proper mealtime with anyone. It made him happy to see her happy.

'Where did you get the salad?' she asked.

'Lauren and Morgan have been doing a pretty good job getting things going here. The tomatoes were growing in the sunroom. All the other stuff was growing in the basements.' As he forked a lettuce leaf, the thought occurred that despite all the drama of meeting Lauren again, they could actually stay there longer than they had intended. The original idea was just finding Lauren and developing a cure, but it could be more than that.

'What're you thinking?' she asked, holding her fork midway to her mouth.

'It's just, we could stay here. For a while.'

Amy cut into a chip and looked up at him. 'I don't know.'

'Things are OK with Lauren, aren't they? You aren't jealous? Because you don't need to be.'

'It's not that. It's how safe this place is.'

'The walls are high enough,' he said. 'There are the gates.'

She watched the waves swelling out the window. 'You saw what happened to Tower Bridge. We need to be underground to be truly safe until the rains are no longer a danger.'

Joel fingered the corner of the tablecloth. 'I get that, I do. But what about the other two? If we find somewhere, would they take a child in?'

Amy looked back to the doorway, just in case Morgan was

around. 'I don't know. They'd have to. She's the key to making this all work. She's immune, remember?'

'Where do we go? What is left out there?' he asked. 'All I found was howlers last time I went out.'

'I don't know, Joel,' she hissed. 'There might be other immune people, or those who have escaped the city like we did.'

He reached out for her hand and squeezed it. 'We'll just have to keep trying the radio and hope someone's out there.'

She nodded. 'Until we figure out what to do next.'

'I think you'll like your new quarters,' he said. 'I've upgraded us.'

After they finished their meal, he led her on a walk through the castle back to the guest quarters. The look of surprised joy on her face when she opened the door to the honeymoon suite was worth every minute he had spent tidying and getting it ready. He had changed the sheets and dusted, and lit some candles.

'Shut up. This is for us?' she asked, gawping at the four-poster bed with heavy drapes and dark wooden frame. The long window went the length of the room, framing the sea. It was Amy's very own moving painting that she could look at for as long as she wanted. It was for her; she deserved it. She deserved to be loved, happy and a little bit spoiled.

He went to the mini bar and found a bottle of champagne and a glass. He popped the cork and poured her a drink. 'Get yourself comfortable,' he said, handing her the glass. She sat on the chaise longue, while he went to the bathroom and filled the jacuzzi.

He returned for Amy, took her hand and led her into the bathroom. The bubbles were just starting to creep over the edge of the jacuzzi. Without waiting, she peeled her clothes off and hopped in.

He turned away and pulled his shirt over his head, leaving him with a naked torso. In front of the mirror, he unpacked his razor from his toiletry bag to have a shave. He lathered up foam onto his cheeks and started to shave his beard off. In the reflection, he found Amy sipping her drink, fascinated in watching the seemingly mundane task. He wondered if she had ever spent ordinary time together like that with another man, or if it really had been just cocktails, dancing and sex in strangers' beds? If no man had ever been in her bed, it seemed the latter was more likely.

He carried on shaving above his top lip, enjoying being her spectacle. He adored her: the wildcat with a foul mouth and a temper, her stubbornness and her vulnerability. They locked eyes. He tried to suppress the torrent of emotions he was unused to, while they whirled round inside him.

'There we go,' he said, dabbing his face with a towel. 'Shiny like a new penny.'

Amy took another sip of champagne and gave him a mischievous look. 'Won't you join me?' she asked, with a grin.

He hesitated. Was she talking about the drink or the jacuzzi? He had made a conscious decision not to drink a while ago. 'I don't need it,' he said, surprised by his own epiphany.

She draped herself over the lip of the tub, bubbles dripping onto the floor. 'Neither do I,' she breathed, her mouth open and cheeks flushed. 'But I want it.'

He turned to stare at her. All he wanted was her, all the time, any opportunity. He could not help himself. He slung the towel in the basin and started to undo his belt. She bit her lip, giggling as he slid his jeans and boxers off as fast as he could and vaulted into the jacuzzi. Water sloshed onto the floor as they locked lips. She took a sip of champagne and then kissed him, swirling the liquid round his mouth with her tongue.

She straddled him as his cock pressed against her stomach. They shared the rest of the glass, feeding it to each other and, when finished, Joel set it down on the side. He lifted her up carefully by her hips and turned her round so she was leaning over the edge of the bath. Her bum was raised just enough so he could scoot his thighs underneath.

He edged her along, lining her up so she was directly in front of a nozzle jet. 'Is this OK?' he asked.

'Yeah,' she breathed. She wriggled her legs wider and he leaned over her back, his wet skin against hers.

He eased himself into her and they began to slowly rock with each other. As she moved, he focused on the way her skin went taut over her ribs and shoulder blades, the soap bubbles sliding down. He reached round to grasp a perfectly round handful of breast. His fingertips found the hard nub of her nipple and he brushed across it.

'Fuck,' she moaned, her head dipping over the edge of the jacuzzi.

He had not gone for that long last time, as passion and urgency had overridden any chance of pacing himself. This time he wanted to keep going as long as he could. *Don't come yet, don't come yet*, he told himself despite her yelps of pleasure.

Slowing the pace down, he hugged her waist, resting his chin on her neck, kissing the heart tattoo etched behind her ear. He wondered when and why she had got it done. Was it her being ironic? He knew she had never had a boyfriend. Had she always wanted love but never found it?

He pulled out and she turned round quizzically.

'What is it?' she asked.

He kissed the tip of her nose. 'Nothing. There's no hurry.' He filled up the glass of champagne and fed her another sip. Then he climbed out the bath and held out his hand to her.

'Where are we going?' she asked. As he led her to the huge bed, she gasped. 'We're dripping wet. We'll wreck the sheets.'

'Hang on.' He came back with an armful of fluffy towels from the linen cupboard and laid them out on the bed. Picking her up, he laid her gently down onto the bed and he eased down on top of her. His chest pressed against the warmth of her wet skin and his hair dripped beads of water onto her throat, running down her collarbone.

She parted her legs and he noted it was the first time he had seen her fully naked in good lighting. A small heart tattoo on her hipbone matched the one behind her ear. He bent down to kiss it and the *ohhh* sound she made seemed to go on forever, as he dragged his tongue along the edge of her bikini line. It was an altogether different experience doing this in the light and he could tell she felt exposed, almost bringing her legs up to his head and shoulders as if to hide her nakedness.

He looked up and brought the towels round her top half. 'Don't get cold,' he said.

She gave an appreciative laugh, which turned into a gasp as his mouth took hold of her hood and he sucked it. His tongue explored her and she moaned his name, her hands grabbing at his hair.

He pulled away and bent over the bed to his bag on the floor and pulled out a condom wrapper. 'I suppose we ought to, right?'

She nodded and reached her hands out for him to return to her embrace. As much as he wanted to come inside her again, he had the luxury of time now and wanted to be careful.

'Help me in,' he said, when he had put it on.

Her fingers judged the right place and fed him in. Her small hands ran from the back of his thighs up round his buttocks. She dragged her fingernails lightly across his back in an S-shape, as if she wanted to explore every inch of him. Pushing in deeper, he gave her his whole length. He took her leg and raised it up as he went faster.

Her hands scrunched up the towelling and he felt her tighten around his cock. She gasped, arched her back then sank back into the bed. Chuffed he had succeeded in his side of the business by satisfying that precious woman, he was ready to let go himself.

Shuddering as he finished off, he breathed in her wonderful perfume. He realised that with the bath and the soap, whatever spray she had put on would have washed off. It was her own unique scent. That smell all along was just her, her own heavenly brand of Amy. He remembered back to sitting down in the auditorium at the summit and he had smelled her, before he saw her. He was amazed at the power that drew him to her.

He dropped the condom into the wastebin by the dresser, then laid down next to her as they both got their breath back. She draped a leg over his stomach and lazily ran her hands through his chest hair.

'When did you get these?' he asked, tracing his finger across the heart tattoo on her hip bone, his other hand brushing the hair from her ear.

'In Soho, when me and Ash left the care home. It was like a celebration to be rid of that fucking place.'

'Why a heart?'

She propped herself up on her elbows. 'Why not?'

'It could have been anything – music notes, a skull and crossbones, Daffy bloody Duck.'

She shrugged. 'I guess I wanted to believe that love was out there, that it did exist.'

'Like it was a myth?'

'No one has ever loved me before. I mean, there were a few boys, but when they tried to get a bit more serious, I chipped them off. I wasn't ready to trust in a fairy-tale.'

He saw goosebumps on her skin and wrapped the towels round her. 'What about now, babe? Will you trust me?' The way her face softened when he called her *babe* was not lost on him.

'There aren't any other wives I need to know about?' she asked, a glint returning to her eye.

He grabbed a pillow and swatted her with it. 'You know everything now. I'm laid bare.'

She smirked, holding the pillow in a hug as she eyed him up and down. 'You are. And you look amazing for it.'

He ran his fingers through his hair. 'Well, I don't know what to say.'

'You don't need to say anything.'

The thought of waking up to Amy every day made him want to have an early night every day of the week so he could spend longer in bed with her. He worried if she would always feel the same. He had changed so much since he was her age. He was already married to Lauren by then.

'Does it bother you,' he asked, 'the difference in our ages? In twenty years' time, I'll be—'

She slapped a hand over his mouth. 'It doesn't matter. This world isn't the one we left behind. We've both nearly died several times. Whatever time we have left, I want to spend it with you.'

Happy with her reply, he kissed her some more. When they broke apart, they lay still in each other's arms.

'What about this?' she asked tracing her fingers across the tattoo on his right arm. 'It looks like a snowflake.'

'It's a Viking tattoo – the Helm of Awe – the sun in eight tridents to represent protection.'

'What about the dragon?' Her fingers traced around the outside of the design.

'It's the prow of a dragon boat. I've always felt most myself when I'm exploring unchartered waters. I got this when I was at college. Lauren hated it.'

Amy leaned over and kissed it. 'A true Viking. I love it.' She laid out and stretched. 'Are you going to be here when I wake up?' she asked, her eyes all soft and sleepy.

The last time they had shared a bed together was back in her flat and he had got up before she woke. It felt like years ago. He wanted to be there when she woke up; to be the first thing she saw. He brushed the hair from her face. 'Be not afeared.'

They spent the next few days in a blissful bubble. Safe behind the castle walls from the howlers, Amy and Joel ran more tests on Lauren, and occupied Morgan as best they could. The tests on Lauren were showing that the treatment was working. Morgan was happy and getting used to them being a foursome.

Amy enjoyed helping Joel cook and they all ate together in the medi-bay, before they said their goodnights to Lauren and Morgan, and retired to the honeymoon suite. Night-time was all about making love as much as possible. It only seemed to make Amy and Joel want it more, now they could, and there was no danger to their lives every five minutes.

They overslept the day Amy was due to do the morning radio call. She showered before Joel and was dressed by the time he got out the shower. She was sat at the dresser, brushing her hair in front of the mirror, when he came out wearing nothing but a towel. He swaggered past, deliberately walking past in her line of sight, looking sexy as hell.

Amy chewed the inside of her cheek, trying to avoid a smirk and succumbing to her urges. Already late, she needed a coffee before she was able to function like a normal person. They had a busy day lined up, running more tests on the detained howlers and checking the hydroponics in the basement.

Picking up her hoop earrings, she had just got the second one in her earlobe when she saw something in her peripheral vision. His towel landed by her feet and she turned round to see Joel laying on the bed, wearing only a grin.

'Professor Harket, don't start what you can't finish,' she warned.

'Oh, I can finish, Miss Weston,' he challenged.

'Don't,' she said and laughed, picking up the towel and throwing it back at him. 'I'm late.'

'What?'

'For my shift, I mean,' she added, quickly.

'It's Sunday. You're allowed a lie-in, aren't you?'

The idea of staying in the suite with Joel all day seemed heavenly, but she had a job to do. She was about to protest, when there was a frenzied knocking at the door.

'Open up,' Morgan squeaked from the other side. 'It's my mum.'

'Just a minute, Morgs,' Amy said, trying to sound calm while worrying about Lauren having a delayed reaction to the vaccine. She checked Joel had made himself decent before opening the door. 'Are you OK?'

She rested on the doorframe as she tried to get her breath back. 'Mummy says you've got to come quick. There's a signal coming through on the radio. Someone's out there. They're on their way – now.'

'Who?' Amy asked.

'I don't know,' she replied in a small voice.

'Go stay with your mum,' Joel said. He looked to Amy. 'Get ready.'

Amy reached under her pillow for her knife and Joel pulled

on his trousers and a shirt. It was happening. She had not expected their own reality to be invaded so soon and she was scared, but glad Joel was with her. He was strong and self-assured. Nothing ever seemed to truly panic him.

Her leg was healing well and it almost did not hurt at all when she had to rush about. They jogged up to the castle rooftop and they looked up at the skies. Nothing yet, but Amy was ready for whoever it was, be it good or bad.

She thought about Lauren and her plans to use Morgan's blood to help people who got bitten. Then she remembered what Sylvia had told her in the War Rooms – that carbon dioxide levels would still increase, despite industrial production having stopped. It would level out eventually but would take time to stabilise. The world just needed to recover, and she knew this was not the place to stay for the interim. She had thought it for a while, particularly in the storm while Joel was away from the fort. Then she thought about how Joel had come back for her, more than once. She glanced over to find him watching her.

'What?' she asked, nervously.

'Do you remember when we were at the hospital and I said you were my fiancée, so I could get in to see you?'

'Yeah,' she said, frowning at him.

He dug his hands in his pockets, not quite meeting her eye. 'I know what I want, and I have done for a while now.' He dropped to his knees at her feet and held a diamond ring in his grip. 'Will you marry me?'

Amy gawped at him kneeling on the ground. She had to put all her faith in him now and she wanted to, but there were too many questions whirling through her mind. 'Why?'

He raised his eyebrows. It was clear he had expected the response to be an easy one. 'Because I love you.' He said it like it was obvious. 'I want to be with you forever. There's no one else. Don't you believe me?'

'But, why now?'

'We never seem to know what is going to happen next. These people could be soldiers, spies, or criminals,' he said, as they could near the far-off buzzing sound of aircraft.

'Honestly, I don't think I'm wife material.' She half-laughed.

He looked her straight in the eye. 'Whatever material you are, I want the whole outfit.'

'You married Lauren. That didn't work out so well.'

He clenched his jaw and shut his eyes, almost as though he was fighting some internal struggle. He opened his eyes again, looking at her straight. 'This is different. *We* are different.'

'How?'

He shook his head. 'This is difficult for me to talk about.'

She knelt down next to him and took his hands in hers. 'Tell me. It's your turn to trust me.'

'I married Lauren because I felt I had to. But, I choose to marry you. I love you and want you to be my wife. I want to be there for you, and seal our love with this,' he said, looking at the ring.

She scratched her head. Was it all going a bit too fast? In a normal situation, maybe it was, she reasoned. This was no normal world anymore and time had a fucking scary habit of going too quickly. 'I've never even had a boyfriend.'

'I'm not a boy; I'm a man. We can be man and wife, if you'll take me on?'

She remembered the loaded look Joel gave Lauren when she mentioned the honeymoon suite. She could not work out a lot of his mysterious looks. Maybe it was part of his appeal. Who knew if she would ever totally figure him out? It did not matter to her. They loved and trusted each other and would fight for each other until the end.

She stood up and brushed the dust off her legs 'If you think I'm going to do the "obey" thing, you can fucking think again.'

He laughed, still on his knees and kissed her. 'You don't strike me as the obeying kind. So, will you marry me?'

She trusted him with her life and her heart. The look on his face told her that she was more than enough for him. Joel was the only man she had ever loved and never wanted to love another. She did not stop him, as he slid the ring on her finger. She was about to answer him, when a black helicopter rounded the headland and flew over the castle. They were coming.

THE END

377

EASTER EGGS AND SOCIAL MEDIA

I listened to a lot of music while writing and editing this book and many songs inspired me to reimagine the characters and their relationships with each other.

Amy and Joel had a special song (Elbow's *One Day Like This*) which meant so much to them and is crucial in the upcoming sequel *The Poison Thieves*. The lyrics are very powerful and, to me, perfectly describe their ever-evolving relationship.

Want to know what the first song was that Amy danced to in the flat? Follow my blog, Facebook page, Instagram and TikTok, where you can find lyrics and learn more about my inspiration for *The Poison Balance*:

lucyghose.wordpress.com

Facebook: facebook.com/LucyGhose

Instagram and TikTok: @lucyghose

Lucy got double E for her Science GCSE, because she was more interested in chatting up the boys and writing erotic novels under the table with her best friend than copying the set text off the whiteboard. When she said she was going to do Media Studies at college, she was told by a teacher that "employers will laugh at you with that qualification". That qualification led her into journalism, and a continued love of writing. Writing and publishing her debut novel is literally a dream come true for her. So don't give up on your dreams, write like no-one is watching, ignore your inner critic and always ask "why". And care less about what other people think.

ABOUT THE AUTHOR

Lucy Ghose started working for local newspapers aged seventeen, and has since written short stories for a national magazine. She loves reading and writing about the '80s, zombies and end-of-the-world scenarios. Having studied in London for university, she later moved back to her birthplace in Dorset, UK, where she lives with her young family.

ACKNOWLEDGEMENTS

Thanks firstly to my mum, a former librarian who brought me up with a love of books. Thank you for being my beta reader and I'm sorry for giving you literal, actual nightmares.

For Rich, my husband, who has watched me evolve from rookie reporter, to mother of our two children, to a woman getting her writing mojo back after the baby-brain fog abated. You knew I could do it, even after nearly a year of rejections from agents, you showed me to think outside the box and never give up. You show me what love is every day, even if we are as stubborn and fiery as each other.

I'd like to thank my publishers for holding my hand throughout the whole process and answering all my never-ending questions (old habits from a journalist die hard!). Thank you for taking me on and making my dreams come true by publishing my book.

And to Morten – if I hadn't been a fan of *The Masked Singer UK* and watched you that season when you were Viking, I truly believe my book wouldn't be what it is today. You might not ever read this (and it might be better if you don't), but I'm grateful you got out of your comfort zone, even if it was just the once.